THE
PHANTOM
FLAME

THE
PHANTOM
FLAME

BRIMSTONE & FIRE, BOOK 2

T. M. LEDVINA

Hardcover: 979-8-9863870-3-1
Paperback: 979-8-9863870-5-5
e-Book: 979-8-9863870-4-8

First published March 2024.

Edited by Lavender Prose Editing (lavenderprose.com)
Cover Designed by Stefanie Saw (seventhstarart.com)
Map Design by Rachael Ward (cartographybird.com)
Interior Formatting by Lindsay Clement (novelitica.com)

OBCC Publishing
Madison, WI 53701

tmledvina.com

For Addy. Without you, I never would have learned to grieve.

For you. I see your grief. The tunnel is long and dark and hard to breathe, but the end is there. You will see the light again.

You reside within me like
the star fragments
of a long-lost galaxy
Sparkling against the void
remind me that we are so small
but also infinite.

TRIGGER WARNINGS

---

*Dear reader, please be advised that this is a
work of adult fiction. Themes include grief,
depression, enslavement, and oppression.
If any of the specific trigger warnings listed
below make you uncomfortable, please do not
read this work.*

Blood
Violence
Description of Injuries
Implications of Sex/Sexual Violence
Depression
Self-Harm Ideation
Suicide Ideation
Panic attacks
Loss/Death of a Parent

THE EASTERN NATIONS OF
ILERON

ALLERSEA ISLAND

THE CERULEAN SEA

USWYE

THE BROGAN MARSHLANDS

THE ENSEN MOUNTAINS

TO THE FAR SOUTH

TO THE UNCHARTED NORTH

DENTEN

LEGEND

◎ CAPITAL CITY

◉ CITIES AND SETTLEMENTS

PROVINCIAL BORDERS

CALLIX

RIVENSTORM

THE ASTRAN PASS

RALIAH

CENTRILIR

LAKA

EBENFELL

NATHCON

NATRON

LACHIA

IVORYMORE

SPIRAL CITY

WEST MISERAN

WOLFWATER

ASTRA RIVER

KAZUTA

KETTLEGUARD

MIDLSET

LANAHEIM RIVER

WESTREACH

EASTREACH

ALDERBURN

GALZAGA LAKE

BALINDAO

SPIRAL CITY

TO THE CERULEAN SEA

NORTH GATE

NORTHWIND MEDICAL

VAN ALDER RESIDENCE

NORTHWIND

UPPER CLOUD

THE GRAND GARDENS

CASSIAN'S SAFEHOUSE

THE GUARD

L U N A D E R E

WEST GATE

BLOOMSIDE

THE MORGENSTERN'S

SPIRA MIRABILLIS

EAST GATE

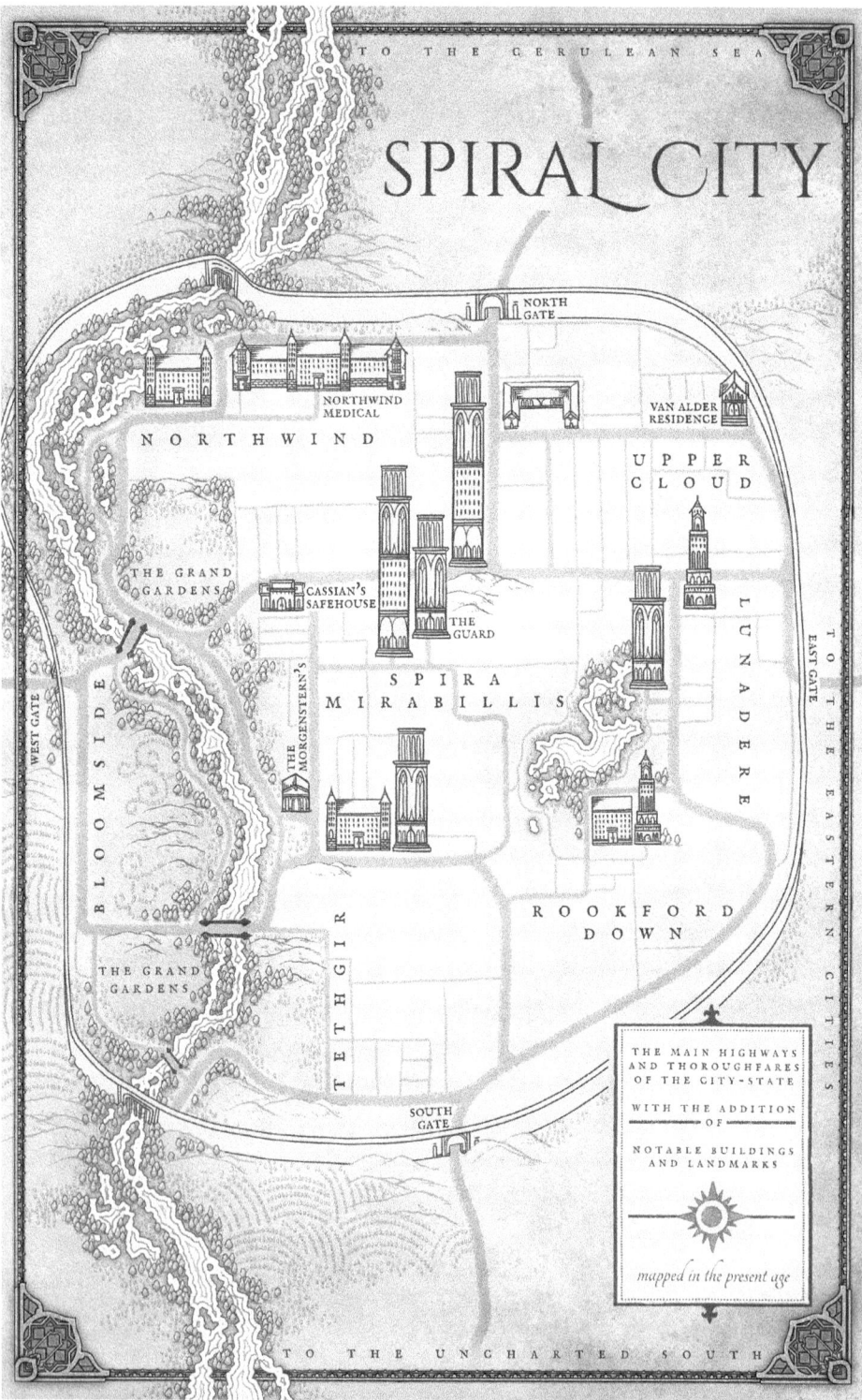

TO THE EASTERN CITIES

TETHGIR

ROOKFORD DOWN

THE GRAND GARDENS

SOUTH GATE

THE MAIN HIGHWAYS AND THOROUGHFARES OF THE CITY-STATE

WITH THE ADDITION OF

NOTABLE BUILDINGS AND LANDMARKS

mapped in the present age

TO THE UNCHARTED SOUTH

THE FREE CITY OF

RIVENSTORM

HILLCREST ROAD

NORTHERN RESIDENTIAL
NEIGHBORHOODS

PENNINSULA
BAY

IVORY
ROAD

RIVERWAY

RIVENPARK PATH

PENINSULA
MARKET
DISTRICT

IVORY HEIGHTS

RESIDENTIAL
DISTRICTS

THE
HOSPITAL

CENTRAL HILL   ROSESTONE

DOCKSIDE
MARKETS

IVORY ROAD

DOWNTOWN
CORE

HARBORSIDE

COMMERCIAL DISTRICT

RIVENSTORM
DOCKS

DIADEM ROAD

TO WESTERN
FARMLAND

AUTUMN
ROSE

DOCKYARD ROAD

THE EAST RANN PASS

LOWER QUARTER

RESIDENTIAL
DISTRICTS

INDUSTRIAL
DISTRICT

THE MAIN HIGHWAYS
AND THOROUGHFARES
OF THE FREE CITY

— OF —

NOTABLE BUILDINGS
AND LANDMARKS

Mapped in the
present age

CHARACTER GUIDE

THE LEGION & SPIRAL CITY

KELLAN MANCHESTER: A private in the nineteenth division as well as a Fallen. Has served as an indentured investigator/assassin for the past four years with the Legion.

VAIDA LARSEN: Another private in the Legion, serving in the eighteenth division as an analyst. Kellan's best friend in the Legion. A woman of many secrets.

THE COMMISSIONER: The leader of the Legion. He has served the Legion for over seventy years, but has only been in his current role for just over twenty years. Strangely attached to Kellan.

SELWYN MORGENSTERN: An heiress to weapons and tech giant, Morgenstern Tech. Her role in the Morgenstern business has only grown since her brother disappeared four years ago.

THE HELLS

CASSIAN EVERMORE: Previously an assassin in Ragnor LeRoche's employ but has since disappeared. Whereabouts are unknown.

ZALMELLOTH: A mysterious and elusive prince of the Hells. Zir's domain is Stygia; is in a pact with Cassian Evermore.

AZ'GOMACK: The de facto leader of Stygia as well as a prince of the Hells.

THE PHANTOM FLAME

ROSALIE DELACOUR: The leader of the Phantom Flame.

LIV AUCLAIR (TIGEREYE): A member of the Phantom Flame, and one of Rosalie's closest friends.

SPIDER (REAL NAME UNKNOWN): A member of the Phantom Flame, and one of Rosalie's closest friends. On Reaper's squad.

BECK AENMAR (REAPER): Actually an indentured Red Guard member in disguise, but is now part of the Phantom Flame. Spider is part of his squad.

FOXTAIL (REAL NAME UNKNOWN): A member of the Phantom Flame, and a part of Reaper's squad.

GREEN WASP (REAL NAME UNKNOWN): A member of the Phantom Flame, and a part of Reaper's squad.

For a hundred days, the trespasser god and the original god fought.

It is said that the sun never set during those hundred days. The fields were scorched, the rivers ran dry, and the people begged their gods to stop fighting.

And when they did, only the trespasser god was left standing.

Although his power was greatly diminished, he won. He prevailed against the original god and trapped the only ones who could try to defy him, locked them away in a now-cursed realm.

Waiting for the day when the Veil finally falls.

SECTION 1

DEMONIC PACTS

Demonic pacts are, regardless of the parties involved, always a symbiotic relationship. Although it may seem that the pact-bearer is getting the better end of the deal, rest assured this is not the case.

Pacts are only formed with agreement from both parties—forced pacts do not exist. The terms of agreement can be as simple as an affirmative response from both sides or much more complex and ritualistic. Since the foundation of the pact is formed with consent from both parties, it is natural that the rest of the pact functions in much the same way.

Betrayals between pact members is impossible. Asking the other member of your pact to cause the other harm is a distinct taboo. In return, pact-bearers gain the powers equivalent to the demon they have formed a pact with. Other, more specific terms can be formed upon the creation of the pact beyond the no-harm agreement.

Summoning a demon and creating a pact is reserved only for those who have innate magical abilities. Lack of magical ability doesn't disclude you, however, from forming other kinds of agreements with a demon.

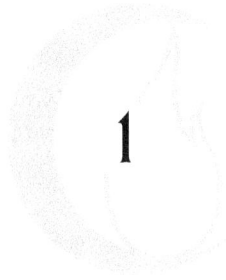

1

KELLAN

Spiral City | 14th of Cresting Moon

That familiar sensation descended upon him without warning; tickling his nose, stinging his eyes, clouding his vision.

Not here. Not now.

The shifter to his left smoothed a finger over Kellan's leather jacket sleeve, their eyes bright. Nothing stirred in him other than disgust.

The disgust wasn't for his companion; it was for himself. But Kellan had long ago learned that disgust was preferable to the deeper, sharper, all-encompassing grief he was suppressing as he leaned in to lock lips with the shifter.

His self-loathing only deepened as the kisses did, each one leaving him more and more empty inside. Each exchange that should have left him breathless instead left him cold.

The black pit inside of him squirmed, its depths writhing with loathing and hatred. It was angry; with himself, with Sol, with Leo and Alvemach. That was good. Anger was another emotion he'd found to keep the grief at bay.

The shifter parted Kellan's lips, flicking a snake's forked tongue inside his mouth. He didn't flinch, but the blackness swarmed with more fervor. He wove a hand through their soft, shoulder-length black hair, letting the strands trail through his fingers like liquid.

"My place is upstairs," the shifter said, finally pulling away long enough to speak. Their tongue flicked over lips swollen from kissing. "Care to join me?"

Kellan didn't much care about where they lived. It was close, which was good. He'd be on the way to momentary blissful distraction sooner than later.

He shrugged nonchalantly. "Lead the way."

The shifter smiled, then stood. They motioned to a group of people, waving their hand in a quick goodbye. None of them gave Kellan a second glance. If they had, they might have seen the black fire burning in his eyes as he followed their friend out of the bar and up a set of metal stairs beside the entrance.

Where was he again? he thought, glancing around. It certainly looked familiar, but then again, all of Spiral City looked familiar by now. There weren't any trees, so Lunadere was out. Maybe Tethgir, in the northern part of the district that bled over into Lunadere? He couldn't tell. Vaida would be furious with him when he'd inevitably call her in the middle of the night or early morning to come pick him up.

Again.

His companion fumbled with their keys, turning back once to shoot him a sheepish yet flirty grin. He didn't return their smile.

Finally, the door unlocked with a soft click and they were inside, lips locked the moment the door closed behind them.

Between kisses, clothing came undone. First, their jacket dropped to the floor with little pomp or circumstance. Kellan's jacket joined soon after.

Their shirts came off slowly, a teasing game to see who could torture the other longest before they caved. Kellan won, allowing the shifter to think they were doing more than serving as a fleeting distraction from the maelstrom of his heart.

His pants were a harder obstacle to overcome. Instead of allowing his partner to fumble, Kellan simply shook his head, gesturing toward the bedroom.

"Go, get ready. I'll be there in a sec."

The shifter nodded, walking toward the bedroom with a single flirtatious glance backward before disappearing.

He gathered his discarded clothes, neatly folding them and placing them on the chair in the living room, placing his pants and undergarments with them. He'd lost enough pairs of underwear by now to know when to take caution.

Kellan paused, the weight inside him heavy as he stared down at the pile on the chair. He was bleeding inside, but his skin was smooth and unblemished. What would it feel like to cut open that skin and let the pressure inside of him spill out? Would he feel some kind of release? Or would the pain distract him from the angry fist that clenched his heart?

His jaw tightened. He already knew the answer. It wouldn't help.

He turned toward the bedroom, leaving his neatly folded clothes on the chair and focusing on the dark before him.

The shifter had already disrobed, lying on the bed in full splendor.

Kellan joined them, crawling slowly across the sheets, a wry grin spreading his lips. "Make me forget everything tonight."

The shifter caught him, nibbling on his neck, just below his ear. "Consider it done."

🜂   🜂   🜂

Several hours later, his techpad was lit with Vaida's hologram. He'd dressed as the shifter slept soundly, the sheets tangled beneath them, the disarray proof of their night together. Not that it would matter in the morning.

"Seriously?" Vaida drawled, then sighed in resignation. "You could just get a taxi, you know."

Kellan tugged his jacket on, shaking his head. "Too expensive. You don't make small talk, either."

"I should strangle you," she retorted. "Be there in twenty."

He nodded, then swiped a hand over his techpad, erasing her hologram and ending their connection. He didn't glance back at his conquest before easing himself out of their door and back down the metal staircase.

Alcohol didn't work on him—a shame, that was. But he couldn't deny that he preferred loud places these days. Noise was a good cover for his thoughts. And this place was loud enough he couldn't hear himself think.

He reentered the bar, smoothing his shaggy hair back from his face. It had a slight curl to it when he let it get longer, and it was over his ears now. People enjoyed weaving their fingers in it in the throes of passion.

Kellan's shoulder bumped against another patron's as he crossed toward the bar from the entrance. He mumbled a half-hearted apology, not bothering to turn and look at whoever he'd run into.

He didn't get far; a large, meaty hand descended on his shoulder, whipping him around to face them. The hand belonged to a hulking man, his hair buzzed short to his lumpy head. His ears were long and pointed, silver hoops flashing at their tips.

"Watch where you're going, shrimp," the man said, squeezing Kellan's shoulder beneath his hand. "Little bitch boys like you should have some manners."

Anger flared brilliant crimson in his vision. The high from sex was fading, and this guy was pissing him off.

He wrapped a hand around one of the man's massive fingers and lifted his hand from his shoulder like he was picking up a soiled rag. "And why should I have manners for some beast like you? You look like day-old roadkill."

The man's cheeks flushed red. Before he could open his mouth, Kellan continued.

"I wish I cared about talking more with you, but I'd need to learn whatever language dogs speak in order to communicate with you. Woof, woof."

Kellan watched with amusement as the man's face went from red to purple, the veins in his neck popping. Excellent. He was in the mood for a fight.

Sensing the tension in the air, the surrounding crowd stepped back. Kellan rolled his neck, popping the spaces between with satisfaction.

The man cracked his knuckles. "I'll make you wish you'd never been born, asshole."

"Oh, great comeback. I'd give you a dirty look, but, ah, you've already got one."

The man roared, swinging his meaty fist wildly toward Kellan, who easily ducked out of the way, his hands stuffed into his pockets. The man was obviously not well trained and had used his size to his advantage until now.

Kellan laughed wryly. "Come on, you've gotta be faster than that!"

He roared again, bringing his other fist up from below, hoping to catch Kellan's jaw in an uppercut. His size hindered him against someone nimble like Kellan, and he easily avoided his swings. Kellan still seethed, but enjoyed taunting his opponent.

The big man swung around to face Kellan where he'd circled behind, practically foaming at the mouth. "Stop dodging and fight me face to face, you little shit! You're underestimating me."

"I find it impossible to underestimate you, *sir*," Kellan said, emphasizing the honorific.

That seemed to enrage the beefy man further. He swung again, Kellan ducking between the double swings he took toward his head and stomach. It was easy to avoid him; his tells were sloppy and obvious. With Kellan's training, it was akin to fighting an oversized child.

He dodged between flying fists with ease, never taking a shot and waiting for the perfect opportunity. The crowd had backed up enough to avoid accidentally impeding their fight, but watched with eager eyes.

Finally, he saw a chance. While the big man took another swing, he dove beneath the man's massive arm and twisted, letting his back roll along the extended arm. They ended face to face. Kellan wore his best shit-eating grin, then brought his knee up into the man's groin.

The man dropped like a stone, clutching between his legs with a strained cry.

Kellan scoffed, clicking his tongue at the man before crouching down to meet his eyes that brimmed with pained tears.

"Next time you pick a fight with someone, maybe reconsider. Your size isn't always an advantage."

The man wheezed. "You—"

"Kellan!" Vaida's voice cut the man off as she emerged from the crowd. "Gods above, I should have known it was you."

Kellan stood, brushing his hands on his pants nonchalantly. He tossed the man one last look over his shoulder before turning to Vaida. "Let's go, V."

She grabbed a fistful of his jacket in her hand, pulling him close, their noses practically touching. "The next time I find you in a bar fight when you beg me to come pick you up, I will castrate you myself. Without anesthetic. Understand me?"

Kellan paled, but nodded meekly.

The man, still clutching between his legs, stared up at Vaida with fear in his eyes. She frowned at him before dragging Kellan toward the door.

Once outside, she nearly threw him onto the sidewalk outside the bar. This was a familiar scene for them. She'd been dragging him from bar fights for three years now. Why she was still putting up with him, he'd never been able to figure out.

She sighed as he righted himself. "Kellan, I don't know what else to say to you that you'll understand. I've tried everything, and I don't know how to help you. But this?" She gestured back toward the bar. "This isn't the answer to your pain, and you know it."

Kellan scoffed again, crossing his arms as he leaned against the building. "It's better than sitting around and doing nothing, alone."

"That might be true," Vaida said, coming to stand beside him, "but my point still stands. You're not solving anything. You're just hurting yourself even more."

"I'm fine." He gestured to his body as proof.

"Physically, maybe," she agreed. "But your head and heart aren't doing so well."

The scowl that turned his lips down was venomous. He knew Vaida wouldn't take it personally, but he couldn't stop the expression once it started. A small voice in the back of his mind told him she was right, but he ignored it by squeezing his eyes shut so hard he saw stars.

He felt a hand graze his cheek, coming to rest just below his ear. "Listen," Vaida said. "We never get over our grief. We just learn to live with it. I'm trying my best—can you do the same for me?"

He knew what she was asking for. She wanted him to talk to her, to release everything he'd been feeling into words. He knew it was stewing inside, a black chasm that sat like a stone in his gut. It had dictated his life for so long now, driving all his actions with a single-minded, selfish motivation.

Maybe it was time to take back control. Maybe Vaida was right.

He sighed, releasing his arms to rest at his sides. "I'll try."

Her smile was brilliant as she turned his face to meet hers. "That's all I can ask of you."

2

BECK

Rivenstorm | 15th of Cresting Moon

He watched the group of women at their usual table in the corner, his eyes resting on the dark-haired woman. He watched her eyes as they followed Alpha, then her hands as they gently picked apart a snarl in her hair.

Alpha's braid swished; the movement reminded him of the day they'd met, when she'd asked him what freedom meant. Reaper hadn't been sure how to answer.

Whatever he'd said at the time had satisfied her, his answer enough to give her pause. She'd welcomed him into their ranks with a smile, but he'd seen the way she watched him out of the corner of her eye for nearly a year afterward.

He knew the three women who sat with the flaxen-haired Alpha well; Tigereye, Rosalie's closest confidant and a brash-mouthed fighter. Harpy, a dark-haired woman of small stature who had always welcomed him with a smile.

Then there was Spider. She was radiant; a skilled gymnast and wicked with her demon-killers, and Harpy's twin sister. He found it difficult to look anywhere but at her.

They'd granted him the codename Reaper when he'd first joined—Tigereye had joked when he'd come on board that he was much too pretty to be a warrior, and thus, he must be a demon instead. Reapers were a deadly breed of devil, able to take the visage of a beautiful humanoid whenever they set foot in the material plane.

He hadn't minded the joke. He'd embraced it, along with the connotations it carried about his character.

He was just like a reaper demon, using a pretty face to infiltrate their organization and ensure its downfall from the inside out. The name, although started as a joke, was more accurate than Tigereye ever could have realized.

He leaned upon it like a crutch, using his codename as a substitute identity to separate himself from the guilt of the mission he was to carry out.

There was another thing reaper demons were known for—they were harbingers of the end.

Reaper really was no different.

He sat in the corner of a bar called the Autumn Rose, the headquarters of the human resistance known widely throughout Ileron as the Phantom Flame.

Although he'd been a member for several years now, he still didn't feel like he fully belonged. He supposed that was on purpose; bringing down an organization from the inside was easier when you didn't become attached to its members.

Don't get attached, he repeated to himself. Even as his eyes followed Spider as she stood, flipping her hair over her shoulder and waving farewell to the rest of the table.

Don't get attached.

His techpad buzzed in his pocket, jostling him from his silent brood. He dared not pull it out here, so he stood as well, following Spider as she made her way to the staircase to the rooms above the bar.

Reaper had a room here too—it was more of a hassle to rent in the city, especially when the room he rented here had been available when he joined.

She didn't notice him at first as they converged on the staircase, but as he grew closer, her expression drew closed. He knew how she felt about him; his presence had always made her nervous, but she'd begrudgingly accepted him at Alpha's behest.

She nodded toward him, expressionless. "Reaper."

His lips never moved, but hearing his codename made him want to scream. Why? He wasn't sure.

"Spider," he replied, eyes locked with hers, "how are you feeling?"

Something had hit her hard during their last sting, an encounter that left her with a large gash in her arm. Spider hadn't complained, barely noticing the wound even after Reaper had pointed it out to her.

They ascended the stairs together as she considered his question. Halfway up, she shrugged. "It's healing fine," she said. "Thanks for asking."

"I was worried."

As they reached the top of the staircase, she flipped her hair over her shoulder, throwing him a small smile. "I'm okay, I promise. You don't need to worry."

Without waiting for him to respond, she peeled off toward her room at the end of the hall. He stared after her, waiting until her door shut before turning toward his own.

🝆 🝆 🝆

Kellan had called.

He'd kept up his relationship with his best friend at great risk to both himself and his operation. But something about letting go of the only family he had left had been simply too much to bear.

But his time was growing shorter, the plans laid in motion many years before finally coming to fruition, and each passing day grew more and more precarious for Reaper's cover. Although he didn't want to, he knew he'd have to let this be the end for the time being.

He could always come back, right?

He fished his techpad out once he'd secured the door and set up the noise-canceling nodule he kept in his room for calls like this. The walls here were thin; he didn't need eavesdroppers.

Kellan picked up on the second ring, his hologram exhausted and haggard. Concern twisted Beck's stomach.

These last few years there'd been a darkness about Kellan, something tugging at the edges of his friend that he'd never been able to ask him about. Something that had turned Kellan's normal shine into something dull and cold. Beck desperately wished to know what had darkened Kellan so, but his friend never offered the information, so he never asked.

"Sorry, Kell, I was tied up."

Kellan's trademark smirk had him relaxing. "Sounds kinky. Was it fun, at least?"

He rolled his eyes at the hologram, setting the device down on the small table in his room. "Not that kind of tied up."

A wheezy laugh from the techpad had Beck's lips quirking up the smallest touch. "I haven't heard from you in weeks, man. What's going on?"

Guilt wiped the smile from his face as Kellan spoke. He couldn't reveal anything to him, regardless of how much he wanted to or who was listening. Even if he wanted to spill his mission's secrets, the tattoo would prevent him. They'd know. They'd always know.

"Doing some undercover work," he finally said. "And speaking of work, I'll be going dark soon."

Kellan was silent on the line, his brows furrowed in a contemplative expression. They stayed silent for several heartbeats, the sounds of the Autumn Rose blocked from his room thanks to the nodule. The silence was…too silent. Unnatural.

His best friend finally released a breath, eyes closing as he did. "I hate undercover shit. But I get it. You can't tell me more, can you?"

Beck shook his head. "Not a peep."

He could see Kellan's hand appear in his hologram, rubbing the back of his neck as he'd so often done when they were kids. Something about the habit being carried over into adulthood made him even more charming.

Kellan had always been what Beck wasn't. He was friendly, charismatic, and their instructors at the Mission had always loved him. He'd never really understood why Kellan had kept him close, but he'd never fought it.

Finally, Kellan sighed. "Fuckin' tattoos," he breathed as he dropped his hand. "Well, I can't say I like it, but I understand. Just—"

Kellan stopped, closing his eyes once more. Beck stayed silent, knowing Kellan needed a moment to plan whatever he was trying to say.

"Just be careful, okay?" The words finally came.

Beck nodded, his heart constricting. "I will, I promise."

They fell into a comfortable silence for a few moments, Kellan fiddling with something off hologram. Beck just watched him, appreciating the comfort and normalcy Kellan brought into his life. He noticed the darkness in his eyes, the way his smile never quite reached his eyes.

The words spilled out before he could think better of them. "Did something happen?"

Kellan tilted his head. "What do you mean?"

"You seem…" Beck searched for the right word. "Off. Sad."

His friend chewed his lip, and Beck wasn't sure he would even answer. Their lives weren't exactly easy, so it wasn't a surprise that something was bothering Kellan. That something had thrown his normally snarky, give-a-damn best friend so far off his usual demeanor.

The guilt for even asking bubbled to the surface. "Sorry, I didn't mean to—"

"I lost someone," Kellan finally said. "Someone important. They're gone now."

Beck didn't know what to say. Apologizing wasn't his place; commiserating would only seem shallow; and he wouldn't know who Kellan had lost, so reminiscing wouldn't help.

He wasn't used to being so useless.

"When?" was all he could ask.

Kellan looked away. He stayed silent for several moments, fiddling with his fingers and refusing to meet Beck's eyes through the hologram. Beck hated the holograms—he wished he could be there in person. He wished he could bump Kellan's shoulder like they had when they were kids.

But they hadn't really been kids. Not since they'd been at the Mission.

"It was a long time ago," Kellan said, almost like a whisper. It was spilling over, his grief; a cup so long overfull that even the slightest shake would send the contents crashing over the sides. Beck could sense the delicate dance Kellan was doing to maintain that balance, to keep the cup from spilling over. He could do nothing to help except watch and pray he could keep it up.

Kellan didn't give Beck the chance to reply before continuing. "I've gotta go, Beck. V is calling."

Beck nodded, then swiped his hand over the techpad. Kellan disappeared beneath his hand. Something about seeing his best friend fade from the screen felt like an ending of sorts. What was ending, he didn't want to think about.

🌢 🌢 🌢

"Please," the woman begged as she kneeled before him. "Please, you know of my son? You must tell me where he is. I need to know."

He stared down his nose at her. She wasn't afraid for herself? She had to know what he was here for, after all. The sword in his hand wasn't exactly subtle.

He didn't reply, knowing he'd said enough already. She didn't know where his other target was, and that was all he needed to know from her.

But something about the image of her begging—not for her own life, but for her child—had Beck in knots. His mother had been his only family for so long until he'd found Kellan. How could they ask him to take someone else's family from them?

The sword in his hand grew heavy, too heavy, like it had turned from steel to pure lead. Like instead of carrying a sword, he was carrying all the lives he'd taken.

He glanced down at the weapon in his hand and nearly dropped it. It was covered with brilliant crimson blood, rushing down in a torrent to pool at his feet. He hadn't even touched the woman yet. Where was it coming from?

"Please," she begged again. "I just want to know if he's safe. I don't care what happens to me."

He shook his head and opened his mouth. But when he tried to tell her, tried to say he didn't know where her son was, she screamed.

She slumped to the floor, the deluge of blood from his sword even stronger now.

He did not wake dramatically; he simply opened his eyes to the cedar plank ceiling of his room at the Autumn Rose. Reaper rarely dreamed about his victims, but she was different, the woman he'd killed three and a half years ago.

She'd begged like she had in his dream, only asking for information about her son who'd gone missing. Her son, who he'd also been sent to kill. Her son, who, even after all this time, had never resurfaced.

He knew that regardless of where Cassian Evermore was, the Red Guard would still expect him to find him and eliminate him. They wouldn't take *he's disappeared* for an answer.

So Reaper threw the covers off and started another day as a beautiful demon.

3

CASSIAN

Unknown

"Cassian, Cassian, Cassian…" The sing-song voice reverberated in his ears.

He ignored his companion, who sat beside him, ice-blond hair falling over zir eyes as ze stared. But Cassian's thoughts were elsewhere, as they had been for…well, he wasn't really sure how long.

Time passed differently in the Hells—he'd learned pretty quickly that there was no such thing as days or nights. And Zal wouldn't heed him when he'd ask how many days had passed. Ze'd deflect or avoid the subject altogether. It didn't matter how many times he asked either; Zal was a master of avoidance.

Zalmelloth, to zir credit, had taught him much about the Hells and what it meant for him to be here. There were nine layers, each with their own distinct geography, government, and social system. Different demons lived on each layer, adapting their bodies to whatever layer they were born upon.

Demons varied wildly from the low-level demons like calpis and imps to the highest-ranked princes like Zalmelloth and Stygia's de facto ruler, Az'Gomack. Since Zalmelloth was a demonic prince, it meant his pact with zem was stronger than it would be with a lower-ranked demon.

Which meant, by proxy, that Cassian's well of power had grown to depths he never could have imagined.

But something about the power inside him felt different. Something had changed when he'd come here. He'd never been able to pinpoint *what*, though. He'd notice at seemingly innocuous times that the pull in his gut was silent.

But his newfound power was overwhelming. Enough so that when he'd first awoken after their pact was struck and Zalmelloth had introduced zemself, he'd immediately collapsed again. It had taken what seemed like years to get his newfound power under control.

And not knowing how long he'd been here gave him many other worries.

He'd gone unconscious in Kellan's arms and woken up here. He didn't know if Kellan was even alive. And beyond that, since he had no concept of time here, he worried about his mother and what would happen to her if he never reported back to Ragnor. He wouldn't hesitate to kill her if Cassian never returned.

"Cassiaaan," Zalmelloth called as ze bent over, hands clasped behind zir back. "I know that look on your face. You're worrying about your mortals again, aren't you?"

Zalmelloth sighed next to him, pouting, when Cassian didn't reply.

The demon wasn't as bad as he'd been expecting, honestly. Ze wasn't ruthless or bloodthirsty like Alvemach, and ze'd been downright kind to Cassian while he'd been here. Ze'd never shared what ze stood to gain from the pact, however, but Cassian hadn't asked.

He turned to face the demon, frowning slightly. "Of course I'm worried, Zal."

"Why?" Zir eyes were bright as ze asked. "You aren't bound by magic, so what's the point?"

"The point," Cassian said, exasperated, "is that you have people to support you and love you even when you don't have magic binding you. It's like…mutual trust."

Zalmelloth stared at him, zir snow-white eyes unnerving, cocking zir head. Before Cassian could say more, Zalmelloth flapped a hand at him. "Seems like a waste of time."

Cassian sighed again. There was no point in explaining it to the demon, anyway. They'd had this conversation before, and it had turned out much the same.

"Anyway, I wanted to bring you here for our next lesson," ze continued, gesturing at the vast expanse of blue ocean. "It's my favorite spot in Stygia."

It looked exactly the same as the rest of the damn plane to Cassian. Not a single defining feature or break in the horizon. Nothing to set it apart from the monotony of the vast expanse of snow and ice. Cassian begrudgingly admitted that, while lovely, it wasn't different. He'd been seeing the same view his whole time here. Nothing changed, no matter how far he traveled.

They were here to teach Cassian how to use the now-massive well of power that lived in his body. They'd practiced many times already, unlearning bad habits Cassian had picked up as he'd learned to harness his power on his own.

Zal stood, facing the ocean, hands clasped behind zir back like some wise professor. Zir eyes swung to him, then ze smiled.

"Begin."

His exercises lay in repetition—diving his consciousness down into the pit behind his navel and threading a small bit of the magic out through his fingers. The trick was not to release a bunch of power at once, but to focus it on a certain area.

He'd never needed such precision before. His well hadn't been large enough to warrant this kind of control; it would never escape him, it would never fight him, it would never let loose and become wild.

But this new well of power was different. It was vast, and if he didn't learn how to control accessing it, it could overtake him easily.

He chose a chunk of ice as his target. He focused his small rope of energy on the ice, letting it strike like a whip. A purple vein of fire rocketed forward, slashing the ice rock in half.

"Splendid work. Again." Zal, although flighty and rather mischievous, was a grueling instructor.

And so he did—for how long he didn't know. But he continued to strike the same chunk of ice over and over until nothing but tiny glittering shards were left. Sweat formed along his brow, immediately becoming bone-chillingly cold as he continued his exercise.

Using his power took more energy than it had before, too. His well before the pact had been small enough that invoking it took little thought or energy. Now it was a mental and often physical exercise that could leave him feeling weak and tired.

"Enough," Zal said, holding a delicate hand up as ze stopped him. "You've got a handle on the small threads, but now I'd like to see how you fare with larger amounts."

Cassian wiped a hand across his brow, the sweat cold to the touch. "What do I need to do?"

Zal gestured to a large iceberg that sat several meters away in the water, the waves lapping gently against its base. "Focus there. Melt it."

He'd never sent magic farther away than he could reach with his hand since gaining his new power. But he knew they'd been working up to this.

Cassian breathed in deeply, letting the cold air soak his lungs, drenching him in the smell of frigid waters and ancient ice. He'd never think of this place as home, but something about the scent was comforting.

He threaded a small tendril of power first, now as easy to him as breathing. Then he threaded another, braiding it into the first. Then several more threads followed until he was holding a rope of power.

It thrummed in his body, vibrating his lungs and making his blood feel jagged in his veins. The strain of holding the large rope of power was immense, but it didn't feel unmanageable.

"Good," Zal said, zir voice thick with pride. "Now release it, with intention."

He did as he was instructed, imagining the rope becoming a bullet of power and flowing through the air like liquefied steel.

The iceberg burst, throwing jagged diamonds of ice into the air. They rained down upon them, glittering in the iridescent light around them like stars.

Pride swelled in his chest. He'd never been this powerful before. It felt good.

But it didn't feel *right*.

🜄 🜄 🜄

Some time later, Cassian walked beside Zal. They meandered through the glaciers, Zal chattering away about everything and nothing. Cassian only half-focused on zem, twirling the silver ring on his pinky.

"An interesting little bauble you have there," Zal said, gesturing to his ring. "May I?"

Cassian glanced at the ring Zal was staring intently at. Even though zir words were calm, he could sense a sort of frenetic energy pouring from the demon. Like ze coveted the ring his father had given him. Why, he couldn't understand.

Cassian shrugged. "There's nothing special about it." He didn't take the ring off, instead lifting his hand to the demon.

Zal took his hand, running cautious fingers over the cold metal. Ze said nothing, zir unnerving pale eyes twinkling with delight as ze twisted his hand back and forth. Zir hands were cold to the touch.

Briar had given Cassian the ring only a few weeks before he'd died. He didn't know why he'd kept it all this time, but every time he'd wanted to rid himself of it, he couldn't. His hands would refuse to take it off, would refuse to throw it away. Whenever he'd entertain selling it, he'd decide against it after only a few moments of contemplation.

The hesitance to get rid of it never struck him as odd so much as sad. He was holding on to a relic of his father, the last connection he had to the man (other than his debt to Ragnor, of course).

He'd never wondered about the ring before. It had been a part of him ever since he was young. It was simply his father's old ring, handed down to his only son as a small, pathetic excuse for an inheritance.

But now, watching Zal's rapt observation of the ring, he wondered why the demon was so interested in this unimportant relic of his past.

"Zal?" he asked, interrupting the demon, who was now twisting it around on his finger. "Why the interest in this? It's just a plain old ring."

Zal released his hand like ze was dropping a hot coal. Although ze didn't wear zir emotions on zir sleeve, it was easy to tell the demon had been enraptured. As if Cassian's question had caught zem in some unsavory act.

Zal brushed off the feeling quickly. "True," ze said slowly. "But I find items with sentimental attachments interesting, that's all."

Cassian narrowed his eyes. Ze wasn't lying; but he could tell it wasn't the whole truth, either. He wanted to press, but he suspected it would yield nothing. He made a non-committal noise instead.

Zal walked ahead, white braids bouncing with each step. Cassian toyed with the ring again as he followed.

Maybe he could…

Cassian dove into his magic, taking a tiny thread and weaving it around his pinky, around the ring. The thread was no bigger than a hair, fine and glittering in the sun like freshly polished steel. Could he tell if the ring was magic this way?

But nothing happened. It simply wrapped around his finger and glistened, taunting him with its ineffectiveness.

They'd tried nothing like this before, anyway; using his magic for non-combative purposes. He knew some things from his magic before the pact, and usually identifying magical objects was a pretty simple spell.

But the ring produced no results, unremarkable as a piece of steel. He let the thread of magic drop. He should have known—despite that, he was disappointed.

4

KELLAN

Spiral City | 24th of Wind Moon

"K, are you in there?" Avalan's voice was deep and rough. It had stayed rough since the day Kindra died.

The sun was still high even though it was late afternoon, streaming through the small window in his room, lighting the stone in liquid gold. The room next to Avalan's was jarringly silent. Kindra was gone, killed in action last winter.

Kellan finished lacing his boots before standing to open the door. "Yeah, I'm ready."

Kindra's absence was a stinging void, a reminder that although they continued to fight, all their efforts seemed in vain. Because, as they'd discovered after months of fighting demons in the city's streets, demons never actually died. They simply dissolved and returned to their home plane in the Hells.

Sometimes Kellan wondered what they were even fighting for.

Avalan nodded, turning on his heel to the doorway. Before he could exit, though, it swung open. Vaida stood on the other side, her dark hair in a multitude of braids that hung midway down her back. She wore a tight red crop top, a keyhole cut out of the chest. Her gray eyes found Kellan's, softening when they met.

"Ready to go?"

Kellan nodded, brushing a lock of hair from his eyes as he joined

Vaida, Avalan following at their heels.

The implications of their fight had haunted him as they discovered more and more about the demons that continued to flood the material plane. The implications that all he and Cassian had done three and a half years ago was for nothing.

He'd thought Alvemach was dead this whole time, but now he knew… He knew that wasn't true. It was an alarming prospect, knowing that the demon and his pact could reappear. It was an equally terrifying realization that giving Cassian up to Leo had also been a useless sacrifice.

The last traces of summer were clinging to life, the trees still verdant as they walked down the city's streets. Cars raced by, their engines a soft hum against the din of cicadas. The pavement shimmered in the heat, mirages appearing in the distance, only to disappear once they got closer.

It was in the small moments like these when Kellan missed him the most—the hours after midnight when all was quiet and still and dark. The silence between sentences when no one knew what to say. The reminder of his eyes in the green of the grass. It was enough to squeeze his heart painfully in an invisible hand.

He focused on Vaida's shoes ahead of him as they walked, using the rhythmic pattern of her footfalls as his guide for breathing. Today was hard. It had been for three years.

They stopped first at a florist to purchase flower wreaths. Wreaths were traditional, their shape representing the Circle of the Gods. Theirs were made of red-petaled flowers, sprigs of tiny white flowers dotted between. They weren't large, just big enough to sit upon the pedestals beside a keystone.

Their next stop was the cemetery. It was on the northeastern corner of Spira, set in a small green space reserved specifically for remembering those who'd left this plane.

Although those who'd passed into the ethereal plane didn't receive individual headstones in the city, there were massive memorial markers for those they'd left behind to mourn. They were often shaped like flames or like enormous gemstones cut into the earth. Flames represented Jupiter's hearth, the flames of eternal rest. Gemstones were also Jupiter's domain, for many believed them to be her tears shed for those who'd suffered.

The city's graveyards were artwork in themselves, built in such a way to bring mourners peace when they remembered their loved ones. Their beauty did nothing for Kellan.

Grief was cobalt blue and had clouded his vision for years now, never quite fading enough to fully see the light.

He'd loved, unashamedly and unabashedly. It had been so brief, enough that he'd not been given time to appreciate it, to understand it. But he'd known, if they'd had time, it would have been perfect. It would have been everything he wanted but didn't deserve.

Cassian was gone, and he wouldn't get him back no matter how much he prayed to the Circle. No matter how he begged them to return him.

Death was not the end, but it certainly was not reversible.

They approached a gemstone carving, painted a shade of stormy green that made Kellan's heart constrict. He kneeled before the stone, placing the wreath on a small hook beside it. He watched as it swayed in the breeze. His knees were dirty from the ground, but he didn't care.

Tears didn't come anymore—they'd long since evaded him. Now all he felt was a hollow sort of emptiness that never filled. All he could do now was simply stare, his thoughts a trickle of half-hearted memories tinged by the blue of regret.

He sensed someone next to him. Vaida took his hand, squeezing it once. Reassurance she was here, with him. It was their secret language, a small reminder that although the world was closing in on them, they were not alone.

Avalan stood a short distance away, his eyes shining. The wreath in his hands looked small compared to his size, but he held the flowers with tenderness.

Kellan turned away from the green keystone and followed

Avalan to a fire carving. He watched Avalan kneel before it, placing his wreath upon a pedestal beside it. The cobalt blue at the edges of his vision grew, closing in on him like he was drowning.

It had been like this for years now, the feeling of drowning even though he was dry. It felt like waves crashing over him as he continued to struggle, threatening to drown him each moment he breathed, then receding when he wanted to succumb.

Grief was a terrible burden. It weighed heavily on him, a pressure he could never escape no matter how hard he tried.

So he stopped trying.

He let it bear down on him, crushing him beneath its weight. It didn't matter anymore if he could keep his head above the water. If he was gone, maybe he could go wherever Cassian had ended up. Maybe he could be released from this weight, this pressure. Maybe his heart wouldn't feel as if it were made of lead.

A hand always reached out when he was close to caving in. A hand that now squeezed his as the edges of his vision went so dark they were nearly black. Even though he wished that burden gone, he couldn't leave. He could never leave her behind.

"Kell," Vaida said softly. "You're okay. I'm here."

He breathed in once, the scent of summer and green grass and grief and pomegranates flooding his nose. She was here. Just as she'd always been.

He squeezed her hand back in silence.

They stood, hand in hand, as Avalan kneeled before the headstone. Wind rustled through the trees surrounding the graveyard, the gold of the late afternoon sun shining through the leaves and casting a kaleidoscope of light upon the ground. Other mourners passed them silently, the entire graveyard quiet.

The sun began its descent, casting the sky in shades of purple and pink and orange. Avalan finally stood, brushing blades of grass from his knees. He looked sallow, the blue tint of his skin leaning toward green.

He'd known how close Avalan and Kindra had been. They'd

been in the Legion together for nearly twenty years, always working closely. For Avalan, losing Kindra was like losing a limb.

Kellan thought he could imagine the pain Avalan must feel.

Vaida squeezed his hand once more before dropping it to turn toward the exit of the graveyard. She only looked back once.

"Shall we?"

◆ ◆ ◆

The Legion dispatched Kellan to the eastern part of Lunadere—apparently, a shopkeeper there had been having trouble with some imps over the last few days.

They'd given him a new sword last year. It was not traditional steel, as he'd been using previously. Instead, the new standard for the Legion were swords with blades that looked to be crafted of hardened light. They vibrated and hummed with every twist and turn, and emitted low light when unsheathed. They weren't hot to the touch, however; they simply glowed.

Somehow these swords, aptly named demon-killers, were especially lethal to demonkind. Kellan couldn't help but wonder how much different the situation with Pontius and Leo could have turned out if he'd had one back then.

Lunadere had changed little; its trees were still evergreen, the houses still wooden and cozy. It was as if time never touched this district; frozen, still living in the past. It was both unnerving and comforting.

Kellan wondered as he stalked down the street if Alvemach was the cause behind all these demonic attacks, if he'd somehow torn a hole in the Veil to let his brethren through. Maybe more demon princes occupied this plane, their presence causing upset between the planes and releasing their hellish minions upon the material.

He rounded a corner, his boots crunching uncomfortably loud in the dead leaves on the sidewalk. It wouldn't matter if he barreled up to them on his motorcycle; they wouldn't flee. Imps weren't the brightest—they were akin to small, angry dogs that didn't quite understand that whatever they were challenging was much bigger and much stronger than they were.

He spotted six of them rummaging through the shop owner's garbage in the back of the store, their grunts and squeals of joy traveling through the air and piercing his ears. Three of them were the most common blood-red color, their tiny horns colored black. Two were purple with yellow horns, and one was black as midnight with a single white horn in the center of its forehead.

They noticed him at the end of the alleyway, and their squeals of joy turned to anger. They couldn't speak well, only the occasional word that Kellan understood. They instead communicated through noises—ones which now were definitely those of agitation.

A red imp flew at him, tiny talons outstretched as it flung itself toward his face. He ducked around it easily, unsheathing and activating his demon-killer with the press of a button. The rest of the imps turned from their rummaging to observe the fight.

The demon-killer sang as it activated in his grip, its brilliant light bathing the alleyway. It hummed as he adjusted his grip, the blue fire of the blade flickering with each movement.

The imp who'd attacked him stopped itself midair and turned to face him once more, baring its small but sharp teeth in a snarl. Kellan smirked and cocked his finger, a gesture for the imp to come closer. It obeyed, screeching as it flew once more toward his face.

This time, he didn't dodge, instead bringing his sword up in a graceful arc as the imp came within reach. The sword vibrated and whistled as it swept through the air, slicing the imp in half from ass to head in one clean cut.

The imp he'd bisected fell to the ground, its halves twitching as it melted into the pavement. Kellan looked at it in disgust, the knowledge that it was simply on an express trip home to the Hells strangling him.

What were they even fighting for?

The other imps screeched at the downfall of their brother, their cries becoming higher pitched as they scattered to surround him. He shook his head—these stupid creatures would never learn, would they? They raced toward him the way the first imp had. He dodged their clumsy attacks easily, swiping his sword each time one of them got close.

The ground was littered with disintegrating demon remains, and Kellan hadn't even broken a sweat. Counting the remains, he frowned. One was missing.

He glanced around, scanning the rest of the alleyway for the little demon and finding no sign of it. It was strange for an imp to be sneaky; they weren't smart enough to consider anything other than a direct approach.

A small white horn barely peeked over the roof of the shop. He grabbed a stone from the alleyway, chucking it as hard as he could in the imp's direction. His aim was true; seconds after launching it, the imp squealed, falling off the roof and plunging toward the ground for a moment before it got its wings out and righted itself.

Kellan lifted the sword once more, its humming filling the alleyway. The imp snarled again, maneuvering itself around Kellan to attack him from behind. It didn't work.

"Stupid human!" it spat in a voice clearer than any of the other imps.

Kellan stopped short, taken aback. "You can speak?"

"Of course I can speak, you stupid human!"

He didn't bother correcting its assessment of his race. He lifted his eyebrows. An imp that could speak? It might have some interesting information for him if he captured it instead of killing it. He adjusted the grip on his sword, reassessing his plan.

He didn't respond to the little demon, instead lunging forward to catch it by surprise. His offense worked, catching the small imp unawares. Instead of slashing the demon in two, he deactivated the blade, then brought the hilt of the sword down upon its head, knocking it out cold.

🜄 🜄 🜄

Kellan wasted no time bringing the captured demon back to the Legion to question it. It stayed out cold for most of the journey back.

The little demon did, however, wake up when he was nearly to the Guard. It squirmed and squealed in his grip, sinking its tiny fangs into his hand over and over. He ignored it, content to let it nibble at his fingers so long as it didn't escape.

No one stopped him as he landed. He marched through the front doors as his wings swept behind him for a moment before fading. The little demon still clasped in his hand was squealing but no one paid it any mind.

He took the elevator down to the interrogation rooms on the second basement floor. It was probably overkill, but he'd rather keep the little monster contained somewhere safer than in his rooms or the labs.

He threw it into the interrogation room, clasping a manacle usually meant for their smaller prisoners around its waist. It couldn't wiggle out, but it could still use its arms. It made several vulgar gestures at Kellan as he took a seat across the table.

"What are you?" he asked, voice low and murderous.

The little demon bared its fangs. "Not tellin'."

Kellan slammed his hand on the table, jostling the creature violently in its shackle. "Try again."

"Nope."

"You really want to play this game?" Kellan leaned forward, flicking his knife open. "How much do you like your fingers?"

The demon squealed and tried to fly away from Kellan, but the shackle stopped it short. It jerked back to the table with a clang.

He didn't reach for it again, instead letting it sit back up and find him there, knife ready. He could practically smell its fear.

"Why do you care? We're just demons to you anyway," it finally said, rubbing its head.

"It doesn't matter. Tell me now. What are you?"

"Fine, fine! I'm an imp."

"*Wrong,*" Kellan breathed, now balancing the knife between his fingers, swinging it back and forth in a threatening arc. "Your shitty little companions were imps. They can't talk, you can. Why is that?"

"I'm an imp, I swear! I've just been promoted!"

Kellan rolled his eyes. They'd discovered, over several years of interrogations, that the power system in the Hells was simply based on who was the strongest. He'd asked the basic questions, standard ones the Legion had instructed them to discuss each time they captured a demon. Now, with a fire burning in his belly, it was time to ask the questions he actually cared about.

"What layer are you from?" he asked, still balancing his knife on his fingers.

The imp scoffed. "Maladomini, but I bet you don't know which one that even is."

Kellan frowned, then brought the knife close to the imp's face. "Imply I'm an idiot one more time and you'll find this knife in places you don't want to imagine."

"I'm not afraid of pain!" The phrase didn't sound fierce in the imp's high-pitched voice.

A feral smile spread Kellan's lips wide. "You should be when I'm the one delivering it."

The imp turned gray, a shudder traveling up its tiny spine. "Okay, fine, fine. I'll answer your questions." It mumbled something under its breath Kellan couldn't hear.

He brought his knife down a hair's breadth away from the imp's tiny hand into the table, a dull thud echoing through the room at the action. The imp squeaked, attempting to take flight and being yanked violently back down to the table thanks to the shackle around its waist.

"I'm being quite nice, imp," Kellan said, voice low in his throat. "I said if you insulted me again you wouldn't like the result."

The imp was writhing now, trying to pull itself from the shackle.

"I only said that our great Prince Sabazios wouldn't stand for this! I wasn't insulting you!"

He'd heard the name before. Although they knew little more than the names of the princes of the Hells, Kellan knew from experience just how powerful a prince truly was.

"Why haven't the princes come to this plane?"

"I don't know! The Veil is thin—all we want is to be more powerful. Our princes are already powerful, especially Prince Sabazios. They don't need to prove themselves."

Gods, was Sabazios all this little imp would ever talk about? Kellan sat forward in his seat. "Do you know of the other princes?"

"Of course!" The imp squealed, still tugging at the restraints.

Kellan yanked the knife from the table and placed it beside him. "Then tell me about Dis' prince, Alvemach. Where is he?"

The imp watched as he laid the knife down, its bulbous eyes following the movement with a single-minded intensity. "He has not dealt with my lord Sabazios in many turns."

Kellan resisted the urge to grab his hair. "You only know of the other princes as it pertains to your own prince?"

"Well, of course!" The imp squeaked. "Why should I care about the other princes? They are not my great prince Sabaz—"

The imp suddenly stopped, cutting itself off in the middle of its sentence. Its milky eyes went wide. A purple tongue lolled out the side of its mouth as it gagged.

And from the toes up, it disintegrated into a fine black powder. Kellan swore.

5

CASSIAN

Unknown

Cassian followed Zal as they wound through the paths cut into the glaciers. They didn't have a home base in Stygia. Cassian hadn't needed to sleep or eat since coming here; time passed, somehow, but he hadn't perceived it.

Zalmelloth hummed as ze walked, hands swinging by zir sides. Although he'd been with Zal for a while now, he hadn't figured the demon out. One minute ze'd be cheerful and mischievous, the next ze'd be serious and brooding, almost like ze'd become someone else.

"Anyway, Cassian, I have some exciting news to share with you," Zalmelloth said, turning to face him. "It's about time we venture into the material plane, don't you think?"

Cassian stopped short. "What?"

"I mean," Zalmelloth continued, not even turning back to see if Cassian followed, "I could have sent you there whenever I wanted, but now we have an easy way to get there without having to use portals. Isn't that exciting?"

Cassian didn't move, his feet frozen to the ice beneath him.

"I'll take your silence as excitement, although it *is* a strange way to show happiness." Zal didn't look back as Cassian followed zem down the path. "Malboge has a Veil breach, we can go through there."

"Why?"

At Cassian's question, Zalmelloth finally stopped and turned back to him. "Because we have a mission to do. Obviously."

"A mission? To do what?" Cassian asked.

A sinister smile spread across Zal's face. "Something only you can do, Cassian." Zir eyes flicked to his hands, then ze took them in zir own. Zal's fingers were ice cold. Ze squeezed Cassian's, then ran gentle fingers over his pinky ring. "It's very important, and I had to present a pretty convincing argument to get our good king to agree."

"I don't know what you're even getting me into."

Zal's smile got wider. "Let me explain." Ze released his hands.

Cassian sat on a glacier, gesturing for zem to continue.

Zal chuckled. "There are three artifacts that we need you to bring back to the Hells. Rosalie Delacour, the human resistance leader, has something that will lead you to them."

He shifted uncomfortably. Pontius had wanted in with them—they'd rejected him. How would Cassian have any sort of success with this? He chewed on his lip.

"They won't accept me, Zal," he finally said. "I'm an elf."

Ze shook zir head. "Don't be so sure of that. You haven't been back for quite some time—you don't know what has changed."

He stood quickly, begging for the chance to ask what he'd wanted to know for so long. "How long has it been, Zal? Tell me. I need to know what I'm going back to."

Zalmelloth chuckled again, staying silent until Cassian caught up to zem. When he finally did, ze turned back down the path, trudging slowly along the ice.

Cassian waited in silence as they walked. Zalmelloth hadn't outright avoided the question or deflected, which meant he might actually get an answer if he stayed silent long enough.

Zalmelloth had a particular way of doing things. Although his understanding of the demon was, at best, surface level, he'd figured out enough of zir tells to know when waiting was to his benefit.

Ze finally spoke, zir voice quieter than usual.

"Time moves differently in the Hells, you know." The silence after their first statement grated on Cassian's nerves. "What might be five minutes here could be three days on the material plane."

Cassian's stomach dropped. Was it that different? While time crawled on here, people might have lived entire lives while he was gone? What would have become of his mother? Of Kellan? Would they be dead already? If he'd been gone for weeks or even months here, surely they'd have come and gone on the material plane.

He stopped again, all sensation leaving his body as the reality sank in. Everyone might be gone. Everyone he'd ever loved.

"You've been here for the equivalent of a little less than four years in the material plane. In Hells' time, you've been here for about four months."

Four years. He'd been gone for *four years.*

The cold hadn't ever sunk in before. It hadn't raised the hair on his arms or prickled the flesh at the base of his neck. But now it was as if his very bones had frozen over.

Stygia went white, his eyes stinging. There was no way his mother was still alive. If he'd been gone for four years, Ragnor surely would have had her killed long ago, as they'd agreed upon at the beginning of Cassian's contract. There was probably a bounty put out for her, and she couldn't defend herself against trained killers.

And Kellan. What would he think? He'd disappeared; Leo had taken him, and he'd never returned. Panic churned his stomach, making him sick. Kellan would never forgive him.

His entire life had crumbled and he hadn't been there to stop it.

His knees hit ice. Fine, powdered snow coated his legs in a dusting.

Zalmelloth's face appeared before his, zir white hair swaying in a non-existent wind.

"Existential crisis?" Ze sighed. "See? This is why I didn't tell you until now. I knew you'd freak out." Ze turned on zir heel, looking dramatically over zir shoulder at him as ze cocked a white-blond eyebrow. "Why don't we discuss something else?"

Cassian couldn't focus—his thoughts cycled from his mother to Kellan and back again, stuck in an everlasting loop of the worst possible scenarios. All he could do was stare at his hands, unsure of how to continue when it seemed there was nothing left for him.

"Oh come now, your life isn't over," Zal said, suddenly beside him and patting his shoulder. "I've given you another chance, Cassian. Don't despair."

"A chance to do what? Betray the resistance? Give you demons more power?" Cassian snapped. The desperation had turned to anger, sharp and jarring in his head.

Zal frowned. "I never shared what these artifacts even do."

"I can't imagine you would want something that didn't benefit you," Cassian scoffed. "So what do they do, Zal? If I'm going to return to nothing, might as well make me even more angry."

The demon said nothing, zir frown only growing deeper. Cassian wanted to push zem, but he knew it would do nothing. Zal was stubborn when ze wanted to be. Instead, the demon turned away, looking out over the vast expanse of nothing as if ze had a great weight upon zir shoulders. Cassian simply watched as ze stayed silent.

They stayed like that for some time before Cassian stood. The desire to rush everything along was stark. He knew now how long every second that passed here cost him. Every moment he spent in the Hells was too many moments lost on the material plane.

A thought occurred to him—if he'd been here while years passed on the material plane, then what had happened with Alvemach and Leo?

His anger was a living thing, squirming and writhing in his abdomen.

"Zal, what about Alvemach? Leo? Where are they?"

Ze didn't respond right away, but he could sense the shift. Moving away from the subject of the artifacts was softening the demon to conversation once more. Typical.

But ze shook zir head in a melancholy way. "I, unfortunately, don't know. The planes are quite separated here. I can only surmise what they might be up to." Ze sighed. "Alvemach is a prince of Dis, and that's four planes away. We can travel there if you'd really like, but…" Ze trailed off, refusing to meet his eyes.

Cassian shook his head. Passage through the planes was a tedious matter, and he didn't want to waste the time, not when he could return home only one layer away. The urgency to return ate at him.

"No, no, that's fine," he said, exhaling and rubbing his face. "Just…let me go back."

Zal turned to face him at that. "That was always the plan. I never planned on keeping you here much longer. Your mission is of the highest priority, but you needed time to manage your powers."

The pit in his abdomen squirmed, the absence of his second sense a yawning maw in his subconscious. It was as if both senses were itching for the chance to leave.

"When?"

Zal nodded, then looked around. "I think now might be a good time, don't you think?"

Cassian flinched. "Now? What do you mean?"

"I mean now," ze said, beginning to walk toward the continual vast expanse of nothing. "Come along. We have a bit of a distance to travel."

There were too many emotions in Cassian, too many for him to make sense of. Anger lived somewhere in his chest, nervousness in his stomach, fear in his head. Hope, though…hope was suspiciously absent.

6

BECK

G reen Wasp and Foxtail sat on the rooftops of buildings adjacent to his own, blending into the surroundings so well no one would see them.

Except for Reaper, of course.

Through the streets below, a demon was stalking. Although Reaper knew his eyes were deceiving him, the creature looked like a regular human. Most likely, it was a subspecies of the naishiek demon.

Reaper had only seen a few of them during their demon hunting trips. They were native to Dis, the second layer of the Hells. Their ability to disguise themselves so thoroughly made them difficult targets to hunt and even harder to spot when they'd infiltrated the material plane.

But this one had gotten a little *too* comfortable. Someone had complained to the local branch of the Guard that someone had been on a crime spree in the northern residential neighborhood of Penninsula Bay. Word had gotten back to the resistance, too.

Winning out against a naishiek demon was a battle of wits more often than not. They could appear as anything to their prey—family, friends, loved ones, and important figures. It took considerable strength to cut down a demon wearing the face of your mother or best friend.

This one in particular had left a trail of grifted victims in its wake, stealing anything it could get its hands on while wearing the faces of their loved ones.

Reaper and his crew stalked it, waiting for the right moment to strike. Spider was ahead, scouting the area for innocents and getting them out. The fewer people for the demon to use as bait the better.

A crackle came through his earpiece. "Reaper." Spider's voice was steady. "Zone's clear. I'll be back in a few moments."

"Nice work, Spider," he said, nodding to Foxtail and Green Wasp. It was time to move.

Fox was first; he swung himself down on a fire escape, not bothering to use the handholds and sliding down with one hand. He landed with a too-loud thump just behind the naishiek demon, who whirled on him, a hand over their chest in mock surprise.

Reaper followed suit but took his time getting down, keeping as quiet as possible to prevent the demon from realizing it was surrounded.

Fox grinned as the demon's visage changed. While it may not know the people whose faces it stole, it could act the part based on the victims' perceptions. It was a cunning demon, but most of its power lay in its ability to deceive. Once the illusion was up, the fight became much bloodier.

The demon took on the face of someone Reaper assumed was in Foxtail's family, maybe his mother or sister. She was pretty, with wide brown eyes and soft auburn hair.

"My son," the demon said, lips spreading wide. "You scared me, coming down like that. Why are you out so late?"

It didn't fool Fox. "I know what you are."

The demon didn't relent. "Whatever do you mean, love?"

Fox wasted no time, leveling his sword to his mother's throat. "Give it up, demon. I know this isn't real."

Tears welled in the demon's eyes, spilling down her cheeks. This thing was good, Reaper thought as he hopped down from the fire escape. It didn't relent under pressure. Maybe the Phantom Flame's members could learn a thing or two from it.

He shook his head and smiled wryly. There was nothing to learn from demons, regardless of their sometimes exceptional deception.

Movement caught the corner of Reaper's eye—Spider had reached them and was creeping up behind the demon, who was still sobbing.

Fox's role wasn't to take out the demon. He needed to keep it occupied while Spider, Green Wasp, and Reaper snuck up on it. The most important thing was to confuse it. If there were too many targets it would have a harder time trying to mislead all of them at once.

Reaper pressed the comm in his ear. "On my signal, Wasp, Spider. In three, two…"

On one, they leaped together.

Spider reached it first, wrapping a hand around its throat and swiping with one of her blades. The demon grabbed her arm with both hands and threw her across the clearing. Fox dove to catch her.

Wasp scrambled to the demon's side next, jamming a syringe full of some kind of poison into its neck. It was viscous and bright yellow and drained sluggishly.

But before it could empty completely, the demon swung its arm around and caught Wasp at the waist, throwing him, too. It yanked the syringe out of its neck and threw it to the ground.

Reaper reached it last, pressing the button on the hilt of his demon-killer and engaging the demon. It transformed, changing into the face of Commander Aluin.

"Stand down, soldier," it said. Reaper's stomach dropped. If any of the others saw…

But before he could react, Spider flew from the side, tackling the demon into the dark of an alleyway. They landed in a heap of tangled limbs and empty crates. Their jumble was hard to see but easy to hear.

Reaper ran to the alley, sword at the ready. From the chaos, both figures stood.

He swore as two Spiders emerged from the darkness. There wasn't a single difference between them, down to the tangle of her hair from the tussle.

The Spider on the left glanced to the Spider on the right, realization dawning on her face. She swore, colorfully.

"Reaper," she begged. "It's me."

"No," the Spider on the right said, "I'm the real Spider, you have to believe me."

His gaze darted back and forth, hand tightening on his sword. Left? Or right?

Before he could decide, the Spider on the left leaped at the Spider on the right, knocking her back into the alleyway.

He swore, and Fox came to his side, panting. "Whoa."

"I don't know which is which," Reaper snarled. "I can't tell the difference."

His mind raced with all he knew about Spider. Her mannerisms, the way she held herself, the exact shade of the red nail polish she was wearing before they left. He swore again. That wasn't enough for him to tell the difference—they were things the demon could easily replicate.

What made Spider *Spider*? And which of them was the demon feeding from to get its information to maintain the ruse? If it was feeding from Spider herself, they were screwed.

Unless…

An idea came to him. An absolutely insane, completely reckless idea.

"Spider!" he yelled. The fighting in the alley paused. "Come here."

They emerged again from the darkness. One held a circular blade to the other's throat. He still couldn't tell the difference between them. But the captive Spider's eyes flashed with fury.

The captive Spider snarled. "Get your hands off me!" Her feet lashed behind her, trying to catch the other Spider in the knees. She missed.

"Shut it, demon," the Spider with the blade snapped.

"Stop it, both of you," Reaper said. "I propose a game, if you dare."

Both Spiders frowned at him. The captive Spider scrunched her nose. "The hells do you mean, Reaper?"

Was she the real one?

"This is stupid," the other Spider said, pressing the blade further into the captive Spider's throat. "I've got the demon in my grasp already. Let me kill it."

Reaper clenched his jaw. "Stand down. If you're the real Spider, you'll have nothing to worry about."

Both Spiders tensed, but the Spider holding the blade released the other Spider, stepping to the side and lowering her weapon.

Fox whispered, "She must be the real one, right?"

Reaper shook his head. "The demon would want to protect itself. It's biding its time."

Wasp had joined them, a nasty gash in his head leaking blood into his eye. "Reaper…" he said in a warning tone.

He held up a hand to Wasp. There was one thing he knew about naishiek demons—memories were impossible to steal from victims, regardless of who they were feeding from. They might replicate mannerisms, appearance, and so much else, but their powers fell short when it mattered.

Reaper breathed, readying himself. "Spider," he began, tensing at her codename, "do you remember what I told you last night? About myself?"

He watched them both carefully. Both remained impassive. The Spider on the left's eyes flashed. She'd been the one holding the blade to the other's throat.

The Spider on the right tensed, her shoulders tight and hunched. Her hands flexed and curled into fists.

Neither gave anything away.

"Are we just supposed to shout something out?" the leftmost Spider asked. "She might try to copy me."

Reaper smiled. "Of course not. Whisper it in my ear. Only I'll know if you're right, of course."

The Spider on the right cleared her throat. "And what if we're both right?"

"You won't be." Reaper crossed his arms. "Whenever you're ready."

Wasp was tense beside him. Fox was smirking, but Reaper could see the strained set of his mouth. Neither one of them liked this. Reaper couldn't blame them.

The rightmost Spider came first. She stalked up to him, hands at her sides in fists. She stood on her tiptoes, leaning in toward his ear. She rested a hand on his shoulder, gripping him tightly.

"You told me your real name," she said, then leaned away, smirking.

Reaper didn't hesitate—he plunged the sword into her belly.

Fox made a strangled noise. The blood poured from her wound onto the ground and sizzled upon contact with the pavement. Wasp stepped back, the blood splashing onto his shoes.

The true Spider gasped from where she stood at the mouth of the alley. But she didn't smile when he withdrew his sword.

The demon fell to its knees, the illusion of Spider melting away like hot candle wax. Below the melting illusion, its crackled charcoal skin glistened with blood. Curling, bone-colored horns sprouted from its forehead over hair as black as the night.

"How?" it croaked as it dissolved.

Reaper looked down his nose at it. "You aren't a very good liar, are you?"

It never got the chance to respond as it faded into black ash on the wind.

🜄 🜄 🜄

Their squad's return to the Autumn Rose was silent. Everyone was rattled, perturbed by the scene with the naishiek demon.

Reaper knew Spider was the most disturbed of them all. The

demon had worn her face, had nearly gotten her killed. He watched as she retreated to her shared room with Harpy the moment they arrived. He wouldn't be her source of comfort, not after he'd killed the demon who stole her face.

Wasp also peeled away after they arrived, ducking out before they went inside.

Only Fox remained, and even he had lost his usual bubbly demeanor. After Spider disappeared, he turned to Reaper, mouth in a grim line.

"You all right?" he asked, running a hand through his hair.

Reaper nodded curtly. "I'll brief Alpha. Get some rest."

Fox didn't move. He watched Reaper with a concerned expression, his eyebrows drawn together in a frown. Fox was young, younger than the other members of the squad. He was a newer member of the resistance, but he was skilled—especially at talking, something Reaper sorely lacked.

"You sure you're all right, man? That was…" He trailed off, lost for words.

Reaper sighed. "I'm okay. Swear to Sol."

Fox nodded and turned away toward the bar. But as Reaper made his way to where Rosalie sat at the fireplace, he felt Fox watching him the whole time.

7

CASSIAN

Unknown

Malboge was, to put it simply, disgusting. He'd noticed the stench the moment they'd passed through Stygia's portal, the muggy heat of the new layer oppressive in its weight. After months of the frigid cold of Stygia, Malboge's sticky humidity was not a welcome change. His skin felt slimy.

He saw a few demons moving in the distance—one that he'd thought was a mass of vibrant green moss opened several blood-red eyes as they moved by, another that looked like a gigantic flying bug with a proboscis as long as Cassian was tall.

They didn't scare him, though. Not only did he know he wouldn't be attacked so long as he was with Zalmelloth, but he was essentially a demon himself by now. He'd promised his life to the demonic prince walking happily beside him.

Or so he thought.

The longer they walked through the plane of decay and rot, the more Cassian felt the demons' eyes following them. The sensation of being watched never faded.

Zal groaned. "I've always hated 'Boge," ze said, flipping zir hair over zir shoulder to look back at Cassian. "It's gross. The muggy air does things I don't like to my complexion."

Cassian didn't respond, letting Zal ramble on about zir dislike of the plane. His attention was split and wandering, jumping between his own thoughts of his upcoming return to the material plane and the demons whose eyes still followed them everywhere.

A nasty pair of sludge demons stalked them, their amorphous graying bodies squirming menacingly in their direction. Multiple eyes on stalks rippled over their bodies, each one of them fixated on the pair making their way to the rift.

Several others watched them too; a skeletal horse with rotting flesh hanging from its bones, a gaggle of what looked like fanged butterflies as large as a dog hovering in the west, and an ominous-looking shadow cast upon the bone-colored trees as they passed by, its shape unknown but foreboding.

"Zal," Cassian finally said, his eyes exhausted from constantly moving around. "There are too many eyes on us right now."

Ze laughed. "That's expected—they're probably waiting for the right moment to attack."

Cassian pulled up short. "Attack?"

Zal didn't stop, zir pace still leisurely as they continued down zir path. "Naturally. I'm a prince of another plane; defeating me would bring great honor and power. Of course they're practically jumping for the chance to spar with me."

"And you didn't think to warn me?"

Zal chuckled, throwing a snarky glance over zir shoulder at Cassian. "You have me. Why would I need to warn you?"

Cassian frowned, resentment for his pact tightening his jaw. He reached down into the swirl of magic in his gut, grabbing hold of a thread in preparation. Zal seemed to sense what he was doing and chuckled, but said nothing.

They continued their journey, Cassian still on edge. The thoughts in his head only grew louder as their destination came closer.

"Cassian," Zal began, slowing to walk beside him. "I can feel what you do, you know."

Cassian glanced up at zem, eyes narrowing slightly. "What?"

"The pact, it feeds me information about your emotional state."

Ze sighed, turning to face Cassian as ze crossed zir arms. "The longer you stay in this pact with me, the stronger the feed becomes."

Cassian said nothing in response. It felt like he would never fully understand what the pact had done to him or how he would fare in the years to come. The tightness in his chest increased as he stared at Zal standing before him, zir head cocked to the side.

"You'll be fine," Zal said, not unkindly. It sounded more like encouragement. "We're almost there."

He was leaving. That fact alone gave him hope. But he had too many questions, questions he didn't think could be answered before his inevitable return. The most important one lingered on his lips.

Zal cocked zir head. "Something the matter?"

Cassian thrust his jaw forward in resolution. "Where will I end up when I go through the rift?" That wasn't what he wanted to know, truly. But they'd get there.

Zal shrugged. "I've never been through, myself, but I've heard you'll end up on Allersea Island." Ze paused, contemplative. "You'll be fine; trust your instincts."

"That's not the issue," he replied, shaking his head. "I—I want to go to Ebenfell. See if my mother—" The fear choked him. He couldn't say it.

The demon's eyes glittered as ze regarded him. Cassian could sense curiosity spilling from zem—the first time he'd gotten such strong emotional feedback through their pact. It was off-putting, the sensation of another's emotions and the distinct separation between zir's and his own.

"Rosalie is in Rivenstorm. Why would you go to Ebenfell?" ze finally asked.

Cassian recoiled. "Because my mother is there?" He didn't know why he framed it as a question.

"But that's not part of the mission, part of our agreement," ze replied, zir white eyes wide like a child's. "You can't detour, Cassian. This isn't a pleasure trip, you know."

A metaphysical cord between them tugged. Their pact—it was

the first time he'd felt it so sharply. He knew if he pushed against it that the recoil could hurt him badly. But if Zal broke any of their terms, it would do the same to zem.

Zir stance was clear. He could only go to Rivenstorm. His journey may take him elsewhere, but only if it was for the sake of his duty and assignment.

Zal sighed. "I recognize this is challenging for you, as a mortal. But everything will be fine in the end. Trust me."

Zal said nothing more as ze turned on zir heel and continued walking. Cassian followed numbly, hardly feeling the sticky air around him and the heat of the sky.

He would be okay. He had no other choice.

🜄   🜄   🜄

The rift was not what he'd expected but somehow not surprising. It looked simply like a tear in space, jagged at the edges like someone had ripped it with their bare hands. It was only a few meters across and just barely taller than himself.

The tear had formed in the middle of bone-colored ruins in an expansive field. The ground was soft beneath his feet; walking on it felt wrong. He couldn't imagine what sort of buildings had once been in a place like this, but the ruins were stark against the pink of the fleshy plain. It wasn't a lonely location, though—the place was swarming with demons of all shapes and sizes. They weren't the only ones with the idea to use the rift to enter the material plane.

He could feel the many eyes of the demons staring at him as they swept through the masses. The demons teeming around the rift were all of low levels, it seemed, and they could sense the incredible power Zal held. The crowd parted like opposing magnets when Zal and Cassian approached, their eyes boring into him with undisguised hatred and loathing.

The hierarchy of the Hells was based on power. All demons sought power, and the lower a demon was on the power scale, the more desperate they became. Resentment brewed constantly and heavily in low-ranked demons. It was no surprise then that they swarmed at the chance to increase their power levels, to prove they were worthy of promotion by their princes.

Zal turned to face the demons closest to the rift, a smirk appearing on zir face to reveal sharply pointed canines.

"You all know it's quite rude to stare, no?" Ze looked around, meeting the hungry eyes of the demons around the rift. "You're waiting for your chance, aren't you? Well then, have at it." Ze spread zir arms wide, challenging the demonic crowd to come after zem.

The crowd obeyed in a sudden wave, the screams of the various demons a deafening din. Cassian blinked and Zal was gone, buried beneath the overwhelming herd of demons itching for a chance to fight the prince.

He stood still, not a single demon paying him any mind. He wasn't sure if he was supposed to help.

Before he could choose to do anything, a burst of white-hot energy exploded from the epicenter of the horde, throwing many of the demons into the air in an almost comical fashion. The rope of power Cassian held mentally was still there, but upon seeing the burst, he manifested it into his hand, willing it to become a flame.

But he needn't worry—at the center of the explosion stood a perfectly unruffled Zal, zir eyes full of mirth, arms crossed over zir chest. Not a single snow-white braid was out of place.

The demons who'd fought scuttled away, tails between their legs, tentacles waving, or scales shivering. The ones who'd simply been looking on decided against trying their hand against the demon prince standing in a crater of zir own power.

The fleshy ground around zem bled, rent open by Zal's display of power. Cassian willed the fireball in his palm to fade.

Zal cleared zir throat. "Leave us."

The remaining demons obeyed immediately, clearing out of the ruins in a matter of seconds and leaving Cassian alone with Zal. Ze turned zir face to the portal, an expression of pure serenity passing over zir features.

"Cassian," Zal began, zir voice softer than he'd ever heard before. "I have taught you so much during your time with me…" Ze trailed off, looking pensive.

Cassian didn't want to interrupt, so he stayed quiet, waiting for Zal to resume zir train of thought.

"You have my power at your disposal—don't forget that. You can call upon me when you need to, but I don't expect you'll need me much, anyway." Zal smiled bitterly. "You know your mission. Get the artifacts, bring them here."

Cassian started to reply, but before he could say anything, Zal gave him a gentle push through the rift and Malboge disappeared, taking the image of Zal with it.

🔥   🔥   🔥

The rift spit him out in a field covered in mud. Freezing rain sprinkled down on his head in a fine mist that soaked him through in minutes. He had nothing on him save for the new battle suit Zal had given him.

He didn't know where he was, but his gut tugged him west. The feeling was achingly familiar but also like a gut punch after so long not having it. He hadn't realized how much he'd missed his intuition.

He followed the sensation, cherishing its tug the whole time.

After an hour his boots were soaked through and covered in mud. Another hour passed and the rain finally stopped. A third hour passed, and he had yet to see anything but mud and snow and the occasional tree. He couldn't tell what time it was, thanks to the sun being hidden behind the clouds.

Yet, instinct wouldn't allow him to veer off course, wouldn't let him venture off the path. He squinted against the wind, and a building appeared in the hazy distance. As he got closer he could see several buildings clustered together.

He breathed a sigh of relief. Although Zal had given him some directions, zir grasp on the landmarks of the material plane was subpar. Cassian knew of Allersea, of course, but he'd never been. He'd never left the Empire his entire life. Ragnor hadn't let him.

The tug in his gut yanked him toward the town. The sensation was much stronger than he'd ever felt before—strong enough that he could have sworn someone was actually pulling on him.

He passed several old buildings that looked like they'd seen better days. They were covered in scorch marks and holes, and one was missing its roof.

There were no signs of life. No noise, no shuffling of doors or chairs, no curtains closing against a stranger in town. In fact, it seemed as if the place was completely abandoned.

It occurred to him then how close this place was to where he'd come out from the Hells. No doubt the demons had found it too, and judging by the state of the buildings, there was a good chance everyone who'd once lived here had died long ago.

But a voice rang out in the quiet, startling him enough to make him jump.

"What do we have here? How is it that you smell so much like my home, elf?"

He turned to where he thought the voice had come from and saw nothing but a half-rotted entryway, a drift of snow covering its threshold. His instincts were almost circular, swirling about him, pulling him forward, then back, then around. It was nauseating.

"Tell me," the voice continued, "how is it you came to smell of Stygia?"

The voice crackled like the dying embers of a campfire; it had a smoky quality to it that gave him chills. It reminded him a bit of Zal's voice, ambiguous and soothing but hiding a dark hint of malice in its cadence.

"Who are you?" he finally asked, turning to observe the rest of his surroundings, consciously keeping his hands relaxed. He ignored his gut as it whirled.

The voice laughed, bell-like, yet cold. "I am surprised you don't yet know, pact-bearer."

His heart stopped in his chest. How did they know?

He continued turning, still searching for the source of the voice when a flicker of movement in the corner of his eye had him whipping around to face a person clothed in a white dress.

They wore no shoes, and their dress was sheer enough he could see the outline of their body through it. It was definitely not warm enough to keep a regular person warm in this kind of weather. His gut stopped its maddening dance, pulling into a taut line toward the person before him. A bubble formed in his chest—joy, and unending, unyielding, gaping sorrow. It was deeper than anything he'd ever felt before.

Their hair whipped out from behind them, white as the snow around their feet. Everything about them was white—hair, skin, eyes. They reminded him of Zal.

That thought led him down another path—Zalmelloth was a prince of Stygia, and during his stay, he'd learned of the other prince of that plane, Az'Gomack. Although he'd never met them, Zal had spoken highly of them.

Was the person before him the ruler of Stygia?

They smiled at him, obviously sensing his train of thought.

"There you are." They took another step toward him, their feet leaving no impressions in the snow. "As you have surmised, I am Az'Gomack. You smell of my home plane. Tell me, why is that? You are not a demon, but it appears you have a pact with one."

He breathed in, then out, calming his thrumming veins. The anguish in his chest hadn't faded; he could hardly think beyond it.

He dipped his head to them. "Zalmelloth is my pact."

They raised their delicate white brows, clearly surprised by this revelation. "Zal made a pact? Interesting."

Their lack of knowledge of Zal's doings surprised Cassian, but he tried not to let that show. If they were here, that meant they'd probably missed most of what happened in the Hells. They must have been gone for many years to have missed his stay with Zal in

Stygia.

But they appeared uninterested in learning more. They turned to face away from him, looking up into the gray sky.

"Wait," Cassian said, reaching his hand out toward Az'Gomack. Why was he reaching for them?

They stopped with a jerk as if they'd been shocked. "Who—"

They cut themselves off, whipping their head toward him and grabbing a hold of his hand. Their grip was like ice, a vice around his fingers crushing the bones and popping his joints. He tried pulling away, afraid they'd crush his fingers into dust.

They seemed to realize when he started resisting that their grip was too tight. They released him, dropping his hand like it had suddenly turned unbearably hot.

"I…" they began, then dropped their gaze, eyes fixed on his hand. "It appears much has happened in my absence. Maybe it is time to return to my plane for now." They sighed, white lashes brushing their cheek. "Goodbye, Zal's pact. We will meet again."

Az'Gomack didn't wait for him to reply, turning around to look at the sky before snapping their fingers once.

They disappeared without a sound.

🔥 🔥 🔥

It took him a week to get to Rivenstorm from the island. After his encounter with Az'Gomack, he'd traveled southward and found a port city, where he'd bartered labor for a ride across to the Empire.

He had yet to find a weapon, but he wasn't without a way to defend himself. In the months he'd spent with Zal, he'd gained an understanding of his magic that he'd never had before.

His previous magic training, if you could even call it that, was taught to him by a grumpy old man in Ragnor's employ whose name he'd long forgotten. He'd given him a few vague instructions like "imagine the magic in the pit of your stomach" and "grab it like a whip and visualize the outcome in your mind."

Of course, magic was more complex than that. Becoming comfortable using it was akin to swordplay or martial arts—it took practice, focus, and small adjustments to make it work properly. Over the years, Cassian had developed habits when using his magic. Since his well had been so small, it had mattered little if they were good or bad.

But now, the well he had to pull from was much larger and much easier to misuse. The habits he'd developed before turned bad as they caused him to use too much power at once or didn't achieve the outcome he desired. He'd simply been throwing magic at things for so long, the precision it required to handle the significant power increase had taken a while to get used to.

And he was still learning. He didn't have a handle on it yet, but he was much more powerful and precise than he'd ever been before.

The only time he could recall feeling this powerful was when that fire he'd been unable to control had raged in Northwind. The power that had completely evaded him ever since. He still didn't know where it came from nor what had triggered it to appear. Zal hadn't known either, but something about the way ze'd avoided the topic had Cassian unsure if it was simply a lack of knowledge or something more.

But the power available to him now was plenty to defend himself with (even if the lack of a weapon made him feel naked).

Rivenstorm had taken him by surprise—even during winter, it was vibrant and full of life. Buildings were painted in a multitude of bright shades of purple, yellow, and orange. Flowers spilled from boxes in windows, giant pots on the streets, and from storefronts, completely unhindered by the cold and snow that had fallen. It must have been like Bloomside that way, he thought. The streets were narrow and cobbled, remnants of a time long before the Conjunction when the world needed less room.

The boat he'd been on for the last week docked in a busy harbor, where hundreds of other boats pulled up alongside them and unloaded wares of all sorts in boxes larger than a single person could handle. He was caught up in the busy wharf crowd when he disembarked without a glance back.

The first step of his mission was going to be a challenge. Finding the right people to contact and convincing them to listen to him was going to give him some trouble, considering his heritage. From what he knew of the organization, they were wary of elves.

The Phantom Flame's home base was here, somewhere in Rivenstorm, hidden under the brightly colored buildings and everlasting flowers. Somewhere, he'd find them.

But he could worry about that in a bit; he first needed to find a weapon and somewhere to sleep. He'd rather not steal, but he was without money, so purchasing a weapon was out of the question.

He ducked into an alley off of a busy street to think. The noise of the crowd was crushing his thoughts, the cacophony weaving through his ears and leaving him feeling scattered.

You've been back for such a short time, yet you're having this much trouble? Zal's voice echoed in his mind.

To his surprise, Zalmelloth could communicate with him while he was in the material plane. Ze'd first contacted him soon after he'd met Az'Gomack to grill him on the encounter. Ever since, ze'd contacted him in random bursts, like ze could tell when he was struggling and sought to make him feel less alone.

It was creepy, if he was being honest with himself.

He thought back to Zal after catching his breath. *You know you don't need to come to my rescue; I know what I'm doing.*

He heard a chuckle, but no response. It was typical of zem to chime in only to give him a hard time. Cassian didn't mind, but the interruption had set his thought process even further back.

He chewed his lip as he leaned against a brilliant teal building and crossed his arms to think. He could probably investigate Ragnor's old safe houses and see if he could still get into one.

A tug in his gut directed him back out to the street, where he was met with an ear-piercing scream.

He glanced around for the source of the sound and found his

eyes drawn to a flurry of movement several blocks down. Although he couldn't spot the source of the shriek, he knew something wasn't right.

Pushing his way through the now-panicking crowd, he slowly got closer to the source of the commotion. When he finally broke through the last of the swarm, his blood ran cold.

Before him stood a monster, a little girl in its jaws, her bright red blood leaking onto the pavement.

8

CASSIAN

Rivenstorm | 12th of Dusk Moon

Cassian's whole body vibrated as he stared down the beast, the little girl still clutched in its maw. A woman screamed next to him, her hands raking down her face in pure terror as she watched the little girl slowly lose consciousness. Her mother, he presumed, since she wasn't running.

He breathed in once, steadying himself. He breathed out, connecting to the pool behind his navel. He sucked in another breath, taking a small tendril and bringing it out through his hand to form a ball. On the final breath out, the ball turned from a soft purple glow into a burst of fire.

He lobbed it at the monster's scaly chest.

It roared, dropping the little girl. He moved swiftly, gliding across the pavement to catch her limp body in his arms, being careful not to knock her head on his shoulder or arm. She was breathing—much to his relief—but unconscious.

The woman screamed again, and he turned back toward her. He closed the gap between them and gently placed the girl in her arms.

"Take her to a hospital, now. She's still alive, but she needs attention," he said, looking the woman in the eyes.

She nodded, looking down to her daughter, then back up to

him. Her eyes grew wide at the sight of his face, the terror only heightening. She said nothing as she turned on her heel and ran.

He didn't have time to worry about the lack of thanks from the woman. The beast was angry—he'd just cost it its lunch.

He took stock of the demon before him, since he'd hardly had a chance to do so previously. It towered over him, its head coming even with second-floor windows easily. It was covered in gray-toned scales resembling steel plates, and its eyes burned a fiery red. It looked like a massive dog, although it was missing ears and its snout was very long and pronounced.

His stomach dropped for a moment, the sight of the four-legged demon with scales reminding him so vividly of the ones they'd fought in Northwind. But this one was much too large, its head the wrong shape and size. It wasn't the same, of that he could be sure.

But whatever in the hells it was, he needed to kill it before it hurt anyone else.

He was already connected to his well of magic, so he didn't need to reconnect, he simply needed to concentrate and pull. The thin tendril that obliged his command came to rest in his palm before turning to fire once more.

The monster snarled, then leaped at him, its paws outstretched and claws at the ready.

He threw the waiting fireball at its chest again, hitting the same spot with deadly precision. The monster stopped mid-attack, yelping as it fell back.

From behind him came a whistling, and before he could think too much about it, he was dropping to the ground, his training taking over. Was someone shooting at him?

Then the monster yelped again, and Cassian looked up to see a long, glowing sword sticking out from the same sore spot in its chest he'd hit moments before. Had someone…*thrown* their sword?

He whipped his head behind him to see a woman with her hands on her hips. She stood with her chin up, her corn silk hair in a plait by her neck. A jagged, dark scar ran from her forehead to her cheek, cleaving her right eye in half. The other was a brilliant blue with patches of white that almost looked like clouds.

She strode up to him, considering him with a cocked eyebrow. How someone could look so haughty with only one eye was beyond him, but she didn't seem too interested in staring at him for long.

"No weapon?" she asked, turning her attention back to the monster. It was trying to dislodge the sword in its chest and failing.

He shook his head as he watched it dissolve in front of him, turning to black ash as if it was burning from the inside out. The smell of sulfur and ash was strong.

She scoffed, approaching the steadily disappearing demon with hardly a second glance at him. She yanked the sword from the ashes, then pressed a button on its grip. The blue blade disappeared, leaving her with only a hilt, which she stuck into her belt.

"Yet you held your own," she said, finally turning back to him. "You're quite interesting. I've never seen you here."

He couldn't find his words; he could only stare dumbstruck as she spoke so casually to him. She'd just taken down a massive demon with a single stab. From a glowing sword. That she'd *thrown*. Who in the world was this woman?

She finally approached him, holding out a hand. "Rose. And you are?"

He took the offered hand gingerly, and she gripped his tightly. "Cassian."

"Cassian," she repeated, shaking his hand firmly before letting go. "I'd like to grab a drink with you. Is that all right?"

A pull in his gut was directing him to her, telling him she was someone he needed to monitor. Not in a suspicious sort of way, more like…she was familiar. The feeling he trusted so deeply was practically begging for this woman before him, a sort of relief flooding through him as he stared.

But he had no idea who she was or why she was even interested in him. It wasn't like he'd done anything so out of the ordinary.

Except fight a giant demon in the middle of a crowded street. But yeah, totally normal. Zal's voice cut through his thoughts.

Shut it, he shot back.

"Cassian?" Rose's voice sounded in his ears. "You can say no, you know."

"No," he said suddenly, the tug insistent. "I'm sorry, that was rude of me. That would be lovely."

She beamed at him before turning on her heel to walk down the street without glancing behind her. He followed, keeping a watchful eye on the surrounding street.

The few people who'd been watching the fight stared at him, but not at her. Even though she'd been the one to take down the demon, it seemed like a normal occurrence to these people. Cassian, however, was an oddity to them.

"It's just up there," she said over her shoulder, pointing to an old inn that looked straight out of a historical novel.

It was built with whitewashed stucco and dark oak, its shutters painted bright orange and filled with brilliant pink flowers whose petals were stark against the white snow. The sign above the inn read *The Autumn Rose.*

Rose ducked inside, holding the door open behind her for Cassian. He thanked her with a bow of his head before glancing around what he could only describe as a tavern.

The inside had much of the same dark oak as outside, with long rectangular tables interspersed between smaller round tables. The place was packed with customers of all shapes and sizes. The windows around the room spilled light into the dark space, and many of the patrons sat haphazardly on the chairs around the room, some on the table's surfaces, some even on the bar top.

The person behind the counter seemed used to this behavior as she weaved in and out between the many patrons, serving drinks in huge old-fashioned tankards that sloshed as she moved. She looked as if she was made of water, her skin translucent and tinged blue, with hair that swirled like waves.

Rose swept through the crowd, heading toward a curtain behind the counter. No one seemed to pay her any mind, even when she lifted the curtain and disappeared behind it.

Was he supposed to follow? He bit his lip and rocked on his heels at the corner of the counter, looking around for any sign that it was all right to go back there.

The bartender noticed him and smiled. "If she brought you here, she wants you to follow her back there, dear," she said kindly.

He bowed his head in quick thanks and followed Rose through the curtain.

Beyond was another barroom, this one much less packed. Gruff-looking men sat at tables and drank. Two more people stood in the corner, throwing rings at a peg in the wall. Three women clustered around a small table, deep in a game of cards.

It was much less noisy here, too, he thought as he glanced around for Rose. He spotted her heading toward the three women in the corner. She sat at their table without so much as a greeting, and the women looked up at her, smirks dancing along their lips as they regarded their newest member.

"Alpha," a dark-haired woman said, "you know you don't need to take care of business yourself all the time, right?"

"I know, but I was itching for a fight," she replied, laughter in her voice. "Besides, I found something quite interesting."

She turned to face Cassian, who hadn't moved beyond the curtain. She gestured to him, and he slowly approached. Every person in the room turned to stare, most focusing on his ears or on his face. He still didn't understand what was so interesting about him.

The women's eyes all grew wide, the dark-haired one jerking her gaze back toward Rose.

"But he's a—"

She stopped the woman with a hand, but never took her eyes away from Cassian. He didn't understand what was happening as she gestured for him to sit beside her at the already-packed table.

He obliged, his mouth going dry as he sat. The dark-haired

woman who'd spoken regarded him suspiciously, her eyes narrowing as she looked down and then back up slowly. Another dark-haired woman next to her looked like her sister. The third woman, whose head was shaved bald, leaned back and crossed her feet on the table.

"Tigereye, I've told you a hundred times to stop putting your feet"—Rose smacked at her feet—"on the damn tables!"

The woman named Tigereye smirked, rolling her eyes as she let them drop back down. "So who's our visitor?"

"His name is Cassian; he helped me today," she responded, looking at him with her good eye. It seemed she was prompting him to introduce himself.

He breathed slowly, letting the air escape through his lips in a steady stream. "Yes, my name is Cassian. I happened to be walking down the street when I encountered the commotion."

"He even lobbed a few fireballs at the thing before I got there. Quite helpful, if I do say so myself." Rose's eye twinkled as she stared at Tigereye, who'd raised her eyebrows.

"Well, I'm Tigereye, as Alpha here has already said." She jerked her chin at the other two women seated beside her. "These two knuckleheads here are the twins, Harpy and Spider. Don't be offended if Spider gives you a nasty look, she's not that sociable."

Spider wore a scowl on her face as he nodded a greeting to her. Her sister, Harpy, returned his smile with a small one of her own. Tigereye seemed to enjoy Spider's discomfort.

But had she referred to Rose as Alpha? None of their names seemed traditional, or really even like names at all.

"Anyway, tell us how you came to throw fireballs at demons, Cassian," Tigereye said. He set his confusion aside for the moment. "Most people with a pact don't tend to fight against their own."

His stomach dropped. How in the world did she know he had a pact? It wasn't like conjuring fireballs was something only pact-bearers could do, so where had she figured out he was in one?

He knew he took too long to answer, the pause pregnant and

uncomfortable. But Rose came to his aid.

"Your eye, Cassian; that's how we know." She tapped her bad eye, a knowing sparkle in the other.

"My what?"

"Oooh," Tigereye interjected, "he doesn't know?"

"Don't know what?" Cassian said, frantically looking between Rose and Tigereye.

Harpy reached into her jacket pocket, fishing out her techpad and turning on the camera function before turning it to face him. When he saw what it reflected, he gasped.

His right eye was completely black—the iris, the sclera, everything. There was no hint of green to be found anywhere.

Took you long enough to notice, Zal's voice echoed in his head.

You knew? he asked in an accusatory tone, still staring at his fully blackened eye.

Zal laughed. *Of course I knew. It changed the moment we formed the pact.* Ze paused, then sighed. *Did you really not know? When you form a pact, it irrevocably changes you. Your eye was just the beginning.*

"I'll ask again," Tigereye said. "How did that happen?"

He was speechless. It wasn't against his pact to talk about it, but he didn't know these women, and if Rose could throw her sword hard enough to kill a demon in one blow, he didn't want to know what her friends could do.

"He's obviously in shock." Rose's voice was even as she admonished the other woman. "Maybe he didn't know about the pact."

"That's impossible," Spider interjected. "You can't form a pact without the consent of both parties."

"Spider is right," Harpy said.

"So he knew about the pact but not the eye?" Tigereye said, narrowing her eyes.

He'd had enough. They were discussing him as if he wasn't even there.

"I almost died," he said, and all four women turned to him. "The pact was to save my life."

He wouldn't go into more detail, but that answer seemed enough to satisfy everyone but Spider. Rose shot her a look that said *don't you dare.* She backed down, her eyes dancing.

"Anyway, you must be wondering why I brought you here," Rose said, gracefully changing the topic away from his eye and the pact. "I have a proposition for you."

The other three women looked at Rose, their expressions a mix of worry and confusion. He couldn't even try to predict what was going to happen, but their faces told him to worry.

"But before I can do that, I need to ask one simple question."

He looked at Rose, focusing on her good eye, and nodded.

"What does freedom mean to you?"

"What?"

She didn't repeat herself, instead staring unblinkingly at him, awaiting his response.

He stared at Rose for a beat too long, the shock of the question sinking into his bones as he thought. Before, he'd thought of freedom as a goal—to no longer be shackled by his father's old debts to Ragnor. He'd thought of it as something attainable and almost tangible—to live with his mother without the fear of retribution or retaliation.

But being in a pact with Zal had changed that opinion a bit. He doubted his mother was still alive, and if Ragnor thought him dead, then wasn't he technically free now?

He sighed, running a hand through his curls once before opening his mouth to answer.

"Freedom is living life according to your own terms," he began. Rose's expression betrayed nothing of her thoughts. "It's holding yourself accountable to ideals that you decide are worthy; to be free to love who you want and do what you think is right."

"What if your idea of doing what you want hurts others?" Rose said.

"Then that's not true freedom," he said. "Freedom doesn't mean you don't have a responsibility to others. It doesn't mean you get to just do whatever, whenever. It means you have the freedom to choose a path that is right for you. That path is yours to forge, and the consequences of your choices are yours to bear."

Rose stared at him for a heartbeat, her face closed and expressionless. Then her chin dipped down as her mouth broke into a wide grin.

"Splendid answer, Cassian. You certainly fit the bill."

Spider made a disgusted noise. "You can't be serious, Alpha."

Rose whipped her head toward the twins, a fire in her eye. "I'm the one who makes these decisions, even if I ask for your opinion. Have I ever been wrong before?"

Spider's face darkened before she hung her head. "No, you haven't."

"And I wasn't wrong about you and Harpy, was I?"

"No."

Rose stared at Spider for a few more moments before turning to Tigereye. "Do you have a problem with this, too?"

Tigereye beamed. "Nope."

"Good." She turned back to face Cassian once more. "Back to my proposition, then. I'd like you to join us."

Cassian felt hot. He didn't know what he'd just gotten himself into. Join? What was he joining? Had he unwittingly joined a cult? A drinking coalition? What did that question about freedom have to do with it?

"I'm sorry," he started, "join…what, exactly?"

Rose smiled and stuck out her hand once more. "It's time I properly introduce myself. Rosalie Delacour, codename Alpha. I'd like to formally invite you to be a new member of The Phantom Flame."

9

BECK

They'd made no progress on the investigation into the disappearances. Reaper found himself frustrated, and not just by their stalled search. His undercover work drew into its final stages, and Brisea grew impatient.

He knew, at the very least, that the Red Guard had been working on a plot to frame Rosalie for something. With his constant stream of information about her activities, whereabouts, and sprawling information network, their ability to plan the perfect frame-up was easy.

They needed something on her to seize her; killing her would never work. She was too powerful, too important. If she mysteriously died, they would have a bigger problem on their hands.

A martyr.

What they needed instead was to ruin her, tarnish her so completely that her arrest and execution wouldn't be taken with offense even by those in her organization.

Of course, Reaper wasn't privy to whatever their plan was. He wasn't important enough for that part, only trusted enough to gather intel and deliver it to Brisea. What was done with it after that was unknown.

Today was a change of pace—a demonic beast of some sort

was rampaging in Ivory Heights. Alpha immediately had headed off to fight, placing the call out to operatives in the area for backup.

Apparently, they'd sent people before him to topple the resistance. But somehow, Rosalie or her predecessors had always sniffed them out before they could do much more than arrive at the front steps of the Autumn Rose.

Reaper hated that he'd been the most successful. They'd never tried a Fallen like him before. Of course, the resistance didn't know his true nature, nor did they know he was a Fallen.

He stalked down the streets of the lower quarter, heading up a steep cobblestone road that would take him from the bay up to the highest part of town, the central part of the city. Beyond that was the upper quarter, which was mostly made up of businesses on the slope leading back toward the rest of the Empire.

Alpha was fighting the beast in the eastern part of the central quarter. By foot, it would take him almost twenty minutes to get there; he had a faster way.

His wings unfurled, pure obsidian speckled with splashes of white that looked like stars. He'd flown sparingly over the last year, unwilling to give away too much of his identity to those who didn't need to know.

He didn't expect the scene that greeted him when he landed two blocks away from the fight. An elven man with wild silver hair threw a fireball directly at the beast's chest and caught the little girl it held in its jaws with a fluidity earned only after many years of practice. He watched as the man handed her off to her mother, then turned back to the beast.

He summoned yet another fireball, throwing it with precision at the spot he'd just hit. The beast roared, its eyes glowing with fire. The man did not flinch.

A glowing sword came from his left, flying past the silver-haired man to bury itself in the beast's chest, in the same spot the man had already hit twice.

Alpha was here.

He smiled as she approached the man and pulled her sword from the beast's chest. He couldn't tell what they were saying, but it looked as if she was introducing herself. Knowing what he knew about her, she was probably trying to recruit him. That kind of power would be useful in the resistance.

After all, they'd stopped caring about who could join their ranks, even elves. Anyone who could fight was welcome, and this man had proven he was more than just proficient.

When the elf turned to greet Alpha, Reaper's stomach dropped to the ground.

He knew this man. He'd been sent to kill him.

♦ ♦ ♦

"Reaper," Alpha's voice came over his earpiece, "where did you end up?"

He was still in the alley, frozen to the spot long after Alpha and the elven man had disappeared. She seemed unruffled, judging by the cool tone of her voice.

He cleared his throat, then pressed his finger to the earpiece. "I must have just missed you. Heading back to base now."

"Good; I've got a new recruit."

How was he going to avoid this one? He knew what he needed to do, according to his orders. He had to kill that man.

He'd been unsuccessful in his search for the last three years, traveling across the Empire on supposed resistance business, hoping to discover where this man had gone. It had been the worst in Spiral City, but the information there had been the clearest.

The man was dead, or so they'd said. He'd been caught up in some scandal involving Northwind Medical, and there was no use looking for him anymore. Reaper had chosen to believe the man named Cassian Evermore dead all this time.

Reaper had killed his mother; the memory of it resurfaced in his vision. The smell of her blood clogging his nose. The sound of her cries drowning all other sounds. It was deafening, the way she'd cried. And not for herself; no, she'd cried when he'd told her that her son was dead.

She cried for Cassian, not for herself. He'd know, because when he'd slid that knife across her throat, she had no fear in her eyes. Only sadness.

Reaper began his journey back to the resistance base. He didn't fly this time.

Foxtail saved him before he arrived—he'd found something.

His voice was uncharacteristically quiet over the comms when he called for the rest of the team. Apparently, another disappearance report had come in during the attack with the massive beast downtown. But this time, there was a witness.

Reaper responded immediately. "On my way."

"Didn't Alpha need something?"

"She can wait. I'll take the blame if she gets mad."

Foxtail laughed. "Your funeral."

Reaper didn't respond, silently thanking Sol and Jupiter and all four goddesses for their grace in saving him from encountering his mark for at least a few hours. Regardless of his status with Cassian, he needed to be there with Foxtail.

It wasn't like Brisea had told him not to investigate, nor had she seemed concerned about his involvement. Although being with the resistance wasn't a choice, he felt satisfaction when he could help them. His own small rebellion against his assignment.

Reaper unfurled his wings once more, leaping up from the street and soaring into the sky on an updraft. Even though it was freezing, he was thankful for the cold. It jarred him from the haze he'd been in since he'd spotted Cassian fighting the demon.

He'd been incredible. His file had mentioned he was magically gifted, but it hadn't said to what extent. From what Reaper could tell, he was incredibly skilled.

Foxtail said nothing else as Reaper made his way over to Harborside, his wings spread wide over the flash of brightly colored buildings below him. He landed a block away from his destination, unwilling still to let even his team members in on his secret. It was easier to pretend he was human; their trust in him came naturally that way.

When he arrived, Foxtail was waiting for him outside an old warehouse. It was nondescript, painted a faded green that blended in with the grassy slopes behind it, and surrounded by similarly painted and run-down buildings.

When he appeared around the corner, Foxtail's expression went from neutral to a frown he wasn't used to seeing on the normally bubbly man's face. A girl stood before him, white as a sheet, fingers twisted around each other. Her eyes darted around, fearful.

Foxtail turned back to her, speaking softly enough that Reaper couldn't hear until he got closer.

"...show us the last place you saw her?" he asked the girl softly.

Her eyes locked onto Foxtail's as she nodded, but she didn't move. Foxtail must have picked up on something Reaper missed because he turned to introduce Reaper even though she hadn't asked.

"Cera," he began, saying her name slowly and calmly, "this is my squad mate, Reaper. He's here to help look for your friend. Is that okay?"

Cera regarded him wordlessly, then nodded.

Reaper walked behind them silently as Cera went around the back of the building. He had questions, but knew now wasn't the time to ask. She'd show them the scene first, then they could move on to the questioning. She was obviously terrified; her hands shook as she walked and her breathing was faster than normal.

"It was here," she said, voice shaky, as she pointed to the sidewalk that ran behind the building. "We were heading to the station down the street. I took my eyes off her for only a few moments." She didn't cry, but her voice quavered at the end. Foxtail patted her on the shoulder.

"This wasn't your fault." His voice was soothing and calm.

"Why were you in the warehouse district if you were heading to the station?" Reaper asked.

Cera turned to him, her mouth a thin line. "I live in the Ward; this is the closest station."

Reaper nodded. "Did you see anyone after she disappeared? Did you look anywhere?"

She gestured down the alley. "There was a man there. But I only saw a glimpse."

"What did he look like?"

She sucked in a breath, then released it slowly, as if remembering was painful. "He was tall and had these horrifying black veins on his face. He was gone so fast, though, I think I was seeing things."

Reaper softened as she spoke. She was doing well for someone who had been through something so awful; her strength of spirit impressed him.

Her description of the man, though, was strange. Black veins on his face? Reaper wondered if she really had been seeing things, if it had been a shadow or maybe even a tattoo. He couldn't think of anyone who might match that description or why someone might have markings like that.

He shot Foxtail a look, then spoke to Cera again. "Thanks for your information. Fox here is going to take you home. I'll look around and see if I can find something to give us a clue about where your friend went."

She nodded. "I'm grateful for your help."

Foxtail gestured to the street, bowing as he swept his arms out. "And now, gentle miss, I'm going to escort you home."

The dramatics of Fox's gesture put a small smile on Cera's terrified face, enough for Reaper to relax. She'd be okay. Fox had an uncanny quality for diffusing tense situations, if not always on purpose. It made him a favorite for reducing panic and comforting children, and he enjoyed the role.

Fox looped his arm through Cera's, then leaned back over his shoulder to give Reaper a dramatic, two-fingered salute. It reminded him so much of Kellan, the melancholy unexpected and sharp in his throat.

Once they'd disappeared around the corner, Reaper shook his head, allowing himself a moment to feel the loss. He let it soak into his bones as he breathed in, then imagined it evaporating off him like steam, rising into the air and out of his body as he exhaled.

He needed to focus. Two more breaths found his center; another one had him open his eyes and roll his head.

Kellan and his grief were gone on the wind. He had a job to do, and although he could guess what Brisea would tell him to do at this moment, he didn't quite care enough to entertain the ghost of her in his mind telling him it wasn't worth it. That this wasn't what he was here to do. That all his work with the resistance would be for nothing, anyway.

He walked through the alleyway, keeping his eyes low on the first sweep. He was looking for a lost shoe, a strange marking, anything that would stand out as strange in this abandoned back alley. He reached the other end of the alley with no leads; he began a second sweep, this time keeping his eyes at mid-level. He scanned the back doors leading to the alleyway; he looked for any markings on the walls that seemed fresh; he tried to imagine what this alley usually looked like.

Halfway down, he noticed one door to the alley was ajar. He hadn't seen it from the other direction since it was only open a crack. He took note of the other doors—none were open. He grasped the handle of the door, pushing it open slowly and waiting for any creak or noise that might alert someone to his intrusion. It was well-oiled and opened silently for him with little resistance.

Reaper slipped inside, lifting his visor from around his neck to cover his eyes. The darkness inside the building was oppressive. Flipping to night vision on his visor was necessary for any sort of mobility.

He'd only just stepped inside when the sense of something very, very wrong came down upon him. It weighed upon him, pressing down on his stomach like he was sinking deep beneath the ocean.

The visor only showed him a warehouse full of metal boxes of varying sizes. He didn't know what this building was for, but at the moment it didn't matter. He continued to pick his way through the warehouse, keeping his steps as silent as possible, hoping for any sign of the missing girl or the strange man Cera had seen in the alleyway.

He passed a particularly tall stack of boxes, and something caught his eye—a strange design on the floor, too pristine and too clean to be something so simple as a scuff.

Reaper circled the boxes and more of the design revealed itself to him. It was a perfect circle, its diameter wider than he was tall. It was segmented by a nine-pointed star, each of its points enshrined by yet another circle.

He recoiled, the feeling of dread from before now threatening to suffocate him. What was demonic symbology doing *here,* of all places? What was it for?

The questions choked him; dread pressed frigid fingers against his throat.

He forced himself to continue his sweep through the building, to search for any more clues like the one he'd just stumbled upon. He prayed silently the entire time that there would be no more. One was too many; multiple would be unbearable.

They already had too much on their plates with the demonic activity in the city at an all-time high, the disappearances, and the many efforts Alpha drove across the country to bring humans their justice. Adding more demonic mysteries on top of it was…

It doesn't matter, a small voice said in the back of his head. *You're not a part of them, anyway. This isn't your problem.*

He could pretend like he saw nothing, like he had simply found an empty warehouse and a bunch of boxes. Like there had been nothing remotely alarming housed beneath the creaking metal roof.

That's it, the voice crooned. It was his training kicking in, the lessons that had been imparted on him since birth. This wasn't his mission. This wasn't his problem. He wasn't here to help the resistance, after all.

As he finished his sweep and found nothing more, he tried to push what he'd found into the back of his mind. He had more than enough on his plate. With Cassian's reappearance, the influx of demons, and his reconnaissance to deal with, this investigation was more than he could handle.

He simply didn't have the time, regardless of what his heart wanted him to do.

Reaper glanced at the markings once more before leaving, committing their shape to memory. Nothing could be done now, but he wouldn't forget.

He couldn't forget.

10

KELLAN

Spiral City | 12th of Dusk Moon

The fluorescent lights of the garage flickered almost imperceptibly, but enough that Kellan had to look at the gray concrete floor as he followed Vaida to her car. She refused to ride the motorcycle with him.

"So, where are we going?" Kellan asked as he pulled open the passenger door. She hadn't told him anything. He owed her dinner for her help on a case, as was their usual arrangement.

But this time she'd requested to go somewhere just outside the city limits, the very tail end of what their marks would allow. He didn't know what awaited them out there or why Vaida had this sudden and urgent impulse to go.

"You'll see," she replied simply.

The drive took them forty-five minutes. The roads outside of the city were empty save for the occasional passerby, trees and grasses as far as the eye could see.

The restaurant was off the main road that led out of Spiral City. It was modeled after old-fashioned diners, complete with long neon lights and a hokey light-up sign that read "Crossroads." Cars lined the parking lot, and it seemed decently busy for a restaurant outside the city walls.

It had seen better days, Kellan noted as they approached.

Several of the lights lining the top of the building were out; the glass was dirty and smudged.

Vaida swung into one of the last empty parking spots, shutting off the car with the push of a button. Kellan exited the car and followed her toward the restaurant, eyes turned to the vast, grassy plain that surrounded the establishment. It had been a long time since he'd seen that much open space.

A tired-eyed server showed them to a secluded booth in the back of the dining room, walking away before they'd even taken a seat. This didn't seem like any of Vaida's usual haunts. He opened his mouth to ask her about it, but she held up a hand.

"I know, not my usual. I've never been here either."

"What?" he said, surprised. "Then why did we come here?"

Vaida glanced around, her large gray eyes full of wariness. "Honestly, this was the best place we could talk."

Kellan cocked an eyebrow at her, even more confused. "Talk? We can't do that back at the Guard?"

"Not for this, no." She clammed up then, taking the menu off the table and perusing it with half-hearted interest. Kellan followed suit; but instead of looking at the menu, he watched the woman sitting across the booth.

She hadn't changed over the last four years. Her hair was still long and dark, and she still wore it in updos, although today she'd gathered her braids into a ponytail at the base of her neck. Her dark skin was flawless, no signs of aging at all. He didn't know how old Vaida was, all he knew was that she was a shifter of some sort. But to not change over many years was unusual, especially for shifters. He didn't even know what her animal form might be, and once again, she'd never offered that information.

A different server came to take their order, this one giving both Kellan and Vaida appreciative looks as she walked away. He pretended not to notice.

"So," Kellan prompted.

Vaida just looked at him before taking a deep breath. "I have a story to tell you, Kellan. One I haven't told in many years."

Kellan sucked in a breath sharply through his nose. Was this the story he'd never been brave enough to ask? He stayed silent, waiting for her to continue.

She did. "It's about how I got my prison mark."

"Are you sure, V? You've kept quiet this long, I don't want you to feel obligated to—"

She cut him off by holding up her hand, shaking her head. "This is not out of a sense of duty. This is because I value you, and…" She paused, putting her hand down slowly. "And, well, you'll see why I am telling you soon."

Kellan nodded, relaxing back into the booth.

"Eighty years ago, I fell in love."

Eighty? She was older than him by a significant amount. He didn't even realize shifters could live that long. Their average lifespan was that of a human. And the fact Vaida didn't look a day over thirty made this revelation even more shocking. Just how old was she? Just *what* was she?

"Her name was Amaris. She was a Fallen, like you. She was assigned to the Legion, as you know, in the sixteenth division. We became friends over several years, and eventually, we fell in love. I was working for the Legion of my own free will.

"She wanted more, though. Amaris was a dreamer—she wanted to travel the world, see Illium and Ellsemere. She wanted more than what she'd been given as a Fallen. And she wanted all of that with me." Vaida sighed, but continued. "I was determined to help her. After several years of research, I thought I'd found a way to break her mark."

Kellan gasped. Break the mark? The only way he knew how was by one of the Red Council's official mages breaking the seal, which was unheard of. Only extreme cases justified mark removal, and a case like that hadn't happened in ages. There was simply no way.

"I was confident in my findings. I was sure that I'd gotten the spell right, the conditions right. I was a fool." Vaida took a deep, shaky breath. Kellan reached a hand forward to touch hers. She smiled weakly at him before continuing.

"It was the Day of the Burning Sun. Amaris was convinced that doing it on a magical day would make it more successful; I agreed to it. We thought it would be all right. We waited for sunset, then drove out to the flower fields west of Bloomside. She wanted it there, where the first thing she'd see as a free woman was one of the most beautiful sights in all the Empire. It was...poetic. I indulged her."

She stopped again, her hands shaking now. Kellan's heart twisted for her as he squeezed her hands tightly. He could sense where this story was headed, but he didn't want to make assumptions.

The server returned with their food as Vaida paused, setting it down on the table with a soft *thunk*. Kellan just nodded their thanks, and the server retreated once more.

"You don't have to continue right now, V. This is a difficult story for you to tell."

She shook her head slowly. "No, I have to tell you. I must."

Kellan squeezed her hands again, then let go. She took another steadying breath and continued.

"It was right at sunset. At first, I thought we'd been successful. The mark faded, and Amaris appeared unharmed. When I told her it had worked, she'd thrown her arms around me.

"But then the alarms began in the city. Inexplicably, they were loudest around us. And then Amaris collapsed in my arms. She writhed and foamed at the mouth like she'd been poisoned, and there was nothing I could do to save her. I tried *everything,* Kellan. Every spell I knew, every countermeasure and stabilization and preservation magic I could think of. Nothing worked. She died in my arms before the Legion found us."

He felt chills travel all over his arms and back, spreading up his neck and onto his face. Vaida had tried to break the prison mark and had ended up accidentally killing her lover. He wanted so badly to reach over and hug her, but she looked as if she had more to say.

"They knew what we'd done; they knew we'd tried to break the mark. And since I'd done it, they punished me by giving me a mark of my own."

"V, I'm—" Kellan stopped, struggling with the words. He didn't know what to say. Everything that people had said to him after Cassian's death had been annoying, fake, vapid. He'd hated it. The sympathy people had shown him had only made him angry.

"It's been decades, Kellan, since this happened. There is no more regret. I did what I thought was right. But I have a reason for telling you this." She looked at her untouched meal, pushing it aside to lace her fingers together on the table. "I've searched all this time for the correct way to break the marks. And I've found it."

Kellan forgot to breathe. "How?"

She shook her head. "I will not discuss specifics now, only because it's too dangerous. You will need to trust me when I give you instructions on how to help me. Can you do that?"

Kellan nodded.

"The knowledge I hold now is incredibly dangerous, so I'm protecting you by keeping you in the dark. But I must ask you— are you willing to risk it with me? Even knowing how the last time went?"

Now he understood. She'd discovered how to do it again, but she didn't want him going into it blindly. She knew the consequences of breaking the mark, and she wanted him to understand them, too.

"I trust you, V. And I'll do what you ask of me."

Vaida smiled at him for the first time since arriving. "Then we'll start as soon as possible. I still need some time to get everything together for this. Give me two months; we'll go from there."

He refused to let himself hope too hard, but tamping down the giddy joy that rose through his veins was a challenge. But what would he even do once they escaped?

Grief settled into his bones again, an unwelcome yet familiar presence. It would have meant so much more to share it with Cassian, to break his own bonds so they could live in peace together. But that hope was gone, whisked away on a dying breath.

Where would they go? Did Vaida have an idea what she wanted to do?

She must have known he was spiraling. Her hands appeared on his, settling gently atop his white-knuckled grip on his utensils. "We'll be okay, Kellan; I won't mess up this time."

Oh. He didn't want her to think his apprehension was because of her skills. He trusted Vaida with his life. He'd lay his heart in her hands if it could still beat outside his body; he knew she'd take care of it.

"That's not—that's not the problem," he began, spluttering the words out to keep up with his head. "It's just…how do I ask this?" He bit his lip, wishing he could scratch at the mark practically burning into the back of his neck but unwilling to leave the safety of Vaida's grip.

She stayed silent, knowing he needed a few more moments to process his half-formed thought. Her grip was steady, and he was thankful for the warmth.

He breathed in deeply, pushing against the grief and guilt clawing its way up through his throat. "What do you want to do after, then?" It was a simple question, but the answer was anything but.

Kellan lifted his eyes to meet Vaida's, watching her as her eyebrows drew together as if she'd never considered it either. She didn't remove her hands, but she didn't speak, either. They spent several moments like that, frozen with their hands joined.

"I…" she began, her mouth parted in a confused half-thought. "I think we should go to Rivenstorm."

Of course. The home of the resistance would certainly be a logical place for two fugitives to end up.

"That's fine, but Vaida, that's not what I asked."

Her face twisted, her lips pursing. "I know what you meant, I just—I didn't know how to answer."

Kellan nodded. "I've never thought about it before, what life would be like if I wasn't chained."

"I used to," she replied, lifting her hands from his now that the danger of a spiral was passed. "But that was before Amaris died. Now…"

The words left unsaid in that space were heavier than anything else they'd said that night. They hung dense and thick between them, resting upon the mutual bond of loss that wove its web around them both.

Something about it was almost pathetic. They'd been bound for so long that the idea of a life without shackles was incomprehensible.

They'd figure it out, together. And as he watched Vaida return to her plate, he thought there wasn't anyone left in the world that he'd rather face freedom with.

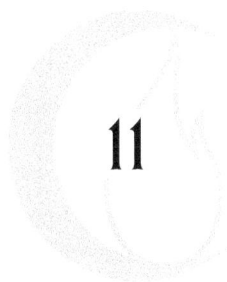

11

KELLAN

Spiral City | 1st of Frost Moon

K ellan awoke in his bare bedroom in the Guard. He hastily kicked off the tangle of sheets wrapped around his legs and hissed when his feet met the cold stone floor. It wouldn't kill the magical facilities team to warm the stones even a little in winter, but they never did.

The snow fell lazily outside his small window, dusting the city in a thin layer of powder. The beauty of the snow was magical; winter made everything feel brighter, he thought. But he hated it too—the cold, the dark, the damp, and worst of all, the loss. It seemed to get worse each year.

Vaida would wait for him, like she did every year. She'd always accompany him to the temple to honor Lyra on the Day of Wishes. Selwyn usually did too, but she was out of town this year—some business trip she'd been tight-lipped about.

He stuffed his feet into his combat boots and tucked a scarf around his neck before heaving a wool coat over his shoulders. They'd be outside for a while today, and he knew he'd freeze without all the layers.

Vaida was in front of the reception desk when he arrived, a vibrant arrangement of dark blue lilies, white daisies, and light blue ranunculus in her arms. She had an eye for things like this, and each year the arrangements were as lovely as the last.

She nodded to him as he approached. "You ready?"

"Let's go."

The walk was a pleasant one, as they'd decided not to brave the drive or transit to Lyra's temple. People were busy preparing for the celebrations they'd be hosting later today. Some were heading to do what Vaida and Kellan were—throwing their wishes down Lyra's well. It was an ancient tradition carried over from the time before the Conjunction, adapted to work with the Circle.

The temple was only a few blocks from the Guard. It was already crowded, but it was early enough that the wait for the well wasn't long.

They stayed silent while they waited, flutters of conversation around them. The silence had become a sort of tradition for them since they'd been doing this each year; Kellan found it more comforting than talking, and Vaida understood.

The well was nothing ornate. Made from a circle of flat gray squarish stones, it was only about ten feet in diameter. It was crowned with a wooden structure that held up a small bell attached to a white rope. Kellan approached the small table full of paper and pens and scribbled the same thing he'd written for the last four years.

Keep Cassian safe.

He hoped wishes applied to those on other planes, that his wish would reach Cassian's spirit in the ethereal plane. But he would never know; he could only hope.

Kellan and Vaida approached the well, wishes in hand, and rang the bell together before tossing their scraps into the inky darkness below. People said the bell would grab Lyra's attention so she would see your wish and acknowledge it for the coming year. He didn't know how much of that was true.

They moved on soon after, heading inside of the temple to lay their flowers at Lyra's feet. An exchange was necessary if you wanted your wishes to come true.

Vaida's brows pinched as they entered. It was crowded in here, too. Worshippers milled about, discussing their plans in excited voices. Some huddled together, cups of steaming hot chocolate in their hands. Others sat on the benches scattered about the large hall.

The temple was beautiful. Soaring, arched windows neatly lined the stone walls, the sun shining brilliantly through them to illuminate a spacious worship center. Oak benches with brilliant blue cushions bordered the walls. The floor was a speckled marble, with swirls of blue and red and gold dotted between the white.

A chorus of blue-green singing stones surrounded the base of a massive gilded statue. Their haunting melody was just above a whisper this time of day, but it echoed in the cavernous space. The statue seemed almost out of place. After all, this temple was pre-Conjunction.

The statue was Lyra, goddess of the sea, and one of Sol's four daughters. A veil shrouded her face, only her closed eyes visible. They'd carved her hair to look like the ocean's waves. The attention to detail in them was so great, Kellan swore he could see them moving as he stared.

By her feet, resting between the singing stones, was an assortment of gifts worshippers had been leaving since early this morning. Flowers, candies, candles, and seashells piled high around her feet as an exchange for their wishes to be granted.

Vaida and Kellan approached, weaving their way between groups of people. Kellan stood back, his head bowed while Vaida laid the bouquet with the others.

She turned back to him. Her face was pinched. "Ready? I'm dying for something warm right about now."

Kellan smiled. "Yeah, I know. My hands are freezing."

They left the temple together, the chatter and singing stones drifting into the air behind them. Vaida found a hot chocolate cart a few blocks away and bought them two cups. Kellan sipped the drink slowly as they meandered the streets.

THE PHANTOM FLAME

The Day of Wishes was the first holiday of the year, celebrated just as the moon reset itself and the world turned a year older. Lyra, being the patron goddess of hope and truth, was the holiday's figurehead. Today was full of joy, laughter, and hope. Or at least, it was supposed to be.

Kellan knew he wasn't alone in feeling like the day was mocking him. Vaida's pinched brows all day weren't lost on him. But he couldn't help it. Today only reminded him of what he'd lost.

He was sure she felt the same.

🜄 🜄 🜄

Selwyn usually accompanied them to Lyra's temple, but she'd seemed distracted when she'd told Kellan she wouldn't be able to go with them. She didn't give details; all he knew was she was out of town.

It didn't alarm him. Selwyn's influence and responsibilities had only expanded since Pontius' disappearance; it seemed she'd tried to at least partially fill the shoes he'd left behind. Although she wasn't nearly as ingrained in the non-profit circuit as her brother had been, she still carried on his legacy through funds, organizations, and a variety of charities throughout the city.

He missed her, though. Other than Vaida, Selwyn had been the most steadfast influence on his life since Cassian's disappearance. She'd kept him from falling apart just as much as Vaida had.

He knew it was partially mutual; something about sharing the burden of losing a treasured person made them closer than they would have been otherwise.

She wasn't the same, not since Pontius had disappeared.

Kellan had made it a tradition to spend the last day of the Feast of Nightfall in late Dusk Moon with the Morgensterns. Selwyn had invited him the year after Pontius and Cassian had disappeared, insisting the table had been too empty the year before.

He'd seen then just how much the family had lost when they'd lost Pontius. It should have been obvious that their grief over losing their son would be sharp and painful.

But nothing had prepared him for the silence of the house, the somber attitude of what was supposed to be a joyous occasion. The Morgensterns' shining star had disappeared completely, enveloped in a night so black it seemed endless.

Kellan didn't know how much Selwyn had told her parents about the circumstances of Pontius' disappearance. Officially, he was a missing person. Kellan suspected they knew it was something more.

Since then, weapons manufacturing had only increased. Morgenstern Tech had developed the demon-killers less than six months after the first influx of demons had wrought devastation on the Empire. They'd since refined their design, making them more and more efficient with each passing version. They now distributed their weapons to nearly every country in Ileron.

Because it wasn't just the Empire that was suffering at the hands of the thinning Veil.

Part of him was grateful for their tireless dedication to the Empire's protection—but a smaller, meaner part of him wondered why they weren't trying harder to find their only son. They had the power to do so.

But money and influence could only get you so far. Even Morgenstern Tech couldn't reverse the metamorphosis into a demon.

He knew he was being unfair, but grief and guilt made him cynical when he never wanted to be. He often had similar thoughts after he'd spent too long with his feelings over Cassian and Pontius. At the moment, he was sitting on his bed, his hands tangled into his nearly shoulder-length hair. His thoughts were vicious knives that cut him more deeply than one wielded by anyone else.

After all, the only person who could even hurt him now was himself.

He hadn't bothered to take his jacket off after their visit to Lyra's temple. Normally, people spent the evening on the Day of Wishes celebrating with their families or friends, eating sweets and baked goods while celebrating the closing of another year and welcoming the new one with joy and happiness.

The idea made him want to choke. He'd spent three Days of Wishes wishing desperately that things had been different. He'd spent three holidays imagining himself into a stupor over what he would have done if Cassian were still here. If Pontius hadn't become a demon.

They'd go to the Morgensterns', of course. Kellan would bring his favorite whiskey and a bottle of red wine for Selwyn. Cassian probably would have made homemade chocolates or baked some delicious cake. Vaida would decline the invitation until she heard Cassian would be baking. Pontius would be in white but would inevitably spill a drop of chocolate on himself during the night. Selwyn would click her tongue at him and demand he change so the maids could get the stain out.

The idea of a happy, fulfilling holiday always made his chest hurt. A whole, blissful Cassian; a perfectly normal Pontius; a Selwyn whose eyes weren't haunted by the ghosts of the past. The daydreams always made him feel like he'd inhaled a mouthful of seawater.

His fingers, woven in his hair, tightened. He pulled at the strands, his scalp burning. Sometimes a bit of pain was all it took to jolt him from a spiral. He'd bite his lip or his tongue, or pinch his arm, or dig his nails into his hands. It was never something that would leave a scar. Never something to remind him later just how badly he hurt.

The pain never dulled; he didn't need another reminder that he wasn't the same person he'd once been. The same person who'd fallen in love with an elven boy and had him ripped away before they'd had the chance to become anything.

It was hard for him to cry anymore, but when he needed to come back from a spiral, when he needed that bite of pain, the tears always followed.

They dripped off his lashes, forcing them to stick together. He couldn't see his hands where he dropped them into his lap. They blurred out like too-thin watercolors, blending into a multicolored swirl of black and tan and nothing else that even mattered.

A door closed; Vaida had returned. She never left him for long, but especially on days like this.

He felt her fingers pry his hands open—he hadn't realized he'd been clenching them.

"Kell?" Her voice was barely loud enough for him to hear over the rushing in his ears. "It's all right, I'm here."

She squeezed his hands, the pressure a welcome reminder that she was with him. This wasn't the first time she'd done this, and he knew it wouldn't be the last. He hoped she'd hold his hands each time this happened. It was the only way he ever felt safe.

Vaida stayed quiet as she squeezed, crouched on the floor before him as his tears fell slower and slower, then stopped completely. She only released him when his breaths slowed and became regular. She stood to wipe the tears from his cheeks with the back of her fingers.

"I made tea, can I get you some?" she asked softly, gesturing to a pair of mugs she'd obviously made in the kitchenette while he spiraled in his bed. "It's cold now, but I can warm it up again."

He didn't have the strength to speak, so he just nodded.

While she returned to the cups, Kellan picked up his techpad. A notification was blinking on the screen:

From: Selwyn Morgenstern.

Kellan, I have something important to share with you. I'm back in town on the fourth, so come over after that. As soon as possible, please.

Vaida returned as he was reading the message again. She peeked at the hologram, squinting her eyes at the message. "I wonder what she has to tell you that she can't share over messages?"

Kellan shrugged. Whatever it was, it piqued his curiosity. And it was a nice excuse to see Selwyn.

He quietly accepted the steaming mug of tea, sipping it thoughtfully.

12

CASSIAN

Rivenstorm | 4th of Frost Moon

In his first few months with the resistance, he'd helped many squads with a variety of tasks. Their most frequent, however, was demon control. Initially he'd been shocked by the frequency with which they were called to a scene, but the surprise wore off as he came to realize the influx was much worse than he could have imagined.

Of course, it shouldn't have been as surprising as it was, considering he'd been at a rift. He'd seen the sheer number of demons that were waiting to cross.

Today, he accompanied Rosalie to their warehouse to receive that week's deliveries. Although they received shipments frequently, this was the first time she'd asked him to accompany her.

She walked ahead of him, her braid swaying with the movement, the wooden bead clacking. She'd donned a heavy peacoat over her jeans and sweater, and had stuffed a fuzzy cream hat on her head. Apparently, Rosalie was not a fan of the cold.

He, however, could hardly feel it. No cold on the material plane could compete with the bone-deep chill of Stygia.

"So, Cassian," Rosalie said, her breath forming puffs in the air. "We've had little chance to talk, you and I. I'm curious about you."

Cassian unclenched his jaw. "What would you like to know?"

Rosalie shrugged. Her boots crunched in the snow as they rounded a corner. The warehouse was only a few blocks away from the Autumn Rose; not enough to drive, but a chilly walk regardless.

"What were you like as a child? Do you prefer your coffee black or with cream? What's your favorite memory of your best friend?" She chuckled. "Maybe not those exactly, but I like to ask more targeted questions instead of saying, 'tell me about yourself.' That's incredibly boring."

Cassian joined her, unable to help the laugh that escaped his lips. "Well, I'm afraid I was a pretty boring kid. I enjoyed stargazing and puzzles, and my mother was happy I wasn't a troublemaker."

"What was she like?" He thought he heard a touch of sorrow in her words.

"She is…" Cassian began, trailing off as he thought of how to summarize everything Eliza was to him. "She smells like a flower garden, and her hugs are like being wrapped in a cozy blanket. Those things alone can give you a pretty good idea of what Eliza is like. Warm, comforting, a hell of a baker."

Rosalie smiled, then looked up at the gray sky. A soft, melancholy smile spread across her face. "My mother wasn't like that at all, even though I wished a million times over that she was. But she was exactly who she needed to be."

He didn't know how to reply, which didn't seem to bother Rosalie.

She met his eyes again, a mischievous smile spreading on her face. "Then what about you as an adult? You said you're from Ebenfell, but I know little else."

"That's pretty much all there is. I've had an uneventful life until now."

Rosalie shook her head, a smirk drawing her lips up. "Fine, keep your secrets. But I intend to figure you out before long."

He chuckled. "I expect nothing less, Rosalie."

They continued the rest of the walk in silence, the snow crunching underfoot. Rivenstorm was wildly different from Ebenfell and Spiral City; its streets were narrower, its buildings older, shorter, and closer together. Cassian never felt like he was being suffocated, though. Something about the city's construction made him feel comforted, instead.

Snow coated the walkways from a storm the previous evening. He tried to count the number of people who'd already walked through it, but the variety of footprints left behind made it impossible to track.

Rosalie stopped before a gray tin building, a white door set in the center. A holographic screen flickered to life at their approach. She punched in a set of numbers with her gloved fingers, swearing softly as she messed up and had to restart. A telltale beep after her second try let them know the door was unlocked.

It wasn't much warmer after they stepped inside, but it was just enough for Cassian to feel a difference. Rosalie puffed warm air into her hands as she moved deeper into the space.

"Come on, Cassian. We're going to take a quick tour before the truck gets here."

Lights flickered on automatically as they moved, tracking their progress through the warehouse. It wasn't much—a massive, open space with a large shipping door on the opposite side. Metal storage shelves lined the long walls perpendicular to the doors, each filled with a variety of cardboard and plastic boxes. He couldn't see what was in them from this far away.

Rosalie pointed a gloved finger to the left. "This side is all non-perishable food items and secondhand clothing. We run a food pantry and clothing drive for locals out of here. We don't keep anything fresh, unfortunately, but what we have keeps people from starving or freezing out on the streets."

He nodded, squinting at the stacks of boxes twice as tall as he stood. They had a lot. "Where do you get donations from?"

"Most of it comes from Rivenstorm, although we get donations from other cities in the Empire occasionally." She tossed her braid over her shoulder as she turned to point to the right. "Over here, we've got supplies for the Autumn Rose and the Phantom Flame. Mostly tools and supplies we need to fight demons, although we've only recently started really using the supply we have here."

He followed her to the other set of shelves on the opposite side of the room. Boxes were stacked in tidy rows, labeled with a neat hand in black marker. He saw glasses, medical supplies, ointments, and a variety of other items on the labels, but his eye snagged on a nearly empty row of long wooden boxes. Rosalie followed his eye to them, then scowled.

"We're almost out," she said. "I've got that on the list for Theo, but I hate to get them. It's a challenge, honestly."

"What are they?" he asked.

Rosalie's smile was not the response he'd expected. "Demon-killers."

Cassian cocked an eyebrow. "You mean those special swords you're using?"

"The very same. They're not illegal to get a hold of, but it is a challenge and can be very expensive. Luckily for us, we have an in."

She didn't elaborate, and he had a feeling even if he asked, she wouldn't tell him. He knew that the resistance had some high-profile backers and donors. It was the only way an operation like this could continue. But Rosalie—and if he was honest, everyone else—had been tight-lipped about *who* those donors actually were.

She weaved back through the boxes to return to the main thoroughfare just as the massive door in the back of the building lifted.

"Shipment's here. Let's go greet our driver," Rosalie said, gesturing for him to join her.

She kept her back rigid, but there was a softness in her eyes as they approached the door and stood to the side to allow the truck inside.

Rosalie turned to Cassian, a small smile painted on the corner of her lips. "I should warn you, Theo is prickly. Just don't ask him too many questions and he'll be in and out with hardly a second glance.

And…use your codename with him."

Cassian nodded and waited for the truck to finish pulling in. As it rolled to a stop, he looked up into the cab, hoping to catch a glance of the apparently prickly truck driver he was about to meet.

The door opened, and a plain man wearing a checkered brown shirt greeted him. Theo was unassuming, with a mop of brown hair and a scowl that rivaled Spider's. He moved with the sort of efficiency born of years of experience and muscle memory.

He didn't acknowledge Cassian, instead turning to face Rosalie right away. His face remained neutral as he spoke. "Only half a shipment today, Alpha. They couldn't spare any more than that. Says the next half will be ready in a few weeks."

Rosalie nodded. "That's expected. Thanks, Theo."

He didn't nod back. His face betrayed nothing as he looked Cassian up and down once with cold indifference.

"Who are you?"

Cassian stiffened. "Frost. New recruit."

Theo scoffed, then turned away to face the truck again. "Help me unload then, Frost."

"Sure," he said as he followed Theo to the back of the truck.

Rosalie came with them, dragging magnetic lifts with her. There were two; they were large and flat and hovered about six inches off the ground. He wondered what they'd need them for, but he understood as soon as Theo opened up the truck.

They'd stacked the back with the wooden boxes he'd seen earlier. This was a weapons shipment.

"Help me get these onto the lifts. Once they're on there, they'll do the rest of the work." Theo's voice was rough and low, brusque, but not unpleasant to listen to.

He nodded, clambering up into the truck. Judging by the depth, he thought there were maybe thirty boxes in the trailer. It wouldn't take long for them to unload. Theo was an efficient companion; he was much stronger than his short stature would suggest, and lifted multiple of the hefty boxes with ease.

Once the truck was unloaded, Theo pulled Rosalie aside, murmuring to her a few times. She nodded, then turned toward Cassian. Theo retreated to his truck, clambering up into the cab without a glance back at either of them. Before Rosalie had even reached Cassian, Theo was already backing out of the warehouse.

She tossed her braid over her shoulder and squinted slightly at him. "So, what did you think of our delivery man?"

Cassian smiled grimly. "Interesting guy, I guess."

"He certainly is," Rosalie replied with a chuckle.

They watched Theo back the truck the rest of the way out of the warehouse before heading back to the front door. Rosalie locked it behind them, her fingers fumbling on the keypad again.

The beginning of their return journey was quiet. They'd been at the warehouse for maybe an hour, yet the sun had already dipped below the tops of the buildings, its light casting long shadows along the sidewalk where their feet landed. It had also grown colder, their breath puffing before them.

Rosalie walked ahead of him. She'd stuffed her hands into the pockets of her peacoat, and her shoulders were nearly up to her ears as she huddled against the chill of winter after sundown.

She slowed as they reached an intersection; the holographic line across the walkway stopped them in flashing orange.

Cassian caught up to her, and she turned her face up to look at him.

"How did you come to form a pact, Cassian?"

She'd been cautious with him, and he'd always felt as if she'd kept a wary eye upon him during his time in the resistance so far. Cassian wondered how long she'd been waiting to ask him that.

"I…" he began, finding the words difficult to say out loud, "I nearly died."

"I know that much," she said. "You said so when I recruited you. I want to know the story."

He chewed his lip. "Why now?"

She smiled as the holographic cordon to the crosswalk turned green, flashing over their hips as they passed through while a mechanized voice ushered them on.

"You've been here long enough," she began, then quieted as a group of people passed them going the opposite direction. "You've...earned my trust. I hope I have earned yours."

He clenched his jaw as they finished crossing the street.

Just answer her, Zal said. *It won't hurt to know how you came to me.*

Cassian sighed, and Rosalie cocked an eyebrow. "That's a no, then?" she said.

"No, that's not it," he said, then tapped his head. "Zal sometimes talks to me. Telepathically, I mean. It's part of our pact."

She nodded like this was the most normal thing in the world. "I don't really know how all this works, but I believe you."

Cassian looked forward, his eyes catching on a storefront with brilliant pink flowers bending under the snow. Stygia would have been prettier with flowers.

He breathed in, then out through his mouth. "I was helping a friend." He couldn't bring himself to speak of Kellan in detail. The pain was still too sharp in his chest. "We were fighting a demon, and it hurt me badly enough that I would have died."

"And then you formed a pact with that demon to save your life?" Her tone wasn't judgmental, just curious.

He shook his head. "No, not the same demon. Zal wasn't there that night. I was taken to zem, and ze asked if I wanted to live."

"You said yes."

"I did."

She turned her face toward the storefronts to her right, her braid swishing along her back. He said nothing more, waiting for her to ask another question. The air between them was thick, tight.

Finally, she spoke again. "It really wasn't for power, then."

"No, it wasn't. I never wanted this."

She nodded, a contemplative look on her face.

They didn't speak again until they rounded the final corner

before the Autumn Rose, when Rosalie suddenly stopped before the bright orange door. She turned to face Cassian, blocking him from the entrance by pressing both hands into the sides of the curved door frame.

"What would you say if I asked you to lead a squad?"

"What?"

"A squad. I'd put you in command of Harpy and Tigereye. You remember them, yes?"

He nodded. "You'd seriously trust me with that?"

She laughed, tilting her head backward. He watched the curve of her throat in the fading sunlight as it bobbed up and down. "I suppose I should say I'm trusting them with you. But I want you to show me your skills in leading others."

He didn't know how to respond. She must have picked up on his hesitance, because she spoke again before he could find his words.

"I'll make sure they don't eat you alive, Cassian. You're going to be fine. I promise."

He wasn't so sure. But he nodded anyway, following Rosalie inside as the midwinter sun disappeared below the horizon.

13

KELLAN

Spiral City | 4th of Front Moon

Her house was as ostentatious as always—the trees still blooming and the flowers vibrant, even coated in snow. The front walkway was shoveled, and an evergreen wreath still adorned the front door, leftover from the Winter Garland celebrations last month. Most people didn't take them down until the end of Frost Moon, anyway.

He pressed the doorbell and stepped back, waiting patiently with his hands in his pockets to keep them from the chill.

Dean, the Morgensterns' butler, answered the door, unsurprised to see Kellan waiting on the stoop. He simply gestured Kellan inside without a word and turned to fetch Selwyn from wherever she was in the house.

He did not follow Dean and instead made himself comfortable on one of the long fainting couches in the sitting room right off the main foyer. He'd told Selwyn of Mina's demise here; the room still held unpleasant memories, even after all this time.

That guilt was a dull ache that never faded. He still dreamed of her shredded throat, the *thunk* she'd made as she fell. He prayed to Jupiter often that she was happy in the ethereal plane.

Selwyn appeared a few moments later, Dean following closely on her heels. She swept into the room, clad in a long-sleeved burgundy dress and house slippers. She'd tied her hair back into a single plait down the back of her neck, and she was still wearing her reading glasses. She smiled warmly at him. Dean closed the doors behind her, promising to bring hot cocoa in a few minutes' time.

"Thanks for coming so promptly," she said as she plopped herself upon the couch opposite him.

He only returned her smile faintly. His mind was running a thousand miles a minute, jumping back and forth between all that had been shared and all that had happened over the last few months. Something twisted in his stomach. Eagerness and apprehension waged a war inside his chest.

Kellan found his voice enough to squeak, "So what did you want to talk to me about?"

Her smile faded a bit, like whatever she was going to say was tough for her to speak of. "Kellan, I'm going to tell you something that will be hard to hear. But I need you to promise me you won't do something stupid when I tell you."

"Stupid? Like what?" he said, innocently.

She made a noise of disbelief. "You know exactly what I mean."

Kellan leaned back into the couch, crossing his arms over his chest. "Fine. I won't do something stupid. Now tell me. The anticipation is killing me."

Selwyn sucked in a shaky breath, but before she could say anything, the door to the parlor opened. Dean reentered, a silver tray balanced on his hand with two white and silver teacups and a pot of something that smelled heavenly. He set the tray before the two of them on the table.

She thanked him and poured herself a cup as Dean retreated once more out of the parlor, shutting the door tightly this time.

She sipped, humming her pleasure as she set her cup back down and turned her eyes back to Kellan. "You want me to pour you a cup?"

He knew she was stalling, which was unlike her. What could this news be that made her want to avoid telling him? Had she found something out about Pontius? Kellan's heart constricted. Maybe Leo and Alvemach were back?

"Kellan?" she said again, noticing his lack of response. "You don't have to have one."

He shook his head. "No—sorry. I'd love one."

Her smile was soft as she poured him a cup, the steam curling in pleasant patterns as she slid it over to him. The smile was small, the corners of her mouth curling just so slightly in the way he'd learned was Selwyn's true smile. She never smiled with her teeth, only ever using the curve of her lips to express her joy.

She sighed deeply, closing her eyes. "All right, enough stalling." Her deep blue gaze met his, the smile vanishing as her mouth set in a stern line. "You remember the rebel movement Pontius was searching for just before we met you?"

"The Phantom Flame? Yeah, why?"

"I did what he could not."

Kellan's jaw dropped. "You—you made contact?"

She nodded. "I did, indeed. And I've been a benefactor for nearly two years now. I'm a part of their information network. It only seemed right to continue the work Pontius was doing before he…" She trailed off, looking down into her cup.

Kellan knew. He gave her a few moments to recover, knowing words or a kind touch would do nothing to help settle her mind. She recovered quickly, looking back up at him and continuing.

"Anyway, that's where I was over the Day of Wishes. I traveled to Rivenstorm and met Rosalie, the head of the resistance. I wanted to confirm a rumor I'd heard."

Kellan cocked his head. "And that rumor is?"

"That they recently recruited an elven man in a pact with silvery hair. A man who'd formed a pact to save his own life, not for power."

He was suddenly drowning. Cassian was *alive?* But he'd been told even if Cassian lived through whatever Leo had planned for him, he'd never see him again. So why was Cassian with the resistance?

Why hadn't he come back for Kellan?

Selwyn continued. "I wanted to make sure the rumors were actually about Cassian, of course. I didn't want to jump to conclusions—although it would be very rare for another silver-haired elven man to form a pact under Cassian's same conditions. I figured if it was him, I could try to find out what he knew about Pontius."

Kellan couldn't breathe. He had so many questions, but his throat wouldn't work. He couldn't ask what he wanted to, couldn't bring himself to take a breath, couldn't will the words to escape his lips.

Selwyn noticed, her brow furrowing. "This is why I hesitated to tell you before I'd confirmed if it was Cassian or not; I knew you'd be like this." She stood and circled the table to sit beside him, grasping his hand in her own. "Kellan, it was him. There's no doubt about it."

He struggled to get his throat to work. "You—you saw him?"

Her hands squeezed his even tighter. "I didn't speak with him. I didn't have the chance. But I talked to Rosalie about him." She sighed. "I know there isn't anything you can do, but I know there are ways to break imprisonment. I can start researching—"

"Selwyn," Kellan interrupted, his voice finally working properly. "I already…I have a way out of this," he said, reaching up to rub the tattoo on the back of his neck. "Vaida's been…"

She cut him off by holding her hand up. "Best I don't know the details. But if there's a way I can help, you must let me know."

They sat in silence for a few moments, their drinks cold and abandoned on the table before them. Something about this room was now almost…poetic. It was like hope was snuffed out here all those years ago, and now it had been returned to him.

Cassian was *alive*.

He bit his lip at the next thought. Cassian was alive, but he'd stayed in Rivenstorm. Why hadn't he come here? Why hadn't he tried to find Kellan? It wasn't like he would be difficult to find, considering his servitude to the Legion.

Kellan could think of a thousand different reasons Cassian

hadn't come back, hadn't sought him out. But one repeated itself over and over in his mind.

He doesn't want you anymore.

It didn't matter. It didn't matter if Cassian no longer wanted to see him—he had to know. And a life on the run, a life with the resistance, would be better than this. It had to be.

And maybe Cassian would take him as he was. Maybe he'd see all of Kellan's broken parts, the ones beyond repair, and would still love him.

He doesn't want you anymore. He doesn't want you anymore. You're nothing to him. He's moved on. He doesn't want you anymore. He doesn't want you anymore.

"Kellan," Selwyn's voice cut off the repetition in his head. "You must promise me something when you get out."

"Anything."

"Find Pontius."

Her statement wasn't unexpected—after all, she'd just revealed she'd been taking over his duties in his stead over the last four years. She might cover for him now, but she certainly would never rest until she found her brother and returned to her.

But Pontius was a demon. Would he even remember them? Where should he begin his search?

He thought back to that awful day in the basement of Northwind Medical. After Pontius had attacked Kellan, he'd stalked toward Selwyn calmly, like he'd recognized her. Even though it had been four years, it was possible a shred of the original man was left within the demon he now was. Maybe he wasn't entirely lost.

But Kellan didn't know where Alvemach and Leo had taken Pontius. They hadn't resurfaced in the last four years. Kellan had been looking. He'd watched for reports of armored dog demons in the news from Spiral City, the Empire, and beyond. But nothing had stuck out to him. After their encounter, Leo and Alvemach had retreated, leaving behind no trace of their experiments.

Northwind Medical had passed into new hands as if nothing

had happened. They'd announced Byre's sudden departure as a family emergency and allowed him to drop from the public eye with minimal fanfare.

The commissioner knew everything, though—and to keep the whole thing under wraps, they'd forced Northwind Medical to shut down their underground testing facilities. They had constructed a new building on the Spiral City University Campus that was open to the public for tours. The commissioner had insisted it would keep them clean.

But that didn't mean Alvemach and Leo had stopped. He was sure that they'd continued their sick experiments, this time using less obvious means. Finding Pontius would be no easy task, and there was no guarantee that finding Cassian would be easy either.

"Kellan?"

He'd gotten so lost in his own thoughts he had forgotten to respond to Selwyn. He relaxed, sighing out his nose and tilting the corners of his mouth upward.

"I will."

10TH OF FROST MOON, SPIRAL CITY

Six days later, Kellan found himself in Vaida's common room on the thirtieth floor, waiting for her to finish changing. They were having a movie night in, but she'd run late this evening, apparently caught up in analyzing some data for the twenty-second.

She finally entered the common suite, dressed in a chunky sweater and baggy old sweatpants. She had a bag of popcorn under her arm as she plopped down on the couch next to Kellan.

"Want some?" she said, offering the open bag to him.

He shook his head. It got stuck in his teeth.

She'd picked a horror flick tonight, and Kellan had reluctantly agreed, but only because he'd been the one to pick their last movie. She knew how much he hated horror films, but she tortured him with them, anyway.

Kellan spent most of the movie with his hands over his eyes, horrified. He didn't understand it himself—he'd seen abominable things in real life, but seeing them in film was so much worse. There wasn't as much suspense in his day-to-day job, especially now.

Vaida went through half of the popcorn bag before closing it up during the end credits. She laughed when Kellan still had his hands over his eyes. She gently peeled them away, chuckling the entire time.

"Come on, you big chicken, it wasn't that bad!"

"V, I love you, but your idea of 'wasn't that bad' is *much* different than mine."

She shook her head at him, rising to put the bag of popcorn away in a cabinet. She busied herself making a cup of tea, turning to cock an eyebrow at Kellan.

He shook his head. They'd spent so much time together that they frequently had these silent conversations. He liked it—Vaida's brand of quiet and calm was soothing to him. It hadn't even been like this with Beck back at the Mission.

The thought of Beck sent an unexpected jolt of melancholy through his heart. Kellan stared down at his hands, eyes focusing and unfocusing as his thumbs twiddled around each other. His breath came in short gasps through his mouth, the sound of his own breath louder than anything else in his ears. His hands were cold, his legs numb. A warm hand came to rest on his own, and a soft voice spoke in his ear.

"Hey, I'm here with you, lean on me."

The effect of it was never immediate; it took a few minutes for his heart to settle back into its usual rhythm, for his eyes to focus again, for his hands to regain some blood flow. Vaida was still and silent while he came back, holding his hands to warm them up.

The first time this had happened was a week after Cassian's disappearance. She'd finally gotten him out of his room and to the dining hall, but he'd taken only three steps out of his room before the panic had set in.

She'd first uttered their code then, asked him literally to lean on her, and he had. She'd propped him up, her hands strong on his back and her shoulder supporting his forehead. The shaking had wracked his whole body. How she'd been able to get him back to his room he wasn't sure, but before he'd known it, he was back in his bed, wrapped in his comforter.

And each episode since, she'd said the same, had supported him while he descended into his own head. Each time, the descent had gotten a little shallower, a little less intense.

Of course, it hadn't gone away. His panic was an ever-present monster, a continual threat he couldn't battle on his own. But Vaida knew that, and she'd fought for him each time, standing by his side with a metaphorical sword in hand.

Enough time passed, and his hands were warm enough that he could move them again. She let them go and stood, brushing her hands along her pants and retreating to the kitchenette to resume making tea.

She never made a big deal about the spirals, either. She was simply there when he needed her, then went back to normal once she knew he was okay. At first it had seemed strange, but he realized later that she was allowing him to do what he needed without her interference.

The tea she made smelled spicy and warm, and even though he'd turned it down, she thrust a cup into his hands with a lemon slice, just the way he liked it.

"Drink," she commanded softly, slumping back onto the couch next to him.

He nodded, sipping at the tea carefully to avoid burning his tongue. It tasted as good as it smelled, and he closed his eyes in pleasure.

Vaida sighed before speaking again, her voice a low whisper. "So Selwyn, huh?" She didn't have to be specific. He knew what she meant.

He'd told her as soon as he'd found out that Selwyn had discovered that Cassian was alive. She'd been as surprised as him, but when he explained her connection to the Phantom Flame, she was even more shocked. Apparently, it hadn't occurred to her that Selwyn would take up Pontius' mantle, especially not with a rebellion.

"Yeah," was all he could muster.

"Think she could help us out?"

Kellan chewed his lip, staring down at the still-steaming mug in his hands. "Possibly."

"Because I'm almost ready."

Kellan set the mug down on the table and turned to her. Her braids were piled into a bun at the top of her head and the bags under her eyes were dark. She'd been busy, and he could tell she was stressed.

"Want me to talk to her?"

Vaida nodded. "I can be ready by next month."

He rested a hand on her arm. "Don't push yourself."

"Since when do I take the easy route?" She chuckled then, a short burst of breath coming through her lips as she smiled wryly at him.

Kellan smiled back, something between panic and excitement roiling in his gut.

14

BECK

Rivenstorm | 10th of Frost Moon

Three times. Three times Reaper had tried to orchestrate a convenient time to kill Cassian.

Three times powers unknown had thwarted him.

He admitted to himself that he wasn't trying as hard as he could have been. He knew that taking Cassian's life was a priority according to his assignment, but he couldn't get his mind off of the disappearances.

They'd still made no progress. He'd tried hunting down the man Cera had described, but no one had seen him. A man with tattoos of black shadows on his face had to be a standout in people's memories, yet no one had seen anyone like that in Rivenstorm.

Even the Phantom Flame's surveillance network had turned up nothing. No one matching that description had crossed their paths. Reaper had considered asking Brisea about him, but had thought better of it. It would lead them down a line of questioning that he wasn't interested in exploring.

He'd been avoiding telling her about Cassian, too. He didn't know why he was doing so, but every time he'd meet with her, the topic never came up.

Tonight, though, he'd taken a break from his failed attempts on Cassian's life and was relaxing in the Autumn Rose. The bar was busy, and as he stepped off the staircase, he scanned the room for a place to sit. He noticed Cera sitting by herself, just to the side of the rambunctious battle rings game in the corner of the bar.

Cera had taken to Foxtail after their rescue. She'd frequent the Autumn Rose, spending many evenings by the battle rings station watching Foxtail play. Reaper felt a jolt of guilt each time he looked at her; her eyes held a sort of darkness that he knew would never go away.

She was watching Foxtail with big eyes, a hand propped under her chin. He hated to interrupt. She looked…content.

"Cera?" he said, cautiously lowering himself down next to her. "Mind if I sit?"

She shot him a small smile, then shook her head, scooting over to give him extra room on the bench.

He didn't speak for a few minutes, letting himself get lost in the game Fox was losing. He was a good sport, though, laughing off his bad throws like he'd meant to do it all along. Something about it reminded him of Kellan.

The twinge of regret over his best friend had long since faded, but it never quite disappeared. It was all Reaper could do to pretend the loss of his best friend did nothing more than make him mildly sad.

He wondered if Kellan had missions like this one. Ones where he'd have to put his entire being aside just to function—ones where he would have to bury himself so deeply he didn't know if he'd ever be able to recover his soul.

Reaper had seen Cassian, too. He'd seen how much good he'd done for the resistance, how much his magic and strength and presence had helped morale against the demons. He *had* to kill him—because it was his life or Reaper's.

Fox threw his last ring, missing the mark wildly, and Cera chuckled. Reaper let the sound sink into his heart, easing some of the tension there. Fox laughed off his loss, asking for another round, to which his opponent happily agreed.

Cera turned to face him. "You all right, Reaper?"

He lifted his eyes to hers, their warm liquid brown reminding him of Kellan and bringing back the tension in his heart once more. He could lie; he certainly knew how to. Lying was as simple to him as breathing. "Yeah. Just…thinking."

"Anything I can do to ease your mind?"

Reaper blinked, then dropped his gaze. "Nah. I'm just…" He trailed off, wondering how he could explain the warring guilt and frustration in his heart. She didn't need to know that, anyway. But something about her gaze was welcoming, comforting.

Her chuckle was light and airy. "A man of few words."

"I'm just concise."

"I didn't say it was a bad thing."

He looked at his hands, fingers woven together in his lap, and tried. "I'm sorry about your friend, that we haven't been able to do anything."

Her lips tightened at his words. He knew that expression—she was holding back tears. "The Red Guard hasn't found a trace of her, either. I'm not expecting a miracle, you know."

He fidgeted. "Still. I'm sorry."

"I appreciate it." Cera gave him a tight smile that didn't quite reach her eyes.

Reaper leaned back against the table, letting his head drop back to stare at the ceiling. He was lost; there were no leads on the mysterious man, no information about the demonic circle he'd found at the site, and each subsequent disappearance yielded no new information.

Cera was still staring at him, but he trained his eyes on the ceiling, unsure of what he'd even say next. She seemed to accept his silence as an end to the conversation, turning her gaze back to Fox's game.

He didn't know how long he stared at the ceiling; the thoughts consumed him. He vaguely noticed when Cera stood, meeting Fox as he approached. What happened to them after that, he didn't know. The bustle of the back bar was like a blanket for his senses, monotonous and comforting.

A body slid beside his on the bench.

Reaper slid his gaze next to him, expecting Cera to have returned. But a shock of adrenaline coursed through him when the person beside him was actually Spider.

"You look pensive," she said quietly. She wasn't looking at him; she was doing the same thing Cera had—the game of battle rings, now without Foxtail as a competitor, was her focus. "Not that I'm asking you to talk, but…" She trailed off, pursing her lips.

Reaper felt himself soften. "Are you offering to listen to me?"

"No, I'm just…" she started, then shut her mouth before trying again. "I'm just making an observation."

He chuckled. "I appreciate—"

He was cut off by a siren from the back bar that indicated a demon attack somewhere in the city. Spider sprang from her spot, Reaper following closely behind her, a hand on the hilt at his hip.

A crackle came over a speaker, and Alpha's voice echoed through the bar. "All available teams to Penninsula Bay as soon as possible."

The flurry in the back bar was well-organized chaos. The resistance knew well how to prepare themselves for a demonic attack by now, and Reaper and Spider were no exception. He was already prepared for the off chance they'd be called into action, but many of the patrons in the bar were not.

Reaper and Spider burst from the Autumn Rose, but she split off toward the road while Reaper turned toward the alleys. Before he could disappear, she stopped, turning back toward him.

"Come on, I'll give you a lift," she said, jerking her head back toward the road. A low motorcycle leaned against a kickstand at the curb.

"I couldn't—"

She didn't listen, turning toward the bike and swinging a leg over the seat. "Hurry, or I'm leaving you behind."

He hesitated again, and she frowned.

"It'll bear your weight, I promise."

That wasn't his concern, but he ignored it. He could have flown, but he couldn't shake his head to refuse once more. It was like some part of him had cemented, begging him not to turn away.

He strode toward the bike with purpose, ignoring the rapid pace of his heart as he swung his leg over the backseat while Spider held the bike steady.

She started the engine, revving it once before turning back to him. "Wrap your arms around my waist; you'll fall off if you don't."

"I couldn't—"

"I swear to Hym if you say 'I couldn't' one more damn time, I'm going to throttle you. Stop wasting time and hold on."

She didn't wait for him to protest or grab on. The motorcycle peeled away from the curb with a squeal of tires, and Reaper threw his hands around Spider's waist, no longer able to overthink the touch.

She was smaller than he expected, but also built of solid muscle. He felt her shift with the movement of the motorcycle and adjusted himself, trying his best to follow her movements. She didn't speak, but he didn't mind—the frigid wind whipping past their ears was deafening. Although it was a cold winter evening, the ride somehow was one of the most pleasant travel experiences he'd had in years.

And even when they arrived at the scene, he didn't feel cold.

They were the first to arrive from the flurry of people that had sprung into action back at the Autumn Rose, and the scene that greeted them was absolute chaos. Alpha was engaged with a towering humanoid demon with gray skin, its face smashed in and black blood dribbling down its chest. Several other members, including Cassian and Harpy, fought smaller imp-like demons. The creatures thrashed against their demon-killers and burst into wisps of black sand that drifted away on the night air.

Alpha's opponent seemed to be the strongest of the bunch, its heavy six-fingered hands smashing into the pavement with seemingly little effort. She was too quick for it, although Reaper noticed she was favoring her left arm, the right hanging limply at her side. The rest of the team members seemed fine against their demons, although the constant flow of fresh adversaries kept them from assisting Alpha in her fight.

Reaper didn't allow the smaller demons to get in his way. Regardless of what the Red Guard wanted, he couldn't merely stand by and let a pack of demons kill the entire resistance.

He slashed his way through the crowd as the demonic stench of brimstone and ash clogged his senses. He culled several demons in his path, giving small respites to the members battling within the chaotic crowd. Spider was nowhere to be seen, but if he knew anything about her, she was at Harpy's side, fighting to protect her sister.

He reached Alpha in a matter of moments, a trail of dying demons left in his path. She looked worse up close—her shoulder was most definitely dislocated, her arm swinging uselessly by her side. She'd gained several red bruises that he knew would blossom into nasty black spots in a few days. Blood trickled from her temple. Yet she stood firm, parrying the demon's clumsy but heavy blows with finesse and grace.

She couldn't hold on much longer, however. She needed more strength to defeat whatever this thing was, and he could tell she hardly had enough to defend herself.

He could say he was too late. He could pretend like the mass of smaller demons had held him up. He could say he'd tried his best, but she'd been killed in action.

It might be a mercy.

But he knew the Red Guard would never let his excuses slide. If Alpha died here today, he wouldn't be far behind.

He leaped in between the demon and Alpha just as it brought its massive meaty fist down, blocking it with his sword. It stopped mid-attack, surprised by his sudden appearance, but recovered quickly. It brought its other fist around to catch him on his unguarded side.

He didn't give it the chance. He swung his sword down upon

the demon's wrist, severing the hand halfway off and getting his sword stuck. The demon roared, flinging black blood as it tried to wrench its hand free. This was exactly what he'd been expecting it to do. Using its movement as momentum, he pushed the blade down further, begging it to continue to cut through and fully sever the hand.

Alpha backed up, keeping her sword raised but relaxing her stance enough to allow herself to breathe. She watched the fight closely. Her eye sparkled in the light from street lamps over head.

The demon finally wrenched hard enough to give Reaper the final bit of leverage he needed to push the sword through. With a yell, Reaper finished the cut, slicing the demon's hand off in a spray of black blood.

His foe screamed, staggering backward as it cradled the stump in its other hand. The severed hand dissolved where it had fallen on the ground.

Reaper was at an advantage now. He brought his sword back up, squaring off with the roaring demon. He raised his demon-killer, leveling it with where he thought its core might be. If it was humanoid, it was safe to assume it would replicate the internal structure of a human.

Diving forward, he brought his sword up in a deadly swipe, aiming for the left side of the demon's chest. His focus was sharp, eyes fixated on his target. The calm he knew so well settled over him as time seemed to slow.

Battles had always been like this for him. He knew what he needed to do—where to go, how to position his body—with little more than a passing thought. Today was no different.

Until the demon's intact fist connected faster than he could have ever expected with the side of his body.

He flew, crash landing into a wall and hearing something crack. The pain was dull in his ribcage, and he could feel warm blood trickle down the back of his neck. He didn't know where his sword had ended up, but it was no longer in his hand.

Reaper's eyes struggled to focus on the demon now advancing on him, tentacles sprouting from the severed hand. Its eyes glowed a fierce, lava-like red. It seemed he'd made a fatal mistake; he'd underestimated his opponent, and he was about to pay the price.

The Red Guard wouldn't care. He was replaceable. He wondered if the Phantom Flame would mourn him, never knowing who he really was.

The demon stood above him, the tentacles of its new hand slithering over his limp body and wrapping around his throat. It was an unpleasant sensation, but he refused to close his eyes. He would face death with eyes wide open.

"Reaper!" A scream came from somewhere behind the demon. His vision was hazy, but he saw two circular demon-killers float before his vision, their effect in the hazy streetlight almost like a neon butterfly.

They descended upon the demon, slicing its head from the rest of its body in a smooth scissoring motion. Without a sound, the tentacles disintegrated from around his neck, and the demon before him fell.

Who had saved him? He couldn't focus, his eyes refusing to cooperate with his brain. A face swam before his—it was beautiful. *She* was beautiful.

"Reaper? Can you see me?" Spider held up a few fingers in front of his face.

He struggled to regain enough breath to reply; all that came out was a wheeze.

He thought he saw her smirk as she turned away to speak to someone else. "He's fine. A bit concussed and probably has a few broken ribs, but not dead."

"You…" he started, and she turned back to face him. Her face was neutral, no concern or fear in her eyes. Like she'd known all along he would be fine. "You saved me?"

She tilted her head at him. "Of course I did."

Beck couldn't help it—he smiled. He closed his eyes and

slumped back against the wall. He was safe. He'd be safe if she was here with him.

"But you did well," Beck heard her say as the black of unconsciousness claimed him.

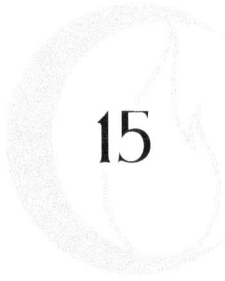

15

KELLAN

Spiral City | 1st of Dawn Moon

It was evening. The sun had set behind the clouds long ago, the night sky painted a shade of inky blue so deep it seemed endless.

Kellan knew just enough to understand—they needed a password to unlock their prison marks; using magic wasn't enough. Paired with a password, the marks could be broken safely. It wasn't foolproof, of course, considering the passwords weren't exactly *accessible*.

And breaking the marks only staved off the alarm. They'd have a few hours at most before someone noticed their marks no longer transmitted their locations. After that, they'd be fugitives.

Kellan wasn't sure he was ready for life on the run. But he needed to know—was it really Cassian? Was he truly with the Phantom Flame? Or had Selwyn somehow been mistaken?

He pulled at his stealth suit as he rode the elevator to the top floor of the Guard, knowing no one would question him going to the commissioner's office dressed like this. Something about breaking in was grating on his nerves. He didn't know why, though. It wasn't the first time he'd trespassed, and it certainly wouldn't be the last.

But he'd never broken into anything in the Guard before. It would be both the first and the last time, no matter how tonight went. Either he'd be free and never return to Spiral City, or he'd be dead.

He'd already packed his bag. His hands had shaken the entire time; he'd be leaving most of his life behind save for the few possessions he could fit in a duffel.

Kellan wondered if he'd ever get to talk to Beck again. They'd agreed to leave their techpads behind too—his best friend wouldn't know how to get in contact with him after this. He'd tried to warn him but hadn't been able to get through. Whatever Beck was up to, he was busy. Vaida had told him not to worry about it, that they would get burners, but something about leaving behind the safety of knowing Beck could always reach him was terrifying.

Static crackled in his ear as Vaida's voice came through the small transmitter. "Okay, Kell, you have ten minutes to get in and out. Just plug the data nodule into his desk pad and I'll run the program. You don't have to do anything but get in and get back out, okay?"

He fiddled with the nodule on his belt. He'd watched her make it a few days ago. She was exceptionally skilled with technomancy, creating instruments and gadgets as a channel for her magic. It was a rare and impressive skill, one that suited her perfectly.

"Right," he whispered, letting go of the nodule and rolling his shoulders.

He could hear Vaida's knuckles crack through their comms. "On my signal, then. Doors open in three, two, one…"

A ding echoed through the empty corridor, ringing in his ears. He winced, then stepped from the elevator.

It seemed the first step of their operation had gone smoothly—the large oak doors to the commissioner's office were unlocked when he tested them. He wore thick gloves that would prevent fingerprints, but if all went according to Vaida's plan, they wouldn't even know Kellan had been here until it was far too late.

He entered the commissioner's suite, footsteps light as he crossed the space to get behind the desk. His heart pounded in his ears.

Kellan's fingers shook as he removed his gloves and fished the nodule Vaida had given him from the pocket on his belt. He crouched beneath the glass desk to attach it. He was acutely aware of how little time he had, and Vaida hadn't told him how long it would take to run the program. The less time he spent here, the better.

After attaching the nodule to the desk, he stood and tapped the techpad's screen, waiting for the program in the nodule to connect. The screen on the commissioner's desk flashed to life, its soft blue glow illuminating everything in the office in a manner he found unsettling.

He watched as the program ran; the time left to upload calculated, then updated to a few minutes. His heart slammed against his ribcage painfully.

The singing stone upon the commissioner's shelf was reaching its peak. Many people put their stones in cases so their song wouldn't keep them awake at night, but it seemed the commissioner never bothered. The stone's pure and high ringing note echoed through the spacious office.

It made it quite difficult to think. And it made other noises more difficult to hear, like the suite door opening and closing behind him.

The final click of the door caught his attention through the singing stone's haunting strain. He whirled to meet the commissioner's placid face. He looked the same as ever, red hair in a smooth coif and beard trimmed neatly.

But his face was unsurprised, a smooth mask of dignity, when he met Kellan's gaze. It was as if Kellan's presence in his office didn't surprise him. As if he'd been expecting him.

"Kellan," he said, leaning against the doorframe. "What are you doing here?"

Kellan's heart was a drumbeat to accompany the melody of the stone. He frantically wracked his brain for an excuse, anything to say to the commissioner that wouldn't arouse his suspicion. But what could he possibly say that would excuse him being in the commissioner's supposedly locked office this late at night? There was no good reason for him to be here; nothing he could say would work.

"Just hold on a few more minutes," Vaida said in his ear, apparently oblivious to the fact he'd been caught. He couldn't reply to her, not with the commissioner's gaze still upon him.

The commissioner didn't seem perturbed by his silence. In fact, he seemed almost…amused? Kellan watched his commanding officer walk into the office, his arms swinging lazily by his sides. He tried to cover the screen, but it was no use. The commissioner would see everything with just a few more steps.

He didn't, however, stop when he reached the desk. Instead, he continued, approaching where the singing stone rested upon the bookshelves and looking up at it with an almost melancholic expression. Kellan simply watched him, eyes wide.

"Did I ever tell you the story of how I got this singing stone, Kellan?" the commissioner asked, ignoring Kellan's silence and the very obvious crime he was committing.

He didn't know how to find his voice, how to respond. But he swallowed hard and mustered the smallest bit of life he had left to respond. "No, you didn't."

"What?" Vaida said in his ear. He ignored her.

"My brother gifted it to me, back before he died," he continued. Kellan clenched his teeth. He'd never known the commissioner had a brother—in fact, he knew almost nothing about this man, even though he'd worked for him for five years.

In the years since Cassian's disappearance, the commissioner had become even more curious to him. He'd spent more time with Kellan whenever he visited than he would with the other legionnaires who reported directly to him. He'd try to get Kellan to open up to him about personal matters frequently, although he'd backed off since Kellan had nearly bitten his head off two years ago when a line of questioning had come dangerously close to Cassian.

He'd never figured out the commissioner's intentions with him. Some days, it was a straightforward boss-subordinate relationship.

Other times, he felt like an overbearing family member.

Regardless of how the commissioner saw him, this topic of conversation made no sense to Kellan. What was he getting at? He'd been expecting an immediate reprimand, a call for someone to arrest him. But…a story? About the commissioner's family?

He felt the question rise to his lips, unbidden. "What happened?"

"The Red Council killed him."

He heard Vaida gasp in his ear. It seemed she'd finally heard that someone else was in the room with him. "Keep talking, Kellan. I'm almost done. I'll figure out how to get you out, I promise."

The commissioner's gaze was on the singing stone now, so Kellan risked a response to Vaida. "Roger."

He heard her groan on the other side of the line. The mission had become all that much harder now that the commissioner had discovered them. How would he get himself out of this without being captured?

His mind finally snagged on what the commissioner had said. The Red Council?

"Wait, what do you mean?" Kellan asked, confused.

Their organization technically worked for the council— albeit indirectly. But something inextricably linked every single governmental figure in the Empire to the council, which meant the commissioner was connected as well.

The commissioner didn't look at him, still focused on the stone on his bookshelf. He clasped his hands behind his back, shoulders relaxed as he gazed at it.

Kellan also stayed still, focused on covering the screen as best as he could while he waited for the commissioner to do or say something else.

"I have a story to tell you, Kellan," the commissioner finally said, turning to face him. "But first, a question. Did you ever know your father's name?"

Kellan recoiled. It had been many, *many* years since anyone had asked about his family. His mother had hardly told him anything about his father; he was elven, he'd left before Kellan was born, and no, she didn't know where he was. He'd never felt a desire to find the man, and after his mother had died, he'd practically forgotten all about who'd sired him.

The commissioner would be privy to his familial history in his file from the Mission. His father's name would be included there. He could have simply opened the file to find out. So why was he asking Kellan?

"Vaeril," Kellan said slowly. His mother had told him once, and he'd never forgotten.

At the name, the commissioner's eyes closed, an expression crossing his face that almost looked like grief. His jaw clenched, exposing the rounded muscle just below his ear, then relaxed.

"Yes, Vaeril," he began, and Kellan's gut flipped. "Vaeril was a good man, a strong man. He loved Amelia very much…" The commissioner trailed off, eyes going hazy.

"Why do you know my father, sir? And my mother, for that matter?"

"Kellan"—the commissioner stepped forward, dropping his hands to wipe them upon his pants—"you must understand. It was for your own good that you never knew."

"Never knew *what,* sir?"

"Vaeril was my brother."

Chills ran from the crown of Kellan's head to the small of his back, traveling down his arms and raising the hairs along them. He couldn't breathe. He was drowning. His vision went black, his senses dulled and vibrating. His ears pulsed.

He couldn't care less about the nodule or the passwords or the program. His knees buckled, and he dropped, one arm still loosely grasping the glass desk, the other slamming painfully into the floor.

"Hey, I'm here, just breathe." A voice in his ears was soft, kind.

Kellan couldn't speak, his throat barely letting in the air he needed to breathe. He completely forgot about the screen behind him and sank to the floor, raising shaking fingers to his eyes. He couldn't see them.

A hand descended on his shoulder, and he shrugged it off on instinct as he breathed in through his nose, out through his mouth. Vaida spoke softly in his ear, but he couldn't hear a word she said.

"Kellan," the commissioner said, his voice softer than he'd ever heard it. "Come." The hand returned to lift him from the floor, hefting him gently into the desk chair.

He stared at his hands, the only thing he could pick out in the sea of black his vision had become. He clenched them into tight fists, his nails digging crescent moons into his palms. They didn't break skin, but they matched small white scars that hadn't faded over the years.

A pair of hands appeared over his, squeezing gently.

"Kellan," the commissioner said again.

The black receded just a little. Enough for him to lift his head and meet the commissioner—his *uncle's*—gaze.

"Your mother and father did everything to protect you. You must understand. If the Council knew about you…"

Kellan's heart skittered. Why had the Council killed his father, anyway? He couldn't muster the strength to speak, and the commissioner didn't offer him the chance.

He squeezed Kellan's hands again. "It's not a coincidence that I'm here tonight—I know what needs to be done to free you. But I can't help you directly, so this is the best I have, the best I can give you." A hand disappeared for a moment, then reappeared to place something in Kellan's now-open palm. "Take it. Take it and go. Find Rosalie in Rivenstorm. Tell her I—Aeryn—sent you. She will know. She'll explain."

Kellan wrapped his fingers around the nodule, disbelief and shock and panic making him entirely numb. But his mind was screaming at him to get out, still not understanding that the commissioner wouldn't arrest him. That, somehow, he would be fine. That the commissioner had given him an out.

He felt the commissioner tug underneath his arms, urging him to stand. "Come. You still have so much to do before you go. You can't stay here forever."

Adrenaline jolted its way through him as the commissioner helped him up, forcing his fingers closed around the nodule at the same time.

"I—" Kellan tried, but he choked on everything he wanted to say.

His uncle, Aeryn, the *Commissioner of the Legionnaires of Spiral City,* smiled at him softly. "It's too much now, but you will understand in time. Now go."

And with one last push, he ushered Kellan out the door toward freedom.

16

KELLAN

Spiral City | 1st of Dawn Moon

He was numb, and not from the frigid wind blowing violently in his face as he flew through the skies. The neon lights of the city below hardly registered. Normally, Kellan loved this view, the bright lights of the city covered in a fine layer of smog and mist. He usually loved the way the sounds were duller up here, the smells almost non-existent.

But that didn't register today. He had a *family*.

At the thought, his mind filled with images of Selwyn, Vaida, and Beck. Their faces were stark in his mind against Aeryn's, the flash of smiles brilliant and blinding. They were as much his family as anyone, but the commissioner was different.

His whole life, he'd assumed his father had walked out on his mom. That he hadn't wanted Kellan, that he'd left to go off and do gods knows what on his own. He'd been so wrong that the truth felt unreal.

But something inside of him knew the commissioner wasn't lying. He'd let Kellan walk away with the data without so much as asking what it was for. It was like he'd known he would be there. But how? Why?

He hadn't realized he'd nearly flown to the city limits until he finally looked down, swearing as he turned around and headed back toward his destination in southern Bloomside.

Vaida hadn't tried talking through his headset since he'd left. She'd most likely heard his end of things, although he'd barely said a word during his conversation with his uncle. He didn't know if he was ready to talk about it, but he knew he must. After all, they'd gotten the data they needed, and it had gone even smoother than they ever could have planned.

Did this mean the Legion wouldn't pursue them? Kellan wondered if, knowing what he knew now, the commissioner would try to protect them.

He landed with a thump on the sidewalk, his wings fading behind him as he stomped into the nondescript building on the corner of a quiet residential street. Four other apartment buildings sat beside this one, their facades all exactly the same gray brick and white shutters. It was a nice area but too quiet for Kellan's taste.

Inside, he rode the elevator up with barely a glance at the buttons. He couldn't even look at his own reflection in the shiny metal.

The chime rang, the doors opened, and he didn't even have a moment to register what was happening before Vaida's soft scent enveloped him as she flew into his arms. Her voice was shaky and weak when she spoke, a tone he'd never heard her use before.

"For the love of all that is holy, Kellan, you scared the shit out of me," she breathed into his ear, hanging onto him with fists balled in his shirt.

He returned the embrace, burying his face in her neck. "I'm all right, V, I'm here," he said, repeating their phrase. She needed it more than he did right now.

She breathed deeply into his shoulder, then pulled away, apparently satisfied he was real and unharmed.

Someone cleared their throat behind Vaida—Selwyn. She was waiting inside, cheeks rosy from the cold, her eyebrows drawn together. She must have arrived only a few minutes before him. Although she'd been kept mostly in the dark about their plans,

T.M. LEDVINA

they'd asked her to be present for the mark breaking.

Vaida broke their embrace, shuffling backward while her face turned serious. Selwyn's expression stayed concerned.

"What happened?"

Where did he even begin? He didn't know how to approach this with them, how to tell them the man they'd worked for all these years was actually his long-lost uncle, that the commissioner had simply *given away* the one thing they needed to escape.

He breathed in once, shakily, then started from the beginning. He told them everything—how he'd thought himself caught, doomed, and how the commissioner had surprised him with the story about his father and who he was to Kellan.

Vaida's eyes widened in surprise as he continued, but Selwyn stayed impassive.

"Kellan, I don't mean to rain on your parade here, but what if…." Vaida sighed, turning toward her techpad on the desk. "What if he's tricking us?"

"I don't think he is, truthfully," he said, handing her the nodule from his pocket.

She took it warily, running her fingers around the outside. "Do you have proof of that?"

"No; call it a gut feeling."

"He's not tricking you," Selwyn said, finally speaking for the first time since he'd arrived. "I can guarantee that."

Vaida stopped fiddling with the nodule as Selwyn spoke, her whole body having gone stiff at the words.

Kellan's ears roared. "What do you mean, Selwyn?"

"The Phantom Flame told him our operation was happening tonight. We didn't ask him to show up, but it seems he took matters into his own hands." She shook her head like a parent talking about a disobedient child.

It made sense. The commissioner hadn't seemed surprised to find Kellan in his office. It would explain why he'd sent Kellan off without so much as a second thought.

But that made so many more questions arise in Kellan's mind. "Is the commissioner…in contact with the resistance?"

Selwyn cocked a delicate brow at him. "I thought that much was obvious, based on what he told you."

Vaida resumed working on the nodule, but her mouth was a thin line. Kellan knew that look—she was angry about being kept in the dark. He knew that was the way Selwyn operated, how this entire operation was supposed to work. But he could tell Vaida wasn't happy about this piece of information being kept from them.

"Selwyn," Vaida began, her voice low, "why didn't you tell us the commissioner was part of the resistance?"

"To be honest, I couldn't," she said, crossing her legs at the ankles. "He wasn't supposed to be there tonight, like I said. His involvement with the resistance is one of their most closely guarded secrets."

Kellan leaned against the wall, the adrenaline that was keeping him standing beginning to fade. The night wasn't over by any means, but he was exhausted, and the information he'd learned so far was becoming too much.

"And," Selwyn continued, rubbing her face in frustration, "I didn't know his relationship to you beforehand. He was tight-lipped about the fact Vaeril had a son at all. No one knew until tonight."

"But they knew he was my dad's brother?" Kellan asked.

Selwyn nodded. "The resistance knew Aeryn long before his rise to power. They never really understood his desire to stick around with the Legion, but it seems there was at least a little logic to it."

Kellan's frown deepened. "I don't understand."

"I don't really either," Vaida said. She'd turned back to her techpad, the nodule lying open on the desk like a metal flower, and was typing quickly. "But now's not the time to worry about that. We can grill the resistance once we're out of here."

They sat in silence for a few moments, the only sound the light clicking of Vaida's nails on the techpad glass as she searched through the program. He didn't know how this was supposed to work, but he trusted Vaida with his life—regardless of how the last time she'd done this had turned out.

The clicking stopped, and Vaida pulled another device from her bag. It looked a bit like a necklace made of metal, open enough to slip around and hang in place. Two half circles of metal hung from the main piece, lit from within with a faint blue glow. She waved a hand over the device, then murmured a string of letters and numbers. Beneath her hand, the device glowed even deeper blue.

A faint purple glow enshrined both Vaida and the metal necklace before fading. Vaida turned from the device to meet his gaze.

"It's ready. Are you sure you want to be first?"

He breathed slowly. "Yes. They won't care if they lose a Fallen. Just do it."

She nodded solemnly, then picked up the necklace. The blue glow hadn't faded. "Turn around; I need to put this on you."

He complied, baring his neck toward her and lifting the hair at the nape of his neck. The metal was cold as she slid it on, the glowing half circles freezing against his back. She murmured something again, and the blue light flared so bright it nearly blinded him.

The back of his neck burned slightly, like a cat had scratched him or he'd been tattooed all over again. But the pain faded just as quickly as it had come.

Vaida didn't remove the collar, leaving it in place for what felt like an eternity. They sat in silence, and Kellan knew she was waiting. His own breaths were shallow, slow. He expected something terrible to happen at any moment.

Time slowed, crawled, scraped by. The night outside the window was neon, the neon he'd once loved so much but had come to resent over the years. It speckled with flashing lights and vague sounds, as if they'd been put into a vacuum and time inside had stopped while the rest of the world moved on without them.

And yet, nothing happened.

Then Vaida moved, and the vacuum was no more. She placed a cold hand on the back of his neck and gently removed the device. Her hand stayed even after the device was gone.

"Did it work?" Selwyn asked in a quiet voice.

Vaida laid the device on the desk again, repeating the same murmuring and incantation she had before putting it around his neck. She ignored Selwyn's question. They'd know soon enough if it had.

Kellan watched as Vaida put the device around her own neck. The subsequent flash of light blinded him again as he waited, breath stuck in his throat.

He and Selwyn watched Vaida's neck, the vacuum of silence hopeful but heavy, weighty but warm. Expectant and damning.

The world stayed silent as the minutes dragged by, perfectly calm and still. Then Vaida removed the device again, placing it on the table with her techpad.

"Kellan," she whispered, and he thought he saw a gleam of something silver in her eyes. "We did it. We're free."

🔥 🔥 🔥

The sun was now peeking its golden-hued head above the horizon, painting the sky in shades of purple and pink and gilding the clouds that hung before them. It was foggy, the first rays of sunlight sparkling off the snow that hung in the fully leafed trees around them.

Bloomside was always unnerving to Kellan, the way everything stayed alive year round, even through the snowy moons of Evergreen, Frost, and Dawn. Even the flowers stayed vibrant through the snow, the pops of color painting an image that looked surreal. No one could deny the scenery was beautiful, though.

Neither he nor Vaida had slept last night. They'd packed most of their things already, but there were loose ends to tie up, people to see, things to pawn. And now that it was morning, it was time to go.

Selwyn left after they'd broken their marks, locking the apartment door behind them for the last time. She wouldn't be here to see them off this morning, either.

But now, as they sat on the train to the warehouse, Kellan's thoughts wandered to the commissioner, to his family, to all the things he'd never dreamed of having.

Aeryn being his uncle didn't explain his sympathy to Kellan's predicament. Aeryn was elven and a high-ranking official within the Empire's government. Theoretically, he shouldn't care about Kellan, even if they were related. And yet…

That brought him to a thought he'd avoided for a while—Pontius. Pontius had been elven, a high-profile activist, and member of Empire society, yet he'd been sympathetic to Kellan's situation. Pontius didn't even have a family member to be concerned about like Aeryn did.

Did that make Aeryn's situation more believable or Pontius' mission less?

The thoughts haunted him until they arrived at their destination, the warehouse built of aluminum and painted dark green, a Morgenstern Tech logo plastered on the far exterior wall.

Vaida elbowed him as they approached the door. He barely felt it.

"Snap out of it, Kell; I need you alert," she said, her voice gentle. "You'll have plenty of time to think once we're on the road."

He sighed, then slowly shifted his eyes to her, giving them a moment to focus on her face. He nodded once, turning back to knock on the door to the warehouse.

A gruff-looking dwarven man answered, his beard braided nearly down to his knees and woven with strips of black ribbon. He gave them a scrupulous stare as his eyes narrowed, taking his time to observe their clothes, their shoes, and their faces.

"You the protection Miss Morgenstern sent?" he said, crossing his arms in front of his chest.

Vaida nodded. "We are. Where do you want us?"

He sighed, then stepped from the door frame to allow them inside. "Docking bay seven. Your driver will give you more instructions."

Vaida thanked him, then pulled on Kellan's elbow to lead him inside. He let her do it, taking the time to glance around at the inside of the warehouse. It was quite bare, more than he expected, although it appeared this section of the warehouse might have been for daily shipments rather than long-term storage.

They walked along the eastern wall, the bay numbers ascending until they found docking bay seven. A truck waited there, a half-elven man leaning against the cab and smoking a cigarette. Kellan watched as the smoke curled around his head and disappeared up into the sky.

The man looked up at their approach, the bored expression he wore never fading. He was quite unassuming—ashy brown hair and a face that could be easily forgotten.

But the look in his eyes made Kellan wary. He grunted at their approach, turning back to the cab as they got close. Vaida narrowed her eyes and called out to him before he disappeared into the driver's seat.

"You must be our ride. Where should we go?" she asked.

The man stopped, one foot on the ground, the other on the step up to the cab. He spoke without turning around. "You're up here, with me." Without pausing for their reaction, he continued into the cab, slamming the door after himself.

"You'll have to excuse Theo; he's a bit of a loner." The dwarf who'd let them in earlier was standing a few feet away, performing a few checks on his truck. "He's not used to having people go with him."

Kellan just nodded to the man, and Vaida shot him a small smile. "Thanks for that," she replied. The dwarven man just grunted in response and turned back to his truck.

Vaida sighed, then jerked her head to the other side of the cab. "Come on, looks like we're getting ready to leave already."

The truck rumbled as they climbed up into the cab. Theo didn't even glance their way before backing the truck slowly out of the warehouse.

Kellan settled himself in the backseat, letting Vaida ride shotgun up front. His heartbeat was a steady thrum in his chest, his stomach empty yet heavy. He was finally leaving, finally free.

SECTION 2

THE
RESISTANCE

The Phantom Flame is the name the human resistance uses to organize their efforts to bring equality to the Empire. Historically, they have been a peaceful organization, utilizing their membership to advocate for equal rights and awareness within the Empire. In the last few years, however, the resistance's efforts have turned more toward peacekeeping and protection against the influx of demons on the material plane.

It has been rumored that the leaders of the resistance, the Delacours, have a connection to the last human monarch, Queen Ameloria. This rumor has never been confirmed, but many people believe it to be true. The current leader, Rosalie, has been in her role as leader for six years. She came into her role at only twenty years old due to the previous leader passing away after she contracted a sickness that slowly ate away at her health.

The Phantom Flame's headquarters has always been in Rivenstorm, as it is the most progressive city in the Empire. However, they do have pockets of membership across the entire country.

17

CASSIAN

Rivenstorm | 2nd of Dawn Moon

Cassian shed the blood-soaked gloves in the back room, dropping them into the bin to burn. His squad had just returned from yet another demon-hunting mission, and he was bone tired. Although he was nearly a demon himself thanks to his pact, it didn't make the endless fights against them any easier.

Cassian, Zal's voice echoed in his head. Zir sing-song tone showed zir annoyance. *You've been dancing around this for long enough.*

I know, he shot back. *I'm exhausted, though. Just let me rest.*

Zal didn't respond.

He sighed, trudging up the stairs to his room on the second floor of the Autumn Rose. What he needed now was a hot soak in the bath, then he'd find Rosalie. He knew what needed to be done—the artifacts and his mission hadn't left his mind since he'd joined. But he'd been avoiding it, content to play the rebel and bolster the ranks of those an old friend had once wanted to join.

Cassian winced as he opened the door to his room. He'd done so easily what Pontius had struggled to do so long ago. How was it fair that he would be the one to betray them in the end?

He filled the tub to the brim with scalding hot water. He stripped the rest of his gear while the water steamed. Stepping in, he hissed, relishing the heat as it seeped into his exhausted muscles.

The demons they'd fought today weren't particularly challenging, but there were many. With the increase in demons flooding the material plane, groups of low-level demons had gotten more and more popular. Despite their relative weakness, it made fighting them more exhausting.

You want a refresher? Zal asked, and Cassian rolled his eyes.

Can't I have a nice bath without you nagging me?

No, Zal replied. He could practically feel zir wink through the pact.

Cassian sighed. *I already know—Rosalie has something that will lead us to the artifacts. Find them, bring them back.*

She will most likely be resistant, ze said. *Human lifespans are so short—asking her about this will be…significant for her.*

Cassian didn't know how to respond. There was another pause, a silence that stretched long enough he wondered if Zal had simply cut off their connection. But he could still feel it, like a taut cord connecting him to the demon, tied to the deepest part of his heart.

He watched his hands float in the steaming water, considering the way they felt weightless. Beneath them, the black veins snaked up his legs to mid-thigh. They'd moved little since coming back to the material plane, but his first few magic lessons with Zal had helped them creep up quickly.

Zal, he said, staring at his wrinkled fingers. *Why me? I'm nothing special.*

You may think that, but we have our reasons. Zal's response was immediate. *You'll simply need to trust me and bring me the artifacts when I ask.*

You're putting an awful lot of faith in my abilities, Zal.

He could feel Zal's amusement through the pact. *Oh no, I don't think it's faith at all. It's something much, much deeper than that.*

Before he had the chance to ask Zal to elaborate, he felt their connection end.

Cassian stayed in the bath until the water cooled, then forced himself out of the bath to do what needed to be done.

🌢 🌢 🌢

Cassian found Alpha twenty minutes later by the fire, reading a book with an intense stare. It was late enough that the barroom was filling with resistance members gearing up for a long night of drinking and games. He knew she wouldn't have peace much longer. Now was his chance.

He sat next to her in an armchair facing the stone fireplace. They were old and worn, the leather faded and cracked on the seats where countless resistance members had sat to chat with their leader. But they were relaxing, squished to the perfect level of comfort.

"Alpha?" he said as he lowered himself into the chair slowly. "Do you have a moment? I'd like to speak with you."

She looked up at him, a soft smile spreading across her face as she met his eyes. She shut her book and gently placed it on the table beside her. "Absolutely."

He chewed his lip, unsure how to even begin. Zal wouldn't mind if he used zem as an excuse to open up this conversation. He was sure no matter how he tried to approach it, this wouldn't be easy.

"I'm going to ask you something that may be sensitive, and I want you to understand that my sources come from the Hells."

She cocked her eyebrow at him but said nothing.

He continued. "You have...something that will lead to relics of some sort. My pact wants me to find them."

He hated such a direct approach, but he couldn't think of another way to get her to entrust him with the information. After all, if she was going to send anyone after them after so many years, it certainly wouldn't be him.

She was calm, watching him with an expression he couldn't name. She glanced around the room once, then sighed as she stood.

"Come with me."

She led him to the opposite side of the barroom, beneath the staircase that led up. Pressing a small knot in the wooden wall once, several panels slid away to reveal a staircase leading downward. She gestured for him to follow. He obeyed.

The basement room was a large, open space interspersed with metal folding chairs and several circular tables. The walls were poured concrete and had never been painted. It was cold down here, but Cassian didn't mind it.

Rosalie, however, shivered as she pulled out one of the folding chairs at the table closest to the staircase. She gestured to one of the other chairs before her. "I'm going to give you a little history lesson." She breathed in and out, closing her eye to steady herself. "But first, how much do you know of Sol and the Conjunction?"

"The basics, but I don't know what you're referencing, I guess?"

She nodded. "Then let me start at the beginning. Before the Conjunction, this world belonged to the humans and our god, Hym. Hym was not like Sol; Hym lived among us, guiding and leading us as one of our own. He believed that the only way to lead was by example, through loving his children directly. The Conjunction displaced hundreds of thousands of new people here, people we'd never even imagined could exist. And that influx forced people out of their homes, displacing thousands more. But not only did it displace people, it displaced the gods."

Cassian frowned. "The Circle?"

Rosalie nodded. "Sol didn't approve of the way Hym ruled his people, especially not when *Sol's* people were now living among Hym's. Sol believed the people could govern themselves and challenged Hym to a duel. The winner would become the only god and would rule as they saw fit."

"The Battle of the Thousand Suns; I know of it."

"Yes, but you don't know the *rest* of it. Hym should have won that battle, but he was losing. He discovered near the end that Sol had three artifacts that fed him power. *The Sword,* which granted him immense strength in battle. *The Staff,* which gave him access to the depths of the ether, giving him nearly unlimited magical power. And last, *The Sphere,* which allowed him to conserve his own energy and use the life force around him."

During Rosalie's story, Cassian fiddled with his pinky ring. He'd never heard of Sol's artifacts. He didn't understand why. If they made their god so powerful, wouldn't Sol want everyone to know about them?

She continued, ignoring Cassian's fiddling. "Before he was finally defeated, and as a last act of defiance against Sol, Hym stole Sol's artifacts. He entrusted them to his angels, who then gave them to the humans to hide from Sol. And then, on the final day of their battle, Sol struck Hym down in anger over his lost relics. Hym was reduced to slivers of his former self. The humans hid the artifacts away so Sol could never wield that power against us again."

He stopped fiddling. He felt...strange. Like the knowledge of this long-lost secret was something he'd known all along. "So this thing you have...you know how to find these relics?"

She folded her fingers on the table, pursing her lips. "Here is where I need to understand something. I have no problem giving you a little history lesson. In fact, I think it is entirely necessary to educate non-humans on our history, especially stories like this one. Sol's violent takeover and subsequent mistreatment of Hym's people is the reason we exist as we do today." She frowned, opening her hands to grip the edges of the table. "But I cannot trust you completely without knowing what your motivations are for wanting something like this from me."

Cassian chewed his lip, twirling the ring around his finger. "But you are confirming you have something?"

"I am confirming nothing. I'd like to understand why you are asking me for something like this."

He closed his eyes, willing Zal to help him out. Ze responded almost instantaneously, as if ze'd been listening the whole time.

Ask if she knows that Hym had a sibling. He'd never heard Zal sound so sincere before.

"Can I ask you something first, Alpha?"

She nodded. "I assume your pact had something to say about my story?"

"Ze did. Ze wants to know if you know of Hym's sibling."

Rosalie's face paled. Her mouth thinned, forming a tight line and aging her face. She didn't respond right away; instead, she stared at Cassian, eye wide. It looked like she'd stopped breathing.

Finally, she loosed a breath, squeezing her eye shut. "This… Their name was struck from the records. No one knows who Hym's sibling was, not even me."

Cassian felt a frown forming between his eyebrows. Then why did Zal ask him to say that?

"But," she continued, "I think I must show you something, now that you have asked."

She stood abruptly, gestured for him to wait, and retreated up the stairs. He sat still as a stone, the weight of something pivotal pressing him down into the cold metal of the chair. The feeling that he'd known all of this hadn't faded; it was as if he was being reminded of something he'd long since known but had simply chosen not to remember.

And for some reason, he wanted to cry.

Did Hym really have a sibling? he asked, ignoring the tears trying to form in his eyes. *Why do you know about that?*

Zal didn't answer.

Soon after, he heard footsteps returning down the staircase. Rosalie reappeared, in her hands a small leather-bound journal that looked hundreds of years old. It was creased along the spine, the leather strip holding it together a different color than the cover. Someone had stamped the front with a symbol—a crescent moon holding a flame between its points.

She sat before him, gently unwinding the leather strap from the cover as she did.

"My ancestors passed this journal down through the centuries. Its contents give hints to the location of Sol's relics. There is a passage in the beginning I would like you to read."

She passed the journal to him, and he took it from her with cautious fingers. The journal was written in a looping hand, flowing enough that the words were difficult to read.

*When Hym's family seeks your aid,
do not ignore their call.*

He read the passage several times, soaking in each word and making sure he wasn't misreading. Rosalie said no one knew of Hym's sibling. But apparently, her ancestors did.

"So…what? Do you think I'm Hym's sibling? Or that I'm a messenger for them?" Cassian finally asked in a halting voice. There was no way.

Rosalie took the journal back, shaking her head. "I don't know, honestly. But you are the first and only person who has ever asked me about them. And that makes me believe that you, or your pact, knows something I don't about this. Maybe this is the sign my ancestors were waiting for."

She gently replaced the leather strap, her fingers shaking. He didn't know what to make of this—that he'd just delivered a sign her family had been waiting literally hundreds of years for. What Zal had asked him to do was immense. It was too much.

Zal and Asmodeus wanted these relics. And Rosalie's family had been waiting for centuries for someone to find them again.

But something twisted inside of him, something nasty and dark and threatening. He didn't know why the demons wanted them. He could only imagine the power they could wield if given these artifacts. After all, Alpha said they'd given Sol enough strength to triumph over the more powerful Hym. But how much of that was true?

He knew that, no matter what, he'd have to find the relics for Asmodeus. It was part of his pact to do what Zal asked of him, and this had been his mission all along. What Zal would do with them was unknown, and he doubted the demon would offer that information up willingly.

Rosalie sighed. "I want you to find these relics. In the right hands, they could be powerful tools to help us fight against the corruption this country has thrived on since the Conjunction. We can use them to turn the tides. And you should be the one to find them, as the messenger of Hym's family."

He wanted to argue. He wanted to tell her that giving him this task would only lead to their ruin. He didn't want to see her fail, not after she'd worked for this for so long.

But he couldn't disobey. He wouldn't tell her that, though.

"I'd be honored. I'll do everything I can to see it through."

She smiled, the color returning to her cheeks. And in her eye he saw it—the first tentative glimmer of hope. Hope that he would personally crush into oblivion.

18

BECK

Rivenstorm | 3rd of Dawn Moon

Reaper sat in an armchair by the wall, Alpha next to him. Her hair was down today, out of its trademark plait. It was still slightly wet, the ends curling in the warmth by the stone fireplace.

They checked in like this often. It was a sign of a good leader, in his opinion. But he rarely saw her this casual, dressed in an oversize knitted sweater, breezy pants, and fuzzy socks. She looked cozy, gathered into the armchair like a child.

Reaper sometimes forgot just how young Alpha was. She was his age, if not a few years older, but carried herself like someone twice her age. Her aura was that of a true commander; someone with the passion and ability to lead in their blood.

After their last demonic attack, Alpha had been injured pretty badly, but she didn't look it now. He could vaguely see a small scar on her forehead, above her eyepatch, but the medical team had done a great job patching her up.

She balanced a techpad precariously on the tops of her knees. Her finger swiped through what looked to be a long letter. He couldn't read much from here; the only thing he saw was the signature at the bottom—Morgenstern.

He wouldn't interrupt her. Her brows knit together as she read, the lip she chewed upon looking redder by the minute. Reaper wondered what kind of news could put such an expression on Alpha's face.

She sighed, shutting off the techpad with a casual swipe of her finger and returning her feet to the floor. He could tell she was forcing the frown off her face as she smiled gently at him.

"Reaper," she began, then bit her lip. "Please give me an update on your team's operations. I need to be distracted."

He was curious, and the desire to ask about the letter and its contents burned at the tip of his tongue. But that's not why he was here. His own personal curiosity was nothing faced with the weight of the tasks set before him. Could he even ask her about the infernal symbology?

He sighed. "We're still investigating the disappearances, but nothing has turned up." It wasn't a lie—since Cera's friend's disappearance, their investigations had stalled. No more demonic symbology had turned up. He'd even revisited some of the other places of interest, but nothing had turned up. They'd almost been *too* clean.

Alpha nodded. "That's expected; I won't get up your ass about it. You're doing well, Reaper, thank you."

Reaper didn't reply, waiting for her to ask another question as she usually did. But she was silent, staring down at the carpet beneath their feet.

"Alpha?" he finally said, his voice just above a whisper.

She lifted her head to look at him, and something in her expression gave Reaper pause. It was as if she was looking through him, not at him, trying to see something that wasn't there. The hairs on the back of his neck prickled; he suppressed a shudder.

"Sorry," she finally said, blinking and breaking whatever spell had settled over them. "I'm just…thinking."

The desire to ask about whatever she'd been reading rose to his lips again. Once again, he tamped down the urge. If she really wanted him to know, she would say something.

"Anything I can do to help?" he asked.

She shook her head. "Not unless you're familiar with the way the Legion operates out of Spiral City," she replied. Her brows slowly wrinkled together as she spoke.

It felt like being stabbed, the mention of the Legion bringing forth memories of Kellan and his toothy grin, of their sixteen years spent together in the Mission. His family, the only one he'd been able to choose for himself, the one that he'd purposefully lost for the sake of this assignment. It was an entirely different pain, the pain of a loss you chose yourself.

Alpha sighed, then flicked the techpad on again. "We're taking in two more refugees. I know they're a risk, but I can't just leave them high and dry." She frowned at the message, then continued. "But the Red Guard will be after them."

Reaper frowned. "Refugees? And why is the Red Guard after them?"

Alpha flicked the techpad off again, rubbing her eyes. "Because they're ex-indentured Legion, that's why."

He ignored the weight that bloomed in his stomach, spreading through his chest and arms, up his neck. He had a million questions, but there was only one he could even think to ask.

"How did they escape? Their tattoos—"

"They broke them."

The weight increased. His chest felt tight. "But—"

"They had help from high places, let's say." She rearranged herself in the chair once more, pulling her feet back up onto the seat. "I'm not sure what I'm going to do with them once they get here, but I have an idea. I trust your judgment, and I'm hoping you might take them in on your squad."

Reaper's reaction didn't show on his face, but his heart nearly exploded from his chest. He would risk much more than his mission getting too close to fugitives. But the impact of successful mark-breaking was significant. And very, *very* dangerous.

It would be suspicious to refuse, he thought. But accepting

might bring down different consequences he wasn't willing to think about at the moment. So he did the only thing he could think of.

"Why not pair them with Frost's team? Normally I'd be happy to accept, but given our current investigation, it might not be the best idea strategically."

Alpha's face went from contemplative to relaxed. "I hadn't considered that angle, but it could be a good one, given their histories." She chewed her lip and stared down at her techpad.

Reaper wasn't sure if she was finished, so he waited, hoping she would dismiss him. She didn't. He sat still, watching the leader of the resistance and waiting for her to say something else.

Several moments passed in silence before she found his eyes again. "I'm sorry, Reaper; I didn't mean to keep you. You're dismissed."

He stood, brushing his pants off sharply. Alpha didn't follow. The techpad sat in her lap, the pattern of her sweater squashed against the glass. He watched her for a moment, expecting her to say something else.

She didn't. She stared at the fire instead, her face unreadable.

He left her alone, retreating toward the staircase in the dining room that led upstairs. He needed a nap and a moment to sort his thoughts.

He'd have to report this to Brisea. The Red Guard may not fully crack the nut that was the resistance, but they kept a close watch on their operations. He would be in a world of trouble if new recruits from outside the city showed up without alerting them of it.

He hated to do it. After all, they were the first people he'd ever heard of breaking their marks.

Reaper reached a hand up to the back of his neck, rubbing the spot his mark still sat with careful fingers. Sure, it was covered now, but it didn't mean the tattoo was no longer there. It didn't just stain his skin; it stained his blood, too. His memories, his choices, his life.

He wondered if they would be able to break his shackles too.

🔥 🔥 🔥

Brisea met him at a ritzy bar in Central Hill every week. It was called the Rosestone, and it lived up to its name. Built with rough, sand-like stone and painted a soft pink, it stood out against the other colorful buildings surrounding it. The windows at its front were as tall as the building itself, their panes made up of hundreds of smaller glass squares set into iron.

They had a table inside—they'd tucked it into a dark corner, far from the windowed front. Brisea was always there before him, sipping a glass of bubbly white wine and tapping her foot against the leg of the chair opposite her.

She was beautiful; her dark skin seemed to glow from within, her rose-colored hair only accenting the dewiness of her skin. Dangling, sparkling gems hung from the tips of her long, pointed ears, and she intertwined matching pins between the strands of her hair. She stood out, a trait not normally sought after for informants of the Red Guard.

But she was good. Better than most at disguising herself, she blended into crowds with an ease even the best changelings couldn't replicate.

She stared him down, the dim lighting of the bar reflecting off the tiny gems embedded in her floor-length black gown. Patrons at every table wore similar outfits; floor-length gowns, fitted suits, the stylish pantsuits popular with nearly every race.

If anything, Beck was the one standing out.

Brisea sipped her wine while he sat, yanking the chair out with more force than was really necessary. Her lips spread into a wide smile.

"Beck," she said, elongating her vowels. "How's life down in the Lower Quarter?" Her t's were crisp but soft, like she pulled away from them just before they could fully form. Her tone was casual, but Beck knew what she was asking. Brisea didn't chit-chat.

"I only have one report for you today," he said, frowning as a black-suited server set a glass of the same wine Brisea had before him. He didn't touch it.

Brisea leaned back in her chair with a casual grace, swirling her wine in one hand. The slit of her dress revealed her leg nearly up to the joint of her hip with the movement.

"Oh? I'm curious," she purred. "Well, then, go on. And don't be shy, I got that drink just for you."

Beck didn't pick up his glass. He watched her, his back tight as she continued to enjoy her wine as if they were simply a pair of old friends wasting the night away. That was exactly what Brisea wanted the club to think. But she knew multiple spells for his tattoo; she literally held his life in her hands. One wrong word, a single utterance she didn't like, and Beck was as good as dead.

He glanced around the room, watching for anyone whose eyes were too curious. It was likely she'd already put some protections in place, probably a spell node of some sort to block anyone from listening in. He wasn't sure how far that spell extended, though.

Brisea noticed his gaze. "The node is active. Speak freely."

He frowned. "Two refugees are escaping from Spiral City soon. They're ex-Legion. And they're headed here."

Brisea's eyebrows raised a touch, the most expression he'd ever get from her beyond a flirtatious giggle or a sly smile. "That's it? Any more information?"

"There was a signature on a letter Rosalie was reading—Morgenstern," he said. "I don't know if it has anything to do with the escapees, though."

"Interesting." She took a long drink from her wine, closing her eyes as she swallowed. He watched her with a cautious gaze.

She was quiet for several moments, losing herself in her wine and acting as if Beck wasn't across the table from her, waiting. This was normal—the world revolved around her, and she took full advantage of it.

"We'll monitor the roads," she finally said. "I'm curious who our runaways are and what the Morgensterns have to do with their escape. We can't have them giving you any ideas, can we?" Her smile was feral, raised eyebrows and curled lips. She was provoking him.

He said nothing. He knew any reply that would come from him now would only serve as fodder for her. Beck wasn't about to give her a reason to use any of the activation spells for his tattoo.

Brisea watched him with a haughty expression, but got bored at his inaction after a few moments. She drained the rest of her glass in a single gulp, then reached across the table for his untouched drink.

"Since you're obviously ignoring my hospitality," she began, bringing the glass to her lips, "I'll be taking this for myself."

Beck shook his head. "I'm just not a fan of wine, that's all."

"Uswyean whiskey, perhaps? Maybe a good liguette from Illium?"

Beck continued to shake his head. "Alcohol does nothing for me."

"Obviously, but you don't even enjoy it for fun?"

He pushed himself away from the table, sick of the conversation. She was always like this, trying to get a reaction from him. He didn't indulge her, but it also didn't mean he had to sit around and take it, especially when he'd already given her the only new information he had.

"If you'll excuse me," he said as he stood.

Brisea shifted, the slit of her dress somehow climbing even higher on her leg. "See you next time, Beck." Her voice was honey, thick and sickeningly sweet.

He said nothing, turning toward the door and making his way through the dark bar to exit into the cool evening air of Central Hill. He took a deep, gasping breath. It was like a hand had been over his mouth the entire conversation, and now that he was out, he could finally breathe again.

Brisea scared him a little. She wasn't afraid to get what she wanted, and he wasn't so blind to not know she found him attractive. Although she'd never admitted that to him, every glance, every gesture, every word she spoke to him was sign enough.

But she was also the keeper of his leash. Even if he wanted to do those things, and even if he wanted to do them with her, it wouldn't be right. The power dynamic was too large between them for him to consider it.

Spider's face popped into his head, unbidden.

He shook his head, trying to rid her image. He couldn't. Although he often wondered what it would be like to run his fingers through her hair, he knew that would never happen. She was off-limits. Everyone was off-limits.

Because he wasn't a resistance member. He was a Reaper, a beautiful demon, a harbinger of the end. It wasn't his place to want her.

His wings exploded from his tattoos and he took off into the skies, leaving thoughts of Brisea and Spider and his chains back on the cold earth.

19

KELLAN

Somewhere in Centrilir | 6th of Dawn Moon

Theo proved to be a rather grueling travel companion. He left at sunrise each morning and would drive until well after sunset each evening. They spent most of their nights in ramshackle roadside motels with truck parking in the back.

Whenever they'd try to start a conversation with him, he'd give them a one-word answer, grunt, or not reply at all. He didn't listen to music while he drove, instead staring at the open expanse of road before them with a single-minded determination that Kellan found unnerving.

The only time Theo would respond would be when they'd ask questions about their journey. He was blunt, and didn't waste time with his responses. Small talk wasn't in his repertoire of skills. After a few days, Vaida and Kellan understood that talking to Theo would get them nowhere, so they would converse in the backseat together.

It seemed no one knew of their escape—or if they did, they were keeping quiet about it. They watched the news and read papers when they stopped at their motels or diners, but it seemed all was normal in Spiral City and the Empire. Not a peep about escaped Legion indentures, nothing about fugitives on the run.

A seed of hope formed in Kellan's heart. Maybe the commissioner was protecting them. Maybe he'd kept their escape under wraps, or had avoided letting anyone find out at all. If that was the case, Kellan was immensely grateful.

But the lack of information made Vaida nervous. She would set up traps at every motel to make a noise if the door opened. She would fall asleep after Kellan did and wake long before him. He wondered if she slept at all; his only comfort knowing she got any rest was naps she'd take on his shoulder in the truck.

Theo didn't seem affected by her paranoia, instead falling asleep almost immediately when they'd enter their room for the night. He never spoke a word about the traps. He only ever watched Vaida set up the contraption once on their first night on the road.

They were nearing the Raliah-Centrilir border, apparently, according to the curt response from Theo when Kellan asked an hour ago. They'd arrive in Rivenstorm sometime the day after tomorrow, most likely in the evening.

The road was empty and the expanse of the Empire stretched out on either side of them, covered in a freshly fallen layer of snow. The roads themselves were clear, but icicles and sparkling clumps of snow decorated the trees lining the roads. It was beautiful and serene. Kellan wondered how long it would last.

Another hour passed in silence. Vaida slept on his shoulder and Theo sat in his cold silence. Kellan simply watched cars and trucks pass as they entered Raliah.

A large truck pulled ahead of them and slowed down abruptly, making Theo swear. It was the first time Kellan heard him express any emotion.

"Everything okay?" Kellan said, gently adjusting Vaida on his shoulder so she didn't fall.

"Fine," Theo said bluntly. His eyebrows were knit together as he stared at the truck in front of them.

He looked out the rearview mirror, checking the lanes and attempting to get around the truck that was still laying on its breaks. Theo swore again as Kellan looked in the mirrors. Another truck had pulled alongside them.

Alarm bells rang in Kellan's head as he looked in the mirror on the passenger side and saw yet another truck closing in behind them. The formation screamed of danger, and he could feel the familiar adrenaline rush coursing through his veins as his body expected a fight.

He gently shook Vaida awake, and she blinked sleepily up at him.

"V, look out the window," he said in a low voice.

She did as he instructed, her eyes narrowing as she took in the trucks surrounding them. Without a word, she pulled out her bag and began tinkering with a device she'd created that looked like a metal canister with several buttons on the side. He didn't know what it did, but he wouldn't want to be around when it did its thing, knowing Vaida.

Theo continued driving, keeping a calm eye on the trucks surrounding them. "Time for you two to be useful." He never took his eyes from the road.

Kellan nodded and pulled the hilt of his sword from his belt. He'd brought along his demon-killer. It was risky to take it from the Legion, but he didn't want to be caught by demons without it.

He didn't activate it yet, instead eyeing the truck beside them. If an attack were to come, it would most likely be on their side.

His prediction came true moments later when a door on the side of the truck flew open and several masked individuals sprang from their truck onto the deck separating the cab from the trailer.

Kellan flung the back door of the cab open, surprising the three people that boarded. Now he activated his sword, the telltale humming resounding in his ears even over the wind whipping around him.

He sensed Vaida approaching, but she didn't move around him. He adjusted his grip on his sword, knowing one wrong move out here would spell death. Fighting on a moving vehicle wasn't something they'd trained for.

The masked assailants readied their weapons at the sight of his sword, their faces impossible to see behind the mirrored full-face masks. He could only see himself in their shiny exteriors.

He gripped his sword tightly, the muscles in his abdomen and legs preparing for the inevitable clash that was to come. He refused to make the first move, however, and instead calmly observed the intruders as they readied themselves to fight.

One of them couldn't stand the anticipation and leaped forward. Their sword cut a swift arc through the air. Kellan moved to meet it, bringing his sword above his head and catching theirs. The clang threw the assailant off balance and they stumbled backward. They swung their arms and nearly fell.

Another intruder on the back shouted to Kellan's opponent, "Keep them occupied," and began climbing the ladder to the truck's trailer. The second assailant stayed put, their blade pointed toward Kellan as if they were holding a gun.

"Vaida!" Kellan shouted, but he knew she'd already seen the person climbing the ladder.

He felt something pass by his head and watched the metal canister she'd been holding fly to the top of the truck. It landed with a metallic thunk, latching on with magnetic force.

The intruder on the top of the truck didn't stop, a mistake Kellan knew would cost them.

The canister exploded, but not in a fiery way. It was a neuro-explosive, one that was designed specifically to target and incapacitate creatures' nervous systems. It was perfect for moving targets as an effective method to detain and capture.

The assailant on the truck's trailer roof collapsed, his legs turned to jelly by the blast. It didn't reach far enough to do anything to the others. But it wouldn't last much longer.

Kellan flipped his sword in his hand again and pressed forward, forcing his first attacker backward. They had little room to maneuver, but Kellan could tell he had the upper hand after the first few swipes.

He quickly cut down the first of the intruders, their body falling to the metal connector with a thud. He turned on the second attacker to find them gone. Kellan whipped around to face Vaida, but she looked as confused as he felt.

A gunshot brought his attention back to the top of the trailer, where another assailant had appeared, standing over their incapacitated comrade's body. They must have approached from the back of the truck. Kellan frowned, then swore under his breath.

He turned back to Vaida and nodded once, then scaled the ladder to the top of the truck. The attacker leveled their gun at him.

These people were obviously well-trained criminals based on their precise movements and weaponry. He had to be careful—he might have the skills to stand off against someone with a melee weapon, but a gun was an entirely different challenge. And to make matters more difficult, the wind was fierce on the truck's roof, and the trailer swayed violently.

The person on the top of the trailer fired. Kellan rolled along the roof to avoid it, heart pounding viciously. It had been years since he'd been this afraid during a fight. The assailant pointed at him again, but the truck's jostling knocked him sideways and the shot went off into the distance. Kellan stayed upright, just barely.

He glanced toward the back of the truck, assessing. He was the only offensive fighter—Vaida's skills lay in creating an advantage before an attack ever happened.

She'd spent some time securing the doors of the truck by Theo's instructions, but Kellan didn't know how skilled the attackers were at navigating traps like Vaida's. For all he knew, they'd already broken into the back.

Although Theo knew their true purpose, they'd still performed the duties that a protection detail would. Kellan found himself thankful they'd taken those precautions as he slowly shifted himself toward the back of the trailer. The person with the gun had regained their footing and was turning back toward him to take aim once more.

Suddenly, Vaida's head appeared on the cab end of the trailer. She waved at him frantically, then made a grabbing motion. He understood her intent and dropped from the roof, holding on to the ladder on the backend of the truck.

The doors were still closed, thankfully, but two more masked individuals were standing on the back of the truck, a grapple securing them as they worked on disarming the traps Vaida had set.

The truck shifted violently as soon as Kellan grabbed on, sending the attacker on the roof flying off the other side to tumble to their inevitable death. The others were thrown off the side, but they stayed attached to the truck as it careened back and forth.

Finally the truck slowed, the armored truck behind them slowing and following suit. They came to a screeching halt on the side of the road, and once they'd stopped completely, Kellan threw himself off the ladder with a graceful leap.

The armored trucks that surrounded them stopped, seven more armored and masked people jumping from them and running to Kellan. He heard the slam of a door and assumed Vaida had finally come out to join him.

What he didn't expect was an assailant to stop before him and take off their mask.

It wasn't someone he recognized, but the insignia on their chest made the shock of recognition clang through him.

It was the Red Guard.

20

KELLAN

Somewhere in Centrilir | 6th of Dawn Moon

K ellan's eyes grew wide, and the grip he held on his sword grew tighter.

"Stand down," the man who'd taken off his mask commanded. He was tall. A bit of stubble peppered his sharp chin, and he carried himself with the air of a man used to being obeyed.

But Kellan wasn't Legion anymore. This man had no control over him.

He didn't do as he was told, instead shifting himself into a defensive stance, his sword humming before him.

The man's eyes narrowed, but he didn't move. "That's a very interesting weapon you have there. It's quite rare for a simple hired security guard to have."

Kellan's jaw clenched. Demon-killers weren't exclusive to the Empire's militaristic organizations, but they were exceptionally hard to get outside of them. Had he given away their entire operation before they'd even reached their first stop? If he backed down, he was sure he'd be killed.

"Stand down," the man repeated once more. "I will not say it again."

"Why? You attacked us," Kellan shot back, his voice low.

"We're searching every Morgenstern truck outbound from Spiral

City. I don't need to give you any more information than that."

Kellan's stomach twisted. They knew. Somehow they knew that he and Vaida were on a truck, that Selwyn had helped them.

The commander laughed at his expression. "It seems we were the lucky ones today. Take 'em, men."

As he laughed, the other men behind him chuckled, but they immediately silenced themselves when the man held up a hand. A commander of some sort, then. He began to sweat.

A door slammed behind them, and the unmistakable sound of a shotgun being cocked reached Kellan's ears.

"*Get down,*" was all he heard before a loud shot rang out from behind him.

The man standing next to the commander went down in a spray of red. One second he was standing, his handgun trained on Kellan, and the next he was dead, the hole piercing his chest seeping deep red.

The rest of the Red Guard members scrambled, their formation breaking so practiced that Kellan knew surprising them again would never work.

Another shot rang out from behind him, a little closer this time, and caught another man as he sprinted toward whoever was behind Kellan.

The commander was shouting instructions as he ran back toward the armored truck. Whatever was back there, he was sure it wouldn't be good.

Kellan leaped after him, keeping his sword out to the side to prevent anyone from getting too close as he ran. He could leave the rest of the men to the marksman behind him. The commander must have known he'd follow, as he shouted over his shoulder to Kellan as they ran.

"You'll never escape," he screamed as he grabbed the handle to the driver's side door. "The Red Guard will hunt you until the end of your days."

Kellan smiled bitterly as he slid to a halt next to the truck. "So be it."

The commander's eyes narrowed as he held a larger gun before him, a blade attached to its base. He'd holstered the handgun on his hip and must have run back for this one.

Kellan glanced down at the gun, then back up to the commander's face. He paused for a breath before leaping toward him and bringing the blade down toward his neck.

The part of him that was trained from childhood to obey his superiors was screaming as he fought—he should stand down, he should take his orders as they were given, what was he doing, why was he disobeying.

But there was a new voice, a new part of him that had emerged over the last three years and gotten stronger as he'd grown closer to freedom. A part of him that urged the bloodlust. A part of him that begged him to continue, to not let anyone stand in the way of him being free.

He jerked his sword right to meet the commander's blade as it swept toward his shoulder, the clash jolting him enough to drown out both of the voices warring inside of him. He couldn't afford to be distracted now, not when he was fighting against the Red Guard.

Another shot rang out from behind him, but he didn't turn to look.

The commander circled him, his blade lowered toward the ground in a position Kellan knew was supposed to look like an opening but wasn't. He wouldn't take the bait.

But as he circled the commander, he finally could see who was shooting from behind him. The hairs on the back of his neck prickled. Theo had exited the truck, a massive shotgun in his arms. It had four barrels and a crescent-moon-shaped blade on the bottom. He wore a bandolier across his chest, fully loaded with spare shells.

But the look of pure death that had crossed his face sent shivers up Kellan's spine. Theo looked apathetic as he pointed his gun at yet another soldier, shooting them down in a brilliant spray of crimson.

The commander took advantage of his temporary distraction and pressed forward, his blade cutting up from below to open him from navel to throat. Kellan barely countered in time, their blades clanging together so that he felt the reverberations through his whole body.

A high-pitched sound erupted around him, and suddenly his knees gave out as he collapsed to the ground. The commander went down with him, his gunblade clamoring to the ground.

Several more shots rang out as he lay on the ground, unable to move. Had Vaida thrown another of her neurobombs? He hoped so, and that it wasn't retaliation from the Red Guard soldiers.

Minutes later, a pair of booted feet appeared before his vision, hauling him up and over their shoulder and leaving the paralyzed commander on the ground.

It was Theo, carrying him back to the truck.

Kellan watched as they walked over several bodies, all in Red Guard uniforms, each with a nasty gunshot wound to the chest. Had Theo really killed them all?

Vaida waited for them back at the truck, her eyebrows scrunched together in a frown. Theo placed Kellan's limp body against the truck before grabbing his shotgun once more.

"What are you doing?" Vaida asked. Kellan couldn't speak.

"Taking care of the last one," he grunted as he walked back toward the commander.

Kellan's heart thudded, and he willed himself to say something, do something. They couldn't kill a Red Guard commander. That was…that was…

Vaida's hand came up to stroke his hair, as if she knew what he was thinking. "It must be done, Kellan. We're fugitives now, and they've seen our faces. We have been lucky until now that our escape has gone unnoticed, but if a Red Guard member made it back alive, we'd be screwed."

A shot resounded through the abnormally quiet air, and Kellan managed to squeeze his eyes shut. What they'd done was something they could never come back from. He tried not to think about the men behind the masks, tried not to consider who they might have been, who they must have served.

A chilling thought coursed through his veins—what if one of them was Beck?

But he dismissed it immediately. He was sure that Beck would have noticed him and done something. He was sure of it.

But a tightening in his ribs made him quiver. What if he'd been under one of those masks? What if he hadn't noticed? Panic made his throat tighten, but there was nothing he could do. He was paralyzed.

Vaida seemed to know he was struggling. She never stopped patting his hair, her long fingers running through the mess atop his head. She didn't seem to mind that he was sweaty or that his hair was tangled. She just continued stroking his head gently and staring at Theo, who'd returned.

"We need to get rid of the bodies," he said matter-of-factly.

"What about the trucks?" Vaida asked.

He shook his head. "Nothing we can do about those. We can stave them off longer by hiding the bodies, but they'll figure out what happened eventually."

Vaida nodded somberly, her hand still on his head. "Help me put him into the truck. I'll help with the bodies."

Theo didn't respond, he just grabbed Kellan under his arms and slung him back over his shoulder before setting him on the backseat of the cab.

Even when feeling returned to his body, Kellan still felt numb. There really was no turning back now.

🜄 🜄 🜄

They didn't stop all night to rest. Theo had stoically burned the bodies in the field. Kellan didn't feel much like talking.

But to his surprise, somewhere around midnight, Theo broke the stillness.

"Rosalie seemed confident taking a chance on you two," he

began, never taking his eyes from the road. "But this won't spell good things for the resistance."

Kellan watched Vaida's jaw clench, but he didn't know what to say. Theo wasn't wrong—the fact it was the Red Guard after them wouldn't benefit them. Although Rivenstorm and Raliah had different laws than the rest of the Empire, the Red Guard's jurisdiction didn't disappear there. They'd still be in danger. And they'd be putting the entire Phantom Flame in danger, too.

Vaida spoke before Kellan could. "We can't help who we are, and they promised us refuge." She narrowed her eyes at Theo in the rearview mirror. "Besides, it's not your place to decide whether the resistance accepts us."

Theo chuckled, a noise Kellan never would have expected to hear from him. It seemed out of place. "I wasn't saying I wouldn't take you."

"Then what were you implying?"

Theo shook his head. "Nothing. I'm just stating facts. It's up to you to do something about them."

Vaida huffed, crossing her arms as she sat back in the seat. Kellan still didn't know what to say. He didn't know what Theo was trying to imply, and Vaida wasn't in the mood to be questioned, judging by the furrow of her brow. He decided to change topics.

"So what are you bringing to the resistance, anyway? The manifest said you're headed to Natron, but I know that's not the case."

And for the first time, Theo grinned. It was a toothy smile full of malice and greed, but the way his eyes twinkled reminded Kellan of the way Vaida would look at puzzles. "Weapons. Lots of weapons."

Kellan swore to himself. They'd been led to believe the resistance was fighting without weapons, violence, or bloodshed. He knew it was impossible to resist on a grand scale peacefully; he knew there was no black and white in war. But this wasn't war.

It led him down another path of thought. Selwyn obviously knew these weapons were going there. How would she have been able to alter the manifest if she hadn't known? An entire missing truckload of weapons would raise questions, but not if Selwyn was in on it.

Kellan dared ask. "Why do they need weapons?"

Theo shrugged. "They're demon-killers. It's not like Rosalie is gonna sit back and watch as her city gets overrun with demons, not when they can do something about it."

Kellan released a little tension. Their approach to freedom hadn't seemed to change, but he understood their desire to protect their home.

Something in him squirmed, a thought he hadn't let himself have since they'd escaped. Kellan didn't have a home. Even though he hadn't chosen Spiral City, the city had ingrained itself within him, becoming a part of who he was. And now, he could never return.

The Mission hadn't been a home, not really. But he'd always felt like he belonged there, so long as Beck was with him. But now, Beck was gone too.

What did he have left?

He glanced toward Vaida, feeling a small bubble of adoration fill his chest. She was the closest thing he had to a home now. If destiny forced him to spend the rest of his life on the run, Vaida was the first person he'd want by his side. She'd become more important to him than even Beck had been, and that thought both comforted him and scared him to death.

She must have sensed his train of thought, reaching over to grasp his hand. "I'm here," she whispered.

He squeezed back, letting his head fall against the cold glass as the world whipped by outside.

21

CASSIAN

Rivenstorm | 10th of Dawn Moon

"Frost, are you sure about this?" Harpy's voice in his earpiece was hesitant. After all, she still didn't trust him completely when he planned strikes.

"I know basilisks freak you out, but I promise this has been effective against them before," he said calmly, a hand on the hilt tucked into his belt.

Cassian found it hard to believe he'd been with the resistance for four months. He'd learned much during his time with the organization, and finding out what Rosalie knew about Hym and Sol and the Battle of a Thousand Suns was only the tip of the iceberg.

He'd learned much about Rosalie as a person, too. She was tough but kind, and would often make choices with seemingly little thought. It was as if she was always looking at the world, the resistance, and him through a magnifying glass, the world blown into infinite detail for her and only her. What she saw through that lens, he could only imagine.

He understood that Rosalie had started taking leadership over the resistance when she was a teenager—her mother had been the previous head. Everyone clammed up when he'd asked the circumstances of her mother's death, though. Even Tigereye, who seemed to enjoy spilling secrets she wasn't supposed to, wouldn't tell him.

"Come on, Harpy, stop being such a baby. You've killed these things on your own before!" Tigereye's voice was bright in his ear.

"Shut it, or I'll smack you over the head myself," he growled, but Tigereye knew he wasn't serious about the hitting part. She simply loved to rile people up, although Harpy wasn't exactly the easiest to ruffle.

He was crouched behind a stack of wooden crates in an alley, his teammates scattered in their own hiding places around the park on the north side of Rivenstorm. A massive snakelike demon was gorging on some poor animal, its cries long silenced as they prepared their attack.

This was most of what the resistance had been doing since he'd joined. They'd captured their fair share of demons and interrogated them, learning all they could about their layers and what their missions here were.

Cassian could verify a lot of their information with Zal, who was surprisingly helpful in their cause. His position as a pact-holder had proven to be a significant advantage for the resistance.

Today, they were eliminating a pack of basilisks that had been causing trouble around the Lower Quarter since late last night. One had even stolen some poor farmer's cow, leaving the half-eaten corpse in the middle of a main road. This one before them was the last of the pack.

"On my signal, in three, two…"

On one, the group sprang forward, their swords drawn and pointed ahead. Cassian didn't draw his, instead conjuring up a fistful of cold to freeze the basilisk's head. While its gaze wouldn't completely incapacitate anyone, it was still a nasty shock to the system that left victims numb in their extremities. Freezing its head wouldn't stop it, but it prevented it from using its numbing gaze.

Tigereye struck first, her sword drawing a long gash down the demon's back. Harpy followed suit, her sword driving in deep just below the basilisk's neck. Tigereye swung again, stabbing her sword down into the demon's tail, preventing it from escaping. Cassian dealt the final blow with a ball of fire.

They watched as the basilisk's body burned, slowly fading into ash as it returned to its home in the Hells.

Harpy clicked her tongue. "Damn bastard will be back before the week is up."

"There's nothing we can do about that," Cassian replied, shaking an ember off his hand. "But we can keep fighting them off until we figure out a way to repair the Veil."

Tigereye flapped a hand at the both of them. "I like fighting them. It's nice to have a never-ending flow of practice dummies."

Cassian threw Tigereye an exasperated look, and Harpy rolled her eyes as they stopped at the edge of the park. But he was satisfied; their strike had gone well this evening. He was finally getting used to being around his teammates.

But he knew this wouldn't last for long. The book Rosalie had—the information she knew—was his priority. After their conversation, she hadn't approached him about the artifacts or finding them. She hadn't said a single word about a plan to him. If Zal didn't remind him of that day constantly, he may have brushed it off as a dream.

A new voice echoed in their earpieces. "Team Arctic, status?" Rosalie had impeccable timing.

"Basilisks are cleared, Alpha," Harpy reported as she sheathed her sword.

"Good work," she replied. "Frost, I need you to return to base. Tigereye and Harpy, you're off for the evening."

"Roger that," Tigereye said, a broad smile cutting across her face as she slapped Cassian on the back. "Good luck."

"See you soon, Alpha," Cassian replied, ignoring Tigereye as she strolled off with Harpy.

He didn't follow them, knowing they were most likely heading home rather than the resistance's base. Besides, he enjoyed walking through the streets of Rivenstorm at dusk. Something about the golden light on the colored buildings calmed him.

The last few months hadn't been what he'd expected at all. The Phantom Flame was a much more well-organized group than he'd ever realized. They ran their organization similar to how a military would, with groups of their members functioning like squadrons complete with codenames in case of a breach. He didn't know anyone's real names besides Rosalie.

Rivenstorm itself allowed their operations to be carried out like this, content to have the resistance act like their law enforcement. Even though there was a local branch of the Guard here, the resistance still proved more effective than an Empire military group could.

It was a nice change of pace, he'd decided, being part of an organization that supported him. He couldn't help but think of how he'd been treated with Ragnor every time he considered his position within the organization. Working for Ragnor had been like being an outcast or a nuisance, only fit for killing rather than protecting.

And that was the resistance's main goal—to protect the citizens of Rivenstorm and, by proxy, the citizens of the Empire. It was noble, and Cassian found himself more and more amenable to their cause with every passing day.

Cassian lost himself in the brightly colored buildings of Rivenstorm, hands in his pockets, taking in the sights of snow fallen on the vibrant buildings. The streets were cobblestone, uneven and treacherous if you weren't paying attention.

As he moved through the city, taking in the sights, the light faded from the sky. Streetlamps with curling iron bases flickered to life as he walked, their light seeming to follow him and guide him on his slow journey through the city.

The more he thought about the resistance's support, the more his thoughts wandered to Ragnor. His mother was surely dead by now. He'd wanted to go to Ebenfell to find her, but Zal had specifically forbidden it. Ze didn't want him to risk being seen by any of Ragnor's operatives in the city and being taken out before his mission had even started.

It made sense, he supposed, but it didn't ease the sting any more.

He breathed in the smell of Rivenstorm deeply to calm himself. A whiff of exhaust, a touch of fresh-baked bread, and the briny smell of the sea. His heart was still heavy, but it wasn't pounding furiously in his chest anymore.

He rounded a corner, finally coming to face the black and orange facade of the Autumn Rose. It was busy inside, but he ignored the hullabaloo and made a beeline for the back bar.

Rosalie wasn't waiting for him. If she wasn't here, there was only one other place she might be. His gut instinct tugged him there, and he followed.

He pressed the pressure plate to the secret stairway in the back of the room where Rosalie had shown him the journal. Muffled voices floated up the stairs, one lower and one that was definitely female but not Rosalie. He wondered who was meeting down there and debated interrupting them when he heard something that made his stomach flip.

"Alvemach isn't the only prince who has slipped through into this plane. I'm sure you must have noticed the rise in demonic activity lately?"

The voice was Rosalie's. But she was talking about something from his past that he'd never mentioned. How did she know about Alvemach? A thought floated to his mind—a dangerous thought that, if he let it, would consume his entire being.

His feet carried him down the stairs as he listened to the voices. They sounded familiar, teetering on the edge of his dreams like a feather on the breeze. A voice he'd only dreamed about for the last eight months reached him.

"And what plan is that? We're just supposed to skip happily off into the sunset, find something that is going to save the world, and do it just the two of us?"

His foot reached the bottom stair, and he opened his mouth before thinking. "You'd have help." He didn't know what he was saying, but it was out before he could stop it.

And sitting there, at a table in the center of the large meeting space, was the face that had kept him alive all this time.

Kellan.

22

KELLAN

Rivenstorm | 10th of Dawn Moon

The free city of Rivenstorm was nothing like Kellan expected. The buildings were all brightly colored, painted in shades of orange, yellow, and purple so vibrant they hurt his eyes after looking at nothing but snow-covered fields for so long. Their destination was in the city's southernmost district, a bar that was apparently the Phantom Flame's headquarters.

Theo parked the truck at a warehouse in the city's Lower Quarter. They double-checked the locks and enchantment spells Vaida had redone after the Red Guard attack before leaving the vehicle behind.

The city was bustling, even at sundown. It wasn't like Spiral City, though. The bustle was denser, like there were the same number of people stuffed into a much smaller space—which, he supposed, was accurate.

After taking the city's mag-lev system, they arrived at a bar named the Autumn Rose. Its exterior was simple compared to the surrounding buildings, save for its loudly painted orange shutters. He could hear how loud the bar was from the street, but Theo didn't hesitate before pushing the door open.

The bar was crowded, stuffed to the brim with patrons of all shapes and sizes. He'd never actually seen another dragonborn besides Sharr, and now there was an entire group of them huddled in the corner. Their hulking frames were hard to miss, especially the vibrant variety of their scales. One was bright red, another silver, and another mottled blue and green.

Behind the oak bar was what he could only describe as a living water droplet. She was translucent and blue, her four arms shimmered as she moved, and her hair ebbed and flowed like the waves on the shore just miles from here. She was one of Avalan's people in her pure elemental form.

Kellan stared for a long while before a sharp jab in the ribs had him shaking his head. Vaida stood next to him, her mouth turned down in a frown. "Don't forget why we're here, Kellan," she said sternly.

"I know. Let's go." He adopted her frown, following Theo as he deftly maneuvered through the packed crowd.

He led them behind the bar and through a curtain Kellan wasn't sure was meant for them to pass through, but Theo entered with such confidence Kellan couldn't help but follow.

No one stopped them as they lifted the curtain, and Kellan turned to face the woman behind the bar. She didn't give them a second glance. He sighed and pulled it back to reveal what looked like another dining room; this time, the majority of the patrons were human.

Several people glanced their way as they entered, their eyes passing easily over Kellan but lingering on Vaida. She had an otherworldly presence.

Theo approached a table of four women seated in the corner. They hardly paid attention as Theo approached, absorbed in a deck of cards. He leaned over to talk to a woman, her corn-silk hair in a braid over her shoulder. She nodded at whatever he murmured to her, then stood and faced them.

The woman approached, the wooden clasp at the end of her braid clacking as she walked. She wore a simple leather outfit with ties up the sleeves and a demon-killer sheathed at her side. She looked like a warrior.

But the thing that caught Kellan's attention were her eyes—or rather, her eye. It was a brilliant blue, with patches of white so startling it looked as if you were staring into a summer sky. But the other, on her right side, was covered by a patch. A massive scar ran from her temple to the corner of her mouth.

Theo stayed at the table, taking the seat vacated by the blonde woman. She smiled gently at Kellan before reaching a hand out to him in greeting.

"Theo tells me you're the guests of the hour. Call me Alpha." Her voice was low and husky, like she'd been smoking a pipe for years. It was comforting.

But weren't they supposed to meet someone named Rosalie?

"Kellan," he replied, taking her hand and shaking it firmly. She had the calluses of an experienced swordswoman; he knew the one at her hip wasn't just for show.

Vaida stepped forward, extending her hand. "Vaida. Pleased to meet you."

Alpha smiled even wider at her, shaking her hand as well. "Why don't we go somewhere quieter to discuss why you're here?" Her eyes narrowed just a touch, enough for Kellan to know not to ask about Rosalie just yet.

They nodded in unison, Vaida gesturing for Alpha to lead the way. She did, taking them toward the back of the room and pressing a wall to reveal a secret door. A staircase beyond led down into darkness.

She didn't speak as they descended. Instead, her steps were even, falling upon the stairs like the beat of a song. It was rhythmic and unsettling, but Kellan knew he was just nervous. They'd already done so much to get here, and now it was finally time.

He'd get to see if Selwyn was right or not. If everything he'd done to get here—if ruining his life—had been worth it. Would Cassian remember him? Would he want to? He'd willingly given him over to Leo; it wouldn't surprise him if Cassian harbored a grudge.

They'd set the basement up like a meeting room. It was large, filled with round wooden tables and hundreds of chairs, all facing a small raised platform at the front of the room.

"Please, have a seat," Alpha said simply before sitting at a table by the stairs.

Kellan observed the room with a careful eye as Vaida moved to join Alpha. He didn't follow, his feet rooted firmly to the ground.

Something was wrong—he could sense it. Like she'd led them into an ambush or an enemy was approaching. Whatever it was, it set his teeth on edge. The hairs on his arms prickled as Vaida and Alpha talked.

"We were told we'd be meeting Rosalie here," Vaida said, finally vocalizing that which had been bothering Kellan this whole time.

Alpha smiled. "You must understand something about how we operate here; we use codenames only. We don't share our true names, even in friendly company. It reduces the risk of our ranks being broken if any of us are ever compromised."

Vaida nodded. "Sure, that makes sense. But it doesn't answer my implied question. Where is Rosalie?"

Alpha's smile turned gleeful. "That would be me. Pleased to make your acquaintance, again."

Kellan's eyebrows raised. This woman was supposedly the leader of the resistance? She barely looked older than him, yet she was one of the Empire's most wanted. Of course, there was nothing they could do about her, but it didn't mean she wasn't any less of a thorn in their sides. Yet, she was so incredibly young.

"I know, astonishing," she said, apparently noting Kellan's surprise. "But I promise you, I am here to help."

Vaida flicked her eyes to Kellan, an unspoken question in them. He shrugged, and she turned back to face the woman before her.

"Look, I'm sorry, but we don't know if we can trust you just yet." Vaida's voice was even. Revealing their situation could be incredibly risky, even if she was truly the Phantom Flame's leader.

"Of course. Your hesitation is perfectly understandable." She paused, tapping her finger against her chin a few times before speaking once more. "Then let me ask you this—what does freedom mean to you?"

Vaida tilted her head slightly as she pursed her lips. "What kind of question is that?"

"One I always ask people who seek me out."

Vaida's expression softened into nothing at all, but Kellan could tell she was calculating her answer. After all, what harm could come out of answering a simple question like that?

"Freedom is no longer holding yourself to the ideals that society imparts on you," Vaida said simply, as if her answer was the only correct one. "Freedom is being true to yourself."

Rosalie smiled softly, her good eye twinkling as she regarded Vaida. "Indeed. Quite the succinct answer." She turned to face Kellan. "And you? What is freedom to you?"

Kellan froze. He had to answer this stupid question too?

It wasn't like he'd never considered it. After all, he'd spent his entire life in shackles of some sort. Freedom wasn't something so easily gained, and asking such a question in such a lighthearted way made Kellan's chest burn.

"Freedom is just that—being free. Everyone's answer will be different, so why bother asking?"

"Because the way you answer reveals much about your character," Rosalie responded calmly.

Kellan scoffed. "Then freedom isn't real. Freedom is an ideal that you can strive toward, but no one is ever truly free. So freedom means nothing to me."

Rosalie raised her eyebrows ever so slightly. "Such harsh words from someone so young. What made you so cynical?"

Kellan stayed silent, glaring at the woman with thinly veiled contempt. He'd answered her question, and until she started answering theirs, he wouldn't speak any more.

She chuckled at his expression, then said, "I'm sorry for prying; that was beyond my line of questioning, so I apologize for that. But your answers are interesting to me. Which is why I'd like to formally invite you to be members of the Phantom Flame."

Vaida nodded. "We accept."

Rosalie turned to face Kellan, a look of expectation in her eye. "And you?"

He gestured to Vaida. "She accepted for both of us."

"Indeed, but she isn't you. I'd like your acceptance as well."

He sighed, shrugging and resisting the urge to scratch his neck. "Oh fine, I accept."

Rosalie clapped her hands together once, her smile polite. "Wonderful."

Kellan's skin prickled; the feeling of wrongness hadn't gone away, but he still couldn't pinpoint what was making him so nervous. Maybe it was the fact they were in a basement or that there was only one exit. No matter what was causing it, he wished the conversation over quickly.

"If you let in anyone who answers your question, then why did you turn away Pontius Morgenstern four years ago?" Kellan asked.

Rosalie sighed. "Despite his wonderful accomplishments, Pontius still had some *proclivities* that we simply didn't know how to handle." She cleared her throat. "Look, Pontius was never a question of if, but when. It wasn't the right time when he came looking for us four years ago."

Kellan felt anger bubble in his stomach. "If you had, he might still be alive right now."

"Kellan…" Vaida said, warning in her voice.

Rosalie whipped her head to him, a spark dancing in her eye. "We do not have the luxury to dwell on what-ifs, Kellan. You would do well to remember that one person's actions are not the fault of another. I won't jeopardize the safety of the organization I've worked so hard to lead, even for someone like Pontius."

He stared at Rosalie's one good eye, her gaze unflinching. He finally blinked, turning back to face the staircase. "You're right— what's done is done."

"Indeed," Rosalie said, turning back to Vaida. "Listen, I hope you understand that we aren't here to vie for the rights of humans; we're here to protect all people. And because of that, I would like to ask for your help."

"Our help? Why?" Vaida asked.

"Selwyn told me about your encounter with The Shadow and Alvemach four years ago, about who you two are," Rosalie said.

"And you didn't think to tell us you already knew who we were when we came?" Kellan snarled. Rosalie was starting to piss him off.

"I wanted to judge you with no barriers first. Like I said, I will not risk the safety of my organization, especially not for two ex-legionnaires on the run."

The phrase dug a knife into his heart. She was right—they were a risk, and it made sense for her to be wary of them—but he still couldn't help the bitterness that built up in his lungs, making breathing steadily more difficult.

"We understand," Vaida interjected, shooting Kellan a look that said she knew how he was feeling and to *cool it* before she did it for him.

"Anyway," Rosalie began, brushing the tense air aside like it was a cobweb, "Alvemach isn't the only prince who has slipped through into this plane. I'm sure you must have noticed the rise in demonic activity lately?"

"We have," Kellan said, turning once more to stare at the stairs. "So what?"

Rosalie gave him an exasperated look. "*So* we have a way to stop it."

That got Kellan's attention. He turned back to face the leader of the resistance, his mouth slightly agape. "How?" The word was hardly more than a growl.

"I've had something in my possession for a long time that I have been waiting for the right moment to use. As ex-legionnaires and fugitives, you would be the perfect choice to carry out my plan."

Kellan gritted his teeth. "And what plan is that? We're just supposed to skip happily off into the sunset, find something that is going to save the world, and do it just the two of us?" He could feel himself getting angrier as the conversation went on. This was *not* what they'd come here to do.

"You'd have help," a voice echoed from the staircase. One he had only heard in his dreams for the last four years.

Kellan snapped his head back to the stairs so quickly he thought his neck might break.

Standing at the base of the steps was Cassian Evermore.

23

KELLAN

Rivenstorm | 10th of Dawn Moon

He'd dreamed of this moment for years—sometimes it was a tearful embrace in a garden under the stars, sometimes it was a random encounter in a club he'd never seen. Other times it was nothing more than an expanse of white, Cassian's hand reaching out toward his face.

Kellan awoke crying each time.

But in all the scenarios, Cassian looked just as he'd always known him—the green of his eyes bright, his silvery hair tucked back into his signature ponytail at the base of his neck, his smile easy.

The man standing before him was not what he'd imagined. His hair was shoulder-length and flowed freely in messy waves. He was dressed in a stealth suit just like the one he'd worn when they'd first met. And when Kellan met his eyes, he gasped.

One was still the vibrant green he remembered. But the other had turned completely black.

"What—" Kellan began, but Cassian held up a hand to stop him.

"Later," he said. His voice was the same except for a hint of roughness that hadn't been there before. He met Kellan's eyes and his expression softened. "I promise."

The wrongness he'd felt moments before burst, Cassian's arrival dissipating the anticipation he'd been fighting.

Rosalie looked unsurprised at Cassian's arrival—in fact, she smiled broadly at him. She spoke like they'd known each other for a long time. "Just in time. We have some new recruits I'd like you to meet."

Vaida cleared her throat awkwardly. "We're, ah, already acquainted."

Rosalie's eyebrows rose. Kellan got the impression she was rarely surprised—but this was something she obviously hadn't been expecting. Her eye narrowed.

"Care to elaborate?" she said, voice dangerous. Kellan wasn't sure who she was angry with; her gaze fell upon Cassian first but shifted between him and Vaida as well. He could barely think straight, but the ire in her eye made bright yellow fear travel up his spine in a shiver.

Cassian shifted, then swept past Kellan, not even sparing a glance as he passed. Kellan started—Cassian's scent had changed. Gone was the smell of coffee and lemon. In its place was the salt of the ocean and something deeper. Something sinister.

Rosalie watched him, her gaze intense and unyielding. "Cassian?"

"I was…involved with the situation in Spiral City four years ago," he said, proceeding to explain in deeper detail the story they all knew so well.

Rosalie's expression didn't change, the mild shock mixed with something deadly beneath the surface never moving as he spoke. But when he reached the end of the story, the part that ended with his being taken by Leo, her eye softened.

"Well, that certainly makes things easier," she finally said. "I dislike surprises, but, unfortunately for me, I have no choice. It's better you all know each other." She rubbed the bridge of her nose, closing her eye against the action. "We need to discuss what I've gathered you all here for, anyway."

Kellan watched their conversation in stunned silence, his gaze bouncing between Vaida, Rosalie, and Cassian. Breathing was a feat of strength, anxiety eating him alive from the inside and coating his lungs in iron. He couldn't take much more than shallow, superficial breaths.

"Cassian has already heard some of this," Rosalie began, leaning back in her chair, "but I need your help to gather certain items."

Vaida leaned in, resting her chin on a fist. Kellan watched her for a moment, focusing on her breaths and trying to match his own to them.

"And how are we supposed to find these things? What are these things?" Her voice was calm, but he heard the excitement behind her words.

Matching Vaida's breathing wasn't working. He was heavy, drowning, falling. Kellan couldn't move, could hardly draw breath into his chest. The black was creeping in.

He didn't even know if this was real anymore—Cassian was alive, and apparently had been this whole time. Why hadn't he contacted him?

Unless he held a grudge against Kellan for giving him over to Leo.

His heart raced, the sound of his blood pumping drowning out the discussion at the table. The only sound that was clear was Cassian's voice any time he spoke. It was like he was being mocked. He couldn't breathe.

He wound up on the floor, on his knees, gasping for air like someone had suffocated him. His hands were at his own throat, willing it to open more, to breathe, to continue this dream where Cassian really had returned. He didn't want to wake up.

It certainly felt real, though. He was getting lightheaded; the gasping coming from his own lips drowned out every sound, including that of his blood pulsing through his veins. Everything was on fire and numb all at once.

There were hands on his face. They were small and soft, hands that had touched his face like this before when he lost himself. He heard his name called gently by a voice that had kept him grounded for so long. But it didn't work this time.

"Wake up, wake up, wake up," he whispered to himself. He could feel the tears on his face. The blackness was creeping over everything now.

"Wake up," he sobbed, then darkness enveloped everything.

♦   ♦   ♦

The sound of a crackling fire woke him from the blackness.

He was warm. Someone had covered him with a plush comforter woven from thick cotton. The bed was soft and squishy, and he found himself uncomfortable after a week of sleeping in crappy roadside motels.

Kellan raised his head enough to see they had put him up in what looked like the bar's guest rooms. It wasn't big, about the same size as his room at the Guard had been, with space for the bed, a small desk, and a fireplace.

Before the fireplace sat a figure. His eyes were blurry enough from sleep that he couldn't see who they were, but their shape was most definitely not Vaida's. Where was she?

"Who are you?" he asked weakly.

He felt like a truck had run him over. Every muscle in his body was sore, straining with the effort of trying to sit up.

The figure stood from the fireplace and approached the bed. Cassian's face appeared above him. He grasped his shoulders gently and pushed him back down on the mountain of pillows at the top of the bed.

"You've had a long day, Kell. Rest." His voice was like a dagger to the heart. It was so good to hear again, but it hurt like hell.

He'd waited for so long to hear his voice again—to not just dream of it, but to hold on to the sound like it was something so precious he couldn't let go.

"Cass, I—" he began, his voice barely a whisper.

Cassian covered his lips with a finger. "Please, rest some more. We'll talk, I promise. Just not now."

The tears came of their own accord, spilling down his face, spreading dark stains on the comforter beneath his chin. They dripped into his hair, pooled into his ears, but they never stopped, rushing as if through broken floodgates.

Cassian stroked his hair, a movement so gentle it made his chest constrict with longing and pain. The touch of his hand was real.

"I'm so sorry," Kellan whispered into the now soaking comforter. He couldn't look Cassian in his mismatched eyes, afraid of seeing something there he couldn't return from. "I'm so sorry, Cass; I'm sorry for everything."

Cassian continued to stroke his hair while he took a seat at the edge of the bed. "What are you sorry for?"

"I left you, I gave you to him. You suffered because of me, because I was stupid—"

Cassian covered his mouth with his other hand, the first still stroking Kellan's head. "You are many things, Kellan. Impulsive, a terrible liar, obnoxious…but you aren't stupid. You did what was right, and it saved my life."

Kellan sat up and reached an aching hand up to stroke the skin just below Cassian's fully black eye. The tears on his cheeks were hot, but he shivered, cold permeating his entire body as the comforter fell away.

"What happened to you all this time? Where have you been?"

Cassian looked away as he suppressed whatever emotion was threatening to bubble up. It twisted Kellan's heart to see him hide his feelings.

"Can I—" Cassian began, the words getting stuck in his throat. "Can I hug you?"

Kellan stretched both hands out to Cassian, a silent plea and acceptance of his request.

He took the invitation, his body flush against Kellan's, the circle of his arms strong and unyielding. Cassian's hands were cold on his back. Kellan buried his face into the crook of his neck, not caring that he would inevitably get his shirt wet. It didn't matter, not when this was *real.*

"Never leave me again, do you hear me?" Kellan whispered through tears.

"Never again," Cassian agreed.

"If I asked you to stay forever, would you?"

"Without a second thought."

The sobs wracked his body, convulsing down his spine. Cassian stroked his back in languid circles, letting him release four years of suppressed emotion. He hadn't known how much he'd been holding back until it was coming out of him in waves. Until the dream he'd had for so long finally came true.

Kellan didn't know how long they stayed there, silently letting his heart spill itself dry.

"I…I thought you'd died," Kellan finally croaked out.

Cassian's slow circles hadn't stopped, and they still didn't as he responded. "I wouldn't willingly leave you, you know that?"

"Even you can't stop death, though."

Cassian's hands finally stopped. Kellan lifted his head then, gazing into the now mismatched eyes he loved so much. He saw sorrow within them.

"Right?" Kellan breathed.

"I think," Cassian said softly, "it's time to tell you what happened."

Kellan's mouth parted, the tears finally slowing at the prospect of finally knowing what had happened to Cassian all these years.

"Please," was all Kellan said.

Cassian stood from the bed, detangling himself from Kellan and retreating to the chair in front of the fire. He leaned both forearms upon his knees, his long locks forming a curtain around his face so Kellan could no longer see his eyes.

"After Leo took me, he brought me to…a place unlike anywhere I've ever been. It was cold, an endless ocean with islands of ice. I met someone there who healed me—but for a cost."

"No," Kellan whispered.

"Yes," Cassian replied. "I created a pact with a prince of Hell named Zalmelloth. My wounds healed when we sealed our pact, but my eye turned black. I even have veins like Leo's on my legs."

Kellan instinctively looked down at Cassian's legs, still fully clothed in his stealth suit. Of course he'd cover what he could.

"But you must have escaped, right?" Kellan said. His heart pounded loudly in his ears. He willed it to quiet, fearful he wouldn't be able to hear Cassian speak.

Cassian stayed silent for a long time before responding. Kellan waited, anticipation draped over his shoulders like a cape.

"No, I didn't."

Kellan's heart dropped into his stomach. "Then how are you here?"

"Zal sent me back."

"Do they…do they know where you are? Do they watch you? Can't you break the pact?"

Cassian shook his head. "Not without both parties willingly breaking the contract, no. But Kellan, it's not the worst thing to have happened. I'm stronger now, and Zal isn't what you'd expect. Ze's… decent."

It was too much. He could feel the panic from earlier rising once more, threatening to claw its way out his mouth and spill onto the bed in front of him. He placed a hand over his heart, pushing on his chest to slow its frantic rhythm. Nothing worked.

"Kellan"—Cassian's voice was soft—"I don't want you to blame yourself for what happened. I know you probably feel like this is your fault—"

"Because it is!" Kellan cut him off, his voice rising. "If I hadn't just handed you over to him…if I'd just taken you upstairs, you would have been free!"

Cassian turned to look at him, the space between his eyebrows deeply creased. "Both you and I know I never would have survived that long. It was an impossible choice, and I don't blame you for what you did. You saved my life."

"But I let you *go,* Cass. I promised I wouldn't and then I did. I was so stupid!"

Cassian jumped up from the chair suddenly, the action so violent the chair toppled over. "Stop," he said forcefully. "Stop blaming yourself. I will *never* resent you for that choice. You saved me, even if it wasn't how you intended. I'm stronger now because of it, even if I am bound to Zal. You did what was right, you hear me?"

Cassian finally turned back to him, and Kellan was shocked to see his own tears mirrored on Cassian's face. These weren't tears of sorrow, though. These were tears of shame, of anger, of regret. Kellan's hands balled into fists, the comforter crumpling between his fingers.

Cassian strode across the room, coming to stand at the foot of the bed. He gripped the footboard tightly; the wood creaked under his grip.

"All I care about now is that you're safe, okay? I never once stopped thinking about you when I was in Stygia. I knew I had to come back, to make sure you survived and that you were okay. I'm only here because of you, and I am eternally in your debt because of it."

Kellan's fists balled tighter into the comforter, clenching so tightly his hands ached. How could he *not* feel responsible for all that had happened? Some part of him knew Cassian was right, though—with the wounds he'd had, he never would have made it upstairs. Only magic could have healed him, and Kellan had none. It had been a futile choice, and he'd choose incorrectly no matter what.

The tears came again, this time out of frustration. He looked at his hands, letting the tears drip off his lashes each time he blinked.

"It's not fair," he finally said. "I have no one to blame for what happened to you. And all I want is to take out my frustration on someone for what's happened. But the only person I can find to blame is myself. After all, Leo only did what I asked of him."

Cassian sighed. "You're not to blame; I don't know how many times I need to tell you that. You made an impossible choice."

"I *know* that. I really do. But do I deserve your forgiveness? Do I deserve to be by your side at all after what I've done?"

"Only I can choose who to forgive, Kellan. And you have nothing to be sorry for, nothing I need to forgive you for."

Kellan lifted his gaze to meet Cassian's mismatched one. He thought he saw a flash of green within the inky blackness of Cassian's right eye.

"Are…" Kellan said, swallowing. "Are you still you?"

Cassian chuckled at that, bowing his head. "You should have asked that a while ago, but yes. I'm still me."

The relief was a weight being lifted from his shoulders. "Then come here." He held out his arms. "It's been four years, I hope you still want me."

Cassian didn't move. Kellan felt his heart drop into his stomach again.

"Kellan," he began, "I didn't deserve you four years ago. I definitely don't deserve you now."

Kellan stared at him, brow furrowing, his arms dropping back into his lap. "I get to determine who is deserving of me and who isn't, not you."

"You couldn't possibly want me now. You don't know what I've become."

"And what of all this talk of not needing forgiveness?" Kellan felt his voice growing louder with each word. "What of all this talk of not needing to forgive each other for things we didn't do wrong? What about me saving your life? Why do you think I did that, you idiot?"

"Kellan…"

"No! No, don't say my name like that! I saved you because you are the one thing in my life that isn't complete fucking shit, Cassian! You are the only thing I had to hold on to for a long time, and I refuse to let that go. You don't get to determine if you're good enough for me—I get to choose that. Because you are the only thing in my life I've *wanted* for myself, do you understand?"

He knew he was shouting now. He wondered if others in the

adjoining rooms could hear his heart spilling out of his mouth.

"I've never had a choice before. I've always been told what to do. But *never* with you. Choosing you was the best thing I've ever done, and it's led me here, to other choices I got to make. It's opened doors I never even knew existed, never thought I could open. I chose you back then, and I'm choosing you again now. So don't you *dare* tell me you aren't worth it—because that means everything I've done until now wasn't worth it. That every choice I've gotten to make for myself was worthless. I don't regret choosing you. I never will. Not for the rest of my life."

Cassian's stunned silence was deafening. Kellan could hear himself breathing heavily in the wake of his outburst. Neither of them moved, Kellan staring Cassian down and Cassian refusing to meet his eyes.

The door to the room opened, and Vaida walked inside. Her timing was impeccable.

"Everything all right? I heard shouting." Her voice was monotone, as if she knew exactly what he'd said.

"Fine," Kellan said through clenched teeth. "Cassian was just leaving."

Because even after all that, Kellan couldn't bear to look at the man he'd given everything up for even a moment longer. He knew what that silence had been. What it had meant.

Cassian still didn't meet his eyes as he turned toward Vaida and the door, slipping out of it silently into the hallway. Vaida watched him leave, then turned on Kellan.

"Want to talk about it?"

Kellan just shook his head, exhausted enough that words simply didn't form on his tongue any longer. He laid his head back on the pillows.

Vaida shrugged as she turned to leave, still holding the doorknob. He waited for the door to shut, but it never did. He turned to face it and saw Vaida still standing in the doorway, looking like she was holding something back.

"Spill it," he said, refusing to sit up.

"You need to give him time," she said quietly. "He looks like he's been through hell and back, and don't forget your journey hasn't exactly been easy either."

"You don't even know," Kellan scoffed. "But everything I've done has been for him. How could he just…*leave?*"

Vaida sighed before coming to sit at the edge of the bed.

"Because people are different, Kellan. And while you've been grieving for him for four years, he's been fighting for his life. He isn't ready to jump into something as quickly as you are."

Kellan turned on his side, resting a hand beneath his face. "So you heard everything then, huh? Insulation in this place is shit."

"Yeah, I think the whole place heard you, dumbass. And while your feelings are valid, so are his. You can't brush them aside just because you love him."

"I know that," Kellan snapped, then softened his tone. "I know. But I can't live with myself if everything I've done is for—"

"Don't you dare say it's for nothing, Kellan Manchester. You know damn well that isn't true, no matter if Cassian is ready for you or not." Vaida's tone was sharper than he expected, and he blinked.

"You are here to serve another purpose, you know," she continued. "Selwyn sent us here to help the resistance, to continue fighting, to make sure that the fates of Pontius and Mina and Tarin never happen to anyone ever again. You have a purpose in life, and you chose this path when you agreed to break your mark with me."

"For Cassian," Kellan whispered.

"What did you say?"

"For Cassian," he repeated, a little louder. "I came here for Cassian, to find out if what Selwyn said was true or not. To see if he was really alive."

Vaida just stared at him, her lips pursed. "So you're just going to ignore the fate of the world being threatened because your crush doesn't like you back?"

Kellan frowned at her. "That's not—"

"That's *exactly* what you're saying. That's exactly what's happening here. You're like a scorned puppy, retreating with your tail between your legs just because he isn't ready for what you are. That's so *stupid,* Kellan!"

He stayed silent as she berated him. He knew, deep down, that she was right. He was being immature, ridiculous, stubborn. But he also wasn't wrong; he had come here for Cassian. The whole saving-the-world bit had been dropped on him without so much as a warning.

"Sulk if you want, but you have this evening to get over this crappy attitude of yours, you hear me? We need to plan for tracking these artifacts down tomorrow, and I will not tolerate you being a lovesick teenager on this journey." She stood, brushing out the wrinkles in her pants as she did.

He listened to her retreating footsteps, heard as she opened the door, paused, scoffed at him once again, then closed the door.

He shut his swollen eyes, the exhaustion of the day's events finally hitting him. Sulk today, business tomorrow. He'd need as much sleep as he could get.

24

BECK

Rivenstorm | 10th of Dawn Moon

The sun had set long ago. Reaper stalked through the streets near Central Hill with a frown on his face. He'd heard about the ambush on the fugitive's transport from Rosalie, but that had been four days ago. He didn't know if they'd survived.

Brisea hadn't been exaggerating when she'd said they'd be watching the roads; he wondered if the escapees had lived through the Red Guard's ambush. If they had, when would they show?

The back of his neck crawled, a nasty reminder that they'd done what he could never hope to do. They'd broken free.

Whatever their fate was, he'd know soon. Brisea had sent an encrypted missive to meet tonight. Even though their usual meeting would be days from now, whatever she had to tell him was important enough to warrant a deviance from their schedule.

He hadn't gotten Rosalie's source regarding the fugitives for her, but it didn't seem like they'd needed it, anyway.

He landed in front of the Rosestone, still as pink as ever in the fading twilight. His night-colored wings faded back into his tattoos, the slits in his jacket sealing themselves as they disappeared.

Reaper knew Brisea probably beat him here, so he didn't bother looking around the waiting area when he stepped inside. He found her almost immediately, seated at their usual table in the darkest corner.

She was like a beacon tonight. Decorated head to toe in white, her dress looked like they'd made it of white scales. A glass of something fizzy and golden sat before her. He noticed with annoyance that a matching glass was waiting for him at the empty chair before her. Her eyes met his, and a sultry smirk spread her full lips wide. She waved at him, the low light of the bar reflecting off the metal she wore on the tips of her fingers.

It was like walking through molasses to reach her. The bar was busy, but the path to Brisea's table was clear. Still, he walked with a casual pace, uneager to reach her.

When he finally approached, her smirk grew into a full smile. "Beck. Have a seat."

He did as instructed without returning her short greeting.

She didn't seem to notice, or if she did, she didn't care. "So, how are you feeling? Everything going all right with the assignment?"

He made a face before he could think about it. "What is this, Brisea? You don't care. Stop pretending like we're friends and get to the point."

She picked up her drink, swirling it around in its crystal glass a few times. She was wearing white gloves that went all the way up beneath the sleeves of her dress. They were pristine.

"It feels so sterile, just getting right to the point with you every time. I was hoping to build some camaraderie."

Reaper snorted. "You hold my noose in your hands. There's no camaraderie here."

"Oh, come now," she began, pouting, "I haven't used it against you yet, have I?"

"I've done nothing to warrant it, so no. But that doesn't mean you won't."

Brisea sipped her drink, closing her eyes as she did. He waited, jaw clenched, for her to be finished. She would keep him waiting as long as she felt it took for her unspoken lesson to sink in.

She was the one in charge.

He wouldn't push, wouldn't ask questions, until she was ready. He didn't know what would send her over the edge and make her use an activation spell.

He was dying to know, though, what had happened to the fugitives. All he knew was the Guard had attacked them somewhere in Centrilir—they should arrive soon, if they'd made it out. Alpha hadn't told them anything else. After he'd recommended them to Frost's squad, he'd assumed that would be the last of his involvement with them.

But he found himself attached to these nameless people, his fascination twisting him in knots. He needed to know how they'd escaped. How they'd broken their marks.

An invisible leash attached him to Brisea. He felt it more keenly now than ever. In his mind's eye, he saw the rope that she held, the one that was attached to his neck. The one that, if he should step out of line even a little, she could pull and end his life as quickly as he'd ended so many others.

Brisea finally set down her glass, opening her eyes to look up at him through dark lashes. He couldn't read her at all. "Our convoy in Centrilir's eastern quarter was wiped out."

He didn't react, but inside he was screaming. "They took out the whole convoy?"

Brisea nodded. "We found the trucks, but no bodies. There's evidence that they were burned, but snow covered their tracks, so the investigation took longer than we'd hoped."

Just who *were* these fugitives? He supposed it made sense that they'd be able to stand their ground if they were Legion, but to have the sort of training it took to stand up against the Red Guard? Few people outside their own ranks could have pulled that off.

"They'll be arriving at the resistance headquarters today," Brisea continued. "I want you to find them."

"And after I do?"

Brisea didn't reply again, swirling her nearly empty drink in the glass. He couldn't guess what she'd ask of him. Would she ask him to kill them? Bring them to the Red Guard?

"I want you to keep me updated on them—who they are, what squad they're on, their codenames. If you can find out their real names, even better." She looked at him pointedly over her glass. "Although you've been slacking on that part of the assignment, 'Reaper.'"

He hadn't bothered. He'd been so focused on everything else— the disappearances and Rosalie's movements—that he hadn't bothered to figure out anyone's real names. He knew Cassian's, of course, and Rosalie's.

But he hadn't told Brisea about Cassian yet. He'd feigned ignorance when he'd joined, pretended he didn't know who Cassian was. And Brisea wasn't privy to the details of his eliminations—she was only his informant for things related to the resistance.

He knew that if he did tell her, it would get back to powerful people, that the request for Cassian's elimination would be renewed in earnest.

Beck wondered if he was unconsciously sabotaging this part of his mission. He couldn't do it on purpose, of course, but testing the limits of what his assignment would allow was something he must be doing and not realizing it. It gave him a small thrill of joy, this little act of his own resistance.

"Fine," he said, sighing. "I'll do my best."

She watched him, swirling the nearly empty glass in her hand. "All work talk aside, how are you?"

Reaper scrunched his nose. "This again? You don't care, Brisea."

She laughed. "No, I don't. But this meeting is drawing to a close and I find myself not wanting you to leave."

"And why would you want me to stick around?"

"Oh…reasons." She crossed her legs, the scales scrunching dangerously high on her white-clad thighs. "Ones I don't think I need to express in so many words."

He clenched his jaw. She'd never made it explicit before that she was interested in him; he'd always suspected, but never confirmed.

He felt trapped by it, though. That leash was growing tighter by the second, his option to decline far out of reach.

He didn't want this.

"I don't want that with you, Brisea."

She pouted, but shifted subtly, letting her dress climb higher up her legs. "It doesn't have to mean anything. It's just sex."

"Regardless, I don't want that with you."

"I know you find me attractive."

Reaper sighed, rubbing his forehead. "That doesn't matter, and you know it. I don't like you, and frankly, you don't like me."

"Like has nothing to do with it."

"Yes, it does."

She opened her mouth to continue to argue, but Reaper stood, hands braced on either side of the table. "I'm not talking about this any further. This relationship will remain strictly professional, nothing more. Good evening, Brisea."

He turned to leave, shouldering his jacket back up over his arms when he heard her speak again, voice colder than he'd ever heard it.

"I could make you, you know."

He froze, still facing the door. He didn't want to give her the chance to say anything more.

Before she could speak again, he lifted a hand to signal his farewell, not bothering to look back.

She didn't call out again.

🔥 🔥 🔥

No one was present in the back room when he returned to the Autumn Rose, his path to his room blissfully free of obstructions or people to talk to. His meetings with Brisea always left him drained.

As he climbed the stairs, he heard shouting. He couldn't determine whose voices they were, but they sounded somehow familiar.

"I don't regret choosing you. I never will. Not for the rest of my life," said the muffled voice from the room next to Rosalie's.

The door opened, and Cassian emerged. He didn't look at Beck, but his expression told enough of a story.

It was agony.

He noticed Reaper, putting a hand over his mouth before turning away. "Sorry if we interrupted you," he said, monotone.

Reaper shook his head. "I just got here." He paused, considering. "Everything all right?"

Cassian's eyes were unnerving, if he was being honest. The green bored into his soul, but the black was nothing short of terrifying. He stared at Reaper without blinking, dazed.

Reaper waited awkwardly for a response, but one never came. Cassian simply stared at Reaper—or rather, *through* him. It was like he wasn't even there.

"Frost?"

Apparently, that startled the other man enough to snap him out of his daze. "Sorry. I'm going to go back to my room now. I apologize again if we caused you trouble."

Without waiting for Reaper to respond, Cassian turned on his heel and walked away.

Reaper didn't investigate the room. He could still hear voices within, much softer this time. He didn't know who was in there, nor did he want to interrupt simply to satisfy his own curiosity.

He continued down the hallway before hearing a door shut behind him. He turned to see a woman standing before the door, her face pinched.

She was new—he'd never seen her before. Was this...

"Oh!" she exclaimed when she saw Beck. "Sorry if he interrupted your night. He's in a bit of a mood, but please don't hold it against him."

Beck just shook his head. "It's really all right."

The woman was beautiful. Not the sort of traditional beauty that Brisea had, but something more ethereal. It was like she glowed from within. Her dark skin and light eyes were a rare combination, one that he was sure made her memorable.

"I'm Vaida. We just got here today."

He had to resist the urge to let his jaw drop. She must be one of their fugitives, a person who'd broken their mark and escaped a life of servitude. He so badly wanted to beg her to help him, to break him free. To release him.

"Reaper," he said, approaching her, shoving his impulsive thoughts aside. They shook hands briskly, and he noted her calluses. Not from swordplay, he decided, but they weren't the hands of someone who'd avoided battle.

She stared at his face for a moment, her brows slightly furrowed. "Reaper? That's a strange name."

"Codename. Standard protocol, and all."

She laughed lightly. "Oh, sorry, I didn't mean for that to come off rude, it's just—"

Rosalie's door opened, cutting her off. The woman emerged, dressed in her regular clothing, even this late at night. She looked between them, her face unreadable.

"Reaper, I see you've met our newest recruit." She shut her door behind her. "And while I encourage this sort of sociability, it's late. You both should get to bed." Her eyes flicked to the next room. "We've had enough excitement for one evening."

Vaida nodded. "I was just thinking the same. It was nice to meet you, Reaper. Good night."

He nodded to her in return. She retreated to the room on the opposite side of the one she'd just left, closing the door with a soft click behind her.

Rosalie turned back to Reaper, a twinkle in her eye. "Quite the interesting woman, isn't she?"

Reaper only nodded, unsure what Rosalie wanted him to say. When he didn't reply further, she sighed, gave him a small wave, and turned back to her room. Her door shut without a sound.

He retreated to his own room, something tickling the back of his mind. Something about Vaida had seemed almost...familiar. Whose voice had been shouting?

The questions persisted, nagging at him incessantly until he could no longer keep his eyes open and sleep overcame him at last.

25

CASSIAN

Rivenstorm | 11th of Dawn Moon

Rosalie called him to breakfast early that morning. Her expression as he sat was calm, but he'd come to know her well over the last four months. She was worried.

He could tell by the way she slouched ever so slightly, the way she pulled the right side of her mouth down, the way she arched her brows.

He wondered if she'd heard his argument with Kellan last night.

"I trust you, Cassian," she said. "So that's why I trusted you last night when those two came here. Why I didn't pry when they said they knew you."

She'd stopped, but he didn't respond. She wasn't finished.

Rosalie sighed, closing her eyes and rubbing her forehead. "But I need to know. What the hells happened between you? How do you know two ex-legionnaires?"

He'd known this question was coming and was prepared for it. He knew she'd been curious last night, but she never asked about his background in front of others, something he was deeply grateful for.

"I've given you some…vague details about my past, but I suppose I can't keep it from you forever," he finally said. His head pounded. "Before Leo took me to the Hells and I entered my pact, I was in debt to a man named Ragnor."

Rosalie jerked at the name, her eyes widening. She knew of him, then.

"He tasked me with a mission to track down, expose, and then kill Pontius Morgenstern. You know him."

Rosalie nodded, her jaw clenched as she waited for him to continue.

"I went to Spiral City, where I met Kellan. We ended up forming a friendship—"

"Sounds like you formed a lot more than that to me, Cassian. Don't leave out details." Rosalie's voice was stern as she interrupted him.

He sighed. "Fine. We had a romantic relationship. And during my time in Spiral City, we helped each other. That was the story you heard about Alvemach. During our final battle with him, I was gravely wounded. To save me, Leo—The Shadow—took me to the Hells. I formed a pact with Zalmelloth to save my life. I haven't seen Kellan since."

Rosalie was silent, her brows knitted together as she considered his story. He'd left a lot of details out, like why he was in Ragnor's employ to begin with and what Pontius' fate had actually been.

Officially, Pontius was a missing person and had been for years. Both the Legion and the Guard were "looking" for him but had long since given up any serious attempts at finding him. Of course, he knew the truth, as did Kellan, Vaida, and Selwyn.

She breathed out through her nose as she tented her hands before her, elbows resting on the table. "Do you trust him?"

He nodded. "Absolutely."

"And what about the woman?"

Cassian tilted his head. "I only met her once in Spiral City, but she was a pivotal part of the fight against Alvemach."

"I see." Rosalie was staring behind him, but not at anything specific. Her eye had gone hazy as she stared into the distance of the barroom.

Cassian watched her, waiting for her to say something else. He knew she was considering their next move and how best to approach sending them on their mission, but something was bothering her. He just didn't know what.

Her eye snapped back to him as she came to some sort of internal conclusion. "I'm proceeding with my plan, then. But I need you to promise me your personal feelings won't impede this. Your mission is of critical importance, and we can't afford any distractions on your part."

He knew this already, of course. After Kellan had collapsed and Vaida had taken him upstairs, Rosalie had explained her plan for retrieving the artifacts.

She couldn't send Cassian alone, but it was hard for her to spare many of her regular members. Cassian had offered anyway, but she'd turned him down immediately. It was too dangerous, she said. When Selwyn had warned of the two fugitives, Rosalie had jumped at the opportunity for more hands, especially ones that would benefit from not staying in one place too long.

Of course, she'd never expected that Cassian would know their two newest recruits. And now, her carefully planned mission had been taken off course by a situation she never could have anticipated. Cassian felt a little bad for her.

She'd made him promise he would stay neutral. He'd understood the gravity of the mission and agreed. He had too much at stake to risk disobeying her orders, anyway.

And it wasn't just Rosalie he'd have to answer to if he messed this up.

Telling Kellan last night that he couldn't possibly pick up where they'd left off had been a choice to honor Rosalie's request as well as to ensure Kellan and Vaida's safety. Because, inevitably, when this mission was over, allowing Kellan to still harbor those feelings for him would only break his heart more.

But, gods, it had hurt to see that utter defeat pass over his face when Cassian rejected him. He'd wanted to reach out once more and cradle Kellan to his chest, to tell him that this was for his own good, that he was only trying to save him from a worse heartbreak later.

But he hadn't. He'd left when Kellan had glared at him, no trace of warmth in those golden brown eyes he'd dreamed about.

Rosalie must have sensed his inner turmoil as she laid a hand on the table before him, palm down. "You're a good man, Cassian, and you've proven as much over these last few months." She balled her hand into a fist. "And I know what you did must have been tough."

"You heard the whole thing, then?"

She nodded, no trace of shame in her expression. "The walls are thin. It was difficult not to hear."

Cassian stared at her fist, the ambient noise of the barroom growing louder as he bit his lip.

Rosalie leaned back in her chair, removing her hand from the table. "I've called them to have another meeting with us to discuss the plan once more in an hour. Take that time to gather yourself." She stood, but before moving away, she looked over her shoulder at him. "Look, Cassian, I can't imagine how you're feeling. But I want you to know that I'm grateful for your help. And that you did what was right."

With that, she swept out of the backroom and disappeared behind the curtain, leaving Cassian alone with his thoughts.

🜄   🜄   🜄

An hour later, they met again in the basement room. Rosalie sat at the table in the middle, Vaida on her left. Cassian took a seat across from them.

And Kellan stood in the corner, arms crossed, observing them with a look midway between disgust and contempt. Cassian's heart ached.

"Thank you for coming," Rosalie began. She turned toward Kellan. "I trust you are feeling better?"

He nodded curtly by way of response. Vaida's face crumpled into a grimace.

"Ignore him," she said to Rosalie before casting a withering look back at Kellan. His expression softened somewhat, but he didn't stop crossing his arms or approach the table.

Rosalie smiled at the exchange. "I wanted to discuss my plan for you in more detail."

She set a journal down on the table; he recognized it from a few weeks ago when she'd told him about Sol, Hym, and the role the humans played in hiding Sol's artifacts. She hadn't shown him more than the first page that day, and ever since she'd waited to give him any further information about the mission.

It might have been from recognition, it may have been something else entirely, but the moment the journal *thunked* upon the table, something in Cassian stirred. A yearning, a longing for something he'd once had.

Rosalie flipped to the middle of the book. This page had been visited often enough that the journal practically opened itself to it, lying flat on the table as she pushed it closer so they could read. Upon the yellowed pages, Cassian could read:

The Sword lies deep in the ancient wood,
protected by those whose souls are good.
Prove thy worth and be awarded its light,
but fall before him with a heart of blight.

The Staff is hidden where our ancestors began,
guarded deep below by no man.
The winter's chill will leave you cold,
but heed its tale and its power behold.

The Sphere is in our blessed palace,
treasured by the ruins of malice.
Hidden in sight you may pass it by,
but its power will call, will sing, will cry.

The familiar feeling overcame him with a stronger pull, the feeling of knowledge already known but long lost. It felt almost like an itch in his brain, urging him to just *remember*.

He shook his head, trying to rid himself of the sensation and instead forcing a shiver down his spine. When he turned to look at the others, Vaida's eyebrows were creased as she observed the words closely.

Rosalie spoke while they considered the riddle before them. "My ancestors created this to lead their descendants to the hiding places of the artifacts. I don't know the exact locations…"

"But we can figure that part out easily," Vaida interrupted. "The challenging part will be understanding what the rest of the verse is trying to tell us. I assume these are warnings for how they protected the artifacts?"

Rosalie nodded. "They were entrusted to officers of the old Albigian royalty, advisors and the like. I don't know what sort of protections might wait for you, though."

Vaida considered the passages again, her eyebrows furrowing more and more with each passing second. Cassian wondered if she had the same question he did.

"Rosalie, why didn't your ancestors just destroy the artifacts when they first found them? Why go through all the trouble of hiding them?" he asked.

The itch was back and stronger than before. It was a warning, an alarm bell in his head begging him to destroy them, begging him to do something. Anything. Cassian suppressed another shudder as Rosalie sighed.

"Honestly, Cassian, I don't know. That wasn't part of the story my mother ever told me. She said they hid them to protect the world, but I often wondered the same thing myself." She shifted in her chair. "But I don't want to destroy them, not this time. I think we could use them."

Using them would be impossible. Zal's voice was colored with humor, like ze was holding back a laugh.

What's that supposed to mean? Cassian asked.

Zal really did laugh this time. *They can't. This is the power of a god they're talking about using. It would be ludicrous to try.* Ze let out another small chuckle. *And perish the thought of destroying them. They can't hope to do that either.*

They could neither use nor destroy the artifacts? Then how were they supposed to—

I told you to bring them back to me. Zal's voice was stern.

And what am I supposed to tell them?

Whatever you want.

Gods, ze was so damn frustrating. Ze'd give him a hint occasionally, but it would often be vague, like this conversation had been. It had been like this when ze'd taught him how to harness his magic as well. Zir directions had been half-baked, like he needed to solve a riddle with each instruction.

He refocused his eyes and noticed Rosalie was staring at him, an eyebrow cocked. "What did ze say?"

"Nothing of use," he replied. Rosalie noticed whenever Zal would communicate with him telepathically.

Vaida glanced between the two of them, confusion written on her face. But she didn't say a word, choosing to move on in favor of asking more questions.

She pointed to the first verse. "This one is the most obvious, in my opinion. They're referencing the Bergamot Forest. It was ancient even back then."

"I agree," Rosalie said, nodding.

Vaida continued. "Verse two has me a little stumped, but I'm sure I can come up with something after a bit of thinking. Verse three is misleading, but I think it might reference Ebenfell. Wasn't that where the old Albigian royalty lived?"

Rosalie nodded. "That's right; the castle is still there. I'm shocked no one has found this artifact yet if that's indeed where it is."

"Strange, but not entirely impossible," Vaida said. "If they hid them away as thoroughly as the story suggests, it's likely in a place no one could access."

Cassian let them discuss—it seemed his input wouldn't be necessary in this conversation, anyway. Instead, he let his attention drift to where Kellan still stood against the wall. His posture hadn't changed, but Cassian could tell he was listening intently.

His fingers itched to work Kellan's hands out from where he'd tucked them into the crooks of his arms. But he figured any chance he had of touching Kellan had gone up in flames last night.

He spun the ring on his finger as he stared absentmindedly. Rosalie and Vaida's voices echoed in his ears, their words hollow and meaningless. The itch was still there, tugging on him as if it wanted him to go now and find the artifacts.

Kellan must have noticed his gaze as his face shifted from one of vague interest to vehement disgust. The look twisted his heart, squeezing it painfully until he forced himself to look away.

I'm so sorry, he thought.

For what? Zal replied.

Not you, he retorted coldly.

"Well, I think we have a plan of action, then," Vaida said, turning to face both Cassian and Kellan. "We'll start in Alderburn, since I suspect it will be our farthest destination. We'll be spending quite a while on the road, so we need to pack some provisions first and prepare ourselves properly."

"I also need to introduce you to the final member of your party," Rosalie interjected. "I didn't get the chance to tell you last night, but I would like to send one more person along with you."

Vaida cocked her head at Rosalie, but didn't argue. "That's fine. Shall we get ready, then?"

Kellan pushed himself off the wall and strode toward Vaida with purpose. "Let's go."

"Kellan," Cassian said, his name painful on his tongue. "It would probably be best if I go with you or Vaida to make preparations separately. Since you are fugitives, it's safer to split you two up as often as we can."

The look Kellan gave him was full of malice, a veritable fire burning behind his eyes. But he simply nodded his head in acknowledgement as he turned toward the stairs. "Vaida, you go with him. I'll stay here and meet with our fourth party member."

Vaida's lips tightened. "Fine. Cassian, let's go."

He nodded and stood, turning to the stairs. But Kellan was already gone.

26

KELLAN

Rivenstorm | 12th of Dawn Moon

He liked Liv. She was blunt, unapologetic, and had a penchant for weapons he hadn't seen since he was at the Mission. Only Beck rivaled her obsession with knives. Or at least, he used to. He didn't know if Beck was even alive anymore.

But Liv was great. She spoke animatedly, using her hands to illustrate her point. She'd asked Kellan about life in the Legion, what it was like to fly, and how he'd evaded capture.

Her codename was Tigereye, but the moment she'd heard what their mission was, she'd told him her real name. She said she refused to be the only one with a codename.

When he mentioned their travels with Theo, she chuckled at his assessment of the efficient yet cold driver. Although Theo was tangentially part of the resistance, it was rare to see him at headquarters. He was their main carrier, traveling more often than not to bring provisions and items other truckers refused to carry.

The weapons he brought were dangerous to transport, and no one else had been willing to do the job. Theo, however, would do just about anything for the right amount. Liv liked him.

He didn't ask what the weapons were. He'd seen enough to know they were more demon-killers, just like the one he wore on his hip.

THE PHANTOM FLAME

When Vaida and Cassian returned from their provision trip, Cassian had avoided his eyes and mumbled something about needing to speak with Harpy, whoever that was. He'd turned on his heel and walked away, not even sparing a second glance at Kellan.

Kellan should have expected it, honestly. He'd been furious for the last two days, sulking and scowling at Cassian every chance he'd gotten. So it really shouldn't have been a shock that Cassian was now avoiding him.

But it still stung.

Vaida pinched his cheek, the pain jarring him back to the moment. They were sitting down for breakfast in the back barroom. Liv had declined his invitation to join, and he hadn't bothered tracking Cassian down, which left just him and Vaida.

Their breakfast was quiet. After she'd scolded him two nights ago, she'd also been icy toward him. He knew she wasn't actually mad. Her frustration was obvious, and he could understand it.

He *knew* he was being an ass, he really did. But the anger that had taken over that night hadn't faded, and that meant something to him. Now he was stuck doing a fetch quest for an organization he didn't know, and the anger in his gut only grew.

She'd stuck with him for so long, yanking him back out of his depression and anger, constantly reminding him he wasn't alone in the world. She'd done it for so long now he didn't know if he'd be able to keep himself afloat without her. She was his lifeline, his raft out at sea.

"Kellan…" Vaida's voice was soft. Maybe she'd finally forgiven him for being stubborn.

He looked up at her, mouth full.

She sighed. "We're ready to go anytime. I've already asked Liv and Cassian, and they said they could move out today. Are you ready?"

He nodded as he swallowed. "Sure."

She looked like she wanted to say something else but stayed silent. He knew she was thinking—her face became eerily calm, her eyes unfocused. What she was thinking about was anyone's guess.

"We've come a long way in just a week," she finally said, her attention drawn back to his face. "But I don't want you losing focus after…everything."

"Smooth, V," he replied.

She huffed, but continued. "I'm *trying* to be considerate of your feelings here, Kellan, but if you want me to be blunt, I will be."

"Try me."

"Fine. I won't tolerate your lovesick puppy bullshit on this mission, you hear me? This is an important task they've asked us to handle, something that could actually change the way the world works. We could fix something."

"I'm not a lovesick—"

"Don't even get me started," Vaida interrupted him coldly. "I get it. You're frustrated. But if your shitty attitude interferes with this even a *little,* I will strangle you myself. Got it?"

"Got it," he mumbled dejectedly.

"Good." Her tone softened again. "Look, I don't want to yell at you, but if you need a swift kick in the ass a few times to get you back on track, that's what I'm here to do."

He scolded himself internally. Vaida was right; he'd been acting like a spoiled child, angry at the fact things didn't go his way. He was supposed to be better now—wiser, smarter, stronger—but he felt none of those things.

She stood, her plate empty, and turned to bring it to the conveyor belt in the front barroom. Before she left, Vaida turned to him once again.

"Pack up your stuff as soon as you can. We're leaving around midday."

He nodded, still staring down at his half-eaten meal. What was he supposed to do now?

Kellan returned to his room after not finishing the rest of his breakfast, his appetite gone after Vaida's lecture. There wasn't much for him to pack, but he double-checked all he had, ensuring he wasn't leaving anything behind.

A soft knock sounded on his door shortly before he was ready to head down to the barroom again. He'd stuffed his pack to the brim, his weapons and gear secured. He was ready to go.

"Come in," he said, buckling the last flap on his pack and turning toward the door.

He expected to see Vaida. What he got was Cassian.

"Vaida sent me to check on you," he said quietly, his eyes trained just beyond Kellan's face. "Are you ready to go?"

His stomach did an annoying somersault at Cassian's appearance, the fire in his heart still burning even after being doused so thoroughly just a few days ago. His lingering attraction to the man standing in his doorway annoyed him.

Kellan frowned. "Tell her if she's so concerned, she can come check on me herself."

Cassian furrowed his eyebrows, gripping the door handle tighter as Kellan responded. "I'll let her know you're coming, then." He closed the door with a soft click.

Damn him. Damn Cassian and his ability to see right through him when he didn't want him to. Why was he so good at ignoring him when he was angry?

It wouldn't be so easy this time, he vowed. He wouldn't let Cassian just waltz his way into his heart, only to rip it out again. He'd made it clear there was no future for them. He'd walked away when Kellan had needed him.

But it had been Kellan's fault to begin with. If only he hadn't let him go. If he'd held on, this wouldn't be happening. They could have been happy.

There was no use worrying about it now. Their status was clear—Cassian no longer had room in his heart for Kellan. And Kellan would respect that, even though it hurt more than any cut, bruise, or wound ever had.

He slung his bag over his shoulder, doing one last sweep of the room before following Cassian out the door.

The other party members awaited him downstairs, gathered around a table in the barroom and enjoying a drink. He stood at the top of the stairs, observing the room before heading down to join them.

Just as he made to head down the stairs, his eyes landed on Rosalie, engaged in conversation with someone. He could only see the man's back, but the set of his shoulders was as familiar to him as his own reflection.

But what the *hells* was Beck doing here, in Rivenstorm, in the headquarters of the resistance?

He opened his mouth to say something, but the words caught in his throat. All he could do was stare, goosebumps traveling up and down his arms and legs.

Kellan hadn't spoken to Beck in a year and hadn't seen his face in even longer. He had to be seeing things; there was no way Beck would or even *could* be here. His mark would prevent him from leaving the boundaries of Kettleguard. What would be the point for him to be here, even if he could escape?

His heart sped up uncomfortably. If Beck had escaped, the natural place to go would be here. Rivenstorm was the "Free City of the Empire," after all.

He stumbled down the stairs, his eyes never leaving the man's back. His legs were wobbly, and he idly wondered if this was what it was like to be drunk. He could barely draw breath as he clumsily stopped at the bottom of the stairs, hands shaking on the railing.

Rosalie called out to him over the man's shoulder. "Kellan, you look pale. Are you all right?"

The man before her did not turn around, but Kellan watched as he tensed at his name.

Kellan felt frozen, like his feet had sunk into the floor and his entire body had turned to ice. The world slowed down as the man before Rosalie turned his head slightly, exposing his profile.

There was no doubt—it was Beck.

The floor seemed to drop out from beneath his feet as he felt all the breath leave his body. He crumpled to the floor, the weakness in his knees unable to support his weight any longer.

He heard chairs scraping as people sprang up to catch him. Vaida made it to him first, her hands coming to cradle his head and cover his ears.

"Kellan, I'm here. Lean on me. Come on, I'm here," she whispered in his ear.

He stared just beyond her as Beck swept out of the room with a quick word to Rosalie. She nodded to him, then made her way over to Kellan, her eyebrows furrowed.

"Kellan," she said, crouching down next to him, "what happened?"

His mind was screaming—it was Beck, Beck was here, Beck was alive and well and here and...

And he'd left without a second glance at him.

Vaida's hands were cool on his cheeks, and he slowly came back to the room, a cluster of concerned faces before him.

Vaida, with her forehead scrunched up, eyebrows pinched together and lips pursed as she spoke softly to him. Rosalie, her eyes wide. She spoke to someone behind her, asking them to get her a glass of water and something to eat.

And Cassian, his green eye brilliant as he stared at Kellan with concern, biting his lip. Damn him, damn him to the Hells.

"I'm okay, V," he finally croaked out, his throat dry.

Rosalie handed him the glass of water she'd asked for, and Vaida helped him to stand. Now that Beck was gone, his legs felt fine again, but his stomach felt empty yet heavy, like a stone had formed at its pit.

"What happened?" Vaida asked as they sat at the table. Liv hadn't moved, but she stared at him, no trace of concern or worry on her face. Why would she be concerned, anyway?

Kellan didn't answer her right away. What should he say? He'd told both Cassian and Vaida about Beck at some point, but neither had actually ever met him. He didn't know what Beck was doing here, either. He didn't know if he'd escaped and was taking refuge here or if he was still under the Red Guard's thumb. He didn't know if any of these people knew Beck's true identity.

Exposing him could mean killing him; he wouldn't do that to his best friend. But he didn't know what to say, so he made up an excuse.

"I'm sorry for being so dramatic," he started, letting the flush creep up to his ears. "I'm okay. I just had, uh, well…I didn't eat much for breakfast."

Vaida patted his hand and pushed a plate of food at him. It was some sort of meaty stew, with large root vegetables and a thick brown soup. The smell was inviting, so he pulled it toward himself and scooped up a spoonful.

"Eat. We'll leave on schedule, then," Vaida said, shooting a glance at the other three that warned them not to ask.

Vaida knew when he didn't want to talk about something. She would never push him if he wasn't ready, and she knew well enough when to leave him be. She'd figured out with hardly a word that now was one of those times. The pit of his stomach warmed, possibly from the soup, but more likely because of her.

Rosalie nodded and left the table, sweeping out through the curtain to the main dining room. Liv watched her go, then sighed.

"Is this kind of meltdown going to be a problem?" she asked, no hint of sympathy in her voice.

"No," Kellan responded immediately. "I'm fine and perfectly capable."

"I'll hold you to that." Liv winked at him, then stood. "I'm going to check the truck one more time. Cassian, come with me. I'll see you two out back in twenty."

Cassian had been hovering the whole time. He looked unsure what to do, but Kellan refused to meet his eyes. He looked like he wanted to say something, but his shoulders sagged as he turned to follow Liv without saying a word to Kellan.

It was better this way, Kellan told himself. There were no distractions now. It was better. But for some reason, he couldn't quite convince himself that was true.

27

BECK

Rivenstorm | 12th of Dawn Moon

W hat had he done?
The question circled around in his mind for hours after he'd seen him at the base of the stairs. The one person in the world who'd kept him grounded. The only person who he couldn't bring himself to betray. His best friend and his brother.

Kellan Manchester.

Why was he here? *How* was he here? And why in the world did he know Cassian?

He realized now what had been bothering him about the voice he'd heard when he'd come back that night, why it had seemed familiar. It was Kellan's voice screaming at Cassian that he'd chosen him and would do so again.

Beck found himself desperate to run to his best friend's side. They'd spoken for the last time a little less than a year ago. Kellan had tried to contact him since, but he'd never responded. He couldn't.

But now he wondered if he could ever repair what he'd intentionally broken.

The question drifted again to his mind—what had he done? He'd heard enough. Cassian had been someone special to Kellan, enough that Kellan had given up everything for him. And now Kellan had seen Beck, and Beck had watched his heart break in real time. But he'd just left him there.

How many times could Kellan's heart break before it would never fit back together quite the same? Had it already gotten to that point? He'd played a part in that fracture, as much as he didn't want to admit it to himself.

But Kellan couldn't know. He couldn't find out why Beck was here and risk exposing him to the rest of the resistance. He trusted Kellan to know not to say anything.

His own cracked heart felt like it was bleeding out.

The question he'd asked himself before was more intense now. *What had he done?*

🌢　🌢　🌢

Spider found him hunched over in his room hours later.

He was broken, unable to delude himself that this was his mission, his duty. Unable to convince himself any longer that what he was doing would go unnoticed if he simply closed his eyes to it. If he ignored it long enough to pretend it wasn't happening, then maybe it wouldn't.

But it *was* happening. And now it wouldn't just affect these people he'd tried to keep at arms' length. These people who'd done nothing to him but welcome him with open arms. These kind people who'd given him a place to belong that he'd hadn't had since Kellan.

Now it would affect the only person he'd ever called home.

His actions would have a direct consequence, one that wasn't simply attached to a faceless codename. Beck didn't know their real names. Beck didn't have any idea who they were beneath their personas.

But Beck knew Kellan.

A hand reached out to touch his shoulder gently. Her hand was small, with long fingers covered in calluses. This hand he knew.

Spider wasn't faceless to him. She was in his vision, always. Her face was there when he fell asleep, her voice haunting him in every interaction with Brisea, with the Guard.

What had he done? Not only had he broken his best friend, but he'd soon break her heart, too. There was nothing he could do to stop the tidal wave. Nothing he could do to prevent the events he'd set in motion.

He would be the reason they would all break.

The enormity of everything he'd done, everything he would do, crashed into him, suffocating him. His breath came in calculated, cyclical rhythms. Even now, his body wouldn't allow him to be anything but perfect, calm, and reasonable.

He was anything but. She couldn't know that.

"Reaper?" she said, removing her hand from his shoulder. "It's nearly dinner time. Alpha wants us gathered in the barroom. I didn't see you so she asked me to—"

He surged up, grasping her hands in his own, tightly. "Beck."

She flinched, trying to draw her hands away. "What?"

"My name," he said, the desperate plea of his heart rendering his voice higher than usual. "Beck."

Spider freed a hand, but left the other as he finished speaking. Her mouth parted just a touch as she looked him up and down. "We're not supposed to know. Why would you tell me?"

"Because I wanted you to know," he replied, relaxing his grip on her hand. "I needed you to know."

She delicately freed her other hand, holding them both against her chest. The crease between her brows was deep, her hesitation obvious.

He expected nothing in return. He didn't need to know her name; he knew her well enough without it. But he needed her to know him, at least one small part of him that was real. One piece of him she could remember.

And remember with disgust when she found out who he really was.

But it was important to him to leave behind something *real,* something tangible that proved he wasn't just a faceless codename.

Something to prove that he really had been here, that he'd known these people. That he'd eventually betray them.

Spider may say his name with disgust someday. She may spit at him, call him a liar. But she would know him as Beck, not Reaper.

"Why me?" she finally said. Her voice was small, quieter and gentler than he'd ever heard it before. "Why would you tell me?"

Beck's hands balled into fists in his lap. "Because it's you."

She snorted. "I'm nothing special." Beck watched her shift, twisting her fingers around each other. "I'm not telling you mine, if that's what you're looking for."

That got a small smile from him. "I'm not. I just wanted you to know."

She nodded, then turned back toward the door. "Then don't wait around much longer. Dinner's almost ready, and we've got a lot to discuss."

Beck watched her go, a faint smile on his lips like a prayer he didn't want to end. He imagined what her name could be, thought of the multitudes of possibilities that would suit her, names of power, names of strength. But in the end, he didn't find one that suited her.

It didn't matter—she was who she was. And what was important was that she knew who he was, even if it was only a tiny piece.

"Oh, and Beck?" She was back, poking her head around the corner. "Thanks. For telling me."

And he thought his name on her lips was the sweetest thing he'd ever heard.

SECTION 3

THE RED GUARD

The Red Guard is the framework upon which all other branches of Empire law enforcement are built upon. Similar in structure to the Legion, with divisions, units, and rankings, the Red Guard is simply an elite collection of the Empire's best.

Generally, the Red Guard accepts very few indentured Fallen each year from the Mission. Oftentimes, they accept none. These indentured are assigned the lowest rank and never advance further than Private, with a clearance level of two.

The Red Guard is mobilized most often as an act of war against other surrounding countries and empires, but also serves in a research and development team, much like the United States military. They are not the nation's regular army, but a special corps designed to enhance the regular military's strength in battle.

Indentured are usually put on the front lines when this happens, used as the first boots on the ground. These indentured groups often do not make it back from these expeditions, as their purpose is to draw out enemy fire and reveal positions.

While the Legion does not treat their indentured well, the Red Guard is much, much worse.

28

CASSIAN

Alderburn | 23rd of Dawn Moon

The week and a half long trip to Alderburn was not a comfortable one. Silence was their most common companion during the drive. Cassian decided early that it gave him entirely too much time to think; an activity he was desperately uninterested in performing, especially when all his thoughts revolved around the man sitting in the backseat.

Vaida and Kellan kept to themselves, often taking turns napping on each other's shoulders. Cassian and Liv took turns driving, although Liv preferred to be in the driver's seat more often than not. When he'd offer to drive for her if she was feeling tired, she'd just throw him a look of exasperation. He'd stopped trying after the fourth day.

He'd steal glances at the backseat when he thought Kellan might be asleep. His instincts were rarely correct. Most of the time Cassian would catch Kellan staring out the window, meeting Vaida's eyes awkwardly, or accidentally meeting Kellan's gaze. The last always made him drop his eyes immediately, his cheeks burning.

It wasn't like his feelings had disappeared—even if he'd wished them gone. But he knew getting involved with Kellan again would only leave them both heartbroken. It was better this way.

Even if Rosalie hadn't asked him to stay impartial, there was no way he could avoid having to return to Zal.

Ze'd been uncharacteristically quiet during the ride as well. Usually, Zal would spring up with a quip now and then, but he hadn't heard from the demon the entire week. It didn't concern him too much, though. A week in the material plane was only a few hours in the infernal plane.

When they finally arrived in Alderburn, something in him softened. Like they'd finally break whatever uncomfortable air had settled over them during the trip once they'd entered the city. He should have known that wouldn't happen, but he was at least trying to be optimistic.

They quickly found an inn on the outskirts of town—Liv and Vaida in one room, Kellan and Cassian in another. He'd nearly begged Liv to switch and stay with him instead, but she'd given him a single glance as they'd entered the establishment that said she wanted no part of whatever squabble was happening between them.

A lively game of battle rings overpowered most of the chatter of the dining room of the inn, the players calling out playful insults to one another as their opponent prepared to throw. He'd never been all that fascinated by the bar game before, but he watched Kellan observe with an interested eye.

A woman with flaming red hair challenged other patrons every chance she got, then swiftly beat them with skill and grace. She was a sore winner, though, bragging about her prowess at a game that required little skill to begin with.

Dinner passed swiftly, and Cassian listened to the babble of the other patrons. Nothing of interest appeared in their conversations, most of them ranging from discussions of mutual acquaintances to farming prospects in the outlying lands surrounding Alderburn.

Most people visiting Alderburn weren't there for the town itself. Rather, they were there to either continue on toward Kazuta or head down into the southern country of Uswye. Alderburn's claim to fame was its forested backdrop, the Bergamot Forest.

Even before the Conjunction, the forest had been ancient to

the original humans of Ileron. The hemlock trees had massively wide trunks that three men could hug at once without their fingers touching. Many considered it a place of magic or a holy place to connect with Avani, the goddess of nature. People found solace in the evergreens' shade.

Cassian retreated to their room before anyone else, considering how they were going to narrow down the location of the artifact in such a giant, sprawling forest. It wasn't carefully mapped out, after all. The Bergamot Forest might be ancient and revered, but people didn't dare venture too deep; most brave travelers never found their way back out of the forest.

So how in the world were they supposed to find an artifact in the middle of it?

He flopped onto one of the two beds in the room, separated by a nightstand and a cheesy wooden lamp carved into the shape of a bear. Everything in the inn was made of wood, from the floors to the walls to the bed frames themselves. It wasn't his taste, but he could see how the campy appeal might attract tourists. It was a little charming.

They could start by talking to the locals, he thought. Maybe someone would know some old local tales about an interesting place within the forest or a legend that would match their only clue.

Of course it wouldn't be easy. Not only was he in charge of their motley crew, he had his own feelings to sort through.

He hadn't realized he'd dozed off until the door opening woke him up. He sat straight up in the bed, his eyes whipping to the door, only to find Kellan standing there, hand on the knob.

"I didn't mean to wake you," he said, his voice hard but not cruel. Cassian shook his head. "It's fine."

Kellan closed the door, making his way to the other bed. Words bubbled up in Cassian's throat, but he couldn't bring himself to say any of them. He was sorry; it wasn't Kellan's fault; this was better for the both of them. That no matter if he allowed himself to feel these emotions for Kellan, it wouldn't matter in the long run.

Because the pact had irrevocably changed him. Unless Zal saw fit to release him, he wouldn't be able to stay with Kellan. He'd have to abandon him again after the journey was over, after their mission was a success.

And his ultimate goal, the one he had to honor or forfeit his life, directly opposed the goal the rest of the group had. His chest constricted at the thought of betraying everyone he'd come to know over the last four months in the resistance.

But his heart twisted even further to think of how devastated Kellan would be after his inevitable betrayal. Part of him hoped that maybe, since he'd cut their relationship off, Kellan would be okay. That he'd react like Liv or Rosalie, with anger instead of sadness. That his heart would be whole enough for him to move on.

Kellan flopped onto the bed with little ceremony, landing face first into the pillows with a small grunt. Cassian felt the corners of his mouth lift, but he didn't speak. It would be enough, he decided, to simply be near Kellan during this trip. It would have to be.

He let sleep overtake him once more, his eyelids growing heavy as he listened to the soft sounds of Kellan preparing for bed.

It was enough, he repeated to himself. It was enough. But he wasn't convinced.

🔥 🔥 🔥

Kellan was gone by the time he woke the next morning, his bed left sloppy and unmade. It was good to see he hadn't changed in the years Cassian had been gone. Cassian's heart warmed at the thought as he slowly rolled out of bed.

Downstairs, the dining room of the inn was bustling. He spotted Vaida and Liv at a table together, chatting amicably and sipping on large mugs of steaming coffee.

He began making his way to them, slipping through the crowded space with murmured apologies. But when he was halfway to them, Kellan joined their table. Vaida said something to him, and a bright smile spread across his face.

It nearly knocked Cassian over to see it—their entire journey, he hadn't seen Kellan smile like that once. Sure, he'd cracked bitter smiles, ones without humor or happiness. But none like this, full of joy and warmth.

Kellan's brown eyes met Cassian's across the dining room, and the smile immediately disappeared. Cassian deflated.

At least you were thorough, Zal's voice echoed in his head as he continued moving toward the table, disappointment beating through his veins.

Oh, you're still alive, Cassian shot back. *I hadn't heard from you for a while, so I assumed they'd replaced you.*

My my, someone's in a bad mood today, ze replied. *Who pissed in your oatmeal?*

Shut it, Cassian said lamely, setting his breakfast down on the table with a thud. *I don't need your sass if you have nothing important to say.*

Touchy. Ze chuckled. *I thought you'd be interested to know that I tried asking some friends about your riddle.*

It's not like they'll know anything, Cassian said. Liv raised an eyebrow at him, but he shook his head. She knew, like Rosalie, when Cassian was communicating with Zal.

You're not wrong, ze replied.

So how is that helpful?

It means the story that woman told you was right, and the humans did their jobs. Just thought you should know.

Cassian sighed, cutting off the connection as he turned his gaze back to Liv. "Sorry. Zal was…chatty this morning."

Kellan didn't spare him another glance, instead focusing on the plate of food heaped high before him. But Vaida raised an eyebrow at him.

"Who is Zal?" she said, frowning.

Kellan must not have told her the story he'd shared that night in Rivenstorm. He supposed it made sense that Kellan wouldn't want to talk about it.

He filled Vaida in on the barest of details, explaining the state of his eye and his pact with Zal. She stayed silent the whole time, her lips turned down in a frown. She didn't ask questions when he was done, apparently content to ponder his situation. Her silence was off-putting, but he couldn't force her to ask questions, not when she so obviously wasn't interested.

But the itch in his mind was back, pulling him incessantly toward her. She was magnetic to him, even more so now that she'd listened to his story. He didn't understand what it was, why it kept happening, or why her. But he struggled to ignore it, struggled to make sense of what he was feeling.

Liv had the decency to change the subject after a long pause. "How'd you sleep?"

"Fine," he replied.

A coffee mug appeared in front of him. He glanced up to see Vaida, her expression still contemplative. He wasn't sure how to react, so he just nodded his thanks.

"You looked like you needed it," she said, a hint of a smirk finally curving her lips upward. "Kellan snores, so I bet you didn't sleep that well last night."

Kellan huffed. "I don't snore."

"You do," she responded without glancing at him. Cassian returned her smile and accepted the mug. The scent of the coffee was enough to make his shoulders relax.

"He wasn't so bad," Cassian said as he sipped.

Vaida chuckled while Kellan made an indignant noise. Liv cleared her throat, and they looked at her. Cassian noted the stern set of Liv's chin and knew she was uncomfortable.

"Vaida and I were just discussing how we should go about finding some clues for this first piece of the riddle," she said, glancing once at the woman seated next to her.

Vaida nodded. "We were thinking it might not be a bad idea to visit some of the tourist spots, see if any of the locals working there know some old legends. It's usually easier to find that sort of stuff in places targeted toward tourists."

He'd come to a similar plan last night. "That's what I was thinking as well. Why don't we split into teams and each grab a handful of places?"

Kellan nodded. "Vaida and I can take one half, you and Liv can take the other."

Liv shook her head. "No can do, buddy. Vaida and I have already picked a few. You and Cassian can check these." She slid a guidebook across the table, open to a page covered in highlights and sticky notes.

Kellan's jaw tightened, but Vaida spoke before he had the chance to argue. "There's a temple to Avani here, and the Alderburn Archives here," she said, pointing to two red-circled spots on the map in the book. "I don't really know what sort of information the temple would have, but it can't hurt to check it out. The Archives have maps; they might have something we can't find anywhere else."

Cassian watched Kellan's face as she pointed out the landmarks, paying close attention to his jaw that never relaxed. He knew Vaida and Liv were pushing them. He knew Vaida wouldn't push too far, either. But he struggled with understanding where that line was and how she knew just how far to push.

But she gambled and won. Kellan finally relaxed, the hard set of his shoulders sinking down as he snatched the guidebook from the table.

"Come on," he said, standing. He didn't look at Cassian.

He stood as well. Vaida shrugged and gave a well-meaning headshake before he followed Kellan out of the inn and into the winter sun.

29

KELLAN

Alderburn | 24th of Dawn Moon

How *dare* she. Kellan's frustration was nearly boiling over as he stomped out of the inn, Cassian at his heels. He'd known Vaida and Liv wouldn't put up with his suggestion, but putting him with *Cassian?*

They were just trying to tease him, weren't they? The frustration boiled purplish pink in his chest as the sun blinded him off the fresh snow on the streets.

And they were supposed to visit, what, a temple and some dreary old archive building? What kind of tourist attractions were those? He was going to give Vaida one hell of a lecture when they returned that evening.

Cassian followed him, quiet and reserved as Kellan stalked toward the station for trolleys that criss-crossed through town. It was faster than walking, considering the Archives were on the other side of the city.

He knew their predicament wasn't Cassian's fault—he knew that. But a little voice in his head screamed at him that Cassian was the reason, anyway. All this hurt, all this anger from the last four years was all his fault.

The station was busy but not overcrowded. The trolleys came every few minutes, their red and dark green exteriors blending in with the natural landscape of Alderburn. They looked old-fashioned but ran on a mag-lev system that Kellan knew they must have retrofitted the cars for. That magnetic suspension made them incredibly quiet; he didn't even hear when a trolley departed just feet away.

"Kellan?" Cassian said, barely loud enough to be heard over the surrounding buzz.

Kellan looked at him but said nothing. He waited, arms crossed, for Cassian to say whatever was on his mind.

Cassian pressed his lips together. "I know you must be… frustrated," he began, picking through the words that left his mouth carefully, as if he was considering each before he said them. "But you have to understand—"

Kellan cut him off, holding up a hand to stop him. "This isn't the conversation we should have now, Cassian."

Cassian snapped his mouth shut, looking away in shame. Kellan clenched his jaw but didn't apologize. He didn't regret cutting him off. A trolley platform wasn't the place to do this. If Kellan was being honest with himself, he didn't want to have the conversation anywhere.

The next trolley arrived minutes later, humming to a halt before them, the gold-trimmed doors opening smoothly for them. Kellan filed in first, checking behind him to make sure Cassian actually followed.

The Alderburn Archives were in an old building on the edge of the city, a backdrop of the Ensen Mountains painting a picturesque scene as they stepped off the trolley. Alderburn's proximity to the border with Uswye meant the town was the first stop on many long journeys. Interesting artifacts and stories had passed through this town, and they kept many of them at the Archives.

The building was well maintained, with a beautifully manicured lawn currently covered in a thin layer of snow. The path toward the entrance was made of a brown stone laced with white and silver, sharply maintained and edged with rock. The Archives themselves were built of the same brown stone as the walkway, with wide arched windows and gold muntins holding the massive glass panels in place.

Kellan went inside first, head swiveling to find an information desk or place to start their search. Cassian turned down a hallway and disappeared. Kellan didn't bother following.

The atrium was old, old enough that the scuff marks in the dark hemlock flooring looked as if they'd been fixed and re-scuffed a multitude of times. A herringbone pattern ran down the center of the wide hallway. Arches split the dark wall paneling every few feet and led to small alcoves filled to bursting with tomes of every shape, color, and size.

Several light wooden staircases that had obviously been built much later than the rest of the building squeezed themselves in just before the alcoves of books, rendering the atrium an almost maze of books versus stairs. Reaching the books in the alcoves would be a skill better suited to a child than a full-grown man.

He wandered, letting his hands trail over the walls with a feather-light touch. The craftsmanship was beautiful, the cuts so precise there were no discernable gaps between the panels.

Someone cleared their throat behind him, and he started, whirling around to face the source of the noise.

A halfling archivist stood before him, Cassian standing just behind. The archivist had half-moon glasses perched upon their sharp nose and, even though they were several feet shorter than him, somehow managed to look down at Kellan.

"You're in search of maps, yes?" they asked, voice clear.

Kellan nodded, and the archivist tilted their head to the side. "This way, then."

Kellan fell into step behind their guide, Cassian moving to create room just behind them. They led them up one of the many staircases in the atrium, striding across the space with confidence.

"It's jus' down this hallway, gents," the archivist said, their voice a pleasant and melodic combination of a Midlset lilt and the bright vowels of an Uswye accent. "Is there a specific map you'll be searchin' for today? We've got some datin' as far back as post-Conjunction, so I'm sure you'll find what you need."

"A map of the forest, if you've got them," Kellan asked.

The archivist's eyebrows rose, a twinkle of scholastic interest in their eyes. "Oh, interested in the Bergamot Forest, eh? I'm sure we can dig somethin' up that will be useful to you."

They prattled on about the history of the forest as they ascended; the sanctity of the hemlock trees to both Hym and Sol; its effect on the city of Alderburn and the relationship to the Ensen Mountains; and how the pre-Conjunction humans had tales of their own, lost to time, about the history of the forest.

Kellan noticed Cassian trailing slightly behind, a look on his face that seemed almost like confusion. It wasn't his job to worry about Cassian, but Kellan still glanced behind him every few steps to make sure he was still there.

The second floor was much like the first, its age obvious in the variety of architectural styles and wood colors. The archivist turned down one of the first arches, leading them into a small room with several tables. Tomes the size of an average humanoid's torso sat upon a solid hemlock table that was stained a deep red and carved with intricate whorls protected by clear resin.

They'd anchored the tomes to the table behind glass, the pages turnable with a device on the front of the glass covering. The archivist led them to one of these tomes, then pointed at the pages displayed beneath the glass.

"This tome contains the first known hand-drawn maps of the trails just on the outskirts of Bergamot Forest," they began, pressing the back arrow of the mechanism to gently turn the yellowing pages of the book backward. "In the very beginnin' there were only a few, and they are quite crude."

The first few maps looked almost comical in their simplicity. The archivist switched to the forward button, pressing several times to advance to a more modern-looking version of the same map they'd just seen.

"Now here's where it gets interestin'," they said, using a small ball between the arrow buttons to shine a gentle spotlight inside the glass. "This map is one of the first that ventures beyond the first few miles into the forest. It seems the early travelers never made it much farther than this, as most of the other maps stay in about the same region of forest. We aren't sure if there were issues or if it's simply unmappable beyond a certain point."

Kellan leaned in. "This is the most the forest has ever been mapped? Or just the most for that time period?"

Cassian stood beside him, leaning over the glass with an intensity Kellan didn't understand. It was as if the drawings entranced him, hypnotized him.

The archivist shook their head. "The most it's ever been mapped. We know its boundaries, but what lies deep in the forest no one truly knows. Anyone who's ever gone in never comes back out. You've heard the tales, right? Of travelers disappearin' beyond the thickest trees? Bein' taken by livin' shadows?"

Kellan certainly had not heard those stories, but the archivist didn't seem like they were paying him much mind as they continued.

"It's probably just made-up tales, things to scare children from venturin' too far. But still, one must wonder why no one has mapped the depths of the forest in any sort of detail. Of course, more detailed maps of the outskirts exist, but these maps were their predecessors, the ones that made current maps as accurate as they are."

If the first artifact was somewhere deep in the woods, then a map that only showed the outskirts wouldn't help them. And if this was all someone had ever mapped—all they'd ever been *able* to map—how in the world were they supposed to find something in the middle of a forest that was full of terrors?

"So how do people make it through the forest? Isn't that the way to Balindao?" Cassian asked. The capital of Uswye lay just beyond the forest and the Ensen Mountain range. The fastest way would be through the forest and mountains.

"Ah, you'd think; but alas, no one goes through. Balindao is accessible only through the northern and southern passes. Each run just outside the outskirts of the forest," the archivist said, flipping the book a few pages further. A new map depicting a simplified version of the Empire and Uswye detailed the safest passages from one city to another.

The northern pass to Uswye ran just south of Kettleguard. The southern pass followed the southernmost boundary of the Empire. Kellan had never realized travel to Uswye overland was so difficult.

Apparently, Cassian had the same thought. "Land travel to Uswye is more challenging than I thought."

The archivist beamed, apparently excited for the new topic of discussion. "Well, you see, most folks take the northern route. It's safest, even in winter. As you know, there's a bit of a natural break in the Ensen range just south and west of Kettleguard. The mountains that actually surround Balindao and back up against Bergamot are some of the tallest in the range."

Kellan wandered, letting them have their discussion. A map of Northreach, the city that eventually became Spiral City, hung in a glass case on the wall. It was much, much smaller than Spiral City, but something about the shape of the original map reminded him of the sprawling metropolis he'd fled only weeks ago.

Some stupid, nostalgic part of him missed the city he knew. But it had only ever been a cage for him. He squeezed his eyes shut momentarily, the old map of Northreach burned into the black in his vision. The stories of living shadows still tickled in the back of his mind, taking shape behind his eyelids in between the ink of the map of Northreach.

"I'll give you a bit to peruse the maps, then," the archivist said, loud enough for him to hear. "I'll be downstairs if you'd like a copy or need assistance with anythin' else."

Kellan opened his eyes and turned to face them as they bowed, crossing an arm over their midsection as they did.

"It was a pleasure to discuss maps with you. It's been a while since anyone has been interested in these."

Both Kellan and Cassian thanked the archivist as they left, somehow taking all the warmth of the room with them. Kellan's gaze drifted to Cassian; he looked contemplative, but the look of concern that he'd seen earlier while coming up the stairs was gone.

It wasn't his place to worry about Cassian like that anymore. He shook his head, his hair flopping with the movement. "Anything strike you as interesting?"

Cassian seemed surprised that Kellan would even talk to him, judging by the way he jumped at the sound of Kellan's voice. It took him a moment to recover and reply.

"Well," he began slowly, just like he'd spoken on the trolley platform, "I find it strange that no one has mapped the forest. It's not like we don't have the technology these days."

Kellan thought the same. It seemed odd that the middle of the forest was an unknown; there had to be some maps out there that had that information. It was surprising they weren't here, of all places.

He waved a hand at the enormous tome the archivist had showed them. "Should we get a copy?"

Cassian nodded. "I want to see what Vaida thinks of all this. She'll have an idea, I'm sure."

"I'll ask the archivist," Kellan said, turning toward the archway.

Cassian stopped him with a choked noise. "I—can I come with?"

Kellan shook his head. "I can go on my own."

He was frustrated enough they had been paired up today. He was angry enough that his feelings felt like a knot inside his chest. The tangle threw him astray, filling him with a swirl of muted and dull colors that mixed into the dull brown of defeat.

He didn't hate Cassian. How could he?

But this? Working together, being in such proximity to him so often…it was too much for his broken heart to handle. It *hurt*, and he didn't relish the pain one bit. He'd spent so long shoving it away, imagining it as a piece of crumpled paper he could throw away. But it always returned, filling him faster than he could ever get rid of it.

Cassian's eyes dulled and returned to the tome when Kellan turned him down. Kellan pretended not to notice the slump of his shoulders or the way his hands fisted in his pockets.

It had to be like this. It had to be.

30

KELLAN

Alderburn | 24th of Dawn Moon

Dinner that evening was a lively affair, just as it had been the evening before. Another rowdy game of battle rings was underway in the corner. Kellan kept a listening ear on the game and its competitors as the rest of the group talked about the map from the Archives.

He'd never taken the game too seriously when he'd played back in Spiral City, but he wasn't unfamiliar with the rules. The crowd was raucous, cheering and hollering as the players took their turns.

One was a younger woman, her hair a fiery shade of copper, pulled back into a ponytail at the crown of her head. She held the glowing blue rings and seemed focused on watching her opponent set up for his next toss. She wore a battered cropped T-shirt layered beneath a beat-up, hole-filled sweater with wide legged pants that tightened around her ankles. Her boots were low, but practical.

Her opponent was an older man, his dark hair graying at the temples. He looked less intense than she, but the luminous red rings he held signaled that he was earning more points than she was at the moment.

There were two rings on the hook, both of them red. Her last two throws had missed, but she was the picture of calm, focusing with an intense gaze on her opponent.

The man threw his third ring, the last one he had in his hands. It knocked off the edge of the peg and fell to the floor with a clatter. The two consecutive rings he'd thrown onto the peg already had earned him six points. Losing out on the third ring now meant he couldn't double his score, but she wouldn't be able to catch him this round with only one ring left.

She rolled her neck and her shoulders, gearing up for her last throw. Just before she set up for the toss, she smirked. She tossed the last ring with perfect accuracy. It swung onto the wooden peg with a satisfying *clack,* earning her two points.

Kellan watched their final round with scrutiny, observing her technique and accuracy. There was no way she'd gotten this good at battle rings only for the sake of the game. She won, handily, in the final round; and when she triumphantly stuck her hand out to her opponent, she watched him count coins into her palm.

Playing for money? Kellan felt an itch as familiar to him as breathing—the one born from that brown sludge of defeat in his gut.

He wanted a fight. She would give it to him.

She cackled as her opponent slunk out into the main bar, then turned to the gathered crowd. Her voice boomed. "Who else wants to try me? I've got a treasure map up for grabs!"

"Kellan," Vaida said in his ear, startling him from his focus on the battle rings game. "We were just discussing where else might have a map of the forest."

He turned back to the table, Liv and Vaida seated on the bench across from him. Cassian had already retired to their room upstairs an hour ago.

Kellan's legs felt restless. He didn't want to sit here talking; he wanted to release all these nerves that had been building since the Archives trip earlier this morning. He'd thought he'd gotten his feelings about Cassian under control, but today's excursion proved he couldn't focus if they were alone. And that was a problem.

What he needed now was a release of some sort. Sex was off the table—it wasn't like he couldn't, but it felt wrong.

So the only thing left was a fight. He wouldn't risk Vaida's wrath by starting a bar fight here, especially with their fugitive status and the risk of attracting the *wrong* attention. But a rowdy game of battle rings wouldn't harm anyone, right?

Kellan shook his head. "I've got nothing. Can we just…please, for a moment, talk about something else?"

The crowd behind him was distracting his thoughts, their chants and the young woman's boasts drowning out whatever Vaida said next.

"I've got a treasure map, yet no one wants to take me on?" The red-haired woman's voice was shrill, a cutting sound through the din of the crowd.

Kellan turned his attention back to the crowd, but Vaida didn't let him ignore her for long.

"Absolutely not, Kellan," she said, following his gaze. "We're supposed to be inconspicuous—you know, *lying low?*"

Kellan scoffed. "A harmless game of battle rings won't set the Red Guard on our tails."

Vaida narrowed her eyes at him. The brilliant orange of fear rose in the back of his mind. He wasn't afraid of Vaida, but of pushing her too far. He would be nothing without her.

So he relented. "Okay, okay. Sorry. I won't."

She shook her head. "I'm only trying to look out for us."

Liv leaned forward, resting her elbows on the table and catching Kellan's gaze. She wore an expression of mischief and curiosity as her eyes flicked back and forth between Vaida and Kellan. He didn't know what she wanted to say, but it seemed as if she was debating getting between them. For whose good, he didn't know.

"Vaida," Liv finally said, cocking her head slightly, "what's the harm in letting him play? It doesn't seem like anyone here gets offended by the outcome of the game, and he looks like he needs to blow off some steam." She sighed. "Besides, we've wracked our brains for hours now. We could use a little fun."

Vaida huffed. Kellan didn't push—he knew anything more from him would earn immediate dismissal, but she was entertaining Liv. He wouldn't push his luck.

His eyes met Liv's. She simply wiggled her eyebrows at him once before returning her gaze to Vaida.

Finally, Vaida closed her eyes, slumping over to rest her forehead in her hand. "Fine. I guess I don't see a problem with a simple game of battle rings." She looked up at Kellan through her fingers. "But Kellan, I am serious when I say don't do anything stupid. If you lose, that's it."

Kellan stood from the table in a hurry, nearly knocking his chair over. "I know, I know."

He made his way to the battle rings, pushing his way through the crowd to approach the red-headed girl, grandstanding for the onlookers.

"Who else wants to try me? I'm undefeated! You'd get bragging rights of the century if you win!"

He stood just in front of the crowd, his arms crossed. "I'll take you on."

She giggled, meeting his eyes with a flash of wild excitement. "A shrimp like you? This'll be interesting."

He sighed and didn't move. "But I won't be betting money."

"Oh?" She seemed intrigued by his proposition.

"How about something else of value?"

She cocked an eyebrow at him, her mouth pulling into a hysterical smile. He could practically see the gears churning in her head as she regarded him.

"Something else of value? Well, if you wanted to sleep with me you could have just said so." The crowd chuckled at her statement.

He didn't rise to it. "You're not my type," he said as he slapped the hilt of his demon-killer onto the table with the rings. "What about this?"

She glanced down at the hilt. Several people in the crowd made confused noises, but he could tell by the look on her face she knew exactly what the weapon was.

"Well," she said, raising her eyes back to meet his, "this is an interesting development. I'll take you up on it." She reached into the bag at her feet and pulled out a folded piece of paper. "This here's a map—supposedly, it shows you the way through the Bergamot Forest, all the way to some hidden landmark in the very middle."

He kept his cool while she spoke, but adrenaline spiked through his veins. This could be just what they needed—so long as it was actually real. He wasn't about to be duped. He held his hand out to her, gesturing to the map.

"You've seen what my offer is with your own eyes, and I can tell you know its value. But I'd like to verify the map with my own eyes first, if you don't mind."

She grinned, her canines pointed. "Sure, sure. Take it. But you get ten seconds to review it, then you gotta put it back. Can't have you memorizing it."

He nodded his understanding and unfolded the map when she handed it over. Kellan's eyes went wide. It was nearly identical to the map they'd gotten from the Archives, but the center wasn't a blank space. There were several landmarks, trees, and other topographical marks that certainly seemed to lead the way through the forest to a—

A hand appeared in his field of vision, covering the center of the map. "All right, ten seconds is up; put it down, shrimp."

He obliged, a flare of annoyance ringing through his head at her nickname for him. He wasn't even that short.

She grabbed the blue rings, then gestured to the red ones in an invitation. He eyed her, sizing up his opponent as he grabbed his set. She had muscular arms, but they weren't huge. Her shoulders were broad and strong. He couldn't figure out where she got the accuracy she showed in the previous game, but he suspected she was an archer.

He'd have his work cut out for him, wouldn't he? The accuracy that it took to be a decent archer wasn't exactly an easy skill to train.

She could probably crush him in an archery contest—it was never his strong suit.

They tossed a coin to see who would get the first move. Kellan lost, but he wasn't concerned. His gut told him he'd do well, anyway. He had to. He had something to prove—both to himself and to Vaida and Liv. This wasn't for fun, not anymore.

She flicked a lock of bright hair over her shoulder, lining up her shot by tilting her head slightly to the side. She held the ring out, brought it back, then tossed it in a fluid motion that Kellan knew would hit the target before it even left her fingers.

It landed with a *clack* on the wooden peg, and she turned back to him, a crooked grin splitting her face.

He returned the smirk, channeling all the anger and frustration that was roiling in his veins. This was what he needed, something that would take his mind off the man sleeping upstairs.

That seemed to spark a fire in her. She leaned on the table between them as he prepared to throw, whispering nonsense to distract him.

He ignored her and breathed deeply, finding the space inside himself he used when throwing knives. This wasn't much different. Kellan tossed his first ring, and it landed with a satisfying clunk on the peg, knocking up against the woman's ring.

Her eyes narrowed as she stared at him. Each ring separately was only worth two points—two of the same color together were worth three each, and all three together were worth four. He'd ruined her chances of getting the most points on this round.

She lined up her next throw, her second ring landing against his with precision. She turned back to him once it was done, a condescending look on her face. She didn't whisper this time, just stared.

He ignored her glare as he prepared the second ring. His also landed against hers gracefully. This wasn't going down without a fight.

They finished the first round with a tie, each with six points. The second round went exactly the same, their accuracy never failing. They'd continued to keep up with one another, no matter who went first, no matter who was watching.

The crowd had fallen silent, watching and waiting with bated breath as they entered the third round. If they tied, the first one to thirty-six points was the winner, regardless of who threw first.

She threw her first ring, swinging around the peg with that incredible accuracy he'd come to envy during their game.

He threw his, once again landing with that satisfying thud against hers.

Her next ring landed against his, the metallic *clack* loud in his ears.

His second ring thwacked against hers. Still even, still tied.

She rolled her neck, the pops and cracks as loud as the rings smacked together on the peg as she prepared to throw her last ring. He silently willed her to miss—he didn't want to play this all night.

She grinned at him, then threw her final ring.

It landed on the floor with a dull thud, having missed the peg by a hair. But how? Her aim had been so perfect the whole game. But it didn't mean he'd won just yet. He still had to throw his. He could see her out of the corner of his eye, her face contorted in fury. Her eyes were wide as she watched him prepare.

"Choke," she whispered, just loud enough for him to hear.

He smirked, not bothering to look at her as he gripped his last ring. He knew it would piss her off to not acknowledge her.

Kellan tossed the ring. The feeling as it left his hand was perfect, the angle was just right, the spin just enough. It would land.

And it did. The entire inn erupted in a cacophony, the roars of the once-silent crowd deafening. He turned back to the red-headed woman and smiled, sticking out his hand to her.

"You played a wonderful game," he said.

She didn't take his hand. "Fuck off."

He shrugged, grabbing his hilt and the map from the table. "Let's play this again sometime."

He didn't wait for a response as he wove his way back through the crowd and upstairs to his room. Satisfaction oozed from every pore, his steps light and airy as he ascended the stairs.

31

ℭASSIAN

Alderburn | 25th of Dawn Moon

Kellan proudly slapped a map down on the table the next morning as they gathered for breakfast. Vaida looked irritated, and Liv didn't even glance at it.

Vaida's attention drifted between Kellan and the map. "I can't believe you wasted your time on this."

Cassian leaned in. "What is it?"

"He played a game of battle rings for it—it's a treasure map," Liv said, a giggle on her lips. "It was a spectacular game."

"A treasure map?" Cassian asked, but he didn't expect an answer. The map looked similar to the one they'd found at the Archives, but there was much more to it.

The text was blocky and dense, written by hand and faded from years of being passed around. He thought he could read some of it; the language was familiar, yet not.

The itch was back as he stared, tugging at the back of his mind like he was supposed to know what this language was. It was as if his eyes were trying to translate it, attempting to make sense of it even when he didn't know it. It was making his eyes hurt, so he finally looked away. The itch eased.

Vaida looked as confused as he did, staring down at the page with the same sort of confused familiarity on her face that he'd felt a moment ago. She looked as if she wanted to say she knew the language, but something was holding her back.

Or maybe he was just projecting.

"It's written in an old form of the common human tongue," Liv said. He hadn't been watching her, but when he turned to her, she'd tilted her head toward the top of the map, squinting as she read. "It says, 'The Bergamonte Tempyl of Hym,' I think."

Cassian stared at the map, but the words stayed just out of his reach. Vaida looked perplexed. The crease between her brows had only grown deeper at Liv's translation.

"It's not surprising you wouldn't know," Liv reassured Vaida. "It's not like they teach anyone the accurate history of humans anymore."

"Can you translate the rest?" Vaida asked.

Liv shrugged. "Probably. It might take me a bit, but my mother taught me a little when I was younger."

Vaida stayed quiet, and Cassian could tell she was deep in thought. Guilt welled at Liv's words, though. She was right. None of them knew anything about human history other than the heavily biased information they'd been fed when they were young. As he'd grown, it became more obvious that most of what he'd learned about humans as a child was incorrect. It still didn't ease the guilt.

Silence descended upon their table, but Liv didn't seem to care. She continued eating, shoveling food into her mouth while the rest of them looked down at their plates in silence.

She finally sighed, pushing back from the table. "Look, it's not your fault. That's how this country functions, and each of you have had your own share of difficulties, so I'm not mad that you don't know." She stood, grabbing the map from the table. "We should compare this to the map we got from the Archives. If they match…"

Vaida nodded. "Kellan may have gotten us exactly what we need."

Kellan preened, looking pleased with himself. Vaida ignored him, but Cassian watched the corner of her lip twitch in a small smile. He wondered what they'd been through together until now—

the thought of Kellan wrecked after Cassian disappeared made his heart ache.

He was glad, though, that Vaida had been there for Kellan. Even though it never should have happened.

There was nothing they could do about that now.

"So what should we do, then?" Kellan asked, his voice dripping with satisfaction.

Vaida shrugged. "Nothing. I'll help Liv. You guys could hang out, play battle rings, and leave us be."

Kellan shrugged, but didn't turn toward Cassian. "I'll figure something out."

Cassian wanted to reach for him, beg him to just talk, but he stopped himself. *He* did this. He'd ruined their relationship, had put them in this position to begin with. What right did he have to pine over Kellan?

It was better this way.

🔸 🔸 🔸

He had nothing to do the rest of the day; Vaida and Liv would be occupied with translation and prepping for whatever their next move would be. Even when he'd asked to help, they'd shooed him away with promises of updates and information. But he saw the sparkle in their eyes. They wanted time away from him.

Cassian supposed it made sense. The tension between Kellan and him wasn't exactly *comfortable*. Zal commented on it every chance ze got. Cassian could feel it more acutely with every moment that passed, a thick miasma hanging in the air between them.

So when Kellan left the inn, Cassian followed him.

Not too closely, of course, but just close enough that he could observe what Kellan was like without the weighty tension that hung between them.

Of course, he'd caught glimpses—that morning at breakfast in the Autumn Rose when Kellan had smiled so warmly he thought the ice around his heart might finally thaw. He'd seen other glimpses, too. Jokes traded with Liv when Kellan thought he wasn't looking. Softer moments with Vaida when Cassian was supposed to be occupied.

Kellan, although four years older and four years more jaded, still had the spark that had made Cassian fall the first time. That little twinkle of mischief in his eyes that spoke of secretive plans and midnight trysts.

But something darker hid there, too. It swelled in the corners of his expressions—the slight downturn of his lips when he wasn't smiling, the way he held his hands rigidly, prepared to strike. Even the set of his shoulders was different.

Cassian was sure he was different, too. But did Kellan bother to notice those things? Did he care enough to notice?

Kellan walked leisurely, hands stuffed in the pockets of his pants, combat boots kicking up snow as he meandered down the stone sidewalks. The town was alive around him. They'd painted buildings in natural tones and lined them with whitewashed wood to contrast the verdant countryside. Residents and visitors alike crowded the streets and the bridges over long-dried canals.

He couldn't know where he was going; it seemed like he was simply following his feet. Even Cassian's abnormally insistent gut was keeping silent, letting him follow Kellan without interference.

Kellan stopped a few times. Once, he paused in front of an old wooden shop on a street corner to watch something through the window. When Cassian passed, he saw an old halfling man in the window, stretching what looked like a massive rope of caramel into a large O.

The second time, he stopped at a woodworker's shop, pausing to look at an intricately carved fox statue. The shopkeeper chatted with him for a few minutes, thrilled someone seemed interested in their artwork.

A third time, Kellan stepped inside what looked like a jewelry store. The display outside was full of delicately crafted silver jewelry, their quality and finery obvious even from across the street. Kellan stayed inside for a while, and Cassian was nearly tempted to chase after him.

But when he emerged nearly an hour later, Cassian noticed the way his eyes sparkled. He remembered that first night in a hotel room so long ago, the curve of Kellan's ear covered in black gems and hoops and spikes. What had he seen that could put that sort of look on his face?

He was lost in thought for a moment too long after Kellan left the jewelry store, and Cassian swore when he looked around the block and couldn't find his golden hair in the crowd.

You've got it bad, Zal said, chuckling. *Stalking your crush while he shops. I didn't know you had it in you, Cassian.*

Shut up, Zal, Cassian replied, scanning the crowd. *I'm not stalking. I'm just…watching.*

That's literally what stalking is, you know.

It's not the same. Now shut up.

Fine, fine. And Cassian felt their connection end.

"What are you doing?" A voice from behind him made Cassian nearly jump out of his skin.

He whipped around to meet Kellan's amber eyes under a furrowed brow. Cassian swore silently. How was he supposed to explain this? Zal was right—he'd totally been stalking Kellan, desperate for a glimpse of him without the contempt and anger he'd worn around Cassian since Rivenstorm.

"I, uh," he began, stupidly trying to think of some excuse and coming up blank.

Kellan waited, arms crossed, but seemed to sense Cassian wouldn't give any kind of satisfactory answer after the fourth "um" from his mouth. His eyes had lost the sparkle from the jewelry shop, Cassian noticed with a sinking feeling. *He'd* done that.

"You were following me," Kellan said simply. "Why?"

"I just—" Cassian began, but Kellan held up a hand, cutting him off.

"Never mind, I really don't care." He waited, chewing his lip and avoiding eye contact. Cassian said nothing, waiting for Kellan to chastise him. But it never came.

Instead, Kellan's eyes drifted around the square, landing on the tiny tourist trap shops and the locals weaving between the tourist hordes. Their bustle and buzz was loud enough to be incoherent, a monotonous soundtrack to this moment.

Cassian felt like they were in a bubble, like the surrounding noise was bouncing off an invisible glass dome that encased only himself and Kellan. If this were a romance movie, he'd take Kellan by the waist and dip him low, kissing him with all the love and passion and fire he kept locked in a tiny box within his heart. They'd stay there as the camera panned around them, snow falling precisely at the moment their lips met, taking the scene from perfect to absolutely magical.

But this wasn't a romance movie. Instead, they were trapped in the glass dome, their gazes drifting around them in search of escape. And that was all he could see as Kellan's eyes darted around the square.

"You know," Kellan finally said, his voice perfectly clear like a bell, "if you were that bored, you could have asked to come with me."

Cassian stared, his focus shifting from the surrounding space to Kellan himself. He was almost…softer.

"You wouldn't have said yes," Cassian said quietly.

Kellan shrugged. "I might have. I'm feeling pretty generous after winning that game last night."

Cassian couldn't help himself—he let himself smile, the fizzle of joy in his chest taking that miasma and blowing on it, sending it drifting into the midwinter sun of Alderburn.

And he could have sworn he saw the corner of Kellan's mouth twist up. It was brief, only a flash of movement, but it was enough.

"Did you see something you liked in that shop?" Cassian said, jerking his head back toward the jewelers.

Kellan shook his head. "Nothing I could hope to afford on my non-existent salary."

Cassian didn't know how to reply to that, so he didn't. Kellan didn't seem offended, either. He just turned toward a coffee shop and cocked his head at Cassian.

"Come on," he said. "Let's grab a cup before we head back. Vaida messaged ten minutes ago that they were done."

Cassian nodded dumbly and followed Kellan into the cafe. He didn't remember how, but before long, Kellan plunked a cup of black coffee down in front of him. All he could think as he sipped at the drink was that it had to mean something that Kellan still remembered how he liked his coffee, even if it was simple.

The thought warmed his stomach more than the drink ever could, and he hoped that this was what Kellan considered a peace offering.

32

KELLAN

Alderburn | 26th of Dawn Moon

The next morning they departed for the starting point of the map, their supplies refilled and additional ones purchased. They'd have to sleep outside, which was horribly unappealing to Kellan. The prospect made his skin crawl.

Vaida drove the van to the beginning of the trail, which allowed long-term parking for those venturing into the Bergamot Forest. Most people didn't venture too deep. Instead, they'd hike along the edge of the forest, which still provided the escape into nature most were looking for.

But their small party was going farther into the forest than that. Their journey to the temple would take approximately three days on foot, according to Vaida's calculations. The trip back, another three. The temple itself rested at the base of a mountain, one of the very first in the Ensen range.

People had traveled beyond the well-worn trails deeper into the forest, of course, but years of ghost stories told to children and warnings from nearly every local about the dangers of the forest proved that they never returned. Whether it was a lack of directions or something more sinister living in the forest, no one could really say. The forest itself was an anomaly that anyone had yet to fully understand, but not for lack of trying.

Kellan could only hope that the map would save them from whatever unfortunate fate had befallen travelers before them. After all, if there was a temple in the middle of this supposedly dangerous forest, it must mean it used to *not* be dangerous, right?

It didn't look foreboding upon their arrival. In fact, it was breathtaking. The snow sparkled on the hemlock branches, the forest floor dusted in a soft coating of brown needles. It was like something out of a fairytale, a serene, sparkling sight that made Kellan suck in a breath of appreciation.

They were one of many groups getting ready to spend their time weaving through the trees. As they divided up the supplies, Vaida gave him an appraising glance. Kellan felt the unspoken question hovering between them, born of her inevitable curiosity over what had transpired with Cassian the day before.

"Spit it out," he said, sighing.

Vaida shrugged. "I'm just waiting for you to tell me about what happened yesterday. Your ice wall is less thick today," she said, rapping her knuckles against the air beside him, as if he really was encased in ice.

He waved her hand away, biting his lip to keep himself from smiling. She might tease him, but he didn't mind. "We just talked. Nothing special."

Her eyes narrowed, but she waved him off. "Sure, whatever you say." She didn't press further. Instead, she turned toward the other two as she hoisted her pack up and onto her back.

Liv lifted her pack with a hand, throwing it casually over her shoulder as Vaida approached. Cassian was finishing with his pack, zipping the top and lifting the straps over his shoulders. Kellan observed him carefully, waiting for him to make eye contact.

He didn't. Instead, Cassian turned toward the trailhead, then cocked his head back to Liv. "Are we ready to go?"

Liv pulled the creased maps from her pocket. "Let's do this thing."

Vaida nodded, falling in step with Liv. Cassian trailed just behind them, Kellan bringing up the rear. Vaida's words about his attitude were stinging still—it made something within him want to rebel, to reach out to Cassian, but also to stay as far away from him as possible. He wanted to prove her wrong, but he didn't know why.

They spent the first leg of the trip mostly in silence, only the occasional chatter from Liv and Vaida breaking the quiet of the forest. Those first few hours were lovely, too—the well-worn paths wound through the trees and gave them a kaleidoscope view of the world from beneath the branches. The sun sent its spindly fingers through the canopy, illuminating the fresh snow like heavenly fire.

Vaida stopped, taking a moment to consult the map and her techpad's compass, then sighed. "Let's take a break; we've gone pretty far, and we're about to depart from the paths, anyway. This is a good time to discuss what might await us in the forest."

Kellan's stomach turned. "What do you mean?"

"You've heard the stories, haven't you?" He nodded, and she continued. "We can't ignore the possibility that there's sinister magic or beasts of some sort in the forest. This map is *old* and definitely doesn't account for changes that may have occurred after its creation."

Kellan shuddered, reminded of the stories the archivist had shared of living shadows that lurked between the towering hemlock trees.

"So what you're saying is we should be ready for anything?" Cassian said. He'd already taken a seat by a nearby tree and dropped his pack on the ground.

Vaida nodded. "I've prepared a few barrier nodules just in case, but my resources are not endless. We need to be cautious and alert. I'd recommend creating a watch schedule as well."

Liv swung her pack down next to Cassian's and sat on it. "Two and two would be best, don't you think?"

Vaida nodded. "Kellan and Cassian first watch, Liv and I will take second."

Kellan opened his mouth to protest, but decided against it. A watch wouldn't hurt, and it might give him the chance to talk more with Cassian. Maybe he could understand just what had gone so wrong between them back in Rivenstorm.

Cassian spoke before Kellan could. "Fine by me."

Liv dug in her pack for some of the food they'd brought along, sticking a piece of jerky in her mouth and waving one toward Vaida. "Sounds good to me. V?"

Vaida nodded, holding a hand out for the offered snack. Liv obliged her, setting a piece gently in her hand.

Kellan turned his gaze back to Cassian. He'd closed his eyes and leaned his head against the tree. Kellan watched him silently, saying nothing.

They spent a little while where they'd stopped, taking the chance to have a light lunch and rest their feet. But Vaida had them up and moving as soon as Liv finished the last of her portion of jerky. She didn't want to waste sunlight; there was no telling what might wait for them in the dark.

Going off-path wasn't as dramatic as he'd expected—they simply followed the compass on Vaida's techpad, taking their time walking between the massive hemlock trunks. Kellan's eyes swiveled side to side, expecting something to jump out of the trees.

But nothing did. It was even more beautiful now, the forest more wild, undisturbed, and quiet. Their footsteps were soft thanks to the bed of needles beneath. The sunlight was just as warm and calming here as it had been several hours ago.

Cassian spoke as the golden sunlight finally turned into a deep amber. "We should stop, use the last of the light to set up camp."

Vaida nodded. "I think that's a good plan. I need to plot where we are on the map, anyway."

They found some space between the trees that wasn't quite a clearing but was enough for their two tents and a portable stove. Kellan got to work setting up their meal for the evening while Vaida calculated their location and Liv set up the tents with Cassian.

The dinner was quiet, and the impending darkness made their meal even quieter. Liv and Vaida both finished their meals quickly, then mumbled something about getting as much sleep as they could. After they headed off to their tent, Cassian and Kellan sat in silence. It was now or never.

"Cassian," Kellan started, his voice quiet. He was positive Liv and Vaida were eavesdropping, but he didn't care.

Cassian looked up at him, the moonlight washing out his hair and making it look like pure silver threads sprouted from his head. An eyebrow raised in acknowledgement.

Kellan continued, trying not to think of running his fingers through Cassian's silver-spun hair. "I wanted to ask about your pact…" He trailed off, not sure where to start.

Cassian cocked his head, his eyes never leaving Kellan's. "What do you want to know?"

Where should he start? "What's it like?" A stupid question, but it was the best he could come up with in the moment.

But Cassian didn't seem to think it was foolish. "I'm...not really sure how to explain it. Zal is me, and I am zem. Everything I feel, ze feels too. What I see, ze sees."

"Are they here with you? Are you one being?"

Cassian shook his head. "No, it's not like that. It's more like we share a consciousness—thoughts, emotions, and sensations."

Kellan bit his lip. "Whatever you know, then ze knows?"

"Mostly. It's not perfect, since our pact is still new, but—" He stopped suddenly, cocking his head toward the dark forest.

A feeling of dread descended upon them, inky black in Kellan's mind, and they sprang apart, hands on their weapons.

"Did you feel that?" Kellan said, his nerves on fire. The hairs on the back of his neck prickled. Were they being watched from the shadows between the trees?

Cassian nodded, his hand on the sword at his hip. "There's something there."

Kellan advanced toward the darkness, his demon-killer drawn but not yet activated. He didn't know what awaited them, he only knew that something was there.

He stepped away from the lamps of their makeshift camp, but before he could fully immerse himself in the darkness, Cassian called to him.

"Kellan, wait! Don't go out there!"

He stopped just short of the thinning light of their lamps. He swore he could feel something just beyond the darkness, but he didn't advance farther. The hairs on his arms stood on end as he squinted out into the dark, hoping to glimpse something. But there was nothing.

He activated his sword, hoping the light from the blade would reveal something, but the instant he did, the feeling of being watched vanished.

Nothing stood before him, only trees and snow.

33

CASSIAN

Bergamot Forest | 27th of Dawn Moon

They spent the rest of their watch on high alert, but nothing else happened. They were both shaken, and Cassian couldn't find words to describe why. It wasn't like they'd actually seen anything; it had only been a feeling.

And tonight, instinct was screaming at him to run.

What's got you riled up? Zal asked while Cassian stared into the darkness for several minutes. His heart beat so fast he was afraid it might explode.

Something's here, Cassian replied. *Do you know what it is?*

Zal was quiet for a moment, but he knew ze was still listening. He couldn't describe why or how he knew their connection was active; it was like knowing if someone was asleep without being able to see their face. You could tell by the way they breathed or the way they stayed still. And right now, he could sense Zal was still there, thinking.

It's not something I am familiar with, but it's hard to tell just based on your perception, ze finally said. *If I was physically there, I might be able to tell you. But you don't know what it is, which makes it much harder for me to figure out.*

Cassian swore out loud, the grip on his sword tightening. But there wasn't a damn thing he could do. The presence was fading by the time Zal chimed in again.

By the way, I see why you were so worried about your…friend while you were here, Zal said, a hint of a smile in zir voice. *The way you feel about him is delicious. Don't stop; I rather like it.*

Cassian promptly ended the conversation there, choosing instead to concentrate his energy on standing watch until the next shift, nervous energy buzzing in his veins.

🝆 🝆 🝆

He rose from the sleeping bag the next morning as dawn's light soaked their tent in liquid gold. Kellan stayed peacefully asleep in the gilded haze. Cassian escaped from the tent as stealthily as he could, hoping he wouldn't wake Kellan as he unzipped the door.

After closing the tent, he found Liv and Vaida huddled before the stove, cooking on the small griddle they'd brought with them. They looked rested, more so than he felt.

"You look like shit," Liv said. He wondered if she could secretly read minds.

"Last night wasn't exactly restful, Liv," he retorted, plopping into a seat next to her and crossing his arms over his chest.

Vaida's brows furrowed. "Tell me again what happened? Kellan was incoherent last night when I tried asking."

He sighed, slumping forward to rest his forearms on his thighs. "We felt…something sinister. But there was nothing there. I'm sorry I can't be more specific, there's just no good way to describe it."

Vaida didn't look any less concerned after his explanation. "That's about what Kellan told me too. I honestly just thought he was exhausted."

Liv coughed. "Did your, uh…pact say anything about it?"

Cassian shook his head. "No, Zal didn't know what it was. But ze said it was probably because I didn't understand it, so ze couldn't either."

"How in the world does that work?" Vaida asked.

Cassian shrugged. "I couldn't tell you the specifics, but Zal can connect with me and experience what I do, but my understanding limits the scope. So even if ze knew what it was, since I don't, ze can't know either."

Vaida nodded her understanding, but Liv seemed confused. She didn't pry further, however, turning back to watch Vaida mix their breakfast in a bowl with water.

"Did anything happen for you last night?" Cassian asked after a moment of silence.

Liv shook her head. "Nothing. Perfectly quiet and calm. Maybe we should take the early shift tonight and see if we can't encounter whatever this strange feeling is."

Kellan saved him from having to reply. His hair was still tousled from sleep, his clothing not quite straightened out. He looked like he'd rolled out of his sleeping bag and walked over half asleep.

Vaida didn't even look up. "Morning. How'd you sleep?"

Kellan made a noise that was somewhere between a grunt and a groan, and Vaida chuckled before scooping a plateful of whatever she'd made and handing it to him.

"Eat, you're annoying when you're groggy."

She plated the rest of the breakfast for Liv, Cassian, and herself, and silence fell over their small camp as they ate.

The next leg of their journey was uneventful; they followed Vaida through trees for what must have been miles, the scenery never changing. The hemlock trees stayed gargantuan and evergreen, the occasional clump of snow dropping from great heights as their party passed by.

They saw no wildlife, save for birds flying high above their heads. Cassian couldn't ignore how his skin crawled the farther in they traveled, and wondered if it had anything to do with what they'd seen the night before. In fact, he was sure of it.

Kellan chatted about demons he'd fought as they continued deeper. Cassian listened with interest and then with guilt as he considered the life Kellan had to lead once he'd disappeared. He hadn't asked what Kellan had been through.

He'd been too caught up in his own problems to consider Kellan's.

Cassian's breath came out in soft puffs as he steeled himself to ask. "How…how did you get your tattoos off?"

Vaida flinched, but softened soon after. Kellan didn't reply, instead turning to Vaida for confirmation. She nodded.

"I figured out how to remove them. It took…many years of hard work, but it paid off, in the end," she said after taking a deep breath.

Cassian didn't press further, but Liv didn't seem to have the same idea. "But they must have known you did it, right?"

Kellan frowned. "They know."

"So why aren't you being pursued?" Liv asked.

Both Vaida and Kellan came to a stop, Liv nearly running into a tree as she stared at them.

"Did I hit a nerve or something?" she asked quietly.

Vaida breathed deeply, obviously struggling with what to say next. "It's okay. Rosalie already knew, and we aren't even sure if we're supposed to say anything… But I guess if Selwyn knew…"

Cassian sucked in a breath at the mention of her name. "Selwyn helped you?"

Kellan nodded. "We couldn't have escaped Spiral City without her."

Vaida turned around, looking at the surrounding forest and then at Cassian. She huffed. "This is as good of a place as any to stop for the evening. We'll tell you more after we set up camp."

They fell silent as they set up, each tasked with their own individual duty to get things settled. When they'd finished, Vaida fished out a pot and began cutting vegetables for dinner. Cassian could feel the tension emanating off her, like something worse than just their escape was impending. What had happened to them?

How else had Kellan suffered while Cassian had been gone?

When the pot was bubbling, Vaida faced Liv and Cassian in the fading afternoon, the tendrils of golden light illuminating her dark hair through the trees. Liv leaned forward, her elbows resting on her knees as she waited for Vaida to speak.

Kellan sat with Vaida, his lips a tight line. His entire body was tense. There was definitely more to the story than their escape.

Vaida breathed in deeply, then looked to Kellan. "Everything?"

He stared back for a moment as if he was contemplating something. "Let me tell that part, at least."

She nodded, then fell silent, letting Kellan speak first.

"Vaida discovered how to break the prison marks. In the grand scheme of things, it was pretty simple. But we needed two parts— the spell to unseal, which she already knew, and the passcode to unlock it, which we didn't have."

He breathed again, as if he was steadying himself. Cassian resisted the desire to move next to Kellan, knowing interrupting him now wouldn't do them any good.

"We made a plan to break into the commissioner's office for the codes. It went…" He trailed off, looking to Vaida for support.

She reached over to place a hand on his arm. The touch seemed to steady him.

"It went worse than we'd expected, but we got what we were looking for," Vaida finished for him.

Liv took advantage of the silence. "So someone caught you?"

Kellan smiled weakly. "Not just someone. The commissioner did."

He couldn't control his noise of shock. It seemed Liv was having trouble containing herself too.

Kellan continued. "But he let me go."

Liv looked like she was about to burst. "He *let you go?* Did I seriously just hear that correctly? What in the hells do you mean he just let you go? Isn't he the leader of the Legion? Seems like breaking into his office to steal passcodes that keep you enslaved to their organization isn't exactly something he'd just overlook."

Vaida threw her a withering stare, and Liv snapped her mouth shut.

"This is…" Kellan looked lost for words. "Honestly, it's really weird and surreal to talk about. Vaida's the only one who knows, but I trust you, and if anyone should know, it's you."

Liv finally stayed silent, waiting for him to continue. Kellan's shoulders softened slightly at the silence.

"The commissioner revealed something about himself to me. He's…he's my uncle."

"He's *what?*" Liv nearly shrieked as she stood abruptly from her seat, sending a flock of birds flying away from their camp.

"Liv!" Vaida scolded her. "Keep your voice down, for fuck's sake!"

Liv had the decency to look sheepish, then sat back down. Cassian couldn't blame her—he'd wanted to spring out of his seat at the revelation as well.

Kellan was related to the commissioner? Then who was Kellan's father? He recalled the times they'd discussed Kellan's family and couldn't remember much about what Kellan knew of his own father. Or who his father might have been.

"That's not all," Kellan continued. "He told me about my dad, too. He was apparently a member of the Phantom Flame. His name was Vaeril."

At the name, Liv's mouth dropped open. "No way," she said, her voice soft and breathy. "Vaeril, The Red Hunter, was your father? But he never had children. How?"

Kellan looked up from his hands and stared at Liv. "You knew my father?"

She nodded slowly. "I was only a child when I met him, but he was legendary within the resistance. Unfortunately, he died after I'd only met him once. I…we all looked up to him."

Kellan lowered his gaze back to his hands, and Cassian felt a pang in his chest at the expression on his face. He couldn't imagine how he must be feeling—to know someone you'd just met knew your own family better than you. It had to hurt.

He'd been silent through the entire exchange. It wasn't his place to ask these questions. He'd been with the resistance for barely four months, he never knew about Vaeril, and he'd lost the right to ask

Kellan about his life when he'd been so focused on his own pain he hadn't bothered to notice Kellan's.

Cassian shoved the despair crawling up this throat back down, determined not to let his own emotions show. Not now.

But his curiosity got the better of him. "Liv, can you tell us more about Vaeril?" He looked to Kellan, hoping for some sort of permission to continue with this line of questioning.

Kellan raised his head, a pleading sort of look in his eyes. He wanted to know more about his father then, too.

Liv sighed, then nodded. "I'll tell you what stories I've heard of him. I can't guarantee they're true, but I'll do my best."

Kellan leaned in as Liv began.

"Vaeril Gildove was an invaluable member of the Phantom Flame. He was one of Rosalie's mother's best operatives and was probably the biggest reason we exist as we do today." She breathed in deeply, continuing on. "They tasked him with infiltrating the White Court; the Delacours had suspicions about their involvement with human trafficking, and they wanted a man on the inside to help take them down. If anyone was going to do it, it was Vaeril. He agreed.

"For years, he worked as an aide for one of the White Court reps for Rivenstorm, Belleth Lancaster. Vaeril was well liked and respected within the court, and no one suspected him of being a member of the resistance, especially not Belleth."

Cassian shifted in his seat. He'd never heard this story—he wondered why. Maybe the outcome was a sore spot within the resistance? Did Kellan's father betray them?

Liv continued. "But what Vaeril uncovered was something far worse than just human trafficking. He discovered that several of the White Court members had demonic pacts and were actively using their powers to do unspeakable things."

His body went ice cold. Members of the government were in pacts? What did that mean? Were they still? He couldn't breathe.

"Vaeril couldn't stand it—he ended up assassinating the

members of the court with pacts, only to discover Belleth was one of them. He couldn't bring himself to kill her, not after they'd formed a friendship. So they fought, and they ended each other's lives."

Kellan's mouth hung open. "Is that"—he swallowed before continuing—"is that why they called him the Red Hunter?"

Liv nodded. "I don't know when he met your mom during all that or when they had time to conceive you. But that's all I know of Vaeril."

The silence was deafening. It seemed even the trees had gone silent during Liv's story. As they'd listened, the sky had grown pitch black, the shadows between the trees lengthening and reaching their dark tendrils out toward their lamps.

Cassian felt the back of his neck prickle, but he couldn't tell if it was from Liv's story or if the presence from last night was back. He turned to face the darkness behind them and saw nothing.

Kellan wilted, like he'd been running on sheer willpower through the story. Now that it was over, all the strength he'd had keeping him up left him. Vaida looked concerned, her eyebrow twitching as she tapped Kellan's arm and murmured in his ear.

He nodded, and Vaida looked at Cassian. "We'll take the first watch. Help him to the tent?"

Cassian stood, not needing a second invitation. He took Kellan by the shoulders and led him to their tent, the prickle never fading even as he closed his eyes to sleep.

34

BECK

Rivenstorm | 27th of Dawn Moon

Heads turned as Brisea swept through the evening crowd at the Rosestone, all except Reaper's. He didn't need or want to watch her walk haughtily toward him. He could hear her, anyway. Her gilded heels clicked on the stone floor ominously.

When she finally sat across from him, he was staring up at the ceiling. She flicked her hair over her shoulder, and the movement caught his eye. Reaper dragged his gaze to her, a frown creasing his forehead.

Brisea said nothing. She only laid a silver nodule on their table and pressed the top with a golden fingernail. The telltale hum of the magical barrier assailed his ears.

He knew she was waiting for him to start. Their last meeting had gone poorly, and he wasn't interested in earning more of her vitriol tonight.

"The new recruits," he started, his throat closing as he spoke. He didn't want to tell her about Kellan. He didn't want her to know about him. But it was a stupid wish, the desire to keep him from her. She already knew.

She noticed his brief pause, her eyes narrowing. "Go on. I'm waiting."

He nodded curtly. "They're already gone."

She frowned. "What do you mean they're *gone?*" Her voice was icy.

Reaper sighed. He hadn't heard much; all he knew was that they were gone, Tigereye and Cassian with them. Rosalie hadn't revealed where she'd sent the small crew of four, and he couldn't fathom a guess.

"Rosalie sent them on a mission somewhere," he said nonchalantly. "I don't know where, but they left Rivenstorm over a week ago."

Brisea's expression turned dark. "And you didn't think to tell me before now?"

"You weren't here," he replied simply. "I can't get in contact with you."

He knew she'd hate that answer. He knew she'd be furious with him. But he didn't really care. He was uninterested in giving her any further information, but he knew he'd be in serious trouble if they found out about this from anyone but him. He'd gotten lucky that she hadn't known about whatever mission Rosalie had tasked Kellan with before, but he knew he wouldn't be so lucky again.

Brisea was fuming. Her hair was slicked back over one ear, a sharp golden earring dangling down far enough that it brushed her shoulder. She'd crossed her legs at the knees, her double slit skirt falling to the side of the chair.

Brisea took her frustration out on a passing server, holding an elegant hand up to him as he walked by. "Bring me a molten six." The server looked bewildered. Brisea snapped her fingers at him. "*Now.*"

He scurried off, and Brisea turned her gaze back to Reaper. Her expression dared him to say something, anything, to her. But he knew she'd snap if he did. His jaw clenched.

"And let me guess," she began, her voice low and dangerous, closer to a hiss than a purr. "You can't deduce where Rosalie might have sent them."

He didn't move.

She took his silence for confirmation. "Then tell me, *Reaper*, who did they send on this journey with fugitives?"

"One of Rosalie's closest operatives and friends, Tigereye," he said without hesitation. He purposefully left out Cassian's involvement.

Brisea lowered her chin. "Tigereye. Livea Auclair, yes?"

Reaper didn't let his surprise show. He hadn't gotten her name; he wondered how she'd found it out.

She continued. "And these fugitives, did you at least get their names? The Legion is incompetent, insisting there's been a clerical error of some sort, that there have been no escapees. Bullshit." She clicked her tongue.

The harried server returned with a strange blood-red drink and set it before Brisea with a small bow. She waved him off and took a long sip. The drink stained her pink lips red.

He swallowed. "Vaida Larsen," he said, slowly, "and…"

She set the drink back on the table with a thud. "And?"

He could lie. He could say he didn't know. That he hadn't gotten the other fugitive's name. If the Legion was really covering it up, then maybe Brisea *didn't* know who they were. Maybe if he didn't tell her, he could protect Kellan.

"I'm sorry," he said. This was the biggest rebellion he'd ever tried. "I didn't catch the other one's name before they left."

Brisea's eyes narrowed again. She tapped the side of her glass with her nail, the *tink tink tink* of the glass like an icepick in his head.

She knew he was lying. His gut turned over itself as she stared at him, waiting.

He said nothing.

"Disappointing," was all she said.

28TH OF DAWN MOON

The disappearances had started back up again; humans and non-humans alike had been reported missing all across the city. Beck had already sent Foxtail and Green Wasp to a different location with specific instructions to look for the infernal symbology he'd seen where Cera's friend disappeared. He'd even tried drawing a copy of the diagram from memory. It was a terrible reproduction, but it would suffice.

Now he was hanging around outside of Spider's door, twiddling his thumbs. He didn't understand his nerves. She was his team member, his friend, and it made sense for them to do this together. And yet, he was pausing.

But he knew he wanted her with him; he knew any opportunity he could take to have her with him, he would. He'd do just about anything to spend time with her.

That alone scared him to death.

Before he could decide on his own, the door swung open, revealing not Spider, but her sister, Harpy. One eyebrow cocked as her eyes met his, but the expression was soon replaced with a knowing smirk.

"Hey," she called behind her, her eyes never leaving Beck's, "you have a visitor, Le-Spider."

Beck didn't stop her—he just nodded. This was fate deciding what he could not. He wouldn't fight it. And some part of him was relieved to have the decision made for him.

Spider appeared from around a corner, techpad in hand, her hair down and unbound. It looked silky and shiny, jet black even under the soft sunlight filtering through the window behind her. Her eyebrow raised in a question, mirroring the expression her twin made when the door first opened.

"Reaper? What are you doing here?" she asked, shutting off the techpad and pocketing it.

He shifted, looking at Harpy with an expression he hoped said *we need privacy*. It seemed to work, as she nodded and sidled around him and into the hallway.

"I'll leave you two to it, then," she said, winking at him for effect.

Spider shook her head, then gestured for Beck to enter. She crossed the space to shut the door behind him, her soft scent washing over him as she passed by. His jaw clenched as he forced himself to stay still while she swept around him.

"So," she began, moving to the table in the corner. It was covered in neat stacks of papers, her black leather jacket thrown over the chair carelessly. "To what do I owe this pleasure?"

His heart tumbled. "I want to check out another spot of interest, down by the docks."

She made a non-committal noise, plopping down in the chair and crossing a leg over at the knee. "What about Fox? Or Wasp?"

Beck shrugged. "You're the first person I thought of." Lies. She was the only person he thought of. "And I already sent them to another site, anyway."

That got him a slightly exasperated look. "An honor to be the first on your mind, I guess?"

"You're always the first on my mind, Spider."

Her expression didn't change, but he swore he saw her stop for a moment, her breath catch. "Sure, Reaper. I'll come. Give me some time to get ready?"

He nodded, and she turned to the stack of papers on the table, a silent dismissal. He turned toward the door, obeying the command.

🜂   🜂   🜂

They were walking through Harborside, the sound of the sea close enough it seemed like they were walking directly beside it. He'd never gotten used to being this close to the ocean, not after spending so much of his life landlocked. Kettleguard was on the Lanaheim River, and while that had been a nice change, it was nothing compared to the vastness of the ocean.

He still remembered the first time he'd seen it. He'd been in Rivenstorm for a single day, and Brisea had already set him up with a contact to get him close to Rosalie. Their meeting had been on the docks, and although he disliked Brisea from the very beginning, he had to hand it to her, she'd chosen well.

The goosebumps flowed up his arms as he remembered watching the waves crash on the seawall separating the harborside district from the Cerulean Sea. Something about the vast unknown of the ocean, this gigantic watery mystery slamming itself upon something they'd built, made him feel small and inconsequential. But not in a bad way. In an immense, cosmic sort of way.

Just the sound was bringing him back to that time, and he didn't notice he'd stopped walking until he felt a tug on his jacket sleeve.

Spider was staring at him, the dimple on her cheek prevalent as she frowned at him. "Where did you go?"

"Sorry," he replied. "I was just thinking about the first time I saw the sea."

He'd never seen an expression like the one she was making now. A mixture of confusion and, dare he think it, joy? The corners of her lips were turned up slightly, her mouth ajar as she stared. Her eyes glittered in the midwinter sun.

"I guess," she started, then paused. "I guess I never realized how incredible the sea is if you haven't grown up with it."

Beck nodded. "I was raised in Kazuta. I'd never seen the ocean until a few years ago."

Spider's eyes turned downward. "I've lived in Rivenstorm all my life. I can't imagine not knowing what the sea is like until I was an adult." She paused again, chewing her lip, looking like she wanted to ask something.

He didn't speak. He waited for her to continue, to finish her thought.

"What was it like?" she finally said, her voice softer than he'd ever heard it. "To see the ocean for the first time?"

He laughed softly, barely a release of breath. She frowned, but he spoke before she could take offense.

"It's hard to describe, if I'm being honest," he began, and her face softened once more. "I was staring into something that could swallow me whole, and I wouldn't leave a trace on it. It made me feel so inconsequential. But I didn't find it scary or overwhelming. It was...I don't know, somehow comforting?"

Her lips had parted slightly while she listened, her eyes never leaving his. She nodded when he finished, like she'd completely understood him through his halting speech.

"I know how you feel," she said, breaking their eye contact to turn toward the sea. "The ocean is home for me. It makes me feel small, like I'm nothing but a drop in this vast, unfathomable thing. But I kind of like that feeling—it means I'm part of something bigger than myself."

He turned his face toward the sea as well, barely visible through the brightly colored buildings along their walk. He understood something about her now, something important. He could feel the realization sinking in, settling against the image of her that existed in his mind, the one he added to every single time he talked to her.

"Is that why you joined the Phantom Flame? To be part of something big?"

She smiled vaguely. "Part of it, yes. Maybe I'll tell you the other reason someday."

"I hope you trust me enough to tell me someday, too."

Their walk continued in silence, but not an uncomfortable one. It was as if they'd broken down a wall, gotten over some invisible hump they'd never been able to breach before. Beck could feel it then—the surrender of himself to a new emotion he'd never felt before.

It made his heart feel like it had doubled in size, tipping him over a precipice of a cliff he'd never seen coming. It was too big for his chest, pulling him consistently and irrevocably toward her.

She was the moon, and he was her blanket of stars.

Just another block and they'd be at the location where yet another girl was last seen. Apparently, there was a spot along the cliffs that was often used for parties. Their latest victim, a human girl, had been last seen there a few nights ago.

Her friends lost sight of her once, and then she was gone, like mist in the early morning. Vanished without a trace.

But Beck remembered what he'd seen at the place where they'd found Cera. He kept his eyes sharp as they approached, watching for anything out of place. Weeds grew through the cracked pavement, and broken bits of stone crunched under their feet as they approached.

The spot itself was nondescript; the alley that led toward it was tight between a red building with peeling paint and a brick building whose mortar crumbled into the street. It was tiered, three levels of smooth, open cobblestone that looked out over the sea. The lowest tier would get wet during high tide and days where the waves were larger than usual.

It wouldn't be surprising if she'd simply slipped on slick cobblestone and fallen over the edge into the water. It wouldn't even be the first time it had happened in a place like this. Rivenstorm was full of treacherous cliff sides like this one. Its rocky shores weren't for the soft-footed. It was easy to slip, to fall, to lose your footing and never return.

But the locals had learned what was safe and what wasn't, and their missing girl was no exception. Her friends had practically started a riot when the Red Guard had suggested she'd simply gone over.

So they would investigate. They'd search every nook and cranny and hope something out of the ordinary turned up.

"Reaper?" Spider's voice was small, timid. He'd never heard her sound like that before. "I don't like this. Are you sure we're in the right spot? It feels…*wrong* here. Like the air is sour."

He thought he had decent intuition and could sense when something felt off accurately. But he felt nothing now. In fact, something about being here felt like he'd gone back to Kettleguard. He wasn't sure why, though. Rivenstorm was nothing like Kettleguard.

"I don't feel anything, but stay close to me, just in case," he said, stepping toward her.

Spider nodded, sliding in next to him and resting a hand on a circular blade she carried at her hip.

His head swiveled, looking for that *thing* that felt so off. The sea was calm today, the waves lapping against the rocky shoreline quiet enough that he could still hear other things. A stray cat leaping from one roof to the next; shutters creaking in the gentle breeze.

Then, a sound. It was small, inconsequential. He might have ignored it if he hadn't been on alert. But it was enough to have him draw his sword and face the alley.

From the shadows emerged a man. His hair was long and black and hung in tangled, greasy strands around his rugged face. He was dressed in what looked like a knockoff version of the Red Guard's combat suits, but his was plated in a dark silver material at the hips, shoulders, chest, and thighs. A sword was strapped across his back and a whip was coiled at his hip.

But the most unnerving part of this man was the pulsing black veins that had crawled up his face, stopping just below his eyes.

Was this the man Cera had seen that night? The veins were distinctive; he could understand why she thought she'd hallucinated. He looked…unreal.

"I see a little mouse has come sniffing." His voice was sharp and rough, like a knife dragged across stone. "Well, you know what they say about vermin."

And with a gleeful chuckle, the man held his hands out at his sides, his wild eyes daring Beck to rise to the challenge.

"Come, little mouse. It's time for you to die."

35

KELLAN

Bergamot Forest | 28th of Dawn Moon

The last leg of their journey faced them today. According to Vaida's calculations, they'd hit the temple in the late afternoon. They could spend the night if needed.

Kellan couldn't sleep; after Cassian had escorted him back to their tent, he'd tossed and turned until Vaida changed shifts with them. Although their watch last night had been uneventful, Kellan couldn't shake the feeling he was being observed from deep within the darkness.

Now it was midmorning, and they'd already trekked through a dense portion of the forest. He'd been more clumsy than usual, tripping on roots and underbrush so often that Cassian had practically glued himself to his side.

It wasn't that he minded the company, but something about his attentiveness knotted Kellan's stomach. He'd known Cassian was following him that entire day back in Alderburn. But he'd let him do it anyway, hadn't felt the need to scold him until he'd gotten bored and decided to tease Cassian. But here, beneath the trees, with something stalking them, Kellan wished it was like that day again. That the only thing following them this time was Cassian.

He said nothing to Cassian, allowing the closeness. And it was most definitely *not* because he found it more comforting to think of that day instead of whatever was stalking them through the forest.

Vaida walked ahead, holding her techpad out with a holographic compass and occasionally consulting the maps in her other hand. Liv was following along, glancing at the surrounding trees, her eyes alert.

Vaida suddenly stopped, checking the map once more before glancing again in front of their party. Liv shot her a concerned glance.

"Everything okay, V?" Liv asked.

Vaida said nothing, only stared ahead, her eyes narrowing. Kellan tried looking in the same direction, but he saw nothing of interest, just more trees.

"Vaida?" he said, stepping forward to rest a hand on her shoulder.

She started, her shoulders tensing up to her ears. "What?"

"You were staring off into the distance," Kellan began. "We thought something was wrong."

Vaida shivered, but shook her head. "No, nothing's wrong. I think we're close to the last landmark, though."

Liv peered around Vaida's shoulder at her directions. "Naktchul Pass? Sounds ominous."

Kellan shrugged. "Well, we shouldn't stop now, we're getting close."

Liv nodded, re-shouldering her pack. Cassian followed her toward the gap between the trees. Kellan stayed while Vaida stared after them, her face bloodless.

"Are you sure you're okay, V?" he asked, brows pinching.

She shook her head, then continued forward. "I said I was fine. Let's go."

He reluctantly followed her, the deep purple of foreboding growing in his head.

They passed through where Liv and Cassian had already disappeared, and when the cover of tree branches was finally gone, Kellan couldn't hold back a gasp.

They were at the base of a mountain long ago split into two.

The pass between them was narrow, just barely wide enough to fit two people walking side by side or one person comfortably. They lost the peaks in the clouds far above their heads, the jagged fissure between them speckled with craggy outcroppings and precariously balanced stones. One wrong move and they would be crushed by falling rocks.

But the worst part of it all was the air; Kellan expected it to be clear and refreshing out here by the mountains, but it was anything but. It was dark, ominous, and nearly suffocating. The unnatural darkness of the path screamed danger, but he couldn't bring himself to tear his eyes away.

"What…is this place?" Liv breathed, her eyes wide as she stared up into the sky at the peaks they could not see.

"Naktchul Pass," Vaida responded grimly. "And we must go through."

"There isn't any way around?" Kellan asked, silently begging the hairs on his neck and arms to stand down.

Vaida shook her head. "No. The base of this mountain stretches for days either way, and attempting to climb them would be deadly. The map specifically says the easiest and safest way is through the pass."

Cassian made a strangled noise. "*Safest?* What kind of monsters were these humans? This is a death trap, we all know it."

Vaida shivered. "I doubt this pass was as dangerous when this map was made. But we have no choice."

Cassian shuddered, but nodded.

Liv leaned against the base of the mountain and observed their group with a scrutinizing eye. "I'll take the front. Cassian can take the back. Kellan, you go before him. V, you're behind me to guide us through if we need it."

Kellan wanted to protest, but found he couldn't come up with a reason. It was strange being commanded by someone he barely knew, but Liv was confident and had a good head on her shoulders. Her plan was solid.

They nodded in agreement, then lined themselves up in front of the pass. Kellan breathed in deeply, the scent of the forest mingling with the scent of death in his nose. A shiver he couldn't stop ran up his spine.

A hand descended on his shoulder—Cassian's. "I've got your back."

Warmth blossomed in his chest, but his shoulder was cold where Cassian's hand rested, like his hand was made of ice.

Liv stepped into the darkness of the pass without hesitation, her head held high.

Vaida followed, her fingers clutching the compass tightly.

Then it was Kellan's turn. As he stepped into the blackness of the twin peaks, a cold like nothing he'd ever felt before enveloped him.

He sensed Cassian step in after him, and the tightness in his chest eased a little.

Then the shrieking began.

🜄 🜄 🜄

They ran. They didn't stay silent; whatever was screaming already knew they were there.

Kellan's heart raced, not just from the physical exertion, but from genuine, amber-colored fear. Whatever made that noise sent panic directly into his core, like a rabbit fleeing from a fox. It was like an old enemy, an ancient one, one that his body instinctively knew would be his ruin.

"Keep going, we can outrun it!" Liv shouted back at them.

No one responded. They bowed their heads and continued on.

But Liv's shout knocked something loose—those massive, precarious rocks they'd seen toppled off their ledges, raining small stones down on their heads as a precursor for what was to come.

"Shit, shit! Kellan, run faster!" Cassian's panicked voice behind him sent his legs into overdrive.

But it wasn't him slowing them down. Vaida wasn't used to this sort of physical labor. She was doing her best, but her strength was flagging. Her breaths were labored as she ran, her face flushed a dark rose.

"Vaida, take my hand," he said, sidling up next to her.

As she reached, a darker shadow passed over their heads. Before he could react, he felt a cold wind push him and Vaida forward as a boulder dropped exactly where they'd been standing.

Kellan looked back, trying to see where Cassian had ended up, but he was nowhere to be found.

Fear gripped his heart as he stopped dead in his tracks. Vaida stopped several steps after him, her breathing still heavy.

"Kellan, let's *go*," she urged before realizing Cassian wasn't with them. "*Shit.*" The techpad creaked in her grip.

"We can't leave him," Kellan said, and Vaida ground her teeth together.

Liv came running back to them, her face pale. "What happened?"

"Cassian pushed us out of the way, but I can't see him," Kellan cried, trying not to scream in the cavern.

The screams that chased them drew nearer, and his legs trembled. Cassian was separated from them, and they were being slowly hunted. His panic was blood red now, seeping through his pores and shaking his limbs. He couldn't think straight.

"We can't wait here," Liv said through gritted teeth. "He's resourceful; he'll figure out a way through."

"But what if he's hurt?" Kellan countered.

The screams from the pass echoed nearer, and Vaida grabbed both Liv and Kellan's hands, her grip tight from adrenaline and fear.

She tugged them along. "Liv is right," she said, pulling them farther out of the pass, "he's got magic and his pact. We will die much more easily than him."

As if they were listening, the screams came again, this time near enough to rattle Kellan's ears. He didn't *want* to leave Cassian behind—he'd saved them, had pushed him and Vaida out of the way. How could they just leave him as thanks for that?

They ran hard, their footsteps echoing loudly off the steep cavern walls and tormenting Kellan as they continued on without Cassian. Each time his foot met the ground, it was like an electric shock ran through his body, reminding him he was a coward, a failure.

It was the basement of Northwind all over again. Kellan was powerless to stop Cassian being taken from him. But there was nothing he could do now; they needed to get away from whatever was chasing them before they ended up dead.

His body betrayed him; it ran, it swerved, it kept Vaida close. Even when his heart screamed to turn back, his feet carried him forward.

Finally bursting into the sunlight at the opposite end of the cavern, Kellan's heart caught up with his body. He collapsed on the ground, Vaida dropping to her knees beside him.

"We," he tried, panting hard enough to catch the rest of the words in his throat. Liv was drinking deeply from a bottle. At his feeble attempt at speech, she handed it to him wordlessly.

He drank, the water so cold it hurt to swallow.

Liv spoke while he drank. "We can't go back for him. But we can wait."

Vaida nodded. "We wait here until nightfall. He's got more than half the day to catch up."

"Besides, I've seen him do some baffling shit with that pact magic of his," Liv said quickly, obviously trying to comfort Kellan.

But her platitudes meant little to him. His panic was orange and hot, stabbing behind his eyes. He'd seen none of what Cassian was capable of with his new magic. He didn't know how Cassian would get out of there or what he was even facing.

What if his magic did nothing to whatever was pursuing them? What if the rock had crushed him? What if the rock *hadn't* crushed him and he was instead begging for help that would never come?

But Kellan didn't know how to voice any of those fears. He didn't know how to put that urgency into words that wouldn't make him sound like he was more afraid for Cassian's life than his own.

Which he supposed he *was*.

"Kellan," Vaida said, placing a hand on his shoulder. She was still breathing heavily, her cheeks flushed. "Trust Cassian. I know it's hard, but you have to try."

Kellan nodded, setting his pack on the ground. His anxieties exploded in his mind like little fireworks, popping against the inside of his skull each time he thought of a new one. But Vaida was right—he had to trust Cassian.

He never took his eyes from the pass, and he prayed.

To whom, he didn't know.

36

CASSIAN

Bergamot Forest | 28th of Dawn Moon

Just melt the rock or blow it to pieces, Zal said. *It's perfectly within your capabilities.*

I know that, Cassian shot back. *But I want to see whatever this thing is. Its presence is like what we felt two nights ago.*

He could feel Zal's exasperation through their pact, but he ignored it, turning away from the massive boulder to face the pass from which they'd come. The screaming had only grown louder, its echoes sending other rocks tumbling down from the skies—none as large as the boulder before him, luckily.

He cracked his knuckles in anticipation, waiting for whatever this was to finally show its face.

He had two options once that happened. First, he needed to determine how powerful this creature might be. If he could manage a fight, he'd stand his ground. After all, they needed to come back this way, and eliminating the threat of the pass would make their return journey much easier.

His second option was to flee. He would have mere seconds to judge if he needed to escape or not, so he needed to be careful about controlling how much power he grabbed. Cassian had some in his grasp already, but he needed more. He reached for the well of magic and threaded it through what he imagined to be a small hole, making the magic more manageable to direct.

The shrieks grew closer by the second, but no matter where he turned his attention, he couldn't see a thing. Then the surrounding air grew cold—as cold as Stygia. His fingertips lost feeling almost instantly, and he felt his entire body tense at the sudden shock of temperature.

A shadow appeared in front of him, a creature made of wisps of black smoke. Its eyes glowed red, set deep into a face that looked like a skull made of shadows. Its body was opaque, but it writhed and swirled like a storm at sea. It had no legs, just a shapeless tatter that drifted in the wind.

It wasn't a demon. He didn't know how he knew that, but instincts told him this was something entirely different. Something he'd never encountered before.

But those same instincts that begged him to run instead made him want to cry at the sight of the creature. As if he somehow knew what it was, what it once had been. A deep urge within him cried out, begging him to do something, *anything,* to help this shadow before him.

Why are you feeling sorry for the thing? Zal said. *It's not your friend.*

Cassian ignored zem. The shadow screeched, reaching a clawed hand toward him. He unsheathed his sword, praying that although it appeared incorporeal, the shadow could be hurt.

Cassian slashed, cutting through the shadows that formed the creature's wrist. It writhed as the shadows dissipated, screaming in a high-pitched tone that threatened to burst his eardrums.

It didn't appear injured, although he couldn't really tell what "injured" looked like for a creature such as this.

He readied his sword again, a tendril of magic wrapping itself around the blade. It was a trick he'd learned while fighting the demonic visitors they'd had over the last four months. He didn't need a demon-killer sword like the one Kellan had, he simply needed to imbue his sword with a touch of his own magic. He assumed because his magic was already demonic, it made his makeshift demon-killer just as effective as the real ones.

But this wasn't a demon.

He lunged, his sword cutting a perfect arc toward the creature. It seemed to shrink away from his blade, rippling away from it like water. It didn't scream this time, and Cassian couldn't tell if his attack had been avoided or if it didn't hurt the creature at all.

They danced around each other for several moments, Cassian laser-focused on the creature's one remaining claw. The one he'd cut off hadn't regenerated, but it didn't seem as if the creature was in any sort of pain.

He also had yet to land another hit like the first one. It seemed as if only his first attack had done anything to the creature. It wasn't showing any signs of fatigue or distress, and no matter how often his sword brushed through its body, it never seemed to cut.

He was severely outmatched and without a good strategy in place. It was time to retreat.

The tendril of magic he'd been steadily feeding was still going strong, and he redirected it from his sword to his free hand. He circled around the creature to put the boulder at his back.

All he could hope for was that the creature wouldn't follow when he ran. But there were no guarantees.

He flung the magic behind him, the intent to destroy weaved into every particle that escaped him. The flash of purple was bright, brilliant enough to cause the creature to scream and melt into the shadows cast by his magic.

The rock behind him disintegrated into dust, unable to bear the pressure of his magical attack. He didn't wait to see what the screaming shadow would do—he fled. As fast as he could run.

The screeches continued, but as he ran, they faded. It seemed they would not pursue him today. Relief swept through him, making him stumble. But he didn't fall. He continued running through the pass, the darkness fading as he continued onward.

Sunlight met his eyes as he stumbled out of the pass at last. His hair was damp with sweat, and when he finally stopped to gasp for breath, it cooled against his head. It was like someone had placed a crown of ice upon it.

Kellan appeared before him, concern written all over his face. "What happened? Are you all right?" His eyes searched Cassian's body.

Cassian shook his head, holding out a hand to stop Kellan from getting any closer. "I'm fine. But I saw whatever was chasing us in the pass. I fought it."

Vaida stood from where she'd been sitting on her pack, her face still flushed but her breathing even. Curiosity made her eyes sparkle.

"And?" she prompted.

"And," he said, taking a deep breath, "I don't know what the damn thing was. It was like a living shadow. Nothing I did to it even seemed to hurt it."

Vaida cocked her head. "A living shadow?"

Liv came to join them, her pack already up and over her shoulders. "How about we don't stand around talking about this, in case those 'living shadows' decide to chase us out here too?"

Kellan nodded his agreement, turning back to face Cassian once more with concern. "Are you okay to keep going?"

Cassian nodded, giving him what he hoped was a reassuring smile. It seemed to placate Kellan, and he turned back toward Liv, nodding once.

They moved out, but Cassian kept turning back to check that his shadow still moved with him. The creeping sensation that someone was watching them never faded.

🔥 🔥 🔥

Hym's temple wasn't what he'd expected, yet, it belonged. It was cut into a crevice and looked as if someone had carved it from the mountain itself.

The trees in the clearing were thinner, cut back centuries ago when the temple was still in use. The growth that had taken over was much younger than the rest of the ancient forest. Browned vines clung to the sides of the stone temple, dead for the winter but not forever. Certain parts of the facade had crumbled and succumbed to time, but the overall structure was still intact.

 His body felt weak, strained, like it was warring with him harder than it ever had before. It pulled at him like a dog on a leash, urging him onward, inside. The need was intense, but he tamped it down. Now wasn't the time to recklessly listen to his instincts, not when they'd just told him to feel pity for the shadows in the pass.

Liv strode toward the door without hesitation, but Vaida called out to her before she could lay a hand on them. "Liv, wait. Don't just go barging into ancient buildings that haven't been visited in literal centuries. It's stupid."

Liv grinned sheepishly and stepped back. "Oops. You're right."

Vaida sighed and reached into her pack to retrieve one of her shiny spell nodules. Cassian didn't quite understand what her magic did or how it worked, but he knew her spells were more practical than the mostly offensive magic he'd been practicing.

She pressed the top of the canister, and a ring around the rim turned blue. He could sense magic expanding from it. Vaida waited, chewing her lip and watching the huge stone door with a mixture of trepidation and curiosity.

Nothing happened. They stood silently, waiting for Vaida to finish her scan. The forest seemed to watch with bated breath, too. It stayed silent, the trees perfectly still and silent.

Cassian turned to watch the pass. It was far enough away that it was difficult to see through the trees that surrounded the clearing but close enough that he'd be able to see any pursuers with plenty of warning. Nothing appeared from the pass. No screaming shadows emerged from the darkness.

Something beeped. Vaida's scan must have finished.

She nodded, holding the nodule up for the rest of them to see. The ring had turned from blue to green. "There's no magic present in the temple. That doesn't mean we can let our guard down, but mechanical traps are easier to deal with than magical ones." Vaida stuffed it back in her pocket as Liv and Kellan stepped forward to join her.

Cassian's eyes met Kellan's, and a small jolt of longing coursed through his veins. He looked beautiful in the fading sunlight, his hair lit with an orange-hued halo of fire. The longing was fierce, tugging at his skin and sending goosebumps over his scalp.

It was a different sort of desire than the one he'd felt looking at the temple. This one he knew was his own.

Delicious, Zal said in response.

You know you don't have to comment on every emotion I have, Cassian replied.

Zal's laugh was breathy. *But your emotions are so delightful, how can I not express my gratitude for giving me all these new sensations?*

Cassian didn't deign to reply. He knew feeding into Zal's moods would only make zem more insufferable. Better to ignore zem and let it drop.

Zal chuckled again but said nothing more.

37

KELLAN

The Temple of Hym | 28th of Dawn Moon

K ellan waited, arms crossed, while he watched his companions. Vaida was scanning the building itself, poking a few nubs of stone cautiously, as if they would suddenly shoot arrows at her. Liv seemed bored, kicking a small stone with her toe.

But his eyes never strayed long from Cassian.

The fear from the pass hadn't faded—his heart still felt too big for his chest, his limbs heavy now that the adrenaline had worn off. He was relieved Cassian was safe, but he was stuck on how he'd escaped.

Was Cassian really that powerful?

Back in Spiral City, the drop of magic Cassian had was just that, a drop. It was barely enough to do much more than the smallest of party tricks. But now his magic had grown to depths they couldn't fathom, and each time Cassian did something new, something powerful, Kellan couldn't help but think about the fire.

Cassian didn't know where it had come from. But it was most definitely not his own, and there'd been no sign of it since.

Kellan bit his lip, lost in thought.

Vaida stood from where she'd been observing a tile by the front door, the movement catching his eye. "No traps here, at least, but we should proceed with caution."

It took all four of them to push open the stone doors that led into the building, their tracks coated in dead plants and dirt. Inside, however, was preserved beautifully.

A plush red carpet ran from just inside the door into the darkness beyond. It broke up the monotony of gray stone that made up most of the interior, adding a splash of color into a drab world. A massive archway marked the entrance just beyond the end of the doors.

"Did we bring lights?" Kellan asked.

Vaida nodded, fetching a few flashlights from her backpack and passing them around. He glimpsed a few other metallic objects in her backpack, most likely more of her spell nodes.

They stepped beyond the archway, treading carefully in case anything was lying in wait. Nothing appeared. Their footsteps were quiet as they walked along the red carpet, flashlights swinging left and right.

Kellan's caught a line of wooden benches, their joints crumbling and rotting away. The intricate carved details on the armrests were unfamiliar to him. One depicted a man holding a lamb in his arms, the animal's coat so realistic he wondered if it would be soft if he touched it. Another showed the same man, surrounded by humans, sharing a meal.

Every bench was carved with the same hyper-realistic, loving precision. Each scene depicted was different but always featured the same man, his radiance palpable even through the carvings.

The others had separated while Kellan observed the wooden benches. Vaida was back toward the entrance once more, her light focused on a single painting hung on the wall.

"What did you find?" he asked, approaching her and adding his light to hers.

When he looked at the painting, he nearly dropped his flashlight.

There was no mistaking it. The woman in the painting was beautiful—and incredibly familiar. Her flaxen hair was swept into an updo, pearls dangled from her ears, and she wore a collar high enough to reach her hairline.

But her eyes were a striking shade of blue, with patches of white that looked almost like clouds. Eyes he recognized.

"Who—" he began.

"Queen Ameloria," Vaida breathed. "The last human monarch."

He stared, openmouthed, as he took in the queen's features. Even if they'd been transformed with time, it would be difficult not to see the resemblance between the leader of the resistance and the woman in the painting.

"Vaida, Kellan," Cassian's voice called as they continued to stare, "come look at this."

They peeled their eyes away from Rosalie's royal ancestor and followed the light of Cassian's flashlight beam down a hallway. It seemed where they'd come from had been the main worship hall, but this led somewhere else. Cassian stood at the head of stairs that descended into blackness, the beam from his flashlight swallowed by its inkiness.

"I don't want to go down there alone," he said as they approached.

Vaida shone her flashlight down the staircase, but the additional light did nothing to ease the darkness swirling below.

"We'll have to explore eventually, but let's wait for now." She turned, heading back toward the sanctum they'd come from. "Where's Liv?"

Cassian pointed his flashlight up a staircase to the left. "She went up. Said it's probably priests' accommodations."

"She shouldn't have gone alone, the idiot." She didn't wait for them to follow before she stormed up the staircase after Liv.

Cassian turned back to Kellan, the flashlight casting harsh shadows along his face.

"Let's go," he said hoarsely, jerking his chin up toward where Vaida had disappeared.

Cassian followed him silently as they ascended.

Upstairs, they found a small dining hall. Long tables sat intact even after centuries of disuse, dishes and cups still scattered along their surfaces. Silver candelabras sat at regular intervals at the tables, their candles long gone and turned to dust.

Vaida and Liv were nowhere to be found, having inevitably disappeared through one of the many doors that lined the dining hall. Unwilling to call out, Kellan shuffled his way through the hall, making a beeline for the largest door in the back. If he knew Vaida at all, she'd go for that door first.

He didn't look back to see if Cassian followed. He'd come if he wanted to.

The door opened with a loud creak, its hinges rusted from neglect. Inside, he found a small library; the walls were lined with shelves stuffed to the brim with hand-bound books and papers. It looked like a harried professor's office rather than a priest's religious study.

He found Vaida and Liv inside, hunched over a desk with more papers strewn about. Liv pointed excitedly at the documents, whispering something about ancient inventions and how this sort of historical documentation could be pivotal in modern research.

"What did you find?" he said, stepping inside the room.

Vaida turned to look at him, her face flushed and eyes glittering with excitement. "You've gotta see this, Kellan."

He obeyed her beckoning, approaching the desk on silent feet. Vaida held out a piece of paper to him, eyes glittering. He didn't understand what he was looking at at first, but the longer he stared, the more it made sense.

"Are these…robots?" he asked, hesitantly.

Vaida nodded. "Or something similar, we think."

He glanced at the paper again. The details were intricate, the measurements precise. It was incredible how advanced the calculations were. But what would something like this be doing in a temple?

"Liv," Kellan began, setting the paper back down on the desk, "why would there be invention schematics like this in…well, here?" He gestured vaguely around them.

Liv sighed. "Yet another thing they wipe from history."

Kellan said nothing, waiting for her to continue.

"You see, Hym was the humans' god. Unlike Sol and the Circle, he was the god of all things—love, the sun, power, knowledge. This sort of invention and progress would have been highly encouraged as a worshiper of Hym. In fact, most priests of Hym were also inventors, engineers, and scholars. It was simply their way of life."

"So they saw an invention like this as, what, prayer?" Cassian asked from behind Kellan, holding up what looked like a blueprint or map.

Liv nodded. "Exactly. In fact, I bet every room off this dining hall looks much the same as this one."

Cassian nodded, turning back to the blueprint. Kellan looked again at the diagram in his own hands. Kellan thought a god that encouraged progress, knowledge, and curiosity seemed worthy of reverence.

Liv collected the papers on the desk, stacking them atop each other as gently as she could. Kellan handed the robotic schematics back to her, and she accepted it with a small smile.

"It's okay, you know," she said in a small voice. "Not to know."

Kellan pursed his lips as he looked at Vaida, whose face was much the same. She looked distressed, her mouth a tight line. The wrinkle between her eyebrows deepened with each passing moment.

"V? You okay?" he asked, laying a hand on her shoulder.

She shrugged him off. "I'm fine," she replied before promptly turning on her heel and walking out into the dining room once more.

"Go," Liv said. "We'll finish up here and meet you back in the sanctum."

He nodded, then turned on his heel after Vaida.

He found her again in the sanctum, running her fingers over the wooden carvings of the man surrounded by angels, their faces smooth and blank as they worshiped him. She'd sat on the floor, her long legs crossed beneath her.

She ran a finger over the lifelike wings and let her nail scrape gently along it. Her face was unreadable, a blank mask. But he could sense it—blue sorrow poured from her in waves.

"It's impolite to stare," she said softly, her hands still on the angel's wings.

Kellan sat beside her. "Remind me to look embarrassed. What's wrong?"

"Nothing. Why would you think that?"

"Because you don't snap at me unless I've done something stupid, and that…well excuse me if I misjudge my own actions, but that didn't seem warranted."

She sighed, her hand finally dropping from the carving. She turned to him, her gray eyes flat and dull. "You're right—I'm sorry. It wasn't you."

"Do you want to talk about it?"

She shook her head, an unruly braid falling from her updo and into her face. "No, I don't."

He stood, dusting off his pants, then held a hand out to her. "Then let's keep going. We have a lot more to explore."

She nodded, but didn't reach for his hand. He waited and kept it extended to her.

He couldn't possibly know what she was feeling; Vaida might be his best friend, might have been able to read him like a book. And while he could pick up on a lot of her moods, there were rare instances where he didn't know what she could be thinking.

Right now was one of those times.

Her face was pinched. It had been like that since they'd entered the temple, a mixture between discomfort and sorrow. He could see it in the blue haze that never seemed to go away, no matter where they went in the space.

Kellan realized there was still so much he didn't know about her. The story she'd told him of Amaris scratched what he could only assume was the surface of the grand mystery that was Vaida. And now this—her strange pinched brows, her odd reaction. He didn't know what to make of it.

But he didn't care. She was still his best friend, still his lifeline. She revealed what she wanted him to know, and that was enough for him.

Finally, he felt her hand in his, and he pulled her to her feet. She gave him a small, shaky smile.

He returned it, not letting go of her hand. Whatever she needed from him, he would give. It was the least he could do for her, after all this time.

🔥 🔥 🔥

Liv and Cassian joined them soon afterward. At Liv's questioning look, Kellan shook his head.

"Shall we?" Liv said, shrugging after Kellan's silent plea. She could be reliable when needed, but he'd been worried she would ignore his direction not to disturb Vaida.

They hoisted the flashlights back up and made their way back to the dark staircase Cassian found earlier. It hadn't gotten any less ominous, and even with four flashlights, the darkness stayed oppressive.

"It's odd we haven't run into any sort of traps," Vaida mused as they stared down the stairs. "You'd think if they went through all kinds of trouble to hide these artifacts that there would be, oh, I don't know, a bit more of a hassle to get them?"

Cassian shrugged. "Maybe the trip to get here was the challenge?"

Vaida shook her head. "No, I don't think so. Remember the verse for this place?"

Kellan's neck prickled. They'd figured out the first three lines—the mountains of old, the woods, even the darkness had made an appearance. But what did it mean to be wary of those who are good?

Liv had the same train of thought. "What the hells is that

supposed to mean?"

"Maybe there are guards here?" Kellan offered.

Vaida shook her head again. "*Think,* everyone. They couldn't have guaranteed anyone would live long enough to continue protecting the artifact, nor could they guarantee the tradition would get passed down. They must have put some sort of failsafe in place—and it's not alive."

Something that wasn't alive...magic? But they'd already ruled out the possibility of magical traps. Vaida had made sure of that. Kellan's mind wandered back to the schematics they'd found earlier. Robots would certainly fit the conditions, but how?

"Vaida," he said, "you don't think they *built* those robots, do you?"

Her eyes widened. "We'd best hope not. If they did...we'd be dead in an instant."

Cassian loosened a breath, the whoosh echoing as it traveled down the dark staircase. They all stared at the impressive darkness, panic rising in Kellan's throat as he stared.

Vaida gripped his hand. "Not now. You can do this."

He nodded. "Let's go, then. We can always retreat if there is something down there."

"Right," Liv added, then took a step down.

Then she was falling, the staircase turned into a stone slide. No one could catch her as she whipped out of sight and into the inky blackness below.

38

CASSIAN

The Temple of Hym | 28th of Dawn Moon

Cassian didn't hesitate—he threw himself down the slide after Liv. Kellan and Vaida's shouts followed him down into the darkness, their fear palpable. But he knew he would have done the same for either of them.

He could hear Liv yell as she reached the bottom, her body hitting the end of wherever the slide led.

"Liv, move!" he shouted down the tunnel, hoping he wouldn't run into her when he reached the bottom.

They weren't so lucky. As soon as the words left his lips, he flew out the end of the slide. Suspended in the air for a few breathless moments, he came to land directly on top of her with a heavy thud.

"Get *off*," she grumbled, breathless from the fall and Cassian's graceless entrance.

He scrambled off as quickly as he could, murmuring apologies the whole time. He offered a hand to Liv, which she gratefully took. Once they'd both stood, Cassian did a sweep of the well-lit room they'd landed in.

It appeared as if it had once been a Room of Reflection. A crumbling stone fountain stood as the central focal point. Four curved stone benches sat around it, the legs filigreed and carved to look as if vines wrapped around their bases.

Torches lit the room at regular intervals, their light a steady, unwavering yellow flame. What they were made of was beyond Cassian. They weren't real flames, but they didn't give off the same hum of energy that electricity did, either. Something about them felt almost…alive.

Between the torches were small alcoves encased in shadow, but he could just barely discern a single faceless statue in each one. The statues wore hooded cloaks and held imposing stone swords, their tips pointed downward.

But the crowning feature was the statue triple the size of the rest across the room from where Cassian and Liv stood. It was gilded, its face lovingly and intricately carved to depict a bearded man with eyes closed and face tilted down. He wore gold and white armor that glittered in the low light.

And in his hands he held a colossal sword. It was gold, the guard an intricately carved helix of twisting metal that covered both hands.

"Do you think that's…" Liv began, staring at the sword.

Cassian cautiously crept toward the statue, eyes fixed on the sword in its hands. "It must be." He didn't get too close, mindful of what Kellan said moments ago.

What if these weren't just statues?

He took another step forward, his guarded footsteps so soft on the stone floor he doubted anyone could have heard them. But as soon as his foot landed, the floor gave way beneath him, and a loud crack resounded through the space.

Behind him, several statues in the alcoves moved. Their swords scraped against the stone floor, the screech sending chills up his spine. They'd been so cautious, so careful to watch for traps. And the moment he'd stopped paying attention…

Cassian swore as he pulled his sword from its sheath.

Behind him, a yelp came, then a dull thud as Kellan shot out of the tunnel and onto the floor. It took him a moment to reorient himself, but he noticed the statues as they moved from their alcoves.

"Uh, guys?" he said, standing and reaching for the sword at his hip. "What are those?"

"'Protected by those whose souls are good,'" Liv recited. "They're protecting the Sword!"

Kellan swore colorfully, pulling his own sword to join them.

The statues wasted no time after Kellan appeared, their slow progress turning to lightning speed. Cassian counted four of them as they stepped from their shadows into the light.

They were terrifying—faceless, featureless, draped in stone carved to look like silk robes. While their stone swords wouldn't cut them, they were heavy and thick enough to break bones.

But the worst part was the wings. He hadn't noticed them when they were in their alcoves, but each statue barreling toward them had a pair of feathery stone wings.

A statue closed in on Liv, who raised her sword to block its attack. She grunted under the strain, her knees buckling the moment their weapons made contact. They were strong. Cassian swore.

Another tried to take Kellan by surprise, but he was too fast for its swing, ducking beneath it and swiping at its back. Although Kellan was a skilled swordsman, Cassian could tell even before the weapon made contact that it wouldn't do much damage. It clanged against the stone and emitted a terrible screech as it scraped along the angel's back.

"My sword is useless," he shouted as he dodged another bludgeoning attack.

Cassian bit his lip as the other two angels made their way toward him, brandishing their swords before them menacingly. He knew his own sword wouldn't do anything; Kellan's unsuccessful attack had proven that much.

Behind him, another thump let him know Vaida had finally joined them. He threw his other hand behind him, warning her to stay away. He heard her suck in a sharp breath at their predicament.

Magic was his only option, it seemed. If these statues were made of stone, he could do to them what he'd done with the rock in the pass. But he needed time, a moment to gather enough of his power to hurl it at the statues.

Luckily, Liv and Kellan were both fast, their speed their only advantage over the angels swinging mercilessly at them. They ducked and weaved and bobbed, keeping just barely ahead of the swinging stone swords.

He heard something metallic fall to the ground and Vaida's soft swearing. "I'm not sure this will even work," she said before throwing a metal nodule toward the two statues advancing.

It landed between them, and neither statue stopped to consider it.

In a burst of brilliant light, the nodule exploded, sending a force field of hazy purple over the two advancing statues. Cassian wasn't sure what it was supposed to do. But the moment the statues' swords touched the edge of the force field, he understood.

They were stuck—he didn't know for how long or how effective it would be if they decided to attack it, but it bought him enough time to build up his attack.

He nodded over his shoulder at Vaida, who was staring at her handiwork with a mixture of tense confusion and pride.

"It won't hold for long," she said, "probably a minute at most."

"That's long enough," he replied, immediately diving into the pool of magic behind his navel and stringing a rope of power from it into his hands.

A ball of magic formed, starting as small as a pebble and growing gradually larger as he fed more and more energy into it. Through the growing ball he could see the force field, and subsequently, the angels now attacking the magical barrier with their swords. It jolted with each strike, the purple fizzling and crackling each time they hit.

The field grew lighter and lighter, the crackling energy fading as they worked on breaking it down. But Cassian was nearly done; the ball he held between his hands was large enough to have broken apart the boulder in the pass. He was confident it would be enough for the two statues.

"Cassian," Vaida warned, her voice low, "they're nearly through."

He nodded, threading a final rope of power between his hands. "Tell me when."

She said nothing, but he could feel her tension behind him as he fed the last of the power into the ball. The sheer amount of energy scared him a little. The well in his gut was as vast as it had been before he'd taken this much out, and yet the ball between his hands was larger than he could have held if it was corporeal. The amount of magic he wielded was terrifying.

He didn't have long to ponder that. Vaida's force field shimmered once, then broke, shattering like glass as the statues succeeded in their single-minded mission.

"Now!" she screamed as the shards glittered into oblivion.

Cassian lifted the ball and hurled it as hard as he could, willing it to fly straight and true and with every ounce of destructive energy he could muster. It sailed through the air without a single hitch or spin and struck between the chests of the angels.

They froze, then cracked, then splintered apart, the arms where the magic had struck directly crumbling into small fragments. They rained onto the floor, more like sand than stone. The angel on the right held their sword in that disintegrated arm, and it clattered to the ground, the hilt splintering apart as it crashed.

Both of the angels stopped when they were hit. Their movement didn't stop abruptly, but slowed, then stilted, then stopped jerkily. It was as if they were wind-up dolls and their energy had finally run out.

Vaida sighed in relief, but her respite was brief.

Kellan, still dodging between the long swipes of his angel, stumbled on a stray bit of rock from the explosion. He lost his footing for a moment, but it was enough for the angel to gain an advantage. Its heavy sword swung around and caught him in the middle. It picked Kellan up off the ground and threw him halfway across the room, slamming him forcefully into a wall. Cassian could hear a distinct *crunch* as he made contact.

Kellan dropped to the floor like a sack of flour. His head lolled, rolling to rest on his chest like a limp doll. He was out cold, knocked unconscious from the force of the impact.

Liv was distracted, turning her attention from her opponent to Kellan slumped against the wall. She yelled, indistinct and feral, attacking her statue with renewed vigor. But she was off, and the angel's sword slammed into her side before she could block it.

She didn't go flying as Kellan had, but she was knocked sideways and onto the ground. The angel wasted no time in towering over her and lifting the sword above its head.

Cassian still had a rope of power in his grasp; he didn't give it as much form as he'd done for the first attack, but it didn't matter. If all it took was damaging the statues to get them to stop, he didn't need to waste all his energy on a single attack.

He threw his rope of power toward the statue's arm, intending to shear it off at the shoulder before it could bring the sword down on Liv. The purple energy whipped through the room and lacerated through the statue's shoulder.

The severed stone arm landed on the ground before Liv's feet, the stone sword still in its unrelenting grip. But the moment it landed, the statue's movements came to a jerky halt.

Cassian was relieved, but his fear was eating away at the small bit of reprieve his success got. Because now, the last angel was only a few steps from Kellan's prone body.

Vaida rushed past him toward Liv while he gathered another rope of power in his hands and lashed out at the remaining angel. It snaked through the air, whizzing over the stone fountain and cutting through the statue's torso like butter. He was getting good at this.

The statue stopped mid-movement, then its upper half slid from the lower, shattering on the ground as it fell.

The room was mercifully still for several heartbeats, and Cassian could feel his own blood in his ears. He held his breath, afraid to move so soon after victory, only to discover this wasn't it. Liv and Vaida, both on the floor, froze, Vaida's hand grasping one of Liv's tightly.

They waited. Their eyes fixed on the other shadowy alcoves around the room, waiting for more angels to step from their daises and wield more stone swords.

But nothing moved. The air itself was still, filled with motes of dust that didn't move; they hung suspended in front of their noses and clogged their airways when they finally took a single, collective breath.

Cassian broke first. He ran, full tilt, toward where Kellan stayed slumped against the wall. There were no signs of blood, although that did little to calm his nerves. He pulled Kellan off the wall gently and laid him on the ground, turning him on his side to check his back and neck for any visible signs of fracture or breaks.

To his relief, nothing stood out. They weren't out of the woods yet, but it was a hopeful sign.

Kellan groaned, and Cassian flipped him onto his back to allow him time to waken.

"Kellan?" Cassian asked quietly. "Can you hear me?"

Kellan groaned again, but nodded weakly. "Did we win?"

"Yeah," Cassian said, a relieved chuckle escaping his lips. "We won. For now, at least."

He held Kellan's head in the crook of his arm, then turned to look for Liv and Vaida. They had stood and were picking their way through the half-crumbled statues toward them. Vaida supported Liv with an arm slung around her waist, Liv's arm draped over Vaida's shoulders.

In the commotion, Cassian hadn't glanced once at the statue of who he assumed was Hym, holding the golden sword. He did so now, and immediately sprang to his feet.

"Liv! Vaida!" he screamed, breaking the peaceful stillness that had settled over them. "It's moving!"

They turned to stare at the golden statue, now lifting a foot to step out of its alcove, both hands gripping the golden sword hilt. Their faces turned from exhaustion to fear as they scrambled away.

But the golden statue did not move as quickly as the angels

had—it took its time stepping from the dais, one foot before the other in sickeningly slow, calculated moves. The Sword lifted from the floor as one of its hands moved to hold the tip of the blade.

When it fully emerged from its alcove, it stopped, holding the Sword across its body as if it were presenting it to someone.

Liv and Vaida had slowed as they all watched the statue's progress, waiting for it to attack them. But it didn't. It stayed perfectly still, sword resting in its hands, eyes closed.

Cassian ground his teeth. Should they approach it and take the risk? Was the trial for this relic to defeat the angels? Or were they simply setting themselves up for another trap? He could sense the Sword's power—the instant the statue stopped moving, it was like a beacon to his soul, tugging and pulling and screaming at him to move, to pick it up and wield it.

Liv and Vaida were still several paces away, halted. Kellan turned his head, although from his vantage point, he wouldn't be able to see the statue. He tried to sit up, and Cassian let him.

No one spoke. Cassian didn't know what to do next, but his gut was impossible and insatiable; he knew he needed to be the one to take the Sword from its place in the statue's hands. He couldn't explain *why*, but the need was aggressive.

He stood, and Kellan made a small noise of protest. Cassian ignored it as he walked slowly toward the statue. He ignored Vaida's message of warning. If not him, then who should take the Sword?

As he approached the statue, it moved again. The spell was gone, replaced immediately with panic and adrenaline that sharpened his focus and had him scrambling for a rope of his power.

But it simply kneeled before him, raising the Sword above its head and offering it to him.

"Cassian," Vaida's voice called, her tone wary.

He hesitated, hand hovering over the golden hilt. It radiated heat as if it had been sitting in the sun for several hours. In fact, the whole statue seemed to be warm, but nothing was as warm as the Sword itself.

He reached forward and grasped the hilt, a small metallic clink from his pinky ring sending chills up his arm and through his entire body. He could feel the power radiating from the Sword as it wove its way through his body. It was like being warmed by the sun—the effect was immediate and almost painful.

It shrank in his grip, turning from a massively oversized sword to one that fit in his hand perfectly. He lifted it gently from the statue's hands, turning the tip up toward the ceiling and running an appraising eye over the length of the blade.

It was made entirely of gold; the double helix guard was, up close, much finer than he'd realized. The gold work was intricate and precise, and he wondered how many hours had been spent crafting such a beautiful decoration for this weapon. The blade itself must have been reinforced. After all, a pure golden blade would be much too soft to use in actual battle.

As he admired the Sword, he grew even warmer; the Sword went from a pleasant heat to almost unbearable. Should he drop it?

But his hand wouldn't release it; he tried to uncurl his fingers from the hilt but couldn't convince himself to let go. It was like he'd been searching for this his whole life—now that he had it in his possession, there was no way he'd ever release it again.

The Sword was *his,* and his alone.

With that thought, the heat became an inferno. And from the hand grasping the Sword came a wave of holy fire.

SECTION 4

DRAGONS IN ILERON

The dragons were an original part of the world of Ileron, inhabiting the lands for millennia before humans. No one knows exactly *how* long dragons have been in Ileron, but many have theorized they were the first living creatures in the world.

Dragons are wickedly intelligent, wise, and incredibly reclusive. They are natural pacifists and will try to talk their way out of a situation before they will muster their strength to fight.

And when they fight, it is a terrifying sight.

Dragons' abilities are determined by their scales, their elemental proclivities tied to whatever color they display. While mottled dragons are possible, it is rare to see one with multiple colored scales.

Before the Conjunction, humans revered the dragons like gods. The dragons lived in harmony with humans, and Hym loved them, too.

But after the Conjunction, dragons were regarded as terrifying beasts by the elves and driven from their homes. No one knows if any dragons still survive, but none have been seen for the last six hundred years. It is possible dragons are extinct, but many surmise they have simply gone deep into hiding.

The last dragon sighting was in the days after the Battle of a Thousand Suns. A single white dragon was seen flying over the scorched hills south of Ivorymore.

39

BECK

Rivenstorm | 28th of Dawn Moon

The wind off the ocean was frigid as they stared down the dark-haired man, the veins on his face pulsating beneath the midwinter sun. He'd stretched his lips thin into a mockery of a smile.

Beck drew his sword, pressing the button on the hilt to activate it. Spider copied him, moving to flank the man. His wild grin only grew at their defensiveness.

"Who are you?" Beck asked slowly. "What is your purpose here?"

The man simply laughed, the noise grating against his ears. It was like broken glass or gears without oil, jarring, sharp, and disconcerting.

"That is for me to know, little mouse," the man replied, the points of his canines poking his lips as he spoke. "But unfortunately for you, you have no purpose here. And I won't have you sniffing around."

The man didn't reach for either of the weapons at his hips. Instead, he threw his hands forward, and black lightning laced with purple shot from his hands. Beck tucked and rolled, the lightning narrowly missing him as it sailed over his head.

He was a pact-bearer, of that Beck was sure. The veins on his face were a dead giveaway. But who he actually was remained a mystery. He was plain but rugged, someone who would blend into a crowd with ease, if not for those marks.

Beck continued moving, unwilling to stay in one place for too long for fear of the lightning striking him. Spider moved around the man, her circular blades gripped tightly in her hands. She'd been using the blades as long as he could remember, and her proficiency with them was nothing short of incredible. The least he could do was distract the man so she could position herself to attack.

"Tell me why you're here," Beck said. He knew it was a shot in the dark to get this man to talk, but it wasn't really about getting information.

The man laughed again, a hysterical sort of sound. "And why should I tell you anything? You're in my way, that's all you need to know."

Beck adjusted his grip on his sword. "I was hoping you'd at least be civil."

"Civil?" The man crouched low, cocking one black-tipped finger at Beck. "This is me being civil. Your ideals of justice and correctness are so outdated."

Beck frowned. Spider was finally in position. She leaped forward, her blades crossed before her. She brought them down in a sweeping arc he knew would leave the man begging for his life.

He was there one moment, then gone the next. Spider leaped through dead air, her blades cutting through nothing.

"Shit," she swore. "Where the hells did he go?"

A flash of purple came from his right; a growl sounded from the alley. It sent chills up his spine. Was it the man, or had they missed something crucial while distracted?

He whirled, turning toward the sound. His grip tightened on the sword. Spider shifted on her feet, preparing for a strike.

From the darkness came a shape; it slunk out into the light on all fours, back hackles raised like a hyena. It had an elongated head, resembling that of a jackal, and brilliant, sickening yellow eyes. Its skin was made of what looked like overlapping scales, like a snake or a dragon.

He'd never seen a demon like it. He could have mistaken it for an animal were it not for the smell that he knew as the demonic stench, sulfur and ash.

It stalked from the shadows, baring its sharp teeth at them. Beck held his sword before him in a defensive stance, his eyes darting from the demon to the alleyways, to the rooftops, and back again. Where had the man gone? Why hadn't Beck noticed the demon sooner?

"Beck!" Spider's voice pulled his attention back to the demon from where it had been fixated on the rooftops. Her warning came just in time for him to raise his sword against the demon leaping toward his throat.

He scrambled away after sword met steely claws. This felt different from the demons he'd fought before—something about this one was wrong. Although all demons felt wrong, this one was especially strange, particularly off-putting.

The demon kept advancing, growling so low that Beck swore the ground beneath his feet vibrated. Its claws scraped menacingly along the stones. He had to keep reminding himself not to look at them lest he be taken by surprise again.

It lunged once more, and this time Beck spun to the side, leaving his sword tucked against his side to drag along the demon. He knew he'd struck true when he felt the telltale splash of warm, slightly acidic blood on his pant leg. It sizzled, not quite acidic enough to eat through the fabric but enough to leave damage.

He rounded on the demon, its side now bleeding freely onto the pavement. It lunged again, apparently uncaring for the massive wound in its side. Beck caught it with his blade once more and threw it to the side. It hit the stones hard, rolling down a few steps to the next level of the clearing. Blood sizzled where it splashed.

Beck turned to make chase, but his eye caught on Spider. She was fighting yet another one of these strange animalistic demons—he hadn't even sensed its presence. Where had it come from?

A bolt of black lightning raced its way through the air, cracking through Spider in a single burst. She screamed, dropping her blades to the ground. Beck felt the air rock with the force of his shout.

The demon she'd been fighting lunged; Beck was faster. He sailed over her, slicing it in two from tip to tail. Blackened blood rained over the stones; some of it splashed onto his own face—it burned, but he didn't care.

Fear sluiced through his veins, slowing his world to a crawl as the demon halves landed with a thump on the ground, twitching. He turned sharply to find Spider unconscious in the arms of the man with the black veins.

Beck saw red. The fear melted into pure rage, red hot and boiling. "Don't touch her, you piece of shit."

The man laughed as Beck started forward, his lungs on fire. He couldn't let this man touch her for a second longer. He was afraid of what would happen to her if he didn't release her from this man's grip.

"She'll make an excellent specimen," he said, running a finger along her cheek and down her neck.

Beck wanted to chop off the man's hands. He wanted to wrap his hands around his neck and strangle the life from him. He wanted to hang him from the dock and let the elements slowly tear away his flesh. How *dare* he touch her? How *dare* he talk about Spider like she was some prize to be won for experiments? Like she wasn't her own living, breathing, beautiful, brilliant human being?

But he couldn't attack—Spider might get caught in the crossfire. He gripped the hilt of his sword tightly, knuckles cracking in protest. How would he get her away?

The demon beside him was still, but movement flickered in the corner of his eye. The other demon had regained its footing and was dragging itself slowly toward him. He couldn't take his eyes from the man and Spider, though, afraid he would lose her forever if he so much as blinked. He'd seen how the man had simply blipped from existence earlier—how could he know he wouldn't be able to do it with Spider in tow?

But he couldn't ignore the other demon. Panic was pinging in the back of his mind, but he wouldn't let it take over. He had to stay calm, had to stay focused.

If he wasn't, he would lose Spider.

The demon attacked, and Beck swung his sword up to catch it, tearing his eyes from the man and Spider. He swung—and someone shot the demon out of the air with an impressive spike of ice.

A sheet of ice coalesced out of nowhere, driving itself forward and encasing the man's legs. Beck nearly lost his footing on it, driving his sword down into it to stop himself from falling. The demon was dead, twitching on the ground beside him.

"Shadow," a voice said. "You aren't supposed to be here." It was full of ice, smooth as a lake on a calm day. It was filled with the promise of deep waters and encroaching ice. An ancient voice that commanded them to obey.

The man named Shadow snarled, "Don't get involved. This isn't your concern."

"It certainly is." The voice was suddenly beside him, echoing in his ear. He turned to face it, jerking at their appearance.

They looked like they'd been carved from ice and dressed in woven snow, glittering under the sunlight. Their hair was pure white, their eyes a pale blue that reminded him of the sky in winter. Their body was draped in a thin, nearly transparent sheet.

If ice were living, it would be them.

Shadow didn't seem concerned about the ice on his legs, his focus completely on the person who'd appeared at Beck's side. The veins on his face pulsed and writhed as if they were mimicking his frustration.

Shadow squeezed Spider tighter. "They came sniffing."

The person beside him cocked their head condescendingly, their face a mask of derision. "He's one of ours, Shadow."

At that, Beck whipped his head toward them. One of theirs? What the hells was that supposed to mean? He didn't know who either of these people even *were,* much less what they were doing here and why they were fighting.

They paid him no mind, and Beck seethed. He wanted Spider back. He wanted answers. He wanted them to leave him be, to get far, far away and get Spider to safety.

Shadow shrugged, seemingly unconcerned with their statement and Beck's apparent status in their unknown organization. "You killed my pet." Beck didn't know the man could pout, but he somehow did just that.

"It was a nuisance," the person beside him said. "Now get out of here. I'll handle this."

Shadow frowned, lifting one hand wreathed in purple and black fire. He used it to melt the ice around his legs, his grasp still tight on Spider. Once he was freed, he waved a hand behind him, opening a portal.

Beck screamed, unable to stop himself. "Leave her!"

The person beside him didn't give him a second glance before snapping their fingers. Spider lifted from the man's grasp on a gust of cold air and was set unceremoniously before Beck's feet. Shadow turned to glare at them again before stepping through the portal. It sucked closed behind him with a pop.

Spider stirred at Beck's feet, and he threw himself to the ground beside her. When her eyes fluttered open, he helped her sit up. Her hand was small in his as she used him for support, but it was warm. She was okay, for now.

Relief flooded through him, turning his insides to jelly.

"Are you all right?" he asked when she'd blinked a few times to orient herself.

She looked up at him blearily, but nodded. "My body's one big bruise, but I don't think anything is broken."

"Oh, thank the Circle," Beck said. He wanted to wrap her in a hug, but resisted. She didn't need to be manhandled more than she already had been.

Someone cleared their throat next to him. He'd already forgotten about the person who'd saved them. They stood next to him, arms crossed over their chest. Their hair and clothes drifted in a non-existent wind. It was as if a gentle breeze constantly surrounded them.

At first, he felt gratitude. They'd saved Spider, saved them from this man who Beck hadn't been sure he could beat.

But then he remembered their power as he looked to their feet, bare upon the sheet of ice. He glanced at the dead demon, acidic blood melting the massive icicle that had impaled it. He frowned at the demon. Why wasn't it disintegrating?

He shivered, involuntarily. They were dead if their savior decided to be their ruin.

They looked down at him, face unreadable. "I will not hurt you, if that's what you're thinking, young man."

It didn't bring him relief. He had too many questions, none of which he could ask now that Spider was awake. He didn't know what they'd meant when they said "one of them." He was afraid it would blow his cover.

The person kneeled beside them and reached out an elegant hand, fingers tipped in frost. "May I?" they asked, meeting Spider's eyes.

She was still leaning up against Beck, her hands in her lap. A few drops of demon blood had splashed on her cheeks, leaving angry welts behind. Spider looked down at the outstretched hand, then back up to the person's eerily pale face.

"It's only to assess," they continued at Spider's hesitation. "I won't hurt you."

Spider gave a terse nod. Beck could feel how tense her shoulders were as the pale person reached forward, resting their frost-tipped fingers on her cheek. Nothing happened—no flash of purple light, no flare of pain, no burst of magic. They simply sat and waited.

Beck squeezed Spider's shoulders gently. It was reassurance for her as much as it was for him. She was awake; she was talking; she was breathing.

They removed their fingers after several tense moments, leaning back on their heels and placing that same hand on their chin.

"You will be fine," they finally said, voice light and airy, as if the confirmation of Spider's health had somehow brought them pleasure. "But, unfortunately, I cannot heal you."

He so badly wanted to ask what they meant, why they'd come, who that man was. But the words caught in his throat. He needed to help Spider; he needed to get her to safety. She swayed in his arms, the tension in her shoulders gone as she collapsed. Beck whipped his head up as she melted into him, glaring at the person who had stood.

"She will be fine," they reiterated. "But she should get medical attention quickly."

"Who are you?" he finally said.

Their lips quirked as if they were holding back a smile. "You may call me Az'Gomack."

Not much information, but he didn't linger. "Why did you help us?"

They smiled then, or the barest hint of one. Their full lips curved upward gently as they replied. "Because I, despite my nature, am on your side. All will be made clear soon, I promise."

He looked down to Spider, making sure she really was asleep before he asked his next question. "What did you mean, that I'm 'one of yours?'"

"You're not all you seem, young man," they replied. "I think you know what I mean by that."

He was thankful for their discretion, but it still didn't answer his question. So they knew he was Red Guard—what else did they know about him? What didn't he know about the mission, about all the moving pieces that seemed to happen without his knowledge?

They smiled again, softly. "Unfortunately, Beck, my time here is short. We will see each other again, I presume." The ice beneath them receded, leaving his knees cold and wet. "Farewell."

Before he could protest, they disappeared with a pop. They left no trace behind, save for the nearly melted icicle in the dead demon.

How had they known his name? What else did they know and hadn't revealed? And what did they mean "they'd see each other again?"

The questions were numerous, and his head was hurting. They hadn't found answers here like he'd wanted, but they'd discovered something interesting. The man named Shadow was obviously involved—his defensiveness and his commentary all pointed toward knowing something he wouldn't otherwise.

He stood, lifting Spider's limp body and cradling her close. She was cold, shivering in his arms, but her breathing was steady. As he stared down into her face, he felt a resolve harden inside of him, like the ice that had melted not so long ago.

Beck would give up his own freedom if it meant protecting her. He'd give up his chance at escape if it meant she wouldn't have to worry about being attacked because of him. This mission for the Red Guard, this betrayal he would inevitably carry out—he wanted none of it. Not if it would hurt her like it had today.

Because he didn't know what he'd do without her.

40

KELLAN

The Temple of Hym | 28th of Dawn Moon

Kellan watched with bated breath as Cassian lifted the Sword from the statue's hands. His head was fuzzy and throbbed like crazy, but the golden image of Cassian was as clear in his vision as crystal.

But that wasn't right—Cassian had always been silver, cool toned. He was like living moonlight. The image in front of him now was made of sun, summer sunsets, and fire. He couldn't make sense of it at all.

A crackle, then a blaze Kellan recognized consumed Cassian, one he'd hoped he'd never see again.

Liv screamed as Vaida turned her body to cover Liv's. But Kellan knew the fire wouldn't hurt them, just like it hadn't hurt him all those years ago in the Northwind basement laboratories. It washed over him, too, a warm tickle that caressed his skin.

But what was causing it? Kellan tried to stand, unsuccessfully, from the ground to see Cassian better. They weren't in danger. They'd gotten the Sword.

Kellan gasped. Was it the Sword? Then how were they supposed to wield it?

"Vaida!" he shouted, hoping she could hear him over the roar of the flames. "The Sword! Get the Sword!"

He couldn't see her, so he could only hope she'd heard him. He tried again to stand, his legs wobbly and weak after the statue's attack. Bracing an arm against the wall, he pulled himself up slowly. The flames were still thick around him.

Kellan couldn't see through the fuzziness of his head and the fire, but he could just barely make out the silhouette of Cassian, sword still held aloft. Behind, another silhouette. Logically, he knew it was Vaida. But she looked like a spirit, her body outlined by the blaze. The way it parted around her made it look like she'd been dressed in a gown of fire, billowing out behind her like wings.

She reached Cassian before Kellan could. He continued, willing himself to step carefully through the rubble and the fire. But the flames didn't stop. They'd gone on so much longer than they had in the basement at Northwind, and he simply couldn't understand why.

Vaida's silhouette was reaching, trying to pry the Sword from Cassian's grasp, but it didn't seem to work. The flames didn't stop; the Sword stayed pointed at the ceiling.

Kellan finally reached them and saw Vaida trying to pry Cassian's fingers from the hilt and having no success. He watched Cassian's face; it was as if he wasn't awake, staring blankly into nothingness, his black eye flickering with the flames dancing around them. He didn't seem to notice Vaida at all. His stance was solid and unmoving.

"Cassian!" he tried, but Cassian didn't acknowledge him.

Vaida didn't stop trying to pry Cassian's fingers from the blade, and Kellan wasn't sure what to do. What had helped last time? He couldn't think; the flames didn't burn, but his mind couldn't stop the panic that flashed brilliant yellow in his mind.

Nothing had caused the flames to stop last time, at least not that he'd seen. Cassian had simply sucked them back in, like water down a drain. Nothing had caused their departure other than Cassian himself.

And right now, it seemed Cassian *wasn't* himself. Maybe, just maybe, Kellan needed to remind him who he was.

He wrapped his arms around Cassian's midsection, burying his face into his back. He was warmer than he'd ever been since they'd reunited, almost unbearable to touch. But Kellan hugged him tightly and forcefully, a reminder to the man in his arms that he was here. He was alive. He wasn't going anywhere.

Somehow, it worked.

The flames died, receding back into the Sword in a vacuum. As they cleared, Cassian's grip on the Sword loosened and Vaida could peel it from his grasp.

Before Kellan could brace himself, Cassian collapsed into him, eyes fluttering shut. They crashed to the ground, Cassian still wrapped in Kellan's arms.

🜄 🜄 🜄

Kellan awoke with a start, his entire body weighed down.

It took him a few moments to realize what had happened—he'd blacked out, briefly, with Cassian still on top of him. Thankfully, Cassian was still out cold.

Vaida stood beside him, the Sword in her grasp. The moment his eyes fluttered open, she dropped it, uncaring that it clanged to the ground. She kneeled beside them and lifted Cassian off him.

"How—" Kellan started, then squeezed his eyes shut against a throb in his head. "How long was I out?"

Vaida shook her head. "Only a few seconds. Are you okay?"

He sat up gingerly, taking stock of how his body felt. It was like a train had run him over, but nothing seemed broken. Just very sore. He rolled his head, grateful to find it only stiff.

"Yeah," he finally said. "Just fuzzy and stiff. Nothing's broken."

Vaida sighed in relief, then turned her focus to Cassian, still out cold on the floor. She was cradling his head after lifting it off Kellan. Nothing seemed amiss, although when Kellan reached out to touch his forehead, it was once again cold as ice.

"We should get out of here," Liv said. She was still sitting on the floor, a line of blood trickling down her face. She was covered in dust and grime, the blood a nice touch.

Vaida nodded, then looked down at Cassian in her hands. "You'll need to help me, Kellan. I can't lift him, and I don't think Liv can either."

"Definitely not in this state," Liv chirped.

Kellan turned toward the slide and realized it had turned back into a staircase. It was a relief; he didn't want to have to figure out how to get back up that stone slide, especially not with an unconscious Cassian.

They each took an arm, slinging Cassian over their shoulders as they stood. He was heavy and limp, so their journey back up the dark staircase was slow. Liv, breathing shallowly, walked ahead of them, flashlight in hand and the Sword strapped to her belt.

When they arrived back in the sanctuary, Kellan and Vaida laid Cassian down gently on one of the intricately carved pews. Liv sat beside him, her breaths still pained. Kellan was feeling the effects too, his side tender where the sword had connected. He could imagine Liv was feeling it more, though. She wasn't a Fallen like him; her resistance to physical attacks like that wasn't as high as his.

Vaida, to Kellan's relief, seemed unharmed. She was covered in dust and debris like the rest of them, but that seemed the worst of it for her. The flames hadn't hurt her, and neither had any of the statues.

Kellan sat too, lifting Cassian's head and placing it on his lap. It probably was unnecessary, but it felt like the only thing he could do while they waited for him to awaken. The panic he'd felt had been real and consuming. He'd been helpless against Cassian's fire—just like he'd been helpless when Leo had taken him all those years ago.

Why was it that whenever it was up to Kellan to protect Cassian, he failed so miserably?

His frustration was dark red, the color of dried blood. He was too weak, too pathetic to protect anyone he cared for. He hadn't even protected Vaida—that had been Cassian.

He shook his head, letting it fall back against the pew. He thought he'd gotten over these feelings of inadequacy. He thought he'd left them behind when hardening his heart was the only thing he could do to keep himself from breaking completely.

But Cassian's reappearance had brought them all to the surface, had forced them back to his heart. He wasn't sure what to do with them anymore.

Cassian stirred in his lap, groaning as he cracked one eye open and met Kellan's gaze. "What happened?" he asked groggily, voice hoarse.

Kellan frowned. "Your...fire."

Cassian nodded. "But how did you get it to stop?"

Kellan felt the flush on his face. He didn't know what he'd done, if he was being honest. He'd simply acted on instinct, hoping that his touch would somehow bring Cassian back down to reality. Explaining that would be mortifying.

Thankfully, Vaida saved him from further embarrassment. "We got the Sword away from you."

Cassian frowned. "The Sword?"

Liv twirled it, holding up the tip toward the ceiling like Cassian had. "This thing. You know, the artifact we came here for?"

"I got that," he said, somewhat sarcastically. "I'm just..." He stopped again, his frown deepening. "You don't feel anything while holding it, Liv?"

Liv shot him a look like he was out of his mind. "What do you mean? It's a sword, not a person."

Kellan watched their interaction, keeping a hand under Cassian's head as they talked. He wondered about Cassian's strange question—as if he was implying the Sword had somehow been sentient. If that was true, what kind of threat did it pose to Liv?

Cassian seemed not to know how to respond to Liv's statement. His eyes met Kellan's, and the realization of his predicament seemed to catch up to him. He sat up quickly, nearly slamming his head into Kellan's.

"Sorry," he said quickly, turning his face away from Kellan. "I didn't mean to stay there so long."

Kellan lowered his gaze. "It's fine. I didn't mind."

Vaida glanced between them, expressionless. But Kellan could practically see the gears turning in her head. He shot her a look, one that begged her to stay quiet. She obliged.

They spent some time gathering themselves; Vaida gave Liv and Kellan both a short exam, checking for broken ribs and other invisible ailments. Ultimately, both suffered from fractured ribs and severe bruising, but nothing life threatening. Cassian was also given a clean bill of health, his brief stretch of unconsciousness seeming to have no ill effects.

Kellan, Cassian, and Liv had ditched their packs in the sanctuary before they'd split up earlier; they retrieved them now, Kellan and Liv both pulling theirs on with grunts of stiffness and a bit of pain. He'd have to endure the discomfort for several days, as they wouldn't be able to bandage or treat any of their wounds until they got back to town.

But now was the next predicament they hadn't planned for—they needed to get back through the pass. Past the shadows that screamed and sent their instincts into overdrive. Kellan wasn't looking forward to revisiting the dark pass and the screeching shadows.

Vaida apparently had the same thoughts as him. She sighed as she adjusted her pack and turned to the rest of the group.

"We need to discuss how we're getting back," she said. "We got lucky coming through, but going back is a different story."

Cassian nodded. "They weren't very susceptible to my magic. I landed one hit, but I don't know what I did to make it work."

Kellan bit his lip. Fighting them seemed out of the question, then. Would they take the long way around the mountain? Could they run?

"What if we use this?" Liv said, swinging the Sword in a lazy loop in front of her. "That fire that Cassian made might be effective against the shadows, too."

Vaida gave her an incredulous look. Cassian looked uncomfortable.

"He can't control it," Kellan said, knowing Cassian would say nothing himself.

Liv frowned. "How do you know?"

"Because he's done it before, and it wasn't on purpose."

Liv stared openmouthed at Kellan while he explained briefly their last encounter with Cassian's mysterious fire. How it had been a desperate situation and how they hadn't known how to stop it then, either.

Apparently, Cassian hadn't included that tidbit in the stories he'd told about his time in Spiral City. Liv already knew about Leo and Alvemach, but she hadn't known about the fire. Kellan wondered why he'd said nothing about it.

Cassian looked pensive but not angry as Liv turned to him once Kellan was done.

"Well," she began, sheathing the Sword at her hip in a smooth motion, "we're just going to figure something else out, then."

The tension in Cassian's shoulders dropped, and Kellan sighed in relief. He didn't think Liv would push, but it was still nice to have her understand so quickly.

Vaida stood, brushing off some of the debris on her pants. "Let's check the weather, see where the sun is at. If we have to, we should spend the night in here."

They all nodded and stood to follow her out to the entrance. Kellan passed by the portrait of Queen Ameloria again, staring up at her beautiful and familiar face, and swore her eyes followed them the entire time.

🔥 🔥 🔥

Night had fallen, and Liv refused to go through the pass in the dark. Kellan had to agree. They retreated inside once more and set up camp in the sanctuary.

They discussed possible options when they awoke the next morning. Going around the pass was simply unfeasible as it would take too long. They could try running through and hoping for the best, but Vaida wasn't keen on the plan as she was slower than the rest of them. Cassian offered to fight them again in hopes he could recreate the first hit he'd landed on the shadow he'd faced; they nixed the idea as being too risky. They simply didn't know enough to predict their behavior.

Cassian looked pensive as Kellan wracked his brain for an option that wouldn't get them killed. He considered the first encounter they'd had. Cassian had escaped unscathed, but how had he done it?

He frowned, a snag in his thoughts drawing his attention. Cassian had escaped. The shadows hadn't followed him out of the pass. Why was that?

"Vaida," Kellan said, grasping the tail end of a thought, "the shadows didn't follow Cassian out of the pass, right?"

Vaida nodded slowly, her eyebrows knit together. "You're right. They stayed back."

Kellan nodded vigorously. "Are you thinking what I am?"

"They're weak to light!" Liv's voice was excited as she sat up on a pew. "That's why they didn't follow him out!"

Kellan wagged a finger at her. "Exactly. And I'm willing to bet they were the same strange feeling we got out in the forest at night. I bet if we keep our flashlights and lanterns on, we can get through without them bothering us!"

Cassian hummed. "It's worth a shot."

They packed their meager camp. Liv kept the Sword on her hip even though Vaida had scolded her for trying to practice with it. They didn't know what other powers it might hold beyond the fire—trying to use it could be disastrous. They didn't know what had triggered Cassian's fire, either. Liv had begrudgingly agreed, but kept it attached on her hip, anyway.

They armed themselves instead with their flashlights and the travel lantern they used in camp. Vaida had asked if Cassian could create light with his magic, but he'd been unsuccessful in his attempts to keep it steady. His specialty now only lay in offensive magic—he'd apparently trained nothing else during his stint in Stygia.

When they pulled the doors to the temple open, Kellan's heart was in his throat. His heartbeat made his skin tight as he clenched the flashlight in his grip. It was impossible to relax like he would have with a sword in hand; resting his life on this small device differed completely from resting it on his sword. With his sword, he was in control. The flashlight, not so much.

They stepped into the pass as one mass, flashlights held tightly before them. Vaida and Liv walked abreast, Cassian before them, while Kellan brought up the rear. Cassian held the lantern before him. Kellan shone his flashlight behind their group, the small beam from his flashlight darting up the steep rock faces on either side.

Nothing approached. It was eerily quiet, as if the pass had been abandoned completely. Kellan supposed that should have comforted him, but it sent waves of dread through his veins instead.

They walked on, the air around them silent and still. No screams, no falling boulders, no trickle of falling pebbles. The hairs on Kellan's arms and neck stood on end the whole time as he listened to the crunch of their boots against the rocks in the pass.

He estimated they'd gone about halfway when he heard a rustle somewhere above them. Their party tensed, slowing down as they listened. But nothing else moved.

Another quarter of the way and they were nearly out of the pass when something moved again, this time closer. It hissed behind Kellan, and he whipped around, casting the beam from his flashlight around the space behind him.

The light fell on the same creatures that had attacked them during the day, a shadow given corporeal form. It sent goosebumps along Kellan's arms. He opened his mouth to tell them to run, but the shadow screamed, flinching away from the light as if it was being burned.

"They really do hate the light," Kellan whispered as the group whipped around at the shadow's cries.

Cassian was the first to turn back toward the end of the pass, now in sight. "Let's get out of here quickly, regardless."

They nodded, holding their flashlights out again with more confidence. And as they reached the end of the pass, Kellan flicked his light around again.

Four more shadows had tried to follow, but as his beam fell upon them, they screamed with the same ferocity as the first one. They scattered back into the pass, leaving their group alone in the forest, sunlight sparkling off the snow.

41

KELLAN

Alderburn | 30th of Dawn Moon

The two-day journey back was blissfully uneventful. They regrouped back at the inn at the edge of the forest in Alderburn.

Vaida found a full leather sheath for the golden sword, knowing if they kept it out in the open they'd be a walking target for people who would covet it. Kellan swore everyone stared at them as they packed up the van, like they somehow knew they'd gained a god's relic and now carried it on them. Like they desired it. But the rest of the group stayed unaffected, so Kellan decided he would have to be, too.

They spent their last evening at the inn by the fire, the Sword safely locked in Vaida and Liv's room under many layers of Vaida's protection spells. Kellan felt it best to have it on them, but he knew the innkeeper would probably balk at them carrying around a weapon in a crowded room like this one.

They sat in overstuffed armchairs, the fire crackling pleasantly next to them in a stone hearth. The riddle, long ago copied onto Liv's techpad, laid before them on a low wooden coffee table covered in water rings and unknown stains.

Liv stared at the techpad, her brow creased in thought. Vaida also stared, her face impassive, but Kellan knew that look well. She was stumped.

Kellan watched Cassian from the corner of his eye. He'd tied his hair back into a low ponytail, a few tendrils falling out and framing his face. He sipped from a carved wooden tankard, his face unreadable. He watched Cassian's tongue dart out to lick froth from his lips.

The heat on his face must have been obvious, as Vaida's lips curved into a smirk.

"Kellan," she said, a mischievous glint in her eye, "any ideas?" She gestured to the techpad, then leaned back in the chair, arms crossed.

He read the second verse again, the one they hadn't been able to figure out just yet.

The Staff is hidden where our ancestors began,
guarded deep below by no man.
The winter's chill will leave you cold,
but heed its tale and its power behold.

Kellan had no gods-damned clue what any of it meant. He'd never been good at logic puzzles and riddles, so asking him to interpret the clues was laughable.

He shook his head.

Vaida sighed. "Liv, you know human history best. Let's start with something tangible. What would they be referencing by 'ancestors began?'"

Liv rubbed her face, brows still furrowed in thought. He could practically see the gears turning in her head as she worked through it silently.

Kellan let her muse, turning his attention subtly back to Cassian in his armchair, sipping the frothy beer in his tankard. The inn leaned into the old-world feel from its dinnerware to the decor. Rustic was Kellan's best way to describe it.

Cassian didn't seem to notice his attention, but it was also possible he was very good at ignoring Kellan. They hadn't discussed his flames again after Liv had suggested using them to protect themselves in the pass. Kellan couldn't tell if he was angry or scared or frustrated by the sudden return of the mysterious power.

The image of Cassian sheathed in flames, Hym's sword held aloft, wouldn't leave Kellan's mind. It had been like watching the birth of a god, one he couldn't recognize as Cassian at all. The idea of losing him in such a manner scared him.

But he couldn't tell Cassian that.

"I have a thought," Liv finally said, interrupting Kellan's thoughts and bringing him back to the present.

Vaida crossed her legs. "Let's hear it."

"You know the old city of Wolfwater?"

Kellan did, indeed. "The one that was leveled a couple hundred years ago? Didn't that used to be an all-human city?"

Liv nodded. "It was. In fact, it was the first city established by the old Albigian royalty when they settled here from Illium. The royal family eventually moved to Ebenfell, but it still stood for hundreds of years after they left."

Vaida stared at the riddle, her eyebrows drawn together in concentration. "So you think the second relic might be there?"

"It's worth a shot," Liv replied, shrugging. "I can't think of anywhere else that fits as accurately as that one."

Vaida nodded, then turned to Kellan and Cassian. "What do you think? We won't go unless we all agree."

Kellan nodded as well. "I trust Liv knows what she's talking about. I'm in."

"I also agree," Cassian said softly, his voice rumbling in Kellan's chest.

Vaida beamed. "We leave at sunrise, then," she declared, then stood from her chair, brushing her pants off with a few efficient strokes.

Liv stood to follow her, and they exited the dining room shoulder to shoulder, discussing something too softly for Kellan to hear.

Kellan and Cassian sat by the fire in silence for several minutes, the rest of the group's departure leaving a void. They hadn't been alone since Cassian's fire in the temple. Words that came so naturally to him were gone in Cassian's presence.

Cassian set his empty tankard down with a thunk, a soft pink blush scattering over the bridge of his nose. "Kellan," Cassian began, his words softer than usual, dulled at the edges by the drink, "about what happened at the temple—"

"I'm sorry," Kellan cut him off before he could say more. "I couldn't think of anything at the moment, and it seemed like the right thing to do. I'm sorry for ignoring your boundaries."

Cassian sighed, and Kellan felt the bottom of his stomach drop out. He'd definitely made him mad. There was no way around it.

Then Cassian's lips broke into a soft smile. "I'm not angry with you."

Kellan blinked stupidly. "You're...not?"

"No. I wanted to thank you for doing that. I wasn't myself when the fire took over. I couldn't have stopped it on my own. You saved me."

Kellan felt the blush rising through his body. What could he say? The relief that Cassian wasn't angry with him was overpowering, leaving him jittery and anxious. He was standing on the edge of something, a narrow ledge that would determine their future. On one side, the twisting pit of anger and resentment he'd been crawling out of for years.

On the other lay the future he hoped for, one where they might recover some of what they'd lost that night in Rivenstorm.

Kellan breathed, feeling the breath expand his lungs into the back of his rib cage. Whatever came out of his mouth next was the jump toward the future he wanted. He could only hope Cassian would jump with him.

"I'd do it again, a thousand times over, if it meant saving you."

Cassian blinked. It was slow, like a cat contemplating whether it wanted to pounce. His face was impassive, but Kellan could feel the consideration like pressure weighing down on his shoulders.

"I think," Cassian began, his words slow and deliberate, "I wouldn't mind having someone like you save me."

THE PHANTOM FLAME

The seasons slowly changed as they moved away from the mountain range. Snow melted away into the brown of reviving growth. Frost still decorated the plains in the morning but faded away quickly as the sun peeked its head over the rolling hills around them.

It took another two days for them to reach the outskirts of Wolfwater. Their car was silent as they grew closer; the anticipation of not knowing what awaited them laid a thick blanket of tension over their group.

On the eve of the second day, as the sun sank once again behind the rolling hills of northern Midlset, they saw something on the horizon.

Wolfwater was desolate.

Kellan had heard the tales. An unknown calamity had leveled the city hundreds of years ago, leaving it in ruins. No one traveled there; no one lived within a hundred miles of it. He watched the ground as they approached; watching how, even though the sun had yet to set, the frost seemed thicker here than it was in the plains.

"Is it just me," Liv said as they approached the outskirts of the ruins, "or is it ridiculously cold for this time of year?"

Cassian simply shrugged from the driver's seat, but Kellan and Vaida nodded their agreement.

The ruins grew closer as the sun continued its descent and the frost grew thicker. Scattered bits of concrete and brick littered the side of the road, spare pieces of iron interspersed between the frozen weeds like some sort of metal growth. The road itself was a bumpy, jarring mess; they could hardly travel a few feet without being jostled in their seats. Cassian drove slowly enough to not break the axles on the jagged pavement.

Before long, a pile of broken concrete halted their approach into the city. They couldn't drive around it, and going over it was out of the question.

Liv unbuckled her seatbelt, her breath puffing before her face. "Looks like we continue on foot from here."

They nodded somberly, unpacking the van with efficiency as they had at the trailhead in Alderburn. They left the Sword; one of Vaida's magical nodules guaranteed its safety, but Kellan doubted anyone was around to steal it in this abandoned city.

Their journey continued over the cracked concrete, their party making hardly a sound. But each crunch of a stray pebble or bit of concrete beneath their shoes felt like a crack of thunder in a silent temple. Kellan swore their being there was a desecration of something sacred.

It surprised him, the stillness of the ruined city. He'd never realized how loud civilization was. He supposed it had been similar in the forest, but something about the eeriness of this town made his hair stand on end.

Conversation felt wrong, like disturbing the silence of the ruins was sacrilegious. To whom, Kellan couldn't guess. So their journey continued in silence, the only sound their footfalls and soft breaths. Eventually, the sun set behind the buildings, and the true cold set in. Kellan shivered, his multiple layers not enough to keep the chill from seeping into his bones. It had been cold in Alderburn and at the foot of the mountain, but not like this.

Something about this chill was more than just late winter's cold. It was as if it was a living thing wrapping its claws around their throats, willing them to freeze if they didn't keep moving. Cassian was the only one who seemed unaffected, trudging along like he was used to it. Just how cold had the Hells been if this was nothing to him?

Kellan didn't know how long they'd been walking, he only stared at the feet in front of him, following them with an almost mindless persistence. But then they stopped, and Kellan finally looked up, unable to stop the gasp that escaped from his lips.

They'd entered the city proper. The buildings were more intact here than they had been at the outskirts, not falling victim to time quite as violently. The frost was thicker here, patches of snow still visible in some of the more shadowy corners between ruined buildings. Glass littered the streets between the fallen rubble like a glittering carpet. It was as if the entire city's windows had blown out at once.

Cassian was the first to break the hours-long silence as they stopped and stared. "What in Sol's name happened here?"

Liv shook her head, her eyes wide as she took in the destruction. Vaida was silent as well, lips drawn into a tight line.

"It looks like some sort of massive blast wiped everything out," Kellan remarked, voice a hushed whisper. "How could anyone have lived through this?"

Liv flinched. "They probably didn't."

Silence fell again, a heavier one still than the one they'd carried from the outskirts.

Kellan looked to his left, staring down a side street at the havoc wreaked there. His stomach was heavy, turning to stone with the realization that thousands, possibly hundreds of thousands of people had died here, and he didn't even know why.

"How..." he began, then trailed off, unsure how to even say what he'd been thinking.

How could the Empire have swept a calamity like this under the rug so easily? Why didn't anyone know about it? Who was responsible for it? His stomach turned from stone into fire, anger seizing his muscles and begging him to fight. It was *wrong*. Kellan felt his teeth creak; he forced his jaw to loosen to avoid breaking them.

A prickle at the back of his mind had him spinning quickly around to face the direction they'd come. He knew this feeling—the feeling of being watched.

It was the same as when they'd encountered those shadows in Bergamot Forest.

Cassian appeared beside him, his brows furrowed as he stared into the darkness beyond the city. "They're here too."

Kellan nodded, a hand on his sword. "What are we going to do? Shine our lights again?"

"It worked last time," Vaida said, holding out a flashlight. "Here."

He accepted the offered light, flicking it on and shining it around the ruins.

The beam reflected off the scattered glass on the ground, glittering like diamonds embedded in concrete. The effect was rather lovely, but turned ghostly in their environment.

No screams echoed. No spectral figures appeared to chase them. But the feeling didn't fade.

"Let's find somewhere to camp," Vaida said. "It will be less terrifying in the day."

They murmured their agreement, Kellan still training his flashlight behind them as they proceeded deeper into the ruined city.

Most buildings had succumbed to time, the roofs they once had long since collapsed. The buildings that were intact were still missing the glass of their windows or doors. No evidence of any sort of inhabitants was present; no long-dead campfires or discarded food. It was like no one had set foot here since the calamity that had destroyed the city. Like no one dared mess with whatever had caused it.

Kellan was surprised. It wasn't like Wolfwater was hard to reach or difficult to enter if one was determined enough. After all, they'd been able to approach with hardly any effort. That worried him. It meant that the ruined city posed enough of a danger on its own to not need protection from entering.

If that was the case, what was waiting for them here?

As they continued to search for a suitable and sturdy place to camp for the night, the feeling of being watched never left them. It was as if eyes followed them through the city. Every building watched them as they picked their way through the crumbled streets, every broken window revealed their location to something within.

Kellan couldn't take it. The sensation was driving him mad.

He whirled on a building to their right, shining his light into yet another broken window. Something moved within the darkness. It wasn't much, a whisper of a shadow, the barest hint of something lurking in the dark. But he'd seen it. And that was enough.

"Show yourself!" he called, voice more confident than he felt.

The rest of the group stopped at his shout, tensing as they waited for the ambush.

Time slowed. Only the puff of their breaths moved within the space, Kellan's flashlight trained in the building where he'd seen the shadow. The beam did not waver.

He could practically hear the frost creeping farther up the buildings. He strained to hear anything, a whisper of cloth, a shifting of weight. But nothing came. Just their breaths in the freezing air. The stuttering silence of the group trying to breathe quietly enough to hear whatever was following them.

Kellan refused to move until whatever he'd seen showed itself. His hand hovered above his sword hilt, ready to draw it at a moment's notice.

Nothing came. The air was still. It was like the chill was mocking him, freezing him to the spot the longer he stood without moving. Like it was determined to hold him there.

Then, a whisper of breath beside his ear.

Chills ran down his body, reaching from his ears to his toes in record time as he whipped around to face the sound. He found nothing there.

"Kellan!" Vaida screamed.

He turned back to face the front and saw a legion of the shadows from the pass waiting for him, unafraid of his beam of light. There were thousands of them, floating in the alleyways and roads behind them like an army waiting to strike. He couldn't see the end of their numbers; there were simply too many of them.

"Run!" he roared, turning back toward the rest of the group without a second thought. They couldn't stay here, not with the shadows being unafraid of the light.

They looked like the ones in the forest, that much he could tell. Their wisp-like bodies, their tattered shapes drifting in an invisible wind. The hollow pit where their faces should be.

They scrambled as fast as their feet could take them over smashed concrete and glass, slipping as they ran on the frost covering the rubble. Buildings flew by, none of them sturdy enough to offer any sort of protection from the army of shadows nipping at their heels.

The shadows were eerily silent; unlike their screaming cousins of the pass, these made no sound. He knew they followed simply by the feeling of constant fear crawling up his spine.

He'd never felt it like this before. It overwhelmed everything else, screaming at him to find cover, to run, to survive. Kellan could hardly contain it, a need to scream at the top of his lungs. But he had to stay focused, otherwise they'd overtake him in a moment. A single slip, a momentary stumble, would send him sprawling and into the icy grasp of whatever these monsters were.

Suddenly, Vaida screamed.

He didn't hear if she said anything, but he saw her veer off their course, pointing frantically at a pristine white building several hundred feet away. It was out of place, but it looked sturdy and well maintained, like time had avoided it entirely.

Something in the back of his head told him this was a bad idea, but they had little choice. It was the strange, perfect building or the shadows. And right now, the fear clawing its way out of his throat was begging him to choose somewhere far away from the wraiths.

Vaida made it first, slamming up against the wooden doors covered in a thick layer of ice. She swore violently, slamming her fists into the ice, begging them to open.

Cassian made it next, his hands already out before him. They glowed red-hot, like he'd made his hands into irons. He grabbed onto the handles. Steam poured around him as the ice melted beneath his touch.

Liv crashed against the doors next, sliding on a sheet of ice beneath her feet. Vaida cradled her to her chest as they crashed to the ground.

Kellan came last, the shadows on his heels just as Cassian melted the ice enough to yank the door open. The other three piled in just as Kellan came sliding across the ice. He hurtled into Cassian with a thud and a groan. They crashed to the ground as the shadows descended upon the door.

It wasn't closed behind them, but the shadows did not enter. They stopped as if held back by an invisible wall. They still made no sound. The shadows floated just beyond the threshold, their faceless figures somehow staring blankly at them.

Kellan stared back at them, hands braced on a cold marble floor. Cassian sprawled beside him, his face turned toward the open door as well.

Vaida and Liv stayed huddled together, Vaida's arms still wrapped around Liv. They squeezed each other tightly. Liv's hands knotted in Vaida's coat.

"What the hells was that?" Vaida breathed, staring out at the floating figures. "Why can't they come in?"

No one answered her. No one dared.

Because beneath their hands, something rumbled. A rhythmic, cyclical sort of sound.

Beneath them, something slept.

42

CASSIAN

Wolfwater | 2nd of Earth Moon

Cassian had never felt fear like this before. It made his skin tight, his blood thick, and filled his head with static. He couldn't breathe as he stared out the open door, watching the legion of shadows waiting for them in the dark.

He didn't think he could feel it more intensely—until the floor beneath him rumbled with the breath of a creature he couldn't fathom.

Whatever waited beneath their feet, it was immense. Its breathing was cyclical, like it was slumbering. But even though it wasn't charging through the floor to swallow them whole, his fear made the rumbling like thunder.

No one spoke. Silence rendered the fear of the shadows secondary to whatever was beneath them, and Cassian knew the others felt the same as he did.

Liv was the first to speak, her voice trembling. "What is that?"

Vaida shook her head. "Whatever it is, it's huge. We should leave."

"And take on the army of shadows outside?" Kellan breathed, his voice shaking. "Face it, we're fucked." His words hung in the freezing air between them like a weight.

Cassian swore softly, and Liv squeezed Vaida's coat even tighter between her hands.

Oh, Zal's voice echoed in his head. *What is that? I'm mesmerized. Be a dear and investigate for me, will you?*

Cassian swallowed hard against the lump in his throat. *So good of you to show up,* he shot back, lacing his words with all the annoyance he felt.

Zal hadn't contacted him for days; he knew the time difference had something to do with it, but it had been unnerving, especially since they'd never gone so long without communicating before. *But you can't just expect me to investigate for your own whims, that's suicidal.*

He could hear the pout in Zal's voice when ze responded. *Cassian, Cassian, don't be so coy. I feel your fear too, you know.*

That's exactly why I'm not listening to you. Besides, I'm not getting anyone killed for your curiosity.

Zal tutted through their connection. *You'd be just fine.*

I won't leave them behind, Zal.

I didn't ask you to.

Cassian cut off their connection with intention, uninterested in keeping the conversation going for much longer. He didn't want to be irritated by the demon's absence during their time at the temple, yet he couldn't help the flare of annoyance in his head when he felt the connection cut.

Liv finally released Vaida to stumble toward the door, feet slipping beneath her. The icy air prickled uncomfortably against Cassian's skin.

He'd known this city was colder than it should be the moment they'd stepped from the van, but it still didn't compare to Stygia. The chill here was simply a taste of what he'd lived in for months. But he could tell the others were struggling.

Liv's hands shook as she made it to the door and pushed it closed. The sliver of light illuminating the space disappeared, extinguished with the final slam of the heavy wooden door.

Kellan sprawled before him, his flashlight pointing toward a far wall. He looked terrified, his face drained of color as he stared at the door. Puffs of air obscured his face as he waited, watching the entrance expectantly.

Nothing broke through. The silence in the space was deafening, terrifying in its purity.

Vaida broke it by shuffling through her pack and tossing their flashlights on the floor with little grace. Kellan's light bounced off the walls, giving them a little light to see by.

Outside, the building had been pristine. Built of a white stucco with a domed golden roof, the building stuck out like a sore thumb in the ruins of Wolfwater. Above them, the dome soared high. It was painted, although he couldn't see what was on it; Kellan's flashlight beam wouldn't reach that far.

The rest of the space was open, held up by soaring columns that melted into high archways leading off to three staircases at the cardinal points, the fourth point being the door Liv had just closed. A plush patterned carpet of reds, purples, and whites covered the stairs, which looked as if they hadn't been touched a day in their lives.

A thin layer of ice coated everything in sight, from the walls to the columns to the floor. It was as if this building had been built and never occupied or used, literally frozen in time for all eternity.

But what slept beneath them, and why wouldn't the shadows enter?

He'd found it strange that the shadows hadn't followed him out of the pass back in Bergamot Forest, and their behavior here had Cassian wondering if it had something to do with the presence of the relics. If that was true, then there must be a relic here holding them at bay.

"What's our next move?" he said, turning his face back to the rest of the group.

Liv and Vaida looked at each other, their faces lit with harsh shadows from their flashlights. Kellan still sat next to him on the floor, eyes wide as he stared off into the direction his flashlight landed.

No one spoke. Cassian didn't even break the silence again to reiterate his question. He knew they'd heard. Now it was a matter of making a choice.

He stooped to pick up a flashlight as he waited. Even Zal was quiet as they waited for the answer. He could feel zem waiting, listening with his ears. Ze was curious, too.

"I hate to bring this up," Kellan finally said, voice timid. "But the verse did say, 'guarded deep below by no man.' It seems likely that whatever is below this building might be our relic's guardian."

"I don't want to go near whatever that thing is," Liv said.

Kellan shook his head. "We can't just send one person down there."

"Oh, come on, does it really matter if I stay behind? I mean, do you hear how big that thing must be?" Liv was nearly hysterical.

Cassian waved his flashlight between them, unable to bear their argument for much longer. "Both of you, stop it. Kellan is right, we can't face whatever that thing is alone. But I don't know what else we can do. We can't leave, at least not until morning. And I know I won't be able to sleep with that rumbling."

Vaida nodded in agreement. "Whatever it is, we can try to be prepared before we go. But if we're going, we should all go together. Who knows if the shadows truly can't enter or if they're just biding their time? Splitting up now would be inadvisable."

"How can you all be so nonchalant about a massive beast? Kellan almost died in the temple, we wouldn't be able to fight whatever that *thing* is!" Liv's voice was reaching a fever pitch. Vaida reached a hand out to rest on her arm.

Cassian felt the frown, but spoke through it. "I know you're scared, Liv, and trust me, I am too. But we have to find these relics."

You have no choice, Zal chimed in.

I don't need you to remind me, Cassian threw back.

Zal chuckled, but stayed silent, their connection still open.

Kellan stood, brushing off his pants. "Down to the beast we go, then?"

Vaida's hand still rested on Liv's arm. She looked down at Vaida's hand, then back up to the rest of the group, worry furrowing her brow.

"We won't go if you say no, Liv," Vaida said quietly, squeezing her arm.

She glanced around the space, taking in the ice and their breaths. Vaida squeezed again, and Liv's jaw tensed.

"Go without me," she finally said. "I'll stay here. Guard the door. If I hear anything—"

She stopped, the unspoken end to her sentence hanging in the air. If anything happened to them, Liv's delayed appearance probably wouldn't change much. Vaida's face softened, and she patted Liv's arm. Cassian didn't want to force anyone—if she wanted to stay, they'd let her.

"But please, be cautious," Liv said, her voice tense.

Kellan snorted. "Did you think we were just going to go traipsing into the beast's lair like, 'Hey! We're here!'"

Liv rolled her eyes. "No, Kellan, I didn't, but I figured you needed specific instructions."

The thick tension in the air was dissipating with their squabble; neither Cassian nor Vaida had the heart to break it up.

Cassian watched as Kellan argued with Liv, their barbs good-natured but sharp. He could see the stress in the way Kellan held his shoulders, pulled tight toward his ears. Liv fiddled with her fingers as they argued, but they relaxed into her lap after a few of Kellan's jests.

I'd do it again, a thousand times over, if it meant saving you.

They'd made up, he thought. They'd turned over a new leaf with that conversation. But something was still missing, still tense between them. He could sense it now, even when Kellan wasn't talking to him. It was like something was missing from Kellan, but he didn't know what it was.

He knew they'd never be like they were four years ago—they both had too much baggage to return to the people they'd been in

Spiral City.

You could always bring him back to the Hells with you, Zal offered.

No, Cassian said sharply. That was why he'd turned Kellan away. He couldn't stay and he couldn't ask Kellan to go. He couldn't risk Kellan's life like that, not for something so selfish.

Vaida cleared her throat, a small noise that brought them back to the present, to the task at hand. Liv and Kellan stopped trading digs, both looking a little more relaxed than they had moments before. Cassian flexed his hands.

She toyed with one of her braids as she spoke. "About this creature..."

Kellan sighed, his respite from their mission going up in a puff of white smoke. He stuffed his hands into his pockets and kicked at nothing.

Cassian watched him while he said, "Let me go first. If this thing is hostile, or if it tries to attack, I'm the one who has the highest chance of surviving the onslaught."

The protest was immediate. "No." Kellan's voice was stern as he shook his head. "We aren't letting you take the full force of an attack, that's just stupid."

Cassian sighed. "It is, but you're forgetting—I have magic. I can try shielding us if need be. Let me go first."

Kellan pouted. "What about one of your force field nodules, Vaida?"

"I used the only one I had in Alderburn," she said, shaking her head. "I could make more if I had the materials."

"I'll go first," Cassian said again. "My magic is mostly offensive, but I can try creating a barrier."

You'll do fine, Zal chimed in. *I'll walk you through it.*

Vaida sighed. "It's the best option we have right now."

Kellan sighed, his agreement reluctant but clear.

"Let's go, then," Cassian said.

🔥 🔥 🔥

Only one of the carpeted staircases led down, and it was coated in a layer of ice. It was a treacherous journey. They stuck to the sides, gripping the wooden handrails and taking the steps one at a time.

The air only grew colder as they descended, the cyclical, slow breathing of the enormous beast growing louder. Cassian's heart slowed, beating in a double-time rhythm to the breaths.

At the base of the stairs was another wooden door like the one leading outside. It was made of a single slab of wood, carved in intricate woven shapes depicting people dancing before a fire, a dragon's serpentine tail curled around the party.

Was it an omen? He didn't know.

He pushed the door in slowly, only for it to be ripped from his hands as the beast sucked in another breath. It clanged open, banging against the wall with a crash loud enough to wake the dead.

Cassian froze in place, hand outstretched, the other holding Vaida and Kellan back. He couldn't see inside the space, but he could sense the gargantuan presence that rested there. Another sigh out, and the beast's breath finally reached them, a gale storm of frigid air that permeated Cassian's already cold bones.

But the next inhale never came.

A rumbling from inside the room began, the sound reminding him of glaciers crashing against one another.

The fear from earlier returned, sinking down from his heart into his feet and gluing him to the floor. He couldn't think anything beyond the fear, not of magic, nor of the people behind him. All he could focus on was the imposing black hole before him where the creature still slept.

Then, a voice came. It was deep, rumbling in his chest and filling his lungs.

"Enter, travelers. Come, hear my tale."

Cassian was rooted to the spot, his feet unable to move. The fear sliced through his veins like thousands of tiny daggers cutting him all over. This was worse than the shadows, worse than the pass.

Neither Vaida nor Kellan moved. He couldn't even hear their breathing as they stood before the open door, eyes straining to see what lay in wait in the darkness.

Cassian, Zal said, a hint of giddiness beneath the words. *Imagine you are weaving a cloth of your magic before you.*

He obeyed Zal's instructions, slowly weaving the threads of magic he gathered in his palm before him. He imagined a spider-like drone running back and forth between the wefts, bobbing in and out as it wove a magical tapestry before him.

Good, good, Zal cooed. *Now imagine it hardening, like all the air and space between the threads are gone.*

He did as instructed, and the wall of purple light before him hardened. Cassian held up a hand, ushering them forward. The voice had not spoken again, even though the shield Cassian had erected wasn't subtle. They couldn't see into the space still, even with the light from Cassian's force field. It was a deep, encroaching darkness. It reminded him of the staircase to the reflection room where they'd found the Sword.

His gut tugged, activating the moment he made the connection, as if it had been waiting for him to realize. It urged him forward into the darkness.

Inside, he gasped at the sight as small orb torches ignited.

A snow-white dragon lay before him, its wings folded along its back, massive clawed feet curled beneath its head. Its snout was long and pronounced, coming to a tapered point with thin nostrils. Spikes fanned out from the back of its neck, covering the soft skin just behind its head. Its scales glittered in the low yellow light of the space, making the dragon appear crafted from the purest snow.

It stared at them as it lay on the floor, pupilless eyes black as the night without stars.

The dragon breathed once more, its mighty chest expanding, the rattle of chains accompanying the sound. Cassian's heart stumbled.

They'd chained it here? Regardless of how one felt about

dragons, it seemed inhumane to treat a majestic creature like this one so cruelly. Especially if it had been like this since they'd hidden the artifacts.

No one had seen a dragon in hundreds of years. For one to be here, chained beneath an old building in a city long charred to ruin, seemed a fate crueler than the one even he'd been subjected to.

Behind them, footsteps echoed. Liv burst into the room and skidded to a stop, her intake of breath sharp as she drank in the sight of the chained dragon. She said nothing.

The dragon breathed again, its slanted eyes closing as it exhaled. Its breath was wintry as it washed over Cassian.

"I will not hurt you," it said, its mouth opening a fraction to speak. "A dragon's promise is binding."

Cassian stepped forward again, cautiously, appraising the creature before him. Words caught in his throat as he took in the chains, the pointed snout, the leathery membranes of its wings. The careful force field he'd erected fell as he took in the state of the majestic beast.

Kellan stepped beside him, brow creased with something between anger and sadness. "Did the humans chain you here?"

The dragon huffed. "This was of my choice, I assure you."

"But why?" Cassian breathed.

It lifted its head and opened its black eyes once more, staring into Cassian's soul. "I shall tell you why. I am known as Gavnith Iceheart, and I am the last of my kind."

43

THE DRAGON'S TALE

Wolfwater | 2nd of Earth Moon

*M*any years ago, dragons once lived in harmony with the people of this land. We did not meddle in their affairs, and they did not interfere in ours. When the humans ruled, they treated us with respect and reverence, nearly like gods. But when the Conjunction came to pass, the elves treated us with fear and loathing.

We did not understand—we had done nothing to make them fear us. We had our mountain homes; they had their river ports. We kept to ourselves, our needs met thanks to the bounty of nature.

But the elves feared us. They hunted our young, stole our eggs, and spread fear and lies about us to the people of the land. They attacked us with fire and stone, chained us with iron and adamantine. They enslaved us to their bidding. They would not listen to our pleas, would not listen to us beg for freedom. They ignored our brethren, the dragonborn, when they pleaded for us to be spared.

We still did not understand.

The humans were no match for their power. They, too, were chained, beaten, enslaved. Tortured to the same fate as we dragons. Their numbers have not dwindled like ours, however.

I was one of the last of my kind when the new sun fought the old star. My brethren had long since died out, quashed under the heel of the elves and driven to insanity and death by the loss of their kin. But *still I prevailed, still I continued to fight against those who'd taken my home and my kin from me.*

It was not an easy fight. We sided with the humans. The elves were devious, wretched, and knew how to wage a war that would not be won easily, regardless of my strength.

And finally, when the sun overpowered the star and day overtook the land, we knew all was lost.

But the humans had one last request, one last act of defiance against those who'd stolen their land. They begged me to take their treasure, to protect it. To ensure that it never fell into the hands of the elves or anyone who could not find the key.

I chained myself here to protect what they've given me. And I leveled the city to keep anyone from finding what has long since been hidden.

The humans here willingly gave their lives to me to sustain me until the day someone with the key found this place and listened to my story. They guided you here to me, allowed you in and ensured you knew where to find me.

I have long awaited the day when I can see the sky with my own eyes. It has been six hundred years since I have flown, since I have tasted the cold mountain air upon my tongue. Many years since I have heard the wind whistle past my face, felt the drafts between my wings.

I am curious about who you are. You four are not all you seem. But you stand before me because you know what lies here. You know what they have charged me to protect.

Two who carry the curse upon them. Two whose fates mirror mine.

Before you can take what I must give, I must receive something in return. To free me, you must give me your memories—the ones that set your heart on fire, that thaw your soul. These memories will serve as a test, a judgment, that you are worthy to bear what I protect.

Offer them to me and set me free, and you will be given that which you desire most.

Once you have offered these things to me, I will be freed.

44

BECK

Rivenstorm | 2nd of Earth Moon

Spider was confined to the hospital for several days. The lightning from the man they'd fought had been as severe as Beck had feared. However, the doctors seemed confident she'd make a full recovery after several intense treatments and lots of rest.

Beck was on his way to visit Spider again today, although this was the first time he was going alone. Harpy had accompanied him twice already, but she'd been busy today. He'd asked Rosalie if she wanted to join, but she'd already had several appointments she couldn't miss.

He didn't know why he wanted someone else to come with him so badly. Time alone with Spider was something he usually cherished.

Maybe it was the guilt. It ate at him—he was the reason she'd gotten into this mess to begin with. He'd dragged her along to the docks, he'd asked her to fight with him, so it was his fault Shadow had hurt her.

The mag-lev trains that crisscrossed the city ran every two minutes, their sleek chrome exteriors a blur when they were in motion. He waited on the crowded platform, hands shoved into his pockets and eyes darting from one waiting passenger to the next.

He spotted a dragonborn with a baby, a fire elemental taming flaming hair, and a human holding hands with a willowy half-elf. Rivenstorm was a melting pot of all the people who shared the Empire's lands. Even though he'd been here for four years, he still found himself swept away by the diversity of people.

And this was what the Red Guard, the Court, and the Council wanted to eliminate? They felt so threatened by such an incredible display of life that they wanted to quash this beautiful enmeshing of people and cultures?

The train hummed into the platform as Beck scowled at his thoughts. He let the crowd drag him forward into the polished train car, unconcerned as he grabbed a hold of the metal poles inside. The fire elemental was sitting across from him, their orange ember eyes meeting his with a flirtatious gaze.

He looked away as the automated announcement system dinged, warning passengers that the doors were closing. Beck was used to the stares. He was just as used to ignoring them.

"Thank you for choosing the Rivenstorm Rail," the automated voice above him said, monotone. "Next stop, Ivory Heights South."

He stared out the window the whole ride; the city flashed by in a mesmerizing kaleidoscope of blues, purples, oranges, and reds. Although he *could* fly, he sometimes preferred the blur of the city as seen from the trains. They twisted and turned through the buildings, but the ride was smooth thanks to the mag-lev system.

Beck had flown after Spider passed out at the docks, unwilling to take her to get help any other way. She'd stayed unconscious the entire short and terrifying flight. He'd never forget the way he felt during that frantic trip. Sick to his stomach; like every breath she took brought her closer to death; like every beat of his heart would make his ribcage crack open.

And Az'Gomack. Their savior had been on his mind ever since that night. They'd been cold, mysterious, and otherworldly. He couldn't make sense of them at all, couldn't reconcile their actions with what Shadow had said.

They knew each other, that much had been obvious. But the nature of their relationship had seemed almost like a disgruntled subordinate and a superior officer. The little he knew of the Shadow told him that Az'Gomack was most likely connected to Ragnor, or at the very least, to the Council.

Beck knew enough about the Shadow and Alvemach from the briefings at the Red Guard. After their disappearance, they'd briefed the entire organization on the situation in Spiral City with the barest of details. He remembered what he'd heard the night he'd seen Kellan at the Autumn Rose—Kellan had *fought* Shadow.

His grip tightened on the metal pole, knuckles creaking with the strain. How much more would he have to sacrifice for the Red Guard? How many more people would he have to hurt just to achieve their goals?

"Next stop, Penninsula Bay Hospital and Market," the automated voice said.

Beck unstuck his hand from the pole. His fingers were sore from the strain, so he flexed them a few times to release the tension.

He departed the train, his head elsewhere, and made his way down to street level. The hospital was two blocks from the station, and he could see the tips of the spires even from here. It had been a clear day, and dusk was closing in on him as he made his way to the hospital.

The Penninsula Bay Hospital was a refurbished building from the Conjunction era, its facade covered in spiky, high-pitched windows and intricate brickwork. It was as beautiful as it was intimidating.

Inside, Beck didn't stop at reception before heading straight for the staircase in the back of the foyer. He turned his face up to the soaring ceilings as he ascended the marble staircase.

Spider was on the third floor in the intensive recovery unit. The hallways were narrower here, the floors made of a white stone with small black diamonds interspersed at regular intervals. Deep mahogany doors lined one wall opposite of the arched windows he'd seen from the outside. The hallway was warm, brightly lit, and empty save for a few medical staff flitting between rooms.

Beck turned left toward a large desk where a nurse was typing away at a holographic keyboard. She smiled when she saw Beck, her eyes crinkling in delight.

"Hello, dear," she said. "Here to see Miss Delacour again today?"

He nodded. He'd used Rosalie's name when he'd admitted Spider to the hospital, embarrassed and unable to explain how he didn't know her true name. None of the resistance members who'd visited her seemed to mind, though.

The nurse's smile grew. "Please, go on in. She's awake and has been asking about you already."

Beck's heart whirled. Spider…had asked for him?

Beck bowed to the nurse and spun on his heel, marching down the hallway to Spider's room. He knew the way well enough by now. Her door was slightly ajar, and he knocked before pushing it open. He felt the pinch of his eyebrows as he took in Spider lying on the bed.

The room was lovely. The same white stone with black diamonds repeated itself on the floor. An old oil-rubbed bronze chandelier hung above her bed, throwing a warm, almost flame-like radiance around the room. She had a window that overlooked what must be an interior courtyard of the hospital.

Holographic displays and glass screens surrounded the head of her bed, although only one monitor was on. It kept pace with the beat of her heart, steady and monotonous.

Spider looked…if Beck was being honest with himself, he hated how weak she looked. He was used to her radiance, her power being obvious behind her eyes and the way she held herself proudly.

But now, she was pale, the shadows beneath her eyes pronounced. She was alert, which he was thankful to see, but she looked like she'd lost weight in the few days she'd been here. Spider's eyes found his immediately as he took a seat at her bedside, lowering himself into the chair and clenching his hands into fists atop his knees.

"Spider, I'm—"

She held up a hand to stop him. "I haven't accepted your apologies either time you've visited before, and I'm not accepting it today." She sighed. "This wasn't your fault. Stop making me comfort you."

He snapped his mouth shut, clenching his jaw against the river of words that wanted to flow from his lips. It was almost a compulsion, how badly he wanted to apologize to her. How badly he wanted to beg her to forgive him for endangering her. How badly he wanted to hear her say that she forgave him for what he'd done.

As if he wanted her to forgive him in advance for what he was eventually going to do.

The realization stopped him in his tracks. It wasn't this situation he wanted to atone for, it was everything he was going to have to do to her in the coming months. The betrayal he was going to put her through.

She may not hate him now. She may not think he was an awful, horrible reaper demon who wanted nothing more than to watch her family burn. She may look at him and not retch at the sight of his face.

But someday…someday she would.

His hands clenched tighter, his knuckles groaning. He hated himself for being the one who would eventually cause her to make an expression he'd vowed to keep from her face.

Beck closed his eyes, took one deep breath, then opened them again. If he wanted to make it through this, if he wanted to live, he had to let go of the inexplicable magnetism he felt toward Spider.

He nodded. "I'm glad to see you're doing better, Spider."

Her eyes were piercing, but at that, they softened. She sighed again, her shoulders relaxing. "That isn't what I wanted to talk about."

She hadn't been awake the first time they'd visited. And the second, he'd been with Harpy. He'd stayed silent the whole visit, watching her sister dote on her while Spider's eyes followed him as he paced by the door.

But this time, they were alone. And she could say whatever she wanted.

"What did you want to talk about, then?" he asked, the weight of his heart crushing as he spoke.

She flushed. "Well, I'd like to thank you," she began, "for saving me."

"No thanks needed. I didn't do much, anyway."

Spider's face fell at his remark. She knew he was right. "That's the other thing I wanted to talk about. Who was that person?"

Beck's thought strayed back to his musings on the train. Az'Gomack was most definitely connected to the Council, to Shadow. But there was no way he could tell her that without blowing his own cover. He had to feign ignorance, no matter how much the lie hurt.

He shook his head. "I don't know. I've never met them before."

"They were really powerful. And…" She trailed off, biting her lip. "I've never seen power like that before, except for Frost. Do you think…"

He knew where her train of thought was leading—that she was a pact-bearer herself. Beck had considered the possibility and thought it likely, although he wasn't sure what that meant for them.

"She's a pact-bearer?" he finished for her.

She nodded and opened her mouth again, but before she could continue, Beck's techpad rang.

Beck made a face, then pulled it out to mute it. Green Wasp's information blinked on the screen. Wasp rarely called him—that honor was usually left to Foxtail. If Wasp was the one contacting him…

Spider noticed the name on his techpad. "Answer it. Speaker, please."

He swiped at the screen, pulling up Wasp's hologram. "What's happened?" Beck said.

"Reaper," Wasp started, sounding out of breath, "Harborside, near the Ward. There's been a murder."

Beck swore.

Spider had practically kicked him out of her room when Wasp ended the call. Beck wasn't sure why they needed him, but she'd insisted. If Wasp was calling, it must be important.

He had a sinking feeling as he sprinted several blocks from the hospital to manifest his wings. Something was *wrong*, but he couldn't pinpoint what. There was a sense of foreboding, a nasty feeling writhing in his gut. Anticipation for what would come next had him in knots.

Wasp sent him a pin with his location while he flew. Beck landed several blocks away from the train station and jogged the rest of the way to meet him.

The streets were quiet. Fewer distractions meant the voices in the back of his head were louder than ever. He couldn't focus on them or he'd spiral into a panic before he even saw what awaited them at the scene.

As he rounded the corner, the situation before him nearly took his breath away.

Blood splatters decorated the walls, climbing higher than his head and spreading across the entire alleyway. It was an excessive amount of blood, as if the perpetrator had wanted people to understand just how much a person could bleed.

In the middle of the alleyway stood Rosalie, crouched over a body. Her boots were flecked with blood.

Green Wasp stood at the mouth of the alley, arms crossed over his chest. He nodded to Beck as he came to a halt, jaw tight.

"What's the situation?" Beck asked, tearing his eyes away from Rosalie and the alley.

Wasp squeezed his eyes shut. "Victim is female, mid twenties. You…" Wasp trailed off, gazing at him with something resembling pity. "You may be familiar with her."

Beck stopped himself from reeling back. Familiar? How?

Wasp gestured toward the alley, inviting Beck to investigate himself. He stood at the entrance, taking in the gruesome sight. Blood splattered on the bricks, sprayed with an almost intentional pattern. But there was something familiar about this place—he couldn't place why.

Before he stepped into the alley, he pulled up the location on his techpad. Warehouse district, near the Ward…

Gods, he was an idiot. The recognition tore through him as he pocketed the techpad. This was where they'd found Cera after her friend had been taken by Shadow.

The sinking in his gut only became more pronounced. He stepped into the alley, taking in the way the blood partially dried on the pavement and the pools that were still wet. He avoided those, running his eyes around the alley in search of more clues.

Rosalie stood at his arrival, her face pinched in concern and frustration. "Reaper," she said simply. "We don't have much time before the Guard gets here. If we want to investigate on our own, now is the time."

He nodded stiffly and finally turned his gaze to the body.

He'd been right to feel anxious. The face that stared up at him was none other than Cera herself. He was going to be sick. What had she done to deserve something so brutal? A death like this was for someone like him, not an innocent girl. She'd done nothing wrong other than associate with the resistance.

"Was it because of us?" he asked, but he already knew the answer. It was because of *him*.

This was retaliation, payment for not allowing Shadow to take Spider. How this man had known about Cera, about any of his movements, was a mystery he didn't want to solve right now. But he knew, without a doubt, that Cera had died because of him.

He squatted down to observe her closely. He started at her head, with her wide-open purple eyes and terrible slashes down her throat and chest. Her body was in tatters, cleaved through multiple times by something sharp enough to leave clean edges on the cuts but large enough to cut through bone like butter. Her face was frozen in a scream, forever immortalized in her last moments by rigor mortis. He wouldn't be able to close her eyes no matter how hard he tried.

His gaze moved to the blood-soaked pavement under her body. He nearly gasped when he saw a design, painted in black ash, beneath the blood. That nine-pointed star was here, at a murder scene?

Shadow was behind the disappearances; that much was obvious. But what had he done with the people he'd stolen? Cera was the only body that had turned up—surely if there were more, they would have found them by now.

"It's her, isn't it?" Wasp had snuck up behind him, quiet as a mouse, and leaned over his shoulder. "I recognize her eyes."

Beck nodded, swallowing hard against the lump that had formed in his throat. He might have been a soldier in the lowest ranks of the Red Guard, but they'd never put him on investigation duty for murders.

He knew Kellan had done this sort of thing before, had dealt with the heartbreak of investigating a murder of an innocent. He remembered the pain in his eyes when Kellan had explained the murder of a girl he'd tried to save, struck through her neck as he'd helped her escape.

He wished desperately that he could just talk to Kellan one more time. Even though he knew he'd betrayed him in Kellan's eyes, he wished he could find that same comfort Kellan had once sought in him.

Because he knew Cera's forever unblinking stare would always haunt him. He knew he'd never get that image from his head. It would prevail in his dreams, lurk behind every thought, stay with him when he closed his eyes.

He released a breath, then stood from her body. As he straightened, several people in dark uniforms stormed into the alleyway, their boots clacking metallically against the stone.

"Civilians, you are tampering with a crime scene. If you do not clear the premises immediately, we'll be forced to take you into custody," one of the uniformed figures said, their voice echoing off the brick walls.

Rosalie nodded to their small group, leading them out the opposite end of the alleyway. They followed, but before they got far, the guard who'd spoken called out to them.

"Wait," he said sternly, his glare razing over them as they retreated, "who was here first?"

Wasp and Beck both turned to Rosalie. She nodded her head. "I was, sir."

The guard narrowed his eyes. "Stay here. You two, leave."

Beck and Wasp didn't wait for another dismissal from Rosalie. They turned and retreated from the alley.

While the resistance might serve as the people's protectors, the Guard had the power here. Any disobedience would be punished, harshly. It didn't matter that Beck was undercover; he'd be treated with the same disdain.

Green Wasp stopped walking a few steps down the block from the alley, and turned back. "I want to know why they held Alpha back."

Beck could make a guess—this would serve as fuel. After all, Cera had associated with the resistance. And that damn nine-pointed star was back, marking the crime scene as part of whatever plot the Guard was cooking up without his knowledge.

He wished he could find Az'Gomack again. He wished Brisea actually knew something. He wished, and wished, and wished, and knew that no matter how hard he might desire it, not a single thing would make sense to him until the end. Whatever they were hoping to accomplish would be done without so much as a finger being lifted in resistance.

Beck was a pawn, and pawns didn't play the game. The game played them.

Before they could consider going back for Rosalie, she rounded the corner, her eyebrows pinched and her lips tight. Her expression softened a touch when she saw them waiting for her, but there was no mistaking the worry and frustration in her expression.

"What did they want, Alpha?" Wasp asked, voice tight.

Rosalie shook her head. "Nothing I couldn't handle. Just a few questions, that's all."

They knew she was lying, but pushing her would get them nowhere. Instead of giving them the chance to press, she breezed past them, her plait bouncing against her back.

Wasp and Beck fell in behind her. As they retreated, he glanced back at the alley. One of the uniformed guards was watching them retreat.

And as he met Beck's eyes, he held a single finger to his lips. Beck turned away, jaw tight, and fear rotting his stomach from inside.

45

CASSIAN

Wolfwater | 2nd of Earth Moon

That which sets your heart on fire.

Cassian bit his lip, staring at the dragon. He slept peacefully, tail curled over his snout.

He'd given them time to consider their offerings in exchange for the relic, then promptly curled up and gone back to sleep.

His first thought had been memories of Kellan. There was nothing else that set his heart on fire like he did. But to give up his memories of Kellan—what would that do to the desire that burned inside of him?

Gavnith hadn't told them what he'd do with their offerings. It seemed obvious they'd lose them. A sacrifice wasn't something easily given, after all.

But why did Gavnith want their memories, anyway? Was the intent to make them forget their mission? Maybe that was the purpose of this exercise, he thought bitterly.

Or maybe, Zal cut into his thoughts, *he needs your memories for nourishment.*

What?

Do you really know so little of dragons? Zal said. *They do not feed like you do. They don't need food, water, or even sunlight. They feed on memories.*

Cassian paused. Then how had Gavnith survived until now? Wolfwater had been abandoned for years. Gavnith himself had mentioned that he'd taken the people's lives who'd lived here.

Realization hit him hard, caving his chest in like he'd been dealt a lethal blow.

Every human in this city had died to feed Gavnith for hundreds, if not thousands of years. The memories he'd fed upon were theirs. How was that even possible?

Cassian pushed off the wall, approaching the dragon on soft feet. "May I ask a question?" he said, voice echoing in the cavern.

Vaida appeared by his side. "What are you doing?"

"You'll see."

Gavnith roused, his black eyes blinking off sleep as he stared at Cassian. "Yes," he said, exhaling a stream of freezing air.

Cassian shuddered involuntarily as Gavnith's breath rolled over him. It was even colder than Stygia had been.

"The humans who died for you," Cassian began hesitantly, "the ones who you say led us here, are…" He trailed off, the words unwilling to leave his mouth.

Gavnith simply blinked, waiting for him to continue.

Cassian swallowed. "Are they the shadows that chased us here?"

The dragon huffed, releasing another stream of frigid air over Cassian. He didn't seem angry or annoyed, but…amused.

"Did I not say they guided you here?"

"But they chased us in the pass—" Vaida began, before cutting herself off.

Gavnith turned to look at her. "The shadows, as you call them, are remnants of the lives given to me to protect this relic. The spirits of Wolfwater will not harm you." He sighed. "Many who died during that time suffered the same fate, but for different reasons. The spirits haunt the resting sites of the relics—such was the humans' sacrifice to protect them. As they were in life, they are in death."

"But—" Liv began from behind him.

Cassian held up a hand. "He's right. The shadows here didn't actually attack us, did they? We ran because we assumed they were the same as Naktchul Pass."

Gavnith huffed. "Naktchul was guarded by soldiers. Their mission was to protect, not guide."

Their group fell silent once more, burdened by Gavnith's words. The dragon closed his eyes once more, breathing slowly, like he'd fallen asleep again.

Kellan was eerily silent as he stood behind a pillar, arms crossed. Cassian met his eyes, nearly black in the dusky light of the room. He wanted to know what Kellan's desire was, what he was considering giving to Gavnith.

Cassian returned his gaze to the sleeping dragon and cleared his throat. "I have more questions, Gavnith."

Immediately, the dragon cracked an eye open. He heard Vaida mumble something under her breath. He couldn't help the smile that tugged at the corners of his mouth.

"I shall answer them, so long as they pertain to your task," Gavnith said.

Cassian nodded. "The memories, do they disappear? Forever?"

"It nourishes me; but you already knew that, it seems," Gavnith continued. "You do not keep your memories once you have given them to me."

"Then why do these spirits still protect Wolfwater, protect you?" Vaida asked. "Wouldn't they simply wander the world, no memories left to ground or guide them?"

"They still desire," Gavnith replied. "Their memories may be gone, but the feelings they gave live on in their hearts. You cannot forget how something made you feel." He stared at Vaida pointedly. "I suspect you understand this better than anyone else."

Vaida was stunned into silence. Cassian felt similarly, unsure what to ask next. What would be a sufficient sacrifice? What would convince Gavnith that they were worthy of the relic? Should he give up something of Kellan? Of his mother? What else would serve as proof that he was worthy enough to bear whatever Gavnith had?

They were all he had.

Before he could move to offer anything, Kellan was beside him. He held his palm up toward the dragon in offering.

"I'm ready."

Gavnith blinked slowly, then nodded his head. "Come forward and touch my brow."

Kellan obeyed. He laid his outstretched hand upon Gavnith's pure white head. As he did, a thin layer of frost appeared over his skin, delicate as a spiderweb. He didn't react—it was as if he didn't feel it at all.

"Ah," Gavnith said, eyes closed, "this is certainly a worthy sacrifice, young one."

Kellan didn't move, his eyes fixed upon the hand resting on Gavnith.

Nothing happened. No flash of light. No booming sounds. No wave of icy air. Kellan and Gavnith simply waited, connected, for what seemed like hours.

Then the frost on Kellan's hand withdrew, and he stepped back, hand dropping to his side. He didn't appear distressed. His eyes were as bright as they'd been before.

But when he looked at Cassian, something was different.

He tried to ignore the worry that washed over him, tried not to let his mind wander to the worst possible scenario. Until Kellan confirmed it himself, Cassian wouldn't let himself speculate.

"Who will approach next?" Gavnith said.

Vaida stepped forward, her mouth set in a grim line. Gavnith blinked once, then lowered his head once more for Vaida to approach. While she stood before the dragon, Cassian watched Kellan, who'd retreated behind a pillar at the edge of the room.

You think he gave something of you up, don't you? Zal said. For once, zir voice wasn't snarky. In fact, ze sounded positively sympathetic.

Cassian frowned. *I don't want to speculate.*

But that's what you believe.

Cassian didn't reply.

You know, Gavnith was right. The feelings are still there, even if the memories are gone.

But who would hold on to a feeling with nothing to back it up? Who would gamble something so precious?

Zal was quiet for a moment, pondering his question thoughtfully. Cassian could feel zir cold contemplation spilling over into his own consciousness, their shared emotions blending together into a strange mix of trepidation and curiosity.

Finally, ze spoke again, zir words softer than he'd ever heard before. *Someone who is so sure of their feelings they will bet the safety of the entire world upon them. If he truly loves you that much, you are incredibly lucky.*

Cassian bit his lip, unwilling to consider what Zal had implied. Kellan was certainly confident enough to do something of the sort. And if that was truly what Kellan had offered, Cassian didn't know what he'd do with himself.

To have someone love him so deeply…he couldn't fathom it.

Vaida stepped back, her eyes downcast as the frost faded from her fingers. She joined Kellan behind the pillar as Gavnith swung his eyes between Liv and Cassian.

"I'll go," Liv said, stepping up to the dragon, her chin held high. "Let's dance, dragon."

Gavnith simply chuckled.

Cassian didn't speak with Zal during Liv's encounter with Gavnith. He watched as she closed her eyes, chin never lowering as she placed a hand upon the dragon's brow. She never flinched, not once.

And when she stepped away, her chin stayed high, proud and strong. He admired her for her strength.

Gavnith's dark eyes met Cassian's. "Cursed one. Are you ready?"

Cassian stepped forward. "I am."

Do you know what you will give up?

Cassian nodded. *I know what I have to do.*

THE PHANTOM FLAME

He laid his hand upon the dragon's brow; the frost crept over his fingers as he closed his eyes, the world behind his lids growing white.

🜄   🜄   🜄

His mother looked back, her smile bright and warm.

"Cassian, come," she said, holding her hand out toward him.

He reached forward, clasping it with his own tiny hand. Hers, although delicate, still dwarfed his. She gripped him tightly as she tugged him along.

The hallway was dark, painted a deep-space blue and dotted with lights in the shapes of the constellations.

He spotted the King, painted by Jupiter in her night sky to represent her husband.

He saw the Stag, Jupiter's beloved pet and protector, to the King's right. Its antlers were the brightest part of the constellation, expanding wide into the sky.

There was the Gale, and next to it, the Flame. They were not as bright this time of year; the lights dimmed to mimic the natural fluctuations in celestial brightness.

They walked further down the hallway, Cassian's head swiveling right and left. There, the Crown, the Wand, and the Eternal Rose. Beyond that, the Dragon, the Wyvern, and the Twin Peaks.

He pointed to each, calling their names out to his mother. He knew she knew them as well as he did, but the joy on her face each time he found a new one was his favorite expression of hers. She never told him she already knew. She always listened, squeezing his hand gently when he'd find another and point it out with a squeal.

Finally, his eyes landed upon his favorite constellation—the Wings. He didn't know why he loved this constellation so much, but ever since his first trip to the planetarium, he'd always waited to see this one in particular.

During his birth season, the Wings were exceptionally bright in

374 | CASSIAN

the sky. They glittered against the deep blue of the painted ceiling, sparkling before his eyes like diamonds in the sky.

"Do you know the legend of the Wings, Cassian?" his mother asked.

He did, but he shook his head. He loved when his mother told him the story of the Wings.

"Long ago," she began, lowering her voice as they stood beneath the stars, "angels roamed the material plane as servants of the humans' god. They had beautiful white wings like gossamer that fluttered in the wind. The most powerful angel, Az, roamed the world as a healer. Her blessings were widespread and wonderful, and many people loved her.

"But when Sol invaded, Az returned to her master's side to fight with him. When he stumbled, Az protected him by sheltering him with her beautiful gossamer wings. They flew off her back and deflected Sol's attack, then shattered into a million pieces, scattering the remains into the sky above."

He'd always loved the story of Az and her beautiful gossamer wings. Something about it reminded him of his mother, how he knew she'd do the same for him.

"Momma," he said to her, "you are like Az."

She turned to him, her eyes filled with sorrow. "You believe so?"

He nodded, but something was wrong. Her eyes. He couldn't remember what her eyes looked like.

"I will always protect you, Cass, my starlight. I may not have wings like Az, but I will do all I can. Remember that always, my love."

He squeezed her hand, her visage becoming more and more blurred with each passing moment. "Momma! Momma, don't go!"

He couldn't see her anymore, but he knew she was smiling as she squeezed back. "I must go, my starlight. But I'm always with you. In your heart. I will always be there."

Then she was gone, and he was alone, no longer in the hallway of the planetarium, no longer a child, no longer holding his mother's hand.

Instead, he was back in the underground room, his hand covered in frost and resting upon Gavnith's brow.

Tears streamed from his black eyes.

"I do not relish taking these things from you," he said. "But you four are strong. Strong enough to have given me such powerful memories and be able to walk from this place without them.

"Take it," he continued, inclining his head toward a trapdoor beneath where he'd lain. "And bring peace to Ileron, which has so long lived without it."

Gavnith shook off the chains, freed now that the last conditions of his self-imprisonment were fulfilled. He took one last look at the four gathered below him, stretching his wings to their full width.

"Wait," Cassian called. "Where will you go?"

Gavnith blinked slowly. "Back to my home in the Icespine Mountains."

The dragon rose, flapping his wings slowly as he did, the gusts powerful. Suddenly, he turned his nose up toward the ceiling and shot through in one go, rupturing out of the top of the building in an explosion of rubble.

Cassian dove beneath the overhang inside the dungeon, where the columns still held firm against the barrage of debris.

And after he was gone, the wind whistled a melancholy tune over the destroyed roof of the building. Almost as if it knew what it had taken to free the prisoner within.

46

KELLAN

Wolfwater | 2nd of Earth Moon

There was a distinct feeling of loss, a hollow ache in his chest. He knew the others felt it too.

When they returned to the surface, crawling up the rubble Gavnith left in his wake, the shadows were gone. It was as if they'd been a representation of everything they'd given up, loss given form, sacrifice taking the shape of the things surrendered. Blown away on the wings of the very thing that trapped them here.

Kellan wondered if it was Gavnith's freedom or their retrieval of the artifact that made the shadows disappear.

Vaida carried the Staff strapped to her pack. It was forged from gold like the Sword and smooth with a pointed, bell-shaped bottom. The top was in the shape of half a sun, its rays swirling, serving almost like the pommel of a sword. It contained a large crystal at the top inside of a force field of some sort. They couldn't see anything holding it in place, yet it floated, contained within the half-circle of the sun design. It gleamed in the fading light as they crawled out of the ruins, a beacon in the night.

No one spoke as they trekked their way back to where they'd left the van. Kellan knew he wasn't the only one who wanted to leave and never look back.

Whatever they'd lost, it weighed heavily on them.

THE PHANTOM FLAME

Cassian looked the worst; his eyes were hollow, sunken. He stared into the distance just beyond Vaida. Even the void of his right eye seemed melancholy.

But it was different for Kellan—when he looked at the silver-haired man walking before him, he felt empty. Like something very important had been taken from him.

He knew, at the very least, that he'd given a memory of Cassian to Gavnith. Possibly several, given the multiple gaps in his memory when he thought of Cassian. He knew they'd met in Spiral City. He knew he'd fallen for him.

But had Cassian ever loved him back?

Everything Kellan had done until now had been for him. He'd broken his mark, fled Spiral City, joined the resistance. But had he done it out of obsession? Or did he really think Cassian would ever feel the same way about him?

It was arrogant, he supposed, to believe that Cassian could ever love him. Their history was fraught with missteps and mistakes. And just when Kellan had finally realized his feelings, Leo took Cassian. And Kellan had allowed it.

There was no way Cassian could love him. Not when he'd stood by. Not when he could have changed their fate.

His eyes burned as he stared ahead, the golden staff mocking him as it flashed in the dusky twilight. He wished he could break it over his knee and fling its severed halves into Galzaga Lake.

Was whatever he'd given really worth it? He didn't know. He couldn't remember.

He watched Cassian from the corner of his eye and wondered what he'd given up. What was important enough in Cassian's life for him to sacrifice it? He felt a sickly silver-green burn of jealousy in his chest when he thought of the possibilities. But Cassian made his own choices, had given something that was of equal importance to the dragon. Kellan couldn't find fault with whatever it had been.

They trudged through the broken city, the frost that covered every surface already fading with Gavnith's departure. Their party's silence bore down on him, weighing on his fractured heart so much he wasn't sure he would have the strength to continue to carry it.

And when they reached the van, they piled into it in silence. Vaida crawled into the back with him, throwing her pack unceremoniously into the trunk, the Staff with it. It seemed she harbored the same feelings toward it he did.

He wondered what she'd given up. Had it been Amaris? He realized he knew nothing about what else Vaida might have given up.

Liv started the van, and in a moment of silent unanimity, began driving away from Wolfwater without asking where they were going. Anywhere, it seemed, was better than here.

Vaida still said nothing as they left the desolate city behind them, choosing to close her eyes and lay her head upon his shoulder.

He didn't realize she'd started crying until a tear landed on his hand.

Kellan laid his head on top of hers, grabbing her hand and weaving their fingers together. The last time he'd felt something like this was in the basement of Northwind Medical all those years ago, after Leo had taken Cassian and disappeared. This sense of mutual loss was not new, and he hated its familiarity.

How much more would they have to give up? How much more would they have to suffer simply because they'd been the most convenient people for the job?

His sorrow festered, turning from a somber shade of midnight blue to a deep crimson. He was so, so angry. Angry with Leo, for starting all this. Angry with Gavnith, for taking something so precious away from them. Angry with Rosalie, for asking them to go.

And angry with himself, for believing he could make it through this unscathed.

Vaida eventually fell asleep against his shoulder, but he had no hope for sleep himself. Liv looked dead inside, her eyes solely focused on the road before them, heading…somewhere.

Cassian stared down at his hands. Unlike on the drive to Alderburn, their eyes never met in the rear-view mirror. He must have imagined all those times he thought it was on purpose.

They hadn't discussed where they were going next. They only had one artifact left, but Kellan wasn't particularly interested in worrying about that now—or ever. He'd had enough, had given enough of himself over for the cause. He didn't care where the last one was.

But he still kept his sense of duty. He knew he had to see this thing through to the end.

He glanced once more at Cassian and realized he was asleep.

He sighed, clearing his throat softly. Liv's eyes flicked to the rear-view mirror once before turning back to the road.

"Wondering where we're headed, huh?" she said, her voice barely a whisper. "The last artifact is at the 'blessed palace,' which can only mean Albiga Castle in Ebenfell. Vaida and I already discussed this back in Alderburn."

Kellan looked down, the question he wanted to ask on his lips. But he was unwilling to say it. Whatever Liv had given must have been deeply personal. It wasn't his place to pry.

She sighed. "I'm sorry."

He finally found his voice. "For what?"

"I know Rosalie put you up to this, and I know you were hesitant," she said, chewing her lip. "This was…more than we ever could have expected. I know if she'd known, she would have insisted on coming by herself."

Kellan frowned. "It doesn't change the fact we were the ones who lost something today."

Liv's smile was melancholic. "No, it doesn't."

Kellan fell back into silence, turning to face the landscape of Midlset passing by the windows.

🔥 🔥 🔥

The journey to Ebenfell from Wolfwater should have taken three days. But that path would take them through Spiral City, and they

—

didn't want to risk passing too close.

So instead, it took them five days, with a two-day detour through the eastern mountains of Kazuta. It was a beautiful drive, but no one seemed inclined to discuss much beyond the journey and where to stay.

Kellan was no better off. He caught himself glancing at Cassian constantly, hoping to find something, some evidence of what he'd lost. But all he felt was a deep, unyielding emptiness.

On the third evening, deep in the mountains, they stopped to make camp. There was nothing nearby, no inns or hotels to speak of.

They stopped on the edge of a small lake at the base of a mountain; its waters were clear and blue and sparkling in the fading light. It was serene, and Kellan relaxed at the sight. Maybe Liv had known they'd needed this and taken them here. Maybe it was chance. Either way, he was thankful for the stop.

They spread their camp out on a grassy knoll a little way off the lake, the view still impeccable. Kellan gathered wood while Liv set about clearing a space for a fire.

The sky darkened to a purplish bruise, spreading slowly across the sky as they sat in silence around the campfire. Vaida picked at her nails, obviously uncomfortable with the tension in the air but unable to do anything about it.

Kellan watched how the campfire illuminated the planes of Cassian's face, how the blackness of his eye stayed blacker than the night. Not for the first time, Kellan wondered just what had happened to him in the Hells. What he'd gone through during his time there. What scars it had left on him.

The fire crackled and danced with the slight breeze; the smoke drifted lazily up and to the left into the sky.

"I'm beat," Vaida finally said, standing and stretching up toward the sky. "It's dark enough now that I don't feel lame going to bed."

Liv nodded, then stood to join her. "Me too. Put out the fire before you turn in, yeah?" she said with a wave of her hand.

After they'd disappeared into the tent, the silence permeated everything. He heard the distant hoot of an owl, the rustle of some woodland creature moving through the underbrush behind them, and the soft *whoosh* of the lake's waves upon the sandy shore.

On a clear day, the lake would have been like glass, reflecting the deep green tones of the mountains and the bright blue of the sky. Tonight, it rippled, the puckered surface reminiscent of pebbled glass. Kellan stared at it for a long time, lost in the silence of nature.

Cassian occasionally shifted, but he never spoke. Kellan so desperately wanted to say something to comfort him, but he didn't know what would help.

He didn't know what Cassian had given up. He didn't know if he'd want comfort from Kellan, if he'd even accept it. Kellan remembered an argument in Rivenstorm, but he couldn't remember what they'd said. He wondered if Cassian hated him now.

Something reflected upon the water's surface that broke Kellan out of his melancholic daydream—a sparkle, a twinkle of light that was so brief he thought he was seeing things. But another glimmer caught his eye a moment later, then another.

He looked up to the dark sky and gasped. Above them, an aurora had formed.

The light wave sparkled with multicolored hues of blue, gold, and green, and interspersed between its waves were falling stars. The stars left trails of glittering gold as they descended, burning out in flashes of pearlescent light.

They fell faster and more frequently until they painted the entire sky in silver and gold. It was the most incredible thing Kellan had ever seen.

He stared at the sky as the stars continued to rain down, somehow never actually reaching the earth. The light from their brief falls reflected in the lake's surface, disjointed and broken up by the dappled waters.

"I was wondering if we'd get to see this." Cassian's voice was soft, reverent, as if speaking too loudly would interrupt the show above them.

Kellan stared at him, eyebrow cocked.

"Don't tell me you've never heard about the infamous Celestial Aurora?"

Kellan just stared at him, dumbstruck.

"It happens once every few years. Some phenomenon with the ethereal plane crossing too close to the material one and sending off sparks. They're not stars," he said, turning back to face the sky. "It's like what happens when two gears grind on each other." He made an exploding gesture with his hands.

Kellan felt the corner of his mouth tug up into a smile as he stared at the side of Cassian's face, finally able to recover. "I've heard of it, but I never expected it to be this beautiful."

Cassian's lips spread into a small smile, and Kellan's heart tumbled.

They watched the sky, the whistling of the sparks the only sound in the valley. The air around them felt charged. If Kellan didn't take the chance to say something now, to ask what was in his heart, he didn't think he would ever be able to.

"Cassian?" he said, softly. He didn't know if he was loud enough to be heard.

Cassian closed his eyes, face still up to the sky. "You want to ask, don't you?"

"What did you give Gavnith?"

Cassian's eyes opened, then he turned to face Kellan, face impassive. Kellan's heart beat too fast in his chest, nerves choking him.

"I…" he began, then stopped himself with a bit lip. Kellan's heart sank lower in his chest. He knew. He knew Cassian hadn't given him up. He hadn't needed to.

"My mother," Cassian finally said. "I don't remember what anymore, but I know I'm missing pieces of her. She's…" He stopped, words catching in his throat.

The weight hit Kellan in the chest viscerally, as if he'd been on the receiving end of a wrecking ball. Whatever he'd thought Cassian had given up, he never thought it would be that.

Guilt welled in his stomach, pushing against him with brilliant yellow fingers. Of course he wasn't more important than family. The commissioner—Aeryn's face flashed in his mind. They had met no resistance on the road so far. There was no doubt it was because of him. Aeryn had protected them this whole time.

He thought then that maybe he understood the magnitude of what Cassian had given up. His mother was all the family he had left, all the blood ties he had left in this world. To give that up was…

"I-I'm so sorry," he croaked out, the grief and guilt tightening his throat.

Cassian shook his head. "Don't be. I'm…quite confident Ragnor already had her—" He stopped abruptly, looking down at his hands. He sighed deeply before continuing. "It may have been for the best that I gave up what I did. Otherwise, my feelings might have led me to seek revenge, and I don't have time to focus on that."

The sorrow welled, bright blue in his veins. Giving up memories of love seemed paltry in comparison.

Kellan sighed. "Still, I'm sorry that you had to give up such a thing for this."

Cassian didn't look up from his hands, balled into fists in his lap.

Kellan said nothing more, instead turning his face back up to the sky. He felt strangled, so many things he wanted to say stuck in his throat and buried deep in his heart. It was like his body was filled with the things he wished he could tell Cassian but couldn't bring himself to say.

He didn't know why he couldn't say them. Why couldn't he just tell Cassian that he'd been the most important thing to Kellan, that he'd given him up even though he was the only thing tethering him to this world anymore?

"The fate of the world seems a worthy cause to give a bit of myself to, you know," Cassian said.

Kellan flinched. "You aren't…angry?"

"No. I know I probably should be, I know it would make sense for me to be. But I'm not."

"Even though you didn't choose this?"

Cassian looked at him then, a sad smile on his face. "I chose few things in my life, Kellan. But Gavnith was a rarity—he allowed us to choose what we wanted to give."

Kellan looked back up to the sky, the words filling his body finally rising to the surface. "I gave you up, Cassian."

He couldn't look at the man he'd loved. He couldn't watch the news settle over him. He didn't want to see his expression.

He didn't want to watch when his heart *didn't* break.

But the other man said nothing. A spark from the sky fell close by. It whistled through the air like a rocket, screaming its descent for the world to hear. Then hands were upon his cheeks, his face forced down to meet green and black eyes.

"You gave the most important thing in the world to him." Cassian's statement was whispered, barely loud enough to be heard over the screaming spark.

Kellan nodded in Cassian's hands.

Cassian let him go, something shining in his eyes. "I—I know I said this before, but I never deserved you, Kellan."

"What?"

Cassian's face smoothed into a mask of confusion; the only wrinkle was the one between his brows. Was this part of the argument he couldn't remember in Rivenstorm?

Something inside of him cracked. What exactly had he given to Gavnith? What memories had past Kellan given that could have taken such a memory away from him? He refused to entertain the idea that this meant what he thought—that Cassian loved him back.

"I see," Cassian said, eyes casting downward. "You must have forgotten."

Kellan shifted. He felt a disconnect, a rift between the Kellan that was and the Kellan he'd become. He'd forgotten something incredibly important, but whatever it was, his past self had wanted it gone.

That which he'd left behind was agonizing, that much was clear to him. The memories were painful but precious—otherwise,

Gavnith wouldn't have accepted them. He'd given up something he no longer wanted. But did he think it could be recovered? Overcome?

Cassian shook his head. "Do you remember what we fought about in Rivenstorm?"

"No," he said, honestly. "I only remember that we fought."

Cassian huffed, turning his face up toward the shimmering sky. "You told me you still loved me," he said.

"Still?" Kellan asked, afraid of the answer but desperate enough to ask anyway.

"I couldn't reply then. I couldn't tell you what was in my heart. Because I was afraid, Kellan. I was afraid of what we'd become if I opened that door again."

"And what would we become, Cassian?"

He didn't reply. Kellan only watched as his jaw clenched, then loosened. His fingers dug into the soft grass, still returning to life after the cold of winter. The dirt lifted for him, although it was hard and compact. It came out in chunks.

"We would crash and burn," he finally replied, fists full of earth. "There's no other way we can come out of this, Kell. I can't stay. I can't stay here, when this is all over. I can't stay with you."

Kellan wanted to scream. He wanted to throw himself on Cassian, beg him not to go. His mind was folding in on itself, twisting him out of every situation he thought of. He could go with Cassian, he could find a way to let him stay. He'd beg Rosalie, he'd beg his uncle. He'd beg Sol himself if that would help. But he didn't know why Cassian had to go. Was it his pact?

He couldn't find the words to say all that was bubbling to the surface. When he tried, a star would scream to the earth, drowning him out and silencing him. What could he say to make Cassian stay? What could he do?

"I think I understand," Cassian said, his voice soft over the descent of the stars. "You forgot my feelings. How I feel about you."

Kellan's lips parted. "You never loved me, though."

Cassian caved in on himself, collapsing over his midsection, head nearly touching the grass he'd yanked from the hard ground. His face crumpled, pain written on every wrinkle, each furrow that appeared on his brow.

"I hate that I made you feel that way. That you felt you had to give up the memories of me ever loving you to save yourself the pain of loving me back." His voice was muffled, filtered through torn ground that mirrored what Kellan thought his own heart might look like. "But you're wrong. No matter how much I know it will hurt, I can't stop loving you. I can't be with you, but I selfishly hold on to you. I can't…I can't let you go. But you had the courage to do just that."

In a rare moment, Kellan was entirely lost for words. Because somehow, he thought maybe he understood.

Kellan reached a hand to rest on Cassian's rounded back, his face still buried in the dirt. "I think, if I know myself at all, the reason I made myself forget is so we could start over."

Cassian was cold beneath his hand, but his skin warmed under Kellan's touch. He first turned to meet Kellan's eyes, then sat up slowly, their gazes held fast. He'd clenched his hands in his lap, still gripping fistfuls of dirt.

Kellan reached down and worked them apart, brushing the dirt away and running fingers over his palms. They were rough, hardened with calluses so much like his own from years of swordplay, training, and hard labor. The knuckles were swollen from overwork and many broken bones. The veins ran smooth beneath his skin, and Kellan could feel the blood pumping as he brushed a thumb along them.

"Do you think we can?" Cassian finally said, staring down at their hands. "Start over, I mean?"

"Only if you want to." Kellan's heart was too big for his chest.

Cassian wrapped his fingers around Kellan's hands. "I think…I'd like that." He paused, breathing in deeply again as he squeezed. "I don't know what I did to deserve you."

Kellan's eyes closed at the pressure. "You didn't have to do anything, you simply were. That was enough."

SECTION 5

THE ALBIGIAN MONARCHY

Prior to the Conjunction, Ileron was a world ruled and inhabited exclusively by humans. Separate countries still existed, each ruled by a different government or monarchy. This period of history is referred to as the Humanistic Period. This time period encompasses most of civilization before the Conjunction and the introduction of other races into Ileron.

Albiga was one of the northernmost countries in Ileron in the Humanistic Period, ruled by a matriarchal monarchy. The lineage was passed down through blood, not by choice like some modern-day countries.

Albiga was established after a war between two factions. The winning faction, led by a woman named Jean Delacour, became the country's first monarch. The Delacour family ruled the country of Albiga for more than four hundred years before the Conjunction.

During the Conjunction and the following Starfallen Rebellion, the nation's last queen, Queen Ameloria, was persecuted by the elven uprising. Although the history books have written her end as a loney death in the cells beneath Albiga castle, the true story has been lost to time.

47

CASSIAN

Ebenfell | 7th of Earth Moon

C assian had nearly forgotten what Ebenfell smelled like. It was noisy and pungent, like engine exhaust and salty ocean and baked bread. But most importantly, it smelled like home.

But something else hung in the air as they entered the city. Something was missing. Cassian didn't need to ponder what that something was—he already knew.

When they arrived at their hotel in Chance's End, Cassian gracefully bowed out as soon as he could. Vaida and Liv both gave him questioning looks, but didn't argue. Kellan, however, insisted on tagging along.

He didn't need a map; he knew this city like he knew his own skin. Kellan said nothing, following him silently as he weaved his way through the streets and dodged pedestrians. The city was busier than usual, buildings and street lamps bedecked in purple and gold for the city's Founders' Day. Storefronts advertised sales for the occasion, holographic displays flashing obnoxiously at the corners of his vision. It was a barrage of noise and light and sound.

Cassian barely noticed it.

They walked for an hour; Cassian never lost speed, and Kellan never lagged. He barely took in the surroundings, his body running on autopilot. It knew where he wanted to go, and he let instinct take the lead.

The cherry blossoms always bloomed in mid-Earth Moon, when the weather in northern Nathcon breathed a hint of warmth into the air. They were blooming a bit early this year. Their petals swirled around his feet as he finally came to a stop before the wrought-iron gate set in a sandy stone archway. The sign above the gate read *Serenity Memorial Gardens*.

His father's headstone was here, in the northwest corner of the graveyard. Cassian had been visiting it for over eighty years.

But if Ragnor had had his mother killed, would she have a headstone here at all?

It was only because of Eliza that Briar had a headstone; his body was never returned to them. A memorial marker was all she'd had to grieve when his father had died, all they had given Cassian to remember the man who'd left him with a life-consuming debt.

The gardens were nearly empty as he walked the familiar paths, the cherry blossoms rustling softly in the spring breeze. Their soft scent reminded him of visiting here each year with his mother, visiting the headstone he now stood before.

Briar Evermore, it read. The final date was eighty-one years ago.

Eliza Evermore's stone stood beside it. The date read three and a half years ago.

He didn't even know who'd bought the stone and put it here. He didn't know who'd taken the time to do such a thing for his mother. His kind, beautiful mother, who didn't have a bad bone in her body, sacrificed because he couldn't protect her.

Whatever he'd given Gavnith of his mother didn't stop the grief from consuming him. It was a yawning, black-edged chasm in the center of his soul, overwhelming him slowly. Fingers gripped at his heart, tearing into the fibers and reconstructing them, creating it anew. It wasn't broken; the pact would never allow that. It was simply changed, a shape he no longer recognized but still knew as his own.

A heart without his mother was a heart he hadn't imagined for a very, very long time.

As he looked inward, he realized he'd known since returning that there was no way she was alive anymore. He'd always known, but something about the reality of seeing it was so much worse than he ever could have imagined.

"Oh?" A voice that was not Kellan's sounded in his ears. A voice dappled with age, a bit shaky, but warm and soft, like butter on bread.

When he turned to face the source, he found himself staring at a decrepit old woman. Her pointed ears betrayed her elven heritage, but her wrinkled skin and tuft of white hair were signs of her obvious age. Her eyes were kind, though. She held a bouquet of white lilies in her arms, and a thick scarf was wrapped around her shoulders and neck.

That itch beneath his skin pulled toward her, nearly yanking him off his feet. It had never been this strong before. The sensation was somewhere between unending sorrow, anger, and an incredible joy.

But he'd never met her before in his life.

"Eliza has wondered where you've gotten off to," the woman continued, shuffling to stand next to him. "You must be Cassian, hm?"

Kellan shifted on his feet. It seemed like he was uncomfortable around her, but she had done nothing to earn his suspicion other than ignore him.

He couldn't find the strength to speak through his pain, but she didn't seem to mind.

"I put her headstone here, so you know. I just couldn't bear the thought of the world not being able to mourn such a lovely woman." She sighed as she slowly bent to place the flowers in a holder next to the grave. "But she hasn't lost faith you'd come back to her. I guess she's right."

Cassian released a breath, staring at the flowers she'd laid down. "How…how did she pass?"

She harrumphed. "Medical complications, they say." He felt a warm hand pat his shoulder. "Malarkey, I say. Regardless, her body isn't here."

"It isn't?" he replied thoughtlessly, finally tearing his eyes away from the stone to look at the woman.

She frowned, then shook her head sadly. "No, they wouldn't release it to anyone but family, and since you weren't here…" She trailed off, leaving the words unspoken, but he knew.

A silence descended over them, the woman's hand never leaving his shoulder as they stood and watched the cherry blossoms drift slowly down to the ground in the breeze. She didn't speak, but it wasn't uncomfortable.

Kellan broke their silence. "Why would you do that for someone you hardly knew?"

Her head snapped to Kellan faster than Cassian thought she was capable of. Her dark eyes twinkled, something in them that Cassian couldn't place.

"I know her better than you could ever fathom, young man," she said, stiffly. Her hand stayed on his shoulder.

Her touch centered his itch, the pull toward her focused entirely on that single point of contact. Something about the touch had pulled him back into himself—but also farther away. He needed to know something, though. Who was she? He didn't recognize her as one of his mother's friends, and she seemed to have a familiarity with Eliza that spoke of years of acquaintanceship. Maybe a neighbor?

"Were you a friend of my mother's?" he finally croaked through the thickness in his throat.

"Something like that," she replied, squeezing his shoulder and then letting go before patting his cheek.

Her hand was cold and soft, leathery but gentle. And when it dropped from his face, she turned to leave. Cassian couldn't let her go without a proper thank you—she'd done this for his mother, and he didn't even know who she was.

"Wait," he said, reaching for her. "I never got to thank you or ask your name."

She didn't turn to face him as she responded. "You can call me Riel. I'm just glad you visited her, dear Cassian. She misses you." And with that, she strode purposefully out of the graveyard before Cassian could stop her again.

Kellan watched her go, his face impassive but rigid. He said nothing, however, turning to face Cassian. His face softened. Their eyes met.

The pull he'd felt toward Riel was entirely gone now, leaving behind only his own rapacious attraction toward the man standing in front of him. His hair was messy from nights spent on the road, but he'd done his best to smooth it down before they came in. It was long enough that Cassian could twist his fingers in it, if he wanted to.

But he didn't want to. He wanted to cry, to use Kellan's shoulder as a resting place, to release this pressure that had been building inside of him all this time. Because now the man before him was all he had left in the entire world.

What a burden to place on someone else. What a weight he would be on Kellan now that he was all Cassian had. Would Kellan grow weary of him? Tire of his constant exhaustion and sorrow? Get bored with his anxiety?

He felt Kellan's warm hand slide into his, then give it a gentle squeeze. "What's on your mind?"

Cassian couldn't look at him. "This…this is all I have to give you, Kellan. All I have left."

Kellan said nothing, his hand still firmly grasping Cassian's. He was waiting—he knew Cassian wasn't finished yet.

"It's scraps," Cassian finally said. "I'm just broken pieces, cobbled together from the man I used to be. That isn't enough for you."

Kellan took his hand away. But it reappeared just as quickly, taking his chin in his grasp. His face was forced up, his gaze meeting Kellan's amber eyes awash in afternoon sun and turning them to burnished gold.

"I'm just parts, too," he replied, breathless. "But isn't that why we find each other, to fill in our gaps? I'm not whole, and neither are you. That's the beauty of it—we don't have to be."

Cassian's lips parted. He was speechless, rendered completely stunned.

Kellan smiled, the brilliance of it almost as warm as the hand still on his jaw. "Come on, let's go." His words were soft, unbothered, as if he hadn't knocked Cassian's heart out of his chest.

He nodded and let Kellan lead him from the gardens and back into the streets of Ebenfell.

🔥 🔥 🔥

They returned to the hotel Vaida had booked in Chance's End, a neighborhood in the eastern part of Ebenfell. The buildings were a mishmash of styles, ranging from a brand-new apartment building with shiny glass and black metal to a building with a circular turret-style tower at its corner built of red brick.

He'd always found the spontaneity of buildings in Ebenfell charming. It gave it a sort of old-world feel, the passage of time obvious in the way the old interspersed with the new. Unlike Spiral City, whose construction had been much closer together, Ebenfell was well over a thousand years old, and the buildings painted a colorful picture of the rich history of the city.

When Cassian had lived here, he'd been in an apartment with his mother on the north side of town. His heart sent a painful pang through his body when he thought of her, her headstone next to Briar's.

If I'd known I'd feel so much of your sadness, I would have come and done this mission myself, Zal griped. *I don't think I've felt this sad in ages.*

Sorry to be such a disappointment, Cassian shot back, annoyed.

Zal laughed. *Darling, disappointments are my favorite.*

Stop talking.

Fine, fine.

When they entered the room they'd booked, Vaida threw open the adjoining door and beckoned them into her space.

She'd set up her techpad and gear on the table in the corner and had several diagrams and photos pulled up of an ancient castle. Cassian recognized it as Albiga Castle. It was smack in the center of the city, surrounded by a park and, ridiculously enough, a moat.

Why the Empire had bothered to keep the old human monarchy's castle was a mystery, but he was thankful for it. It had stood through the centuries, serving as both a museum and governmental building for the White Court. When they needed to meet in one place, they gathered at Albiga Castle, along with the Red Council.

But how in the world were they going to get in? He couldn't imagine the artifact was just out in the open in the museum, and every other part of the castle was off-limits to the public.

Vaida was already a step ahead as she cleared her throat and brought up a map of the castle on her techpad.

"I've been doing some digging about how we're going to get into the castle's off-limits sections. And it seems we're in luck," she said, smirking as she turned the map sideways. "In celebration of Ebenfell's Founders' Day, the Court is holding a ball at the castle."

"Okay, how do we get in?" Liv said.

Vaida's smile grew wider. "Well, that's easy enough for me to handle. It's by invitation only, but I can forge the invites for the four of us. It's going to be an impressive party, four extra guests won't arouse suspicion."

Cassian scratched his chin as he considered the plan. It was a good one, but there were still so many details to figure out. And they only had three days to finalize their plan.

"Won't there be extra security that day because of the ball?" Cassian asked. "It will make sneaking away and exploring the rest of the castle a challenge."

"That's why we're going to the ball," Vaida began, her smile turning feral, "as part of the festivities. They are giving guests a *full tour* of the castle."

That certainly changed things. Cassian had never attended the Founders' Day ball—he never knew it existed. He'd be going into this just as blind as the others would be.

Vaida turned back to the techpad, flicking a finger back to the blueprints and zooming in.

"I have a hunch we're going to need to look in one of two places; first, the queen's chambers, which are in the north tower." She pinched the blueprint and zoomed in on one of the castle's five towers. "Or somewhere in the maze of dungeons below."

Cassian cocked an eyebrow. "Why the dungeons?"

Liv answered before Vaida could. "In the Humanistic Period, the monarchies of Albiga, Illium, and Ellsemere all practiced keeping their valuables in a vault beneath their dungeons. They figured it would be the safest, since one would need to get through massive amounts of guards and prisoners alike."

Kellan huffed a laugh. "I mean, I guess that makes some sense."

"I find the practice ridiculous, but that's irrelevant," Vaida said. "We'll need to split up and investigate while we're there. That's what I wanted to discuss with you two."

Vaida's gray eyes flicked up to meet Cassian's, then shifted to Kellan standing beside him. Although they hadn't told Liv or Vaida about what had happened at that mountainside lake, it seemed like Vaida already knew, judging by the soft smirk that spread across her lips.

Liv picked up where Vaida left off. "Vaida and I were thinking we would take the queen's chambers while you two took the dungeons."

Kellan scoffed. "You just don't want to dig around in the mud and dirt. Rude."

"You're right, that sounds like an awful time. I'd rather *not* be where the bugs and dead people are, thanks." Liv's tone was mocking, but Kellan was smiling at her, anyway.

Cassian looked down at his hands, a frown spreading across his lips. "That's a fine plan. What does the tour schedule look like? How much time will we have?"

Vaida's smile dropped, and she furrowed her brows. "That's the part I'm not sure about. There isn't much information about the tours, only that they will take place each hour on the hour. I don't believe there are assigned groups, but we should go in separate ones just in case. Two people missing is less conspicuous than four."

He scratched his chin. "Then let's assume the tours are forty-five minutes; that gives the guides enough time to regroup and collect the next tour with time to spare. We'll be moving quickly, then."

Vaida nodded. "I can build us comms, but I need time." She sighed. "If we find something, we'll need to get out immediately."

"After we finish searching, we'll regroup with the next tour and leave under the radar," Liv said. "If we can get out without causing a fuss, that's for the best."

Kellan nodded. "I guess this means we have a plan?"

Liv nodded in agreement, Vaida copying the motion. Cassian just hummed his assent.

Kellan clapped his hands together. "Excellent. That means we'll need to dress up for this thing, won't we?"

Cassian felt the chuckle bubble up through his chest, bursting from his lips in a short gasp of breath. Kellan pouted good-naturedly at him, but he wasn't angry. The soft set of his eyes told Cassian enough.

I told you, Zal said softly. *You are, indeed, a lucky man.*

As he stared at Kellan's honeyed eyes, he felt affection burst within him like fireworks. He'd known all those years ago that every choice he'd made had led him to Kellan.

Even though he couldn't stay once this mission was over.

But in his heart he held that small, flickering spark of hope. He covered it with his hands and cherished it, kept it safe and dry. If that was all he had left when this was over, it was enough.

48

KELLAN

Ebenfell | 10th of Earth Moon

Albiga Castle was, frankly, exactly what Kellan expected a castle to look like.

The humans had built it upon a jutting mass of stone surrounded by a moat. A *moat*. No one had moats anymore, not with the magical security of the modern age. Magic made most forms of traditional security irrelevant—like moats.

The castle was built of a dark, wide-cut stone stacked in neat alternating rows. He could tell they had restored parts where the stone was lighter. Massive towers sat at the corners of the building, each with an open-roof patio and lit with gargantuan signal fires. They were lit tonight in honor of the ball. Because of the castle's location on its own small island, there was only a single entrance onto the castle grounds, a stone bridge that could easily fit ten people abreast.

They blended in with the crowd sweeping down the walkway. Vaida walked before the group, her stride confident as her purple suit swished about her legs. Liv followed closely on her heels. She'd opted for black pants and a bright pink asymmetrical jacket; the look flattered her curvy figure well. Cassian walked beside him, his outfit reminiscent of the one from so long ago at a gala where he'd nearly died. Midnight blue suited Cassian; it made a pulse flutter in

Kellan's throat.

The crowd swept them along, excited chatter filling the evening air as they made their way slowly to the entrance. The guards at the end of the bridge stood solemnly as they checked invitations, scanning them before waving the guest through the holographic cordons and into the castle courtyard.

Kellan could feel his nerves sparkle yellow in anticipation, but he couldn't doubt Vaida's handiwork when she'd gotten them this far.

The guard scanned Vaida's invitation with a bored look on his face. Kellan held his breath, waiting for the beep that meant they were in.

Moments passed, stretching on for what Kellan was sure was too long. Any moment now alarms would blare, sirens would wail, and a whole battalion of Red Guard soldiers would descend upon the bridge to take them into custody.

Any moment now.

Beep.

The relief was drastic, like he'd been teetering over the edge of the bridge, waiting to fling himself into the murky waters of the moat below. Cassian reached a hand over and squeezed his shoulder as Liv handed the guard her invitation.

Another beep, and she was in, trailing behind Vaida as they sidled through the holographic gates.

Cassian was next; he handed his invitation to the guard and relaxed his hands at his sides. Kellan wondered if he was nervous. His behavior suggested nothing other than a man waiting to enjoy a relaxed evening.

The beep sent a shiver through him, and Cassian passed through the gates as well.

He handed his invitation to the guard, his face as neutral as he could make it. He stuffed his fists into his pockets to stop himself from touching the back of his neck. The tattoo wasn't there. The guard wouldn't see anything.

Beep.

He smiled tightly at the guard and passed through the gates, joining Cassian on the other side.

"You look tense," Cassian said softly. "Loosen up. It's a party."

He shot Cassian a withering stare. While under any other circumstances Kellan would have loved this event, he was wound too tightly to enjoy himself, regardless of what Cassian said.

"Kellan, come here." Vaida's voice was light, but he sensed tension there.

He approached her, jaw tight, but she didn't even look at him before pointing toward a portcullis to their west. "The tours will meet over there. Liv and I will go in the first one. You and Cassian stay here." She pulled a small box from her pocket and handed each of them a small device. "Put this in your ear. Tap it to activate the voice comm; it's the best I could do with such a short timeframe."

Kellan nodded, taking a comm. Liv took Vaida by the hand, leading her off into the darkness of the courtyard. Cassian stayed next to him, waiting for him to make the first move.

The courtyard was a circular cutout in the center of the castle, the building built up around it. At the center of a perfectly manicured lawn stood a fountain in the shape of a crescent moon with a flame in the center. Partygoers mingled about, scattered between the vibrant green bushes and wandering the small pebbled pathways between.

The ball itself was to be held in a grand ballroom just inside to the west, beyond the portcullis Vaida and Liv had disappeared through. A steady stream of elegantly dressed partygoers headed that direction, and Kellan allowed himself to be swept up into the crowd, Cassian by his side.

Inside, an elegant hallway of white and green marble greeted them, the windows overlooking the moat and the interior courtyard. Gold filigree wound its way up stone pillars at even intervals, taking the form of vines with flowers shaped like flames.

The crowd moved toward a set of heavy green-painted doors on the right side of the hallway. They'd been flung open, and inside he could hear the sounds of a live band playing.

Cassian gripped his hand as they moved toward the ballroom. Kellan looked at him in surprise; he was greeted with a melancholy smile.

"We have at least an hour and a half before we need to join a tour," Cassian whispered into his ear, "so we might as well enjoy ourselves before then."

Kellan squeezed their intertwined fingers. "We might as well."

When they entered the ballroom, Kellan gasped. The crescent moon and flame motif was inlaid in the green and white marble of the floor. The same marble continued up the walls, elegant white pillars holding up a domed ceiling full of skillfully carved statues.

Kellan thought he recognized a few; they looked similar to the carvings he'd seen in the temple of Hym. It made sense, after all. This had been the seat of the human monarchy for hundreds of years. Why the Council hadn't destroyed it was a curious phenomenon, but if the entire castle was this splendid, Kellan thought maybe he understood why they'd preserved it.

The band was along the far wall of the space, set atop a small stage. One woman played a stringed instrument made of a shiny silver metal, its melody smooth and melancholy. Another man played a glass keyboard, his fingers flying across the keys at a surprising speed.

The chatter of guests and music filled the space. Kellan's ears rang with the sound. It wasn't as bad as the clubs of Spiral City had been, but he found it difficult to concentrate on one thing at a time when there was simply so much to look at.

Cassian was now gently tugging him toward a table opposite the band. It was laden with refreshments and holograms of the city's history.

"Here," Cassian said, grabbing a tall flute of a bubbly pink liquid and handing it to him. "Try it."

Kellan sipped. It sparkled on his tongue, fizzy and sweet. "Tastes like I will be sick of this stuff after one glass."

Cassian was staring at the table of glasses, his mouth a taut line. "It can't be that bad." He grabbed a glass for himself, downing half of it in one gulp.

The resulting face nearly made Kellan double over—a mixture of immediate regret and a hint of contemplation at the taste.

"I think I hate it," Cassian said, setting the glass back down on the table. "That's absolutely disgusting."

Kellan drained the rest of his glass for posterity's sake. He didn't like sweets, but it was a gift from Cassian, however small. Once finished, he set his empty glass by Cassian's.

He held a hand out to Cassian, the other behind his back as he bowed. "Dance with me?"

Cassian looked hesitant, regarding Kellan's offered hand for a moment too long. But Kellan didn't move. He waited, his palm up, a gesture of trust.

He could see the storm behind Cassian's eyes. He was putting up a brave face, had been trying his best to act as if nothing was wrong. But Kellan knew that look. He'd seen it too much on his own face for the last four years not to know—he was grieving, and trying to hide it.

Cassian finally moved, placing his hand gently in Kellan's offered one. "Sure. I'm terrible at it, though."

The center of the room already held many dancing partygoers, their garments spinning to the beat of the music. Kellan pulled Cassian in close, a hand wrapped around his waist, the other weaving their fingers together at their sides.

Kellan smiled, pulling up against him, their chests nearly touching. "Well then, it's a good thing I'm an incredible dancer. Follow my lead."

And they spun. Kellan directed Cassian with subtle shifts of his shoulders and gently squeezing their joined hands. Cassian followed his lead, melting into a rhythm that matched the music soaring above their heads. The music swelled; he spun Cassian with a twist of his wrist. The music softened; he gathered Cassian in close, his chin tilting up just enough to hover above his shoulders.

He could feel Cassian's heartbeat in his palms, one rested against the small of his back. It was frantic, pulsating an entirely different rhythm than the music.

Kellan let his hand slide down from Cassian's shoulder to his upper arm, pulling his shoulder in so he could lean his head against it. He felt Cassian stiffen, then soften against him. He rested his chin on top of Kellan's temple.

"You weren't kidding," Cassian said, voice rough.

Kellan chuckled. "Why would I joke about being an amazing dancer?"

He felt Cassian's lips through his hair, then they grazed against his temple in a soft kiss. "I never doubted it for a second."

Kellan tilted his chin further down, nuzzling into Cassian's chest.

They continued to twirl and sway, sweeping between the other dancers on the floor, their bodies in perfect sync. The music melted from one song into another, then another, and another. He didn't know how long they danced for, but he thought he could have danced forever.

He tilted his head up to look at Cassian when the song drew to a close. A crease furrowed Cassian's brows, his mouth a hard line.

"What is it?" Kellan asked.

Cassian hesitated, then replied, "Am I allowed this?"

"Allowed what?"

"To be happy, even though she's gone."

Kellan's heart stopped for a beat. He couldn't imagine what was going through Cassian's mind. Sure, Kellan had lost his mother too. But he'd been hardly more than a child, barely old enough to understand the permanence of death.

But Cassian had grown up with that love, that parental influence that Kellan had never known. To lose that, and to lose it after so much fighting against it… The fact Cassian hadn't entirely crumbled from the weight of it forced Kellan to see him in a new light. He glowed iron-hot, like he was being forged anew.

He squeezed Cassian's shoulder as another song began. "Would she want you to spend the little time you have to be carefree forcing yourself to be miserable instead?"

Cassian shook his head. "No; no, she wouldn't."

"Then think of it as a way to remember her, yeah?"

Cassian said nothing else.

They danced for two more songs before Cassian glanced at his wrist and declared it almost time for their tour to begin. He pulled away from Kellan mournfully, but strode from the dance floor with purpose.

Kellan wandered after him, his heart constricted.

🔥 🔥 🔥

They'd heard nothing on their comms from Liv or Vaida, meaning they'd likely found nothing. Kellan and Cassian's tour was walking up the tower's stairs toward the queen's chambers, partygoers' heels clicking against the marble floors.

Their tour had gone through the chapel, which they'd converted into the meeting hall for the Red Council. They'd seen the solar and the lesser hall, where the White Court met when they convened. The dungeons were the last part of the tour.

The queen's chambers were next, up the staircase that seemed to go on for miles. Kellan's eyes swam with the endless spiral.

Cassian nudged him as they finally, blissfully, reached the top of the staircase. "There," he said, inclining his head toward an oak door with inlays of woven wrought iron.

"Think they've gotten out?" Kellan asked, voice low.

Cassian nodded sternly. "I'm sure they have. If not, they'll stay out of sight."

Kellan nodded, turning back to the tour guide, who droned on about keeping the queens of the human monarchy away from the main parts of the castle in order to best protect her.

"We didn't find anything," a voice said quietly in his ear—Vaida, in his comms.

He didn't glance around the room, forcing himself to focus on the tour guide instead as he whispered out the side of his mouth, "Dungeons it is."

"Be careful."

"We will."

They followed the tour guide back out of the queen's chambers. Kellan stared at the soaring ceilings above him and wondered what life had been like all those years ago. He'd learned almost nothing about Ileron before the current era, the Humanistic Period consistently shrouded in mystery. Most teachers brushed it off, saying knowing human history was unimportant, save for the Battle of a Thousand Suns and the subsequent enslavement of the Fallen and humans. Kellan knew they did it on purpose. Giving them no information meant there was less for them to rebel against. If things had always been this way, who would challenge the status quo?

They descended the long spiral staircase from the tower, coming once again to the main level of the castle. He scanned their group casually, noticing Vaida and Liv seamlessly blending themselves into the group. He glanced over at Vaida, watching as she leaned into Liv to whisper in her ear every few minutes.

The guide led them to another staircase; it was less grand than the spiral staircase, carved roughly from a dark stone and worn down to smoothness in the center from hundreds of years of feet. The banister was also smooth, although that seemed by design.

The guide continued to speak. "The dungeons are one of the most famous parts of this castle. Once used to house prisoners from the nations across the sea and prisoners from the old country, the dungeons are nearly impregnable. After the fall of the matriarchy, it is said that Queen Ameloria herself was kept here until her death ten years later."

No one seemed surprised, but Kellan felt the same sense of wrongness from whenever he'd received a history lesson about that time period. It was like someone had methodically stripped the story down to its barest form, sanitized it, then re-released it to the public. Like what everyone believed to be true simply…wasn't.

They continued down; the guide droned on about what the first Red Council had done with the prisoners and what they'd eventually done with the dungeons. Although no longer in use, they'd kept this part of the castle with as much fervor as the rest.

"You think," Cassian whispered in his ear, "that they continued upkeep on this place because they knew about the artifact?"

Kellan shook his head. "How could they have known?"

Cassian shrugged, but said nothing else.

The dungeons were deeper down than he'd expected. On the blueprints, they'd looked as if they were just below the main floor. In reality, they were several floors down. The air grew cold, and Kellan shivered against it, although it was nothing compared to the bone-jarring cold that had been Wolfwater. The thought of the ruined city brought melancholy down on his heart.

Finally, they reached the depths of the castle; the group clustered together in their finery, obviously unprepared for the dungeon's chill. The guide acknowledged this, regaling them with tales of how the most common cause of death in prisoners had been hypothermia in the winter.

Kellan glanced around, eyes searching for something, *anything* that could help them find what was "hidden in plain sight." What that even meant, he couldn't guess.

They swept through the rows of cells, the metal well polished and maintained. The dirt floors looked as if someone had tended to them lately. Each cell door was closed and locked with what looked like old-fashioned mechanical locks, but Kellan guessed there was more to them than met the eye.

They finally stopped next to a cell that looked like all the others. But on the wall, he noticed, was a grand design carved into the stone. He gasped.

"This," the guide said, pointing to the symbol, "was the very cell Queen Ameloria lived and died in. It's said that she carved the symbol into the wall before she died. Do any of you recognize it?"

A crescent moon with a flame between its points. Wasn't that the same symbol he'd seen at the fountain in the castle courtyard?

Someone else mumbled an answer, and the guide smiled. "Correct! This is the symbol of the monarchy. If you remember, there were several motifs in both the solar and the queen's chambers that included this symbol."

They moved on, toddling down the row of cells and pointing out several others of interest. But Kellan found his feet rooted to the spot before the queen's cell. He stared at the symbol on the wall, eyes narrowing.

Cassian also stood beside him, staring at the cell. His face was slack.

Kellan turned to face him, grabbing a hold of his jacket in one hand. "I think—"

"This is it," Cassian said, cutting him off. "It has to be."

Kellan nodded sharply, then tapped the device in his ear. "V, Liv, we've found something."

49

BECK

Rivenstorm | 10th of Earth Moon

Beck hadn't seen Brisea for nearly two weeks—after their last meeting, she'd disappeared from Rivenstorm without so much as a word. When he'd gone to the Rosestone the week before, a different Red Guard operative had told him she wouldn't be there. It wasn't necessarily a welcome surprise, but he was glad he didn't need to deal with her.

But she'd returned, and he'd demanded a different meeting place, someplace far away from prying eyes. He knew his mission was ending soon, and he needed answers, ones he wasn't sure Brisea could give.

She'd offered her home in Rivenstorm as an option. Unfortunately for her, he wasn't stupid enough to take that request. After the proposition he'd turned down and her subsequent threat, he refused to take any chances with her. Instead, he'd asked to meet near the harbor at an old office building his benefactor from Ebenfell, Ragnor, owned.

Brisea had agreed, promising to meet at their usual time.

He was leaving his room at the Autumn Rose. The usual bustle of the back bar was a calming agent to his nerves. Those nerves were to blame for his eyes swinging around the bar in a practiced gesture he hadn't done here for months.

He was safe here, but the events of the last few weeks had him paranoid. Before he reached the door, a hand landed on his arm, gently stopping him.

"Reaper," Rosalie said softly, her eye mournful. "I know you're on your way out, but…when you return, I'd like you to come see me. Okay?"

He couldn't fathom what she wanted.

He nodded. "I'll do that. I shouldn't be too long."

Rosalie didn't smile. She looked troubled as she nodded him off.

Beck couldn't focus on her cryptic request for long—the flight there was cold, the wind forcing tears to eyes before he finally put glasses on mid-flight. The spring air was nice when he wasn't moving at top speed, but he couldn't waste time. He wanted to arrive long before Brisea did.

His effort paid off when he entered the empty building with a special key from Ragnor, the security spells flaring purple when he opened the door.

The space was open, empty, and clean. There were no chairs, no desks, not even a stray piece of paper. It was as if Ragnor had bought this property only for the locale and hadn't bothered to do anything more with it.

He wandered, a hand on his sword hilt. The windows on the northern wall overlooked the slope that led down to the water, and the view was rather striking. Only a few blocks of city lay between the building and the water, but at this height he could easily ignore the buildings between.

White-capped waves crashed angrily against the docks, the midafternoon sun sparkling off the water. He remembered his discussion with Spider about the ocean and how it made her feel like she was part of something bigger than herself.

His heart tightened at the thought of her smoldering on the ground after the attack. How had he let it get that bad? He should have been better, should have protected her. It was his fault she'd been there to begin with.

"My, I do love a brooding man," Brisea said, surprising him out of his spiral. "What's got you all tied up in knots? Not that I don't love it."

He turned from the windows, facing her. She stood by the closed front door, wearing a form-fitting black bodysuit with a cropped yellow sweater over top. A pair of triangular sunglasses hid part of her face. He could see the digital sheen on them—they weren't just for fashion.

"Keep the commentary out of the conversation, Brisea," he retorted. "I don't know how many times you need me to tell you I'm not interested."

She laughed, patting herself down as if looking for something. "Whether you are or aren't, I can still have my fun."

Beck ground his teeth. "I need you to enlighten me on a few things."

She found a column to lean against, crossing her arms over her chest as he spoke. She pouted. "Well, you're no fun."

"I'm not here to be fun."

She sighed dramatically, then gestured for him to continue.

Beck sighed, clenching his teeth. Brisea might not have the answers he was looking for. She was cold yet coquettish; she might simply decide she didn't want to reply. He also knew he was toeing a very dangerous line—she held his leash, and she wasn't afraid to pull on it.

But he had to try. The Red Guard's plans were leading them into territory he didn't want to explore blindly.

"The Guard's plan for Rosalie," he started, voice low, "includes demonic symbology. Why?"

Brisea's face was unreadable. She didn't raise her eyebrows, purse her lips, or even narrow her eyes. She stayed perfectly still, perfectly calm. But it took her too long to reply.

He watched her face, waiting for her to say something, *anything*—the activation words or an angry outburst. The back of his neck prickled in anticipation, like it had a mind of its own.

When she finally moved, it wasn't to reply, but to adjust the glasses on her face. With each agonizing, silent moment that passed, Beck's stomach turned to stone. He was going to die here for asking the wrong question.

"Show me," was all she said.

He handed her his techpad, the terrible rendition of the markings he'd drawn for Wasp and Fox displayed on the holograph. She regarded it for several tense, breathless moments before handing it back with little fanfare.

Brisea sighed. "It's unimportant for you to know the specifics of the Council's plan for her," she said. "You have done just fine without knowing the details."

Beck slammed his fist into a wall, the sound dull but loud in the cavernous space. "Don't bullshit me, Brisea. How am I supposed to play my part convincingly if they're going to throw demonic involvement around in this case without telling me? People are getting hurt—*innocent* people—for this crap, and I can't do anything about it!"

Brisea's eyes narrowed. He knew he'd gone too far, revealed too much, and he regretted it the moment the words left his mouth. Brisea would have no sympathy for anyone he considered dear. Attachment was a luxury he couldn't afford in her care.

"I hope you realize," she began, her voice full of venom, "that the people in the resistance aren't innocent. I heard your dear teammate was injured in a fight—her survival isn't of any importance to the Council. In fact, her death would be just another win in their eyes." She pushed off the pillar and strode toward him, her shoes squeaking on the polished concrete. "It concerns me greatly to hear of your attachment to her. Might I remind you that you are not part of the Phantom Flame. You are nothing but a reaper in their ranks; do not forget your place, Beck."

How did she know? He'd never spoken to her about Spider, never mentioned his relationship with her beyond the fact she was on his squad. Beck had been so careful not to let his feelings for her show—but that had just gone up in smoke.

He wanted to rebuke her accusations. He wanted to tell Brisea she was wrong, that there was nothing there. He tried to open his mouth to speak, tried to say Spider wasn't important to him. But his throat was frozen; the words caught in his chest.

Brisea was in front of him now, close enough that she could reach out with her chrome-colored nails and rip his throat out if she wanted.

She continued, a sinister smirk appearing across her lips. "Regardless, I'm thankful for your information from last time. Because of you, the Red Guard in Ebenfell will apprehend those runaways tonight. What were their names? Oh yes, Vaida and Kellan."

Beck locked his knees. He forced himself not to cry out. She'd known he was lying when he'd told her about Vaida. He should have known she'd find out about Kellan. He'd given her this information. He should have known that it would come to this, result in Kellan's capture. But he'd made a choice—protect those he loved or protect himself?

He regretted it. He wished he'd never said a word to her, wished he'd died instead. It would be better if he wasn't involved; Rosalie would be safe, Kellan wouldn't get arrested, and Spider…

Brisea snapped her fingers. His spiraling thoughts jarred to a halt. Her smile was wicked. "You left out some very *important* information last time, didn't you, dearest Beck?"

She knew. She *knew.*

"Kellan Manchester; Twenty-five, Fallen. Raised at the Fallen Crown Mission. Assigned to the Legion during the 623rd Draft. Known associate at the Mission, Beck Aenmar."

He wanted to scream. He wanted to tell her she was wrong, that he'd never known Kellan. That she could kill him instead. To take his life and leave Kellan alone.

Her smile was gone. "You lied to me. You know what the punishment is for liars."

He wouldn't beg for her to forgive him. He wouldn't try to earn her appeasement. Beck knew whatever he said now would make no difference.

She murmured a word, one he didn't know the meaning of but recognized from his years at the Mission. His body tensed, bracing for what he knew came next.

Pain lanced through him. It started in his neck, wrapping around his windpipe and squeezing. He tried to stop himself from falling, but there was only so much he could withstand. The pain traveled down his arms and into his fingers. It was like fire along his veins, like a thousand tiny cuts in his muscles.

Usually, this was when his teachers at the Mission would give the release word, when they'd allow them to recover from the pain inflicted by their marks. But Brisea didn't waver.

The pain moved from his arms to his legs, and he couldn't keep himself upright any longer. He collapsed to the floor at her feet.

He didn't cry out. He writhed, his back arching up off the floor. Brisea stood above him, her face impassive. Her lips moved, but he couldn't make out what she said over the fire in his veins.

Then, it stopped. It was a sudden thing, almost like he'd been knocked unconscious. But his pulse rocketed; his breath came in short gasps. The memory of the pain wouldn't soon fade.

Brisea stepped back, then crouched down on the floor next to him. A smile spread across her lips again, this time flirtatious. "You know, Beck, you've already done a much better job than any other operative has in the past. You've actually secured us a path to arresting Rosalie and even got us information about the Legion fugitives." She pressed a hand to his chest, still heaving. "The Guard might even reward you for such incredible work. I'll be sure to put in a good word for you."

He couldn't move. His muscles were watery from exertion, and her hand was still on his chest. She'd already revealed how much she knew. Everything he held dear was at risk of crumbling, of breaking completely.

But she didn't push any further. She laughed, then backed away, flicking her soft pink hair over her shoulder. "This has been quite the informational meeting. Since you're so insistent on knowing everything, we'll be making our move on Rosalie in a week. If you give her any sort of warning, I'll pay your *innocent* friend a visit in the hospital."

She didn't wait for his response; she sashayed out of the room, hips swaying like a tiger retreating from its latest kill. He was numb, still sprawled on the floor. Everything was wrong. Everything was ruined. Spider was in danger, and Kellan would soon be in the Red Guard's clutches.

And it was all his fault.

50

CASSIAN

Ebenfell | 10th of Earth Moon

Although Cassian had done nothing to his eyesight, the symbol at the back of the queen's cell glowed like a beacon. It tugged at him just like the other artifacts tugged at him. It was voracious, hungry and imposing and almost obsessive. It urged him to hurry, to dig into the stone walls and find whatever was hidden beneath them. It was insistent, almost like it knew this was the last of the artifacts they needed to find.

Kellan let go of his jacket. He reached a hand to the padlock on the cell, obviously much newer in design than the rest of the cells. Cassian figured they must have added it in anticipation of these tours. After all, he didn't know how often they ran tours in Albiga Castle—preventing unwanted damage to the history down here made sense.

"I don't have lockpicks," Kellan said, still holding the padlock.

Cassian sighed. "Let me."

The hallway was eerily quiet, the sounds of the tour group nonexistent. They must have moved on. That was ideal; he needed to focus, and being caught breaking into the cell wouldn't exactly bode well for them.

He'd practiced his magic more as the months had passed in the material plane, Zalmelloth instructing him telepathically. It wasn't as good as his lessons in the Hells, but it meant his prowess with his magic was steadily improving.

You know I can hear when you're thinking of me, Zal said, a smirk in zir tone.

Cassian rolled his eyes. *You just know when I'm thinking positively about you.*

A chuckle. *Indeed.* A pause, then Zal spoke again in a softer tone. *I know you're feeling melancholic about coming back, leaving him behind.*

I'll be fine.

Sure, Zal replied sarcastically. *But it doesn't change how your heart feels. And I can feel what's there. You have a duty, you know.*

Cassian sighed, resisting the urge to snap at zem. *I know. We agreed to this, you and I. I know what I have to do. I'm not planning on ditching.* He paused, biting his lip. *It's not like I could, anyway.*

I promise I'll help you, Zal said. *I wouldn't force this on you unprepared.*

How much do a demon's promises mean, Zal?

Ze scoffed. *More than most mortals'. More than you know.*

Something pinged in the back of Cassian's mind, something the dragon had said about him when he'd offered the memory of his mother.

Zal, Cassian said hesitantly, *what did Gavnith mean when he said I was cursed?*

I was wondering when you'd ask, Zal replied, zir voice tight. *That's a long story, one I don't want to tell you this way. When you return, I will explain.*

But you know why he said that?

Of course. I'm an all-knowing being with immense and immeasurable—

Zal was cut off by someone laying a hand on Cassian's shoulder. He jumped, only to be met with a shallow chuckle.

"It's just me," Kellan said. "You looked far away. Everything okay?"

Cassian tapped his head. "Just Zal."

Kellan nodded, letting go of his shoulder. "I'll let you at it, then."

He tugged at the ball of magic in his core, threading out a small piece and directing it at the mechanical lock on the cell door. Unlocking a door wasn't a difficult thing to do, so long as you knew how to pick locks. It was an easy spell.

Or so he thought.

He could see the magic on the lock when he directed his thread toward it. It appeared like a complex tangle of threads, an intricate knot, in his vision. Adding his own to the mix would complicate things. Instead, he wrapped his thread around his hands, weaving it over top of his skin.

He slowly picked at the tangle, threading the pieces back out, around, under, and over each other. He'd grab one thread, tug until he could loosen it, then find yet another knot before he could get far.

Unraveling this complicated, impossible knot would be complex. Magic may be convenient and powerful, but it was also challenging. He couldn't burn the knot away or cut the threads, they'd only repair themselves. He knew if he tried it wouldn't end well for them.

So he tugged. He took the threads one by one. He pulled them out from one another, biting his lip in concentration. They obeyed his beckoning, slowly unweaving themselves from the knot. As he worked, the knot became smaller, shrinking with each gentle pull of his fingers.

Finally, his tug unraveled the last knot, and the line fell flat. The lock clicked open with a satisfying sound.

Kellan's eyes gleamed in the low light of the dungeon.

"I don't think I've ever watched you this closely while you're doing magic," he said softly.

Cassian's heart was in his throat as he sucked the last of the threads back into himself. He tried to think of all the times Kellan had actually watched him do magic. It wasn't often.

He felt a blush color his cheeks. "It's really not that interesting to watch."

Kellan's smile was crooked, the one Cassian knew meant he

was about to receive some witty or snarky remark. "I would watch you do absolutely nothing all day, Cass. Everything about you is interesting."

Not witty or snarky. His heart was rapid now, the blush on his cheeks so hot he thought he might have done his spell wrong and accidentally burned his face.

Cassian turned away while Kellan pulled the lock from its hook and opened the door with a too-loud creak. Both men winced, freezing in place as they waited for a guard, a guest, or the tour guide to come running around the corner and find them.

Moments passed in a tense silence, neither of them daring to move or even breathe. But nothing came, not even a whisper of a noise, the hallway eerily quiet.

"Shall we?" Kellan whispered, breaking the quiet stillness around them.

Cassian nodded, gesturing for him to go first into the cell.

It wasn't big inside. Up close, the carving on the wall was even larger than he'd expected. It was the size of his head and hewed several inches into the wall. He ran a tentative hand over top the design. It was rough on the edges, as if it had been chipped away slowly over time with a dull chisel.

Kellan shifted around softly, checking beneath the stone pallet hanging from the wall in the dusty, cobwebbed corners. He ran fingers over the stone, possibly hoping for a loose stone or something to give them a clue where to look.

Cassian sighed, hand still over the insignia on the wall. The feeling was back, tugging him toward the symbol. But it didn't give him an idea of what he was supposed to do.

He shook his head, swiping his hand down the insignia and catching his palm on a sharp edge. Blood welled in the deep engraving from a shallow cut on his hand.

A flash of white. A rumble from the wall.

"What," Kellan breathed, eyes narrowing at the wall, "in the hells was that?"

Cassian turned to look at where his blood had puddled in the wall, now glowing slightly where it filled part of the design. What had the verse said? Treasured by the ruins of malice? Hidden in plain sight?

The insignia wasn't hidden, and it made sense there was some sort of sacrifice one needed to make to gain the artifact. But the verse hadn't been specific about what *type* of sacrifice.

Blood seemed…fitting, somehow.

But before he could voice his suspicions to Kellan, a whisper cut through the air. It slithered over his ears and coated his spine in ice. It was nothing he'd ever heard before—cold, malicious, deadly.

It spoke, its tone even but breathy, like it couldn't fully manifest a robust tone. He didn't understand its first few words, but after he focused, he realized he could.

Blood of the conqueror cannot open the gate. Who are you? What are you?

The slithery voice repeated its questions over and over. One whisper turned into many, and suddenly, Cassian couldn't breathe. It was like the air in the cell was being sucked away. He couldn't gasp for breath quickly enough.

Kellan grabbed his arm, brow wrinkled in concern. "Cass? Cassian? Are you okay? What's wrong?"

He gasped for breath again, staring at Kellan with wide, fearful eyes. "I…can't…breathe."

Kellan whirled, searching for something, but Cassian didn't know what. He couldn't focus on anything but Kellan's face, watching as his eyes grew from frantic to fearful, then melted into pure terror.

He'd watched that expression pass over his face once before—many years ago, when he'd been run through. When Cassian had almost died the first time.

Cassian reached a hand to grasp Kellan's sleeve, trying to reassure him he'd be fine this time, that he wouldn't leave him.

Well, that's not entirely true, now is it? You can breathe, Cassian. This is only in your head. On my signal, take a deep inhale. One, two… three.

He sucked a deep breath in. The whispers stopped suddenly, like his first breath had flipped some sort of switch.

Kellan's hands were on his shoulders, holding him up and guiding him to the pallet to sit.

It was easier to breathe now, he noticed with relief. He sat upon the hard stone. He could feel the air rushing in and out of his lungs, blissfully cold and tasting of stone. Kellan's face was pinched in fear as he held onto Cassian, hands trembling on his shoulders.

"What was that?" Kellan said, voice thick and low. "I could breathe just fine."

Cassian shook his head. "Did you hear the whispers too?"

Kellan's eyes grew even wider. "What whispers?"

They stared at each other for a beat, a chill traveling over every inch of Cassian's body. Zal had saved him, commanded him to breathe, he knew that much. But what were those whispers?

You're welcome, Zal's voice drawled in his head. *And I think I have some idea of what that was.*

Cassian frowned. *Blood of the conqueror cannot open the gate. It requires a blood sacrifice, just not…my blood.*

Good work, Zal said, mockingly. *Seems the humans were thorough, at least.*

Cassian's head pounded, the loss of air and the cut on his hand throbbing and making him nauseous. Kellan's hands were still on his shoulders as Cassian continued his silent conversation and contemplation. He lifted a hand to cover one of Kellan's.

"I think," he began, then coughed, still not fully recovered. "I think you need to open that blood portal."

Kellan turned to look at the wall. "What in Sol's name is a blood portal?"

Cassian nodded toward the insignia. "Blood must be spilled to access the treasury, I bet. Blood portals are a type of spell that only open with a certain type of blood."

"And you think…"

"That I can't open it because I'm an elf. If this was a human-made portal, why would they include elves in the allowed blood types?"

Kellan's expression softened from fear and anxiety into trepidation. He thought he understood—who knew how much blood the portal would require? Would Kellan's celestial blood even work?

"I suppose I can try," he said, releasing Cassian's shoulders reluctantly.

He pulled the tie pin from his lapel and broke it in half, jamming the sharp end of the clip into his pointer finger and letting blood well. He turned to face the insignia, then glanced back at Cassian.

"Here goes."

He stuck his finger into the carving in the wall, starting at the lowest point and tracing upward into the outer curve of the moon. He dragged his blood down the inside of the moon, then up through the flame in the center. His blood shimmered inside the design in the low light of the dungeon.

The instant he pulled his finger back, smeared in blood, the design shimmered in a different sort of way. A light from within glowed, illuminating the entire design. Kellan stepped back, expression unreadable.

A crack splintered the air. The wall moved backward, then sunk down into the floor. It revealed a set of crude and weathered stairs that led into darkness. The movement was loud, louder than the door had been.

Kellan and Cassian both froze again. They sat in silence, waiting, listening for the telltale sound of boots or swords. Nothing came. Cassian released a breath, and they both turned back to the staircase.

These hadn't been maintained like the rest of the dungeons. They were covered in a thick layer of dirt and dust; mold grew up the sides of the staircase, and tiny plants had grown in the cracks of disintegrated mortar.

Cassian stood, his head still throbbing. "This must be the entrance to—"

Kellan shoved him back down onto the pallet. "I'll go by myself.

You stay here."

"You know I can't do that." Cassian's head pounded with every word.

"Too fucking bad; you're staying and that's it."

Cassian wanted to protest, but Kellan's eyes filled with worry and longing. His shoulders relaxed. Kellan lifted a hand to Cassian's face, stroking a thumb along his jaw before reaching up and tucking a lock of his silvery hair behind his ear. The featherlight touch sent a shiver down Cassian's spine.

"Please. Stay here. I can't…I won't…" Kellan stuttered, hands tightening in Cassian's hair. "You scared me earlier."

Cassian stayed still, eyes still locked on Kellan's face. He wasn't looking at Cassian, his beautiful amber eyes downcast and filled with something between fear and longing. His head still hurt, and his throat was sore.

But he couldn't let Kellan go alone.

Kellan's hands released his head. "I promise I'll come back as quickly as I can. I'm begging you, Cass, stay here. Wait for me."

Cassian opened his mouth to argue, but Kellan covered it with a finger. "I will chain you here if I have to. Please."

He sighed, relenting. "Fine. But if you don't come back in ten minutes, I'm coming down for you." Kellan's finger tickled his lips as he spoke.

Kellan's smile was forced, appearing more like a grimace than a smile. "It's a deal." He leaned forward, not removing his finger from Cassian's mouth as he traced the shape of his lips. He looked as if he wanted to say something else, but didn't.

Kellan turned his back on Cassian and faced the door, squaring his shoulders and standing up straight. He clenched his hands into fists; they didn't shake.

Kellan stepped forward and down the stairs, disappearing into the dark.

51

KELLAN

Ebenfell | 10th of Earth Moon

The staircase was dark, the air damp and thick. It was difficult to take a deep breath; the smell of mildew was overpowering. It was cut off from the rest of the castle with no air circulation. No one had been down here in hundreds of years.

His shoes clacked against the stone of the stairs, too loud in the darkness. He wished he had a flashlight or something, but he hadn't thought to ask before he'd left Cassian behind.

Kellan hoped he'd stay away. The fear he'd felt when Cassian was choking in front of him had been unmanageable. It had been overwhelming, that hot, brilliant orange of panic that gripped him by the throat.

He didn't know what awaited him in the treasury; he hoped he wouldn't need to fight. They hadn't been able to sneak in any weapons, so he was totally unarmed. Knowing that made his stomach clench.

It wasn't totally pitch-dark. His descent was lit dimly from above, and he could make out a soft, barely there yellow light from far below. As he descended, it grew.

The staircase leveled out after several minutes, opening into a wide room he couldn't see well. Judging by the drop in temperature, it was much larger than the cramped staircase, but he couldn't be sure without a better light source.

The yellow light he'd seen turned out to be a single sconce mounted on the wall immediately inside the room. It shone steadily but weakly, its pseudo-flame nearly extinguished. Kellan wondered what sort of magic it was. It certainly wasn't run on the electro-magic system everything else ran on, as there was no bulb, but it didn't flicker like a magical flame would have.

He inspected the sconce closely, hoping he might detach it from the wall to use as a torch, but it seemed like he'd need tools to take it off. He didn't want to risk breaking his only light source, so he turned around to face what he thought might be the center of the room, the light from the sconce just barely reaching. The floor beneath his feet was patterned with the same flame and moon motif he'd seen everywhere else, cut in geometric shapes from huge slabs of stone. In this light, it was hard to tell what type or color the stone was, but it was hard and polished beneath his shoes.

Kellan didn't want to venture too far out beyond the light, but he wouldn't make much progress that way. He considered returning to the cell to ask Cassian for a light, but he knew if he returned now he'd never be able to convince the other man to stay behind again.

A small squeak sounded as he continued his tentative exploration. He whirled, but saw nothing. Was something lurking in the darkness?

The light from the sconce flickered.

Fear rose in his throat once again, and he automatically grasped for the sword that wasn't on his hip. What would he do if he had to fight?

The sconce flickered again, then rose into the air.

He watched in slack-jawed awe as a small orb of light rose out of the glass, then jumped in midair. It bounced several times above the sconce, almost like an excited puppy. He couldn't explain why, but something about it was…cute.

It bounced again, then another chirp sounded through the space. Was the light *alive?*

The small orb hopped through the air toward him, then rested on his shoulder with another small chirrup. It was warm, like a tiny sun.

"Are you friendly?" he said, immediately feeling stupid for talking to a ball of light.

It squeaked, rising up slightly off his shoulder in what he could guess was delight. He watched the tiny thing as it wiggled. It was no larger than the palm of his hand, perfectly round and lacking any sort of distinguishing features. The core of the creature was a pale yellow and dense, unblemished. It radiated a soft light that looked almost like a fuzzy blanket. It seemed, all things considered, harmless.

He offered a finger to the orb, and it twirled against it. It chittered, then flitted off his shoulder and a few paces ahead, stopping to bounce back to him when he didn't follow.

He obeyed the light, cocking his head as the orb skipped along ahead of him at eye level. Kellan tried wracking his brain for any knowledge he had of such a creature, but he came up blank. He'd seen nothing like it.

It led him across the space that proved to be as cavernous as he'd predicted. He still couldn't see much, but the orb's light was consistent. The floor shone as they continued on.

The orb stopped before a wooden door, its iron hinges perfectly preserved and polished. It bounced twice, then hovered near a large handle.

"You want me to go in there?" he said. "Is the artifact in there?"

The orb bobbed, then chirped. He took that for a confirmation.

Grasping the iron handle in his hand made him hiss; it was cold, the sensation sharp and painful against his skin. He tested the door, and to his surprise, it opened with little resistance. The orb chirped, then zipped through the small opening he'd created, plunging him into darkness.

"Hey!" he objected, pulling the door further open to get back some of the orb's light.

It must have heard him; it came zooming back out, bounced

near his shoulder twice, then hovered near the door frame.

He pouted. "Stick close to me, okay? I can't see anything without you."

The orb zipped around in a few circles. The longer he watched the tiny thing, the more it reminded him of an excitable puppy.

When he stepped through the door after the orb, light flooded his vision. Enormous sconces flared to life all around the gigantic circular room. Their light was much stronger than the orb's, but they were also nearly six times its size.

The small orb floated toward the center of the room, coming to a stop over yet another royal symbol inlaid into the floor. Orbs as large as Kellan rose from their glass interiors to surround him. His heart pounded—if they were attacking him, he had no way to fight back.

They continued to gather around him, their heat making him sweat. They stayed in a circle around him, creating a dome as more joined the fray. It was almost as if they were observing him.

The small orb darted between its family, coming to rest once again upon his shoulder, wiggling happily next to him.

The orbs simply hovered around him, moving minimally. The tiny orb on his shoulder hopped up and down, back and forth between his shoulders, and shimmied through his hair. It seemed as if it was waiting for something and unable to sit still.

"Are they watching me?" he murmured.

It wriggled a few times on his shoulder, each bounce taking it higher until it hovered just above his head, spinning in a small circle.

He took that as an emphatic sort of yes, so he continued. "What do they want to see?"

The orb spun again, a slightly larger circle than the last one. He wasn't sure what that meant.

He turned back to the surrounding orbs, observing each with a careful eye. Before he could take another breath, one orb broke free from the dome and headed toward the motif at the center of the room. It sank slowly through the floor.

Then, the other orbs dispersed with it, sinking into the same spot, one after another. He turned to the tiny orb, waiting for it to do the same, but it didn't move. Instead, it spun lazily, circling his head like a halo.

"Do you not have to go with them?" he said.

The orb bounced off his hair once, then resumed its orbit around his head. It was a little silly, the small flutter of happiness at its insistence on staying with him.

The orbs continued to descend into the monarchy's symbol. The room cooled with each descending orb, he noticed with a small touch of relief. When there were only a few orbs left, the tiny one still dancing around his head, he heard a noise from behind him. A soft gasp, then a scream.

The orbs disappearing into the floor froze. Kellan whipped around to find the source of the sound, fearing the worst.

Cassian.

He'd followed him down here, apparently adhering to their ten-minute rule. Kellan hadn't realized he'd been gone for so long. He'd been too wrapped up in the orbs, their comforting light, their strange ritual. But now that Cassian was here, everything seemed to halt, as if whatever had been set in motion wasn't sure it could continue.

The orb floating around his head stopped. Even though it had no face, he somehow knew it was observing Cassian with something like fear.

Kellan spoke softly, "He's okay—he's a good person. He won't hurt you."

The orb didn't move. It hovered, its movement minimal. Then, another scream.

Kellan squinted back at Cassian and saw shadows moving around him. These, he recognized. They weren't touching Cassian, but Kellan could just barely see through their haze.

Cassian's head was in his hands, his hair between his fingers and being pulled painfully to either side. The screams had been

Cassian's.

He didn't think—he ran. The orb sprang into action with him, bounding along behind him as he skittered across the polished floors toward Cassian. He hoped that these shadows were susceptible to light like the ones at Naktchul Pass. He had little hope, though.

When he was nearly there, he lost his footing, collapsing in a tangle of limbs and sliding to a halt just beside Cassian.

He writhed in pain, his face contorted as he laid his hands over his ears. His eyes were squeezed tightly shut, his mouth open and spread wide. Whatever was happening to him was immensely painful. Kellan didn't know what to do.

The tiny orb fluttered around him, spinning around his head, then around Cassian's, then back to his own. Almost like…

He never got to finish his thought. The room burst into flames, ablaze with a fire he recognized. It was Cassian's fire. The fire from Hym's temple, from Northwind. The fire they'd never been able to figure out or understand.

But it wasn't coming from Cassian.

It came from the orb.

🔥 🔥 🔥

The shadows dispersed with the flames, their frayed figures dissolving into nothing. The flames lasted only a few moments, and when they died down, the orb spun in a tight circle once more over Cassian's head.

He'd calmed down, Kellan noticed, his chest tight. His face was no longer contorted in pain. His hands dropped to his sides, shoulders slumped. And when Cassian fell, Kellan caught him gently with both hands.

"Thank you," he said to the orb, holding Cassian to his chest. "You saved him."

The orb chirped and spun, then came to rest in Cassian's upturned right palm. It nuzzled in, squeaking in contentment as it did.

"So you like him now?" he said with a smile.

The orb chittered in response.

He held on to Cassian as he regained consciousness, blinking his eyes slowly against the dim light of the orb in his hand. It waited for him to reawaken, snuggling into his slightly curled fingers.

Kellan glanced back toward the large orbs. They were waiting for something, still suspended in the air. His gaze fell back to Cassian.

"The shadows…they were here too," Cassian said, voice hoarse.

Kellan nodded. What had Gavnith said? As in life, so in death? "They were protecting the artifact from you, weren't they?"

"Probably," Cassian agreed. He lifted his hand, the orb of light still resting within, and brought it close to his face. "The fire made them go away. But it…it wasn't mine."

Kellan looked at the orb, cocking an eyebrow at it. "I don't know what these things are, but it saved us, so it can't be all that bad, right?"

Cassian didn't respond right away. He turned his hand, observing the orb closely from all angles. His brow furrowed, then relaxed, then furrowed again as he continued his surveillance. But the orb stayed put; it didn't bounce or squirm from his palm. It stayed silent, too; no squeaks to be heard as it allowed Cassian to turn it this way and that.

Finally, he seemed satisfied he would get nothing more from mere observation. He shrugged. "Seems harmless, I guess."

The orb seemed delighted by his declaration, chirping several times and flipping from his palm. It headed back toward the center of the room, where the large orbs had resumed their journey into the floor.

Kellan stood, reaching down a hand to help Cassian up. He took Kellan's hand tightly, his hand still warm from where the orb had rested. It was a startling change from the ice-cold skin Kellan had become accustomed to. The warmth reminded him of old times, before the Hells, before everything had gone to complete shit.

But then Cassian let go, and the moment was gone, fleeting like a petal on the spring breeze.

He watched the last of the large orbs disappear into the floor, mouth slightly parted. "What are they doing?"

Kellan shrugged. "I don't know. You missed the part where they surrounded me, though."

"Did they hurt you?"

Kellan shook his head. "No. It was more like they were…I don't know, observing me? Judging me?"

Cassian made a sound in his throat, obviously confused. Kellan didn't know how to explain it any better, so he let the topic drop with the last of the orbs.

When all that was left was the first tiny orb, Kellan waited with bated breath. The room was, strangely, as bright as it had been when they'd entered. It was an ambient sort of light with no specific source. It simply was.

A grating noise came from the floor, then the monarchy's symbol cracked, splitting in half down the center. It opened slowly and revealed a rising pedestal. Atop the pedestal lay their goal: a shining golden sphere that was barely bigger than the tiny orb floating beside it.

"It's…" Kellan began, staring at the sphere on the pedestal. It was so small. The other two artifacts had been almost comically large, but the Sphere was small enough to fit in the palm of an average humanoid's hand. It was gold like the rest of the artifacts and shaped to look like it was still molten.

The floating orb bounced a few times by the pedestal, chittering excitedly and spinning in the air. It seemed like it wanted them to take the Sphere. Kellan obeyed, stepping forward with his hand outstretched.

His fingers connected with the Sphere, and a flash of power drove itself through him. It was as if the Sphere was warning him what it could do. It was enough to send him to his knees, the power he'd been shocked with too much for him to handle. Hands were on his shoulders before he could fall further. Cassian's smoky scent curled itself around him.

"Kellan?" Cassian's voice wobbled with worry.

Kellan reached his free hand up to steady himself, gripping Cassian's arm. "I'm okay, just…don't let go. Give me a few moments."

He threw the orb in his jacket pocket, hoping letting it go would help with the weakness. The moment it left his hand, the pressure he'd felt upon grasping it was gone. He felt steadier.

Tapping at Cassian's hand, he pushed himself off his knees. Cassian hovered, offering a hand to help him up. Kellan shook his head, hair falling into his eyes as he stood unassisted.

"Better?" Cassian asked quietly.

Kellan nodded. "Better. Let's get back to the party."

The orb hung by them, lighting their way back to the stairs. Kellan walked slowly, but his strength had nearly returned in full by the time they reached the stairs. Pride swelled in his chest as the Sphere bounced against his hip—they'd done it. They'd gotten all three artifacts. They could be free and done with all this "saving the world" bullshit. He could stay with Cassian.

A growl sounded from the top of the staircase, halting him in his tracks.

Another came from much closer, and in the light from the orb Kellan could see something stalking down the stairs on four legs. It had the head of a jackal, a scaled body, and long talons that scraped along the stone.

It couldn't be.

The demon before him looked at him with brilliant yellow eyes and lunged.

52

KELLAN

Ebenfell | 10th of Earth Moon

Four years had passed since the last time Kellan had seen these demons. Four years of dreaming about Pontius' ocean blue eyes turning yellow. Four years of seeing Cassian's stomach ripped open by one of those talons.

Cassian wasted no time—he grabbed Kellan's jacket and pulled him back before the demon could snap its jaws around his throat. The demon snarled. It circled them but kept its distance. The orb at Kellan's shoulder shrieked in protest.

"I'll take this one. Get upstairs," Cassian said.

"I won't leave you," Kellan argued, even though he knew Cassian was right. He was unarmed and unprotected. Fighting these things without his demon-killer would be impossible.

Cassian shook his head as purple energy gathered in his palm. "You have to."

Kellan frowned, clenching his fists. Of course he had to. But that would leave Cassian alone in a dungeon, fighting against the very creatures that nearly destroyed him last time they'd fought.

His heart was screaming not to leave, but logic needed to win. If the demons were here, then chaos would follow. The people at the ball were in danger. Kellan needed to find Leo—he was surely behind this, surely the cause of these demons showing up now.

"Fine," he conceded. "But if you're not behind me in five minutes, I'm coming back for you."

"Just go!" Cassian shouted. The ball of energy in his palm exploded into flames, and he lobbed it at the demon. With his other hand, he shoved Kellan toward the stairs.

Kellan ran. He sprinted up the staircase, the sounds of battle and snarling and ripping cloth chasing him up the stairs. He squeezed his eyes shut for a single breath, nearly tripping on the uneven steps.

Another demon waited for him at the top of the stairs, fangs bared and snarling. The orb raced ahead of him and bounced off the demon's scaly snout before Kellan could react.

This did nothing to actually hurt the demon, but it was taken by surprise. Kellan saw his chance and took it, using the stone pallet in the cell to leap over the demon and racing his way to freedom. The orb followed, squealing as the demon turned and chased him.

He ran faster than he'd ever run in his life. He didn't know where to go. Heading back up to the ball would cause chaos and put the partygoers' lives at risk. He had no other choices, though, with the only entrance to the castle being the stone bridge over the moat. And he couldn't leave without Cassian.

Kellan tapped the device in his ear, not waiting to see if Vaida could hear him. "V, Liv—we're in trouble!"

No response.

He tried again. "V, Liv! Get out of here, now! There are demons!"

Again, nothing.

Goosebumps spread up his arms as he pushed on, the snarling demon still close at his heels. He couldn't stop to catch his breath even for a moment, or it would overtake him.

He frantically looked around the dungeons flying by for anything he could use as a weapon. They'd been thorough in cleaning out the cells; there was nothing.

He was running out of time to think of something to help him escape the demon. And Vaida not responding to his comms was of equal concern. Too many things were going wrong, and he couldn't think fast enough to solve any of them. It was all he could do to keep ahead of his pursuer.

Kellan finally reached the staircase leading back up to the castle proper. He took the wide marble stairs two at a time. The demon behind him slowed, their long claws making the slick surface hard to gain purchase on.

He took advantage of the demon's difficulties, pushing himself even faster. He rounded a corner of the stairs, then another, and the demon was soon two flights below him.

Kellan burst from the staircase in a flurry of movement, panting heavily and shaking away the sweat that dripped into his eyes.

The scene that greeted him was worse than anything he'd encountered since the basement of Northwind Medical. He skidded to a halt, heart thundering in his chest.

A team of Red Guard soldiers awaited him at the top of the stairs, dressed in blood-red jackets with dramatic bell sleeves and polished gold buttons. Three pointed swords at the staircase; two more held Liv and Vaida captive. Four guards in black stood facing the courtyard, arms raised. A final guard, wearing a star on their breast, stood at the center of the archway, their hands tucked behind their back.

Behind them, chaos reigned. At least five of the demon dogs were snarling at party guests, several already sporting bloodied wounds and ripped finery. No one appeared severely injured, but Kellan couldn't be sure how they'd fare in the next moments. He didn't know why the hounds weren't attacking, but judging by the faint purple haze around the black-coated guards, he assumed they were controlling the beasts somehow.

"Kellan Manchester," the person in the center said slowly, as if the pandemonium behind them was nothing more than a passing butterfly. "You are hereby under arrest for crimes against the Empire and the Legionnaires of Spiral City. Come quietly."

He braced himself, stance widening on the stairs as he prepared to fight. He was screwed; without a weapon, he didn't know what he could do against the Red Guard.

The Sphere weighed heavily in his pocket, but he refused to even entertain touching it. It was a god's tool—he didn't know how to use it, nor did he believe himself capable. The moment he'd held it in the dungeons had proven he wasn't compatible. Being weak right now would only spell doom.

Behind him, the demon had caught up, growling low in its throat. But it didn't attack—it stayed behind him, snarling yet unmoving.

He had to think of something, but his brain felt sluggish, turned to dirt after leaving Cassian behind. Unfortunately, Kellan didn't have the luxury of worrying about him now.

"What crimes am I accused of?" Kellan asked, and he saw Vaida twitch in her imprisonment.

The person he presumed to be the squad's captain frowned. "Your crimes are too many for us to speak of here. Come quietly; I will not ask again."

"See, the funny thing is, I'm not a criminal."

They stiffened. "You most certainly are."

Kellan shrugged. "I really don't see it that way. Here's the thing—I never asked to be born a Fallen. Why should I have to keep paying for something that happened hundreds of years ago?"

"I'm not here to debate ethics with you."

"But isn't it fun to debate?"

Movement from behind caught his eye; either the demon was breaking its statuesque watch over him, or Cassian had caught up. He wanted to scream at him to get back, to stay away, but anything Kellan did would only endanger him.

Vaida's eyes were pleading, a guard's hand over her mouth. She kept looking down the hallway, a gesture for him to run, and run *now*. But he couldn't leave her behind, not when they'd gotten this far.

He fingered the orb in his pocket once more, debating if, now that the situation was different, the Sphere would suddenly obey him. If it would do something other than sap his strength.

A flash of purple and searing heat behind him; the demon

yelped and tumbled down the stairs.

Cassian appeared beside him, a handful of flames in his palm.

"Stand down," the captain said, eyes narrowing on Cassian. "Aren't you—"

Cassian didn't wait for them to finish their thought. He hurled the flames at the captain.

Another of the sword-wielding guards thrust forward, forcing Kellan to duck out of the way just in time for the sword to graze along his tie, cutting it in half.

"I rather liked that tie," Kellan said offhandedly, finally pulling the Sphere out of his pocket.

The guard said nothing, spinning on their heel to dash forward in another thrust. Kellan just barely dodged their swipes and earned a few cuts in his suit along the way. The other guards tried to engage, but Cassian was too fast, throwing fireballs at their feet and forcing them to dance out of the way.

The Sphere sat in Kellan's hand, slightly warm from resting against his body since the dungeons. It did nothing.

The guard made several more maneuvers toward him. Kellan could tell they weren't trying to kill him, only incapacitate him enough to arrest him. Well, at least they didn't want him dead, he supposed.

His desperate hope the orb would do anything for him faded with each passing sword swipe, but he couldn't dwell on it for long. Not if he valued his life.

The guard swung again, catching him across the bicep and splitting his jacket open. Kellan swore and nearly dropped the orb.

When the guard tried to swipe again, they stumbled. Kellan scrambled away, hoping to regain some distance and buy himself moments to get the Sphere to work. Around the guard's head, the tiny orb zoomed, bouncing off their face as if it was trying to attack them.

Kellan stopped, mouth hanging open before snapping it shut and wrenching the ball up. It still did nothing.

he guards in black didn't turn, but their hands twitched; the demons, who'd been still before, sprang into action. Several of them went for the party guests, their screams blending in with the yells and shouts of the guards trying to fight Cassian.

The orb stopped circling and smacking the guard, turning to face Kellan instead. It chittered, then sped toward the Sphere.

"Wait!" he cried, but the little orb didn't listen.

It collided with the Sphere in his hand, melting into it as if it had turned to liquid. Fire poured from the Sphere.

It didn't hurt him. It was warm and comforting, like being covered in a heated blanket. The guard, however, was not so lucky. They screamed, waving their hands around their body frantically to put out the flames.

Kellan took a test step forward. The fire that spiraled around him went with.

"Keep this up, little guy," he said to the Sphere, then ran.

Vaida, Liv, and Cassian seemed unaffected by the fire as well, but the rest of the Red Guard unit were panicking. Although none of them burned, it seemed to give them the impression they were.

The demons, however, weren't as lucky as the guards. The moment the fire touched them, they burned to ash, smoldering cinders on the marble floor that Kellan secretly hoped would leave stains. Just as Alvemach had turned to ashes in the basement of Northwind Medical, the demons burned.

Vaida was next to him in an instant, tugging at his jacket and begging him to run. In the chaos, she and Liv had broken free from their captors.

Cassian followed close behind, still shooting fireballs at their pursuers' feet, although the flames pouring from the orb were more than enough to keep them at bay.

They sprinted through the hallways of the castle, the sparkling elegance around them made hellish by the Sphere's flames. Partygoers screamed as they ran through the courtyard, people diving out of their way in their haste to avoid a fiery fate.

KELLAN | 441

They were nearly to the gates when shouts from behind them indicated actual pursuit. The Red Guard was catching up to them.

"The van!" Vaida yelled over the flames.

They'd parked the van a few blocks away, their essentials stashed in the back. They'd left most everything else at the hotel, save for the artifacts and a spare set of clothes. Vaida had set up a force field around the artifacts inside the van, unwilling to risk leaving them completely alone for even a few hours.

It seemed they'd been right to be cautious.

The Red Guard unit gained on them as they stepped onto the bridge, and Kellan felt the warmth of the flames diminish.

"No no no, don't run out on me!" he pleaded with the Sphere, but it seemed the orb was nearly out of energy as the surrounding flames shrank.

"Kellan?" Cassian said, cocking an eyebrow.

They were only about halfway across the massive stone bridge when the flames died entirely. He shook the orb once, hoping his friend would reemerge, but it seemed the flames had taken all the little orb's power. A flicker of sadness passed through him, but he didn't have time to dwell on it as a bullet shot past his head.

Vaida swore, fumbling in the pockets of her pantsuit for anything she could use for a spell. Kellan could hardly think, the heart-pounding chase taking all his energy just to stay ahead.

But they weren't staying ahead—in fact, the Red Guard, emboldened by the disappearance of the flames, were steadily gaining on them.

Liv stopped, and Kellan nearly screamed.

She looked over the side of the bridge, then back to the group. Then she stepped up onto the stone railing and gestured downward.

"Follow me!" she said, then jumped off.

"Is she insane?" Cassian yelled, running to the railing and looking down, then back at their pursuers, growing closer every second.

Vaida looked over as well, then threw her hands in the air. "It's the only choice we have. Go! Quickly!"

Kellan cried out in frustration, looking back once and ducking as another bullet whizzed past his head. With one last sigh of exasperation, he vaulted himself over the railing, free falling into the night.

53

CASSIAN

Ebenfell | 10th of Earth Moon

Kellan had jumped, and Cassian followed right after, a bullet grazing his shoulder as he leaped. The pain was sharp, jarring him off course and making his fall anything but graceful.

The moat was below. Its water was dark and freezing cold. When he slammed into it, his body wanted to break apart, shatter like glass on concrete. His shoulder's throbbing was visceral, an ache that made it impossible for him to tread water on his own.

So he sank. He tried pushing out his lungs to get himself to float, but with hardly any air to begin with, it was a worthless cause. He could hardly think. His self-preservation slowly bled out with the pain in his shoulder, numbing thanks to the water.

Cassian. Zal's voice was in his head, stern. But was that a touch of worry he heard? *Grab a thread. Wrap it around yourself and imagine it expanding. You aren't dying again.*

Again? His mind snagged on that word, but he couldn't think on it for long. He focused his addled mind, grabbing a thread and wrapping it around himself, just as Zal instructed. He imagined it expanding as if he'd pumped it full of air.

The purple thread obeyed, expanding outward to surround him. Suddenly, he could breathe again. The bubble had pushed the water away. He could see some, too. Kellan was swimming toward him, a frown creasing his face in worry.

Kellan burst through Cassian's air pocket, coughing as he collapsed at the bottom.

"Handy," was all he said between coughs and gasps for air.

Cassian was still freezing, his suit soaked through. The wound on his shoulder was colder than the rest of him. He looked around for Liv and Vaida, eyes snagging on Liv treading water a few meters away and above them. He directed the bubble toward her, hoping she'd notice.

As he got closer, his stomach tightened. She was holding Vaida, and Vaida wasn't moving. The surrounding water was stained with blood.

Liv noticed them and dove, dragging Vaida with her. When she burst into the bubble, they landed where Kellan had been at the bottom, a tangle of limbs and dark water and blood.

"What happened?" Kellan said, voice thick with panic.

Liv was shaking violently, her hands pressed against Vaida's side. "I don't know; they must have shot her as she jumped." Liv turned to Cassian. "Did you see anything?"

He shook his head. "No, but they grazed me too." He pointed to his shoulder, but Liv just frowned.

"Looks fine to me—are you sure?" She shook her head. "Whatever, it doesn't matter. We need to get out of here and back to the van. We have some supplies I can use to stitch her up."

Cassian nodded and directed the bubble through the water, circling to where he hoped they'd be out of range of the Red Guard.

Their journey through the water was a quiet frenzy; Kellan and Liv both worked on staunching the blood flow from Vaida's side. Kellan handed Cassian the Sphere before shrugging his jacket off. He folded it carefully and tied it around the wound in Vaida's midsection.

Cassian pocketed the orb, a strange sensation prickling his fingers when they closed around the warm metal. It was like static electricity, but hotter, sharper.

Watching Kellan reminded him of the basement laboratory, the pool of blood, the smell of burned flesh. Vaida's wound wasn't nearly as serious but…

The thought reminded him of what Zal said earlier about him not dying again.

I meant nothing by it, Zal said, obviously eavesdropping on his thoughts.

Cassian frowned. *That didn't seem like a slip of the tongue, Zal.*

It wasn't, but it means nothing. Please, just focus on getting the artifact out of there.

He sighed. The desire to understand, the need to know just what Zal was hiding, burned in his veins like lava. But he knew pushing now would get him no answers, nor would it help with his wavering focus on the bubble. They couldn't afford his distraction.

They reached the shoreline far from the bridge and pulled themselves free of the water, Kellan doing his best to lift Vaida out without getting her any wetter. Cassian could see her tremors.

The Red Guard and the demons were nowhere to be seen on the bank, a small blessing after a series of unfortunate trials.

"Let me," he said, helping Kellan to lift Vaida. "I want to see if I can do anything for her."

Our magic doesn't work like that, Zal said.

I have to try.

He held his hands over Vaida, focusing his magic into his hands. He imagined the ropes like a needle and thread, hoping he could stitch the wound closed. Purple magic flowed from his fingers in a tiny thread. But the moment it touched Vaida's skin, it disintegrated.

Cassian tried again, then again, and again, each with the same result. Frustration built up in his chest—what good was this magic if he couldn't heal?

I told you, that's not how it works. Zal didn't sound mean; he could sense the small bit of compassion and understanding in zir words.

"Cass," Kellan said as he laid a hand on Cassian's shoulder, "it's okay. We don't have that much time. We need to go."

He nodded, stepping away from Vaida and allowing Liv and Kellan to pick her up gently. He could feel his magic flickering; he'd used more today than he ever had.

The van was several blocks away, although it was a mostly straight shot from where they'd emerged from the moat. "Should I lead?" Cassian asked softly, noting the tightness in Liv's eyes and mouth.

Liv nodded curtly. "You know this city better than I do. Keep us in the shadows?"

They set off, taking an indirect route through the city streets clogged with traffic and decorated heavily in purple and gold for Founders' Day. People crowded the main thoroughfares, heading to and from the parties that would take place well into the small hours of the morning.

His heart was tight; the people who'd attended the Founders' Day Ball would forever have this day ruined. How many of those innocent civilians had died simply because they'd been there? How many more were injured? How could the Red Guard do this to the people they were supposed to protect?

It was a pointless question—after everything they'd seen, the Red Guard didn't have the people's best interests in mind. They'd do anything, it seemed, to achieve their goals.

Including summoning those demons.

Why had they been there? He'd eventually dispatched the first demon that attacked them in the treasury, but there had been so many. They'd heard nothing about Leo for so long. This was most definitely his handiwork—if that was the case, where was he now?

Cassian clenched his teeth. There were other things he needed to worry about; they could discuss the implications of the demons later. He led them through alleyways between the towering buildings. His sense of direction was at its sharpest in his home city, pulling him where he needed to go. He followed the tug in his gut, keeping his eyes peeled for any sign of the Red Guard or the demons.

The pull was stronger than ever, amplified by a thousand here. Each time a reveler would get too close, it would tug him in another direction. Although their path wasn't straight, he knew they were headed the right way.

It seemed they'd escaped for now. No one followed, nothing lurked in the shadows, no one got too close.

He glanced behind him, where Liv and Kellan still supported a barely lucid Vaida. Kellan's jacket was still tied around the wound at her side, but he could see it had already grown dark with her blood.

They needed to hurry. The frustration from his inability to do any sort of healing for Vaida festered in his stomach, but he couldn't focus on it now.

The van was only a block away now, and he could hear Vaida's labored breaths behind him. Keep going, he urged himself, feeling more and more like he was losing his tether to the world as they kept marching forward.

They pressed up against the wall of a building, the concrete cold and rough on his back. He was thoroughly chilly by this point, the tips of his fingers nearly blue from wet clothes and crisp spring evening air. He knew the others must be freezing, too.

Cassian poked his head out from the alleyway, swinging his eyes left and right to take in the busy street before them. No sign of the Red Guard. He breathed out slowly, turning back to the rest of the group.

"Coast is clear. We need to move quickly."

Liv nodded solemnly, adjusting her grip on Vadia's limp arm. Kellan's eyes were dark with determination, their usual sparkle replaced with something more sinister. Cassian sucked in a last breath, then stepped into the street, the other three following behind.

They had to cross the street to get to the van, but the streets were busy enough that they could try to blend in with the crowd. It was harder to go unnoticed with Vaida in her state, but Cassian didn't have time to worry about how they'd get her to meld with the crowd.

They shuffled along with the people crossing the street, allowing their shoulders to brush against the other pedestrians, letting themselves be swept away by their movement.

Finally, *finally,* the van was in his sights. Their pace increased with the goal in sight.

The tug in his chest turned from a gentle pull to a violent yank so strong it nearly knocked him off his feet. Pedestrians screamed as a demon tore its way through the crowd. Its muzzle was smeared with blood; several people already lay bleeding in its wake. He saw two more creeping up behind the first.

"Go!" Cassian screamed, positioning himself between the demon and the rest of the group. "Get in the van, we'll make a run for it!"

Kellan scrambled. Liv nearly tripped over Vaida's feet as they dragged her toward the van, no longer trying to keep her upright. Speed was of the essence now, and if getting her to safety meant a bit of mishandling, so be it.

If only he could summon the mysterious fire at will—it would make quick work of the demons. But he'd never figured out the trick to it. His magic was waning, too. He'd used it too much today already, and he could feel it flickering in his gut like a sputtering, dying flame. His weapons were in the van, and he was left without defense.

Still, he had to make sure Kellan, Vaida, and Liv were safe. He was their best line of defense.

He turned toward the demons, crouching into a fighting stance and picking at the waning well of magic in his gut. The orb, still in his pocket, knocked against his leg as he turned.

The demons growled, all three stalking him, hunters cornering their prey. He felt naked without a sword, but he didn't have the luxury of running to the van to grab one. Too many people who would die if he didn't fight.

The demons lunged. Cassian threw a fireball, singeing the scales of a demon. Another leaped toward his side and sank its sharp teeth into his arm. The third tried to leap for his face. A well-timed throw of the one attached to his arm had both of the demons in a tangled heap several meters away.

He heard the van's door slide open somewhere behind him and the thump of weight being dragged inside.

"Cassian!" Kellan's voice was tight as he yelled. "Vaida's in, I'm taking the wheel. Let's go before they attack again!"

People were still screaming, still surrounding him, still watching with panic in their eyes as the demons recovered from his attacks. He couldn't leave them like this. They would die.

Cassian remembered the weight of the orb in his pocket. He dove into the puddle of magic in his gut, grabbing all of it at once and shoving it unceremoniously into the orb. If he was going to do this, he'd have one shot.

Cassian, this is dangerous. You shouldn't drain your reserves, and you don't know how to handle the orb, Zal warned him. *You could die.*

Kellan was still yelling at him, screaming for him to get in the car, to get out of harm's way.

I have to, he replied to Zal. *For him. For us.*

He could hear Zal's frustration. *You're an idiot. Why did I have to have a pact with you?*

I'm concentrating.

Zal said nothing more, and Cassian could feel zir frustration and annoyance, but there was also a small undercurrent of concern. He couldn't consider the implications for too long. The ball of magic had grown enough that his reserves were empty.

He wasn't sure how to use the orb, but he hoped it would do something like what had happened at the castle. Fill it with magic, get fire. He couldn't channel his own strange fire on command—this was the next best thing.

Cassian had one shot, one chance to get the demons in his range and burn them to ash and dust. They had recovered now and were slowly closing in on him.

He held the orb aloft in his right hand, aiming at the demons and willing the magic's release.

The explosion rocked the street, raining glass down around Cassian. He watched the dust without blinking. But as glass and debris fell around him, he found he suddenly couldn't keep his eyes open.

He heard a final shout of his name before his knees buckled underneath him and he collapsed to the ground, vision fading to black.

54

BECK

Rivenstorm | 12th of Earth Moon

The day of Spider's release from the hospital dawned bright and clear, but Beck's nerves were tangled. He knew his frenetic energy was putting everyone on edge. But no matter how much he told himself to relax, he couldn't.

Harpy walked beside him as they exited the rail station. She'd asked him to accompany her to the hospital, and he'd agreed without hesitation. But Brisea's threats had him obsessively staring down dark alleyways and flinching at the tiniest sounds, convinced that the Red Guard would appear at any moment.

He'd been scanning all the newsfeeds for any word of Kellan and his companions' arrests, but nothing had come through. There had been a disturbance at the Founders' Day Ball in Ebenfell, but the reports had called it a gas leak. If they'd actually captured Kellan, they would have reported just that.

Beck supposed the lack of news on Kellan was probably a good sign.

But now his worry was laser-focused on Spider and the impending threat Brisea posed to her. He couldn't warn her without blowing his own cover.

He didn't know how they'd move forward from here. She'd been attacked under his watch, yet she'd forgiven him with no fuss. He was sure she harbored some sort of resentment toward him.

The hospital looked the same, old and beautiful and slightly haunting. Harpy led them up the stairs toward Spider's room, not bothering to check if Beck was following. She knew he would be.

Spider waited for them in her room, sitting sideways on her bed. Harpy must have brought her clothes at some point; she'd dressed in a pair of soft suede pants, a black T-shirt, and a pair of shiny black boots halfway laced. Her hair was down, still drying and leaving it more curly than usual.

Spider's dark eyes found his the moment they stepped inside. His stomach clenched, twisted between guilt and relief in a vice grip.

She didn't smile at them, but finished lacing her boots before standing and brushing her legs off. "Thanks for coming, Sis, Beck."

Harpy opened the closet, drawing out a knee-length jacket hanging inside. "Wouldn't miss it," she said with a wink before tossing the jacket at Spider.

She caught it with less grace than she usually had, and Beck could tell the sudden movement was hard for her to perform. Harpy seemed to realize her mistake as she watched her twin's face; the smile dropped from her lips.

Spider frowned as she put the coat on. "Don't look at me like that."

"Like what?" Harpy said innocently.

"Like you pity me." Her eyes swung to Beck. "You, too."

Beck held up his hands. "Whatever expression you think I'm making, I can assure you I'm not."

Her face was impassive, but he could see the usual spark in her eyes. That little flash of defiance, of stubbornness, that he'd been missing. The tightness in his torso loosened a bit.

"I'm fine," she continued with a sigh. "The doctors cleared me; I can handle myself."

Harpy shook her head. "Just because you're coming home doesn't mean you're completely healed."

"And because I'm going home it means I am well on my way."

Spider finished zipping her jacket, pulling the fuzzy hood up over her damp hair. "Let's go; I'm ready to get out of this place."

Harpy frowned, and Beck mimicked her gesture. It was obvious Spider was in a better place than the last time he'd visited, but Harpy was right. If he knew anything about Spider, she would push herself too far too soon. Her stubbornness was a trait he absolutely loved, but it could very well prove detrimental to her healing.

She blatantly ignored their worry and swept past them into the hallway. Harpy trailed behind, casting a single glance at Beck before rushing after her sister.

🜂 🜂 🜂

The Autumn Rose was bustling. This was not surprising.

What *was* surprising was the crowd in the back bar, gathered around a single table near the back. The crowd was so thick Beck couldn't see who sat there. If he had to guess, it was Rosalie. But Rosalie's announcements rarely caused this much muttering.

He caught snippets of conversation as they headed toward the hubbub, resistance members murmuring as they stood on their tiptoes, trying to get a peek of whoever was in the center of the crowd. People didn't act like this for Rosalie—if it wasn't her, then who was causing such a commotion?

An instinct of sorts caught hold, twisting his insides and reminding him of when Spider was hurt at the docks. It hung around him like an irritating bug, persistently buzzing in his ear. Protectiveness overtook him. He stepped in front of Spider and Harpy, reaching an arm backward to touch Spider. She let him.

Rosalie appeared from the crowd, her brows drawn together in contemplation. The knot of anxiety loosened a bit. If Rosalie wasn't worried, he most likely didn't need to be, either.

But his hand never left Spider's arm.

Their leader approached, stopping before Beck to peer around him dramatically, her trademark plait falling to the side as she found

Spider.

Her eye crinkled, and she opened her arms. "It's wonderful to have you back," she said, casting a pointed look at Beck, who stepped out of the way to allow them to hug. Spider's face went into the crook of Rosalie's shoulder, her fingers digging into the soft leather of her corset.

Beck observed their reunion, waiting for them to break apart. When they did, he could see Rosalie's stern demeanor return. Beck tensed as she opened her mouth to speak.

"We have a…guest." Her tone betrayed nothing. "And Beck, remember when I said I needed to speak to you? It's time."

He couldn't reply before she turned on her heel, heading into the thick of the crowd. Instead, he stared after her, mouth slightly agape.

Spider followed in her wake. Her movement snapped him back to his senses, and he followed her, Harpy bringing up the rear.

The crowd did not part for Rosalie, at least not right away. When she approached, she cleared her throat. The people in the farthest back turned around and had the decency to look sheepish.

"All of you," Rosalie began, her voice barely loud enough to be heard over the chatter, "this is enough. Leave our guests in peace."

The crowd dispersed, leaving behind Rosalie, Beck, and the twins. He had to resist the urge to gasp when he saw who awaited them.

Az'Gomack sat in a wooden chair, their ethereal beauty not dampened in the space. They wore more than they had last time, dressed in a white wool sweater and dark fitted pants. Their hair still glittered, somehow, even in the low light of the back bar.

"You," Beck began, and they acknowledged him with a slight incline of their head.

They smiled. "Me, indeed. I promised we would continue the conversation we started, Beck. And I am here to make good on that promise."

Az'Gomack gestured an elegant hand to a woman seated next

to them. She was just as beautiful, although in a more earthly way. She had fiery red hair that curled nearly to her waist and was dressed smartly in a wool coat and pointed boots that were tapping against the floor impatiently. Something in his brain tickled, a memory of this woman he couldn't quite place. He recognized her, but he didn't know why.

Az'Gomack spoke again, nodding their head toward their companion.

"This is Selwyn Morgenstern, my bond."

Selwyn was a household name, even outside of Spiral City. Beck had never paid close attention to her, but he knew who she was, regardless. But…who or what was a bond? Why was Selwyn, of all people, speaking with the leader of the resistance and this mysterious magician like they were her friends?

Beck felt Spider slide next to him. She pressed against his side, a gesture of comfort, before she spoke hesitantly.

"You saved me that day," Spider said, inclining her head toward Az'Gomack. "And I never got to thank you."

"It was both my honor and my pleasure, daughter of Hym," they said, smile turning saccharine.

An awkward pause had Beck looking between Selwyn and Az'Gomack, unsure who to address or what to even say. Rosalie stared at Selwyn, waiting for someone to say something.

Beck felt like a balloon about to burst—he had too many questions. Az'Gomack was in league with the Shadow, a man who'd proven his crimes against humans four years ago in Spiral City. He knew Rosalie knew of it. So why were they here, in some weird partnership with Selwyn Morgenstern, in the headquarters of the resistance? None of it made sense.

He bit down on his lip. It wasn't the place to ask, but he needed to know sooner rather than later.

Selwyn spoke first. "We have important matters to discuss with certain members of the resistance, but Rosalie has informed me they aren't here."

Rosalie nodded. "Correct. Some of our members are out of state on a mission of great importance."

Selwyn frowned. "Is there somewhere else we can talk? I'm not sure whose ears are listening here."

Az'Gomack smiled. "You know I wouldn't let anyone listen who shouldn't be."

"Still, I would like to be somewhere more private." Selwyn seemed practical and had taken the words right from his mouth. He warmed to the fiery woman almost immediately.

Rosalie turned toward the staircase to the basement. "Follow me." Before they could follow her down, she turned to the twins. "I'm sorry, Spider, Harpy, but I'll need you two to stay behind."

Harpy looked confused, but Spider's face went from hurt to angry in seconds. Beck wanted to keep his hand on her back, to guide her down the stairs with him, but she shook her head and slipped from his hold.

Spider turned her gaze on Rosalie, anger burning in her eyes. "There had better be a damn good reason for this."

Rosalie looked apologetic but said nothing more. Spider threw up her hands in anger and stomped from the bar, Harpy rushing off at her heels.

Rosalie sighed, turning again toward the staircase and gesturing for Beck to proceed. She closed the door behind them, and Beck saw Az'Gomack make a gesture, sealing it with a blue glow.

They settled in the expansive basement room. Selwyn had perched herself on a folding chair, making it look like the most regal throne with her straight-backed posture. Az'Gomack, however, draped themself across their chair. He found the flourish unnecessary, but it seemed to suit them.

Az'Gomack spoke again, turning their unsettling eyes on Beck. "You have many questions, no?"

He looked to Rosalie for confirmation he could speak. She nodded, settling back into her chair, hands folded in her lap. She was not here to talk, but to listen.

"Who are you?" he said, eyes locked with Az's unnervingly white ones.

They nodded their head. "It is only natural that you are curious. My name is Az'Gomack, and I am what you call a demon prince of the fifth circle of Hell."

Beck balked. He stood from his chair, but both Selwyn and Rosalie stayed seated, as if they'd already known. Just what was happening? Why had a demonic prince saved Spider and him? Why had they even been there?

"So you're…you really are in league with the Shadow?" Beck couldn't stop the question. "Why didn't you kill us?"

Az'Gomack smiled, their face a mask. "Because that's not my goal. I thought that much was obvious."

His eyes swung to Rosalie. "You knew about Az'Gomack?"

She nodded once, curtly. "Az has been imperative to our work over the last three years. Same with Selwyn."

His eyes then turned to the redheaded woman sitting before him. Her elegant hands were clasped in her lap, chin tilted up in a manner that was begging for him to challenge her.

"What is a bond?" Beck asked.

Selwyn's lips spread, thinning out into a look of disapproval. "I don't have magical power, so I couldn't summon Az for a pact. A bond, however, is a mutual agreement between a demon and a person of the material plane. A mutual exchange of sorts."

"So you two are…what? Exchanging information?" He felt the panic rising. He didn't understand—how could the resistance be hiding something like this? How had he never known?

The Red Guard was already trying to pin Rosalie with demonic crimes. Their accusations wouldn't even be false. She really *was* colluding with a demon. Suddenly, pieces fell into place. The markings, the disappearances, Cera's murder, and the Guard's singling out Rosalie. Had they already known?

Selwyn didn't reply, and Az'Gomack stayed silent, turning to Rosalie and tipping their head toward him as if to ask her to calm him down.

"Beck," she began, pursing her lips as she paused, "Az is not here for a malicious purpose like the demons we've been hunting. I need you to understand this."

"They're a demon. What else could they possibly be doing?"

"Helping us!" Rosalie snapped, her posture rigid.

He'd never heard her raise her voice before. As soon as she finished, she relaxed back into the chair. She closed her eye before speaking again, and he watched her regain her usual calm, noting the softening around her eye and the relaxing of her mouth.

She sat up straight as she began again. "This is why we wanted to speak to you. There are many things you don't yet know, many things that we need your help with."

"And why should I trust you?" he asked, swinging his gaze to Az'Gomack. The question was more for the demon than anyone else.

Az'Gomack smiled. "Well, isn't it obvious? It's because I saved you."

Beck frowned. "Coincidence. Why were you even there?"

"Because," they started, then glanced at Selwyn. She nodded, and Az'Gomack continued. "I've been tracking Alvemach's magical signature. Leo still carries it, for now. So when it appeared on the material plane, and in Rivenstorm, I went to head him off."

Beck huffed, sitting down in a chair and leaning his forearms on his thighs. "But why was Leo there?"

Az'Gomack shrugged, but somehow the gesture was more elegant than any other shrug he'd seen. "That I don't know, and I'm sorry I don't."

He didn't know what else to say. Spider had come with him to investigate and was caught in the crossfire. No one else was to blame for her injury more than he was. He wanted to blame someone—blame Az'Gomack or Shadow—but the truth was, if he hadn't asked her to go, she wouldn't have gotten hurt.

"Beck," Rosalie began, "I'm going to ask you a question. And I want you to answer me truthfully."

He schooled his face into a neutral mask of calm. What was the meaning of this? Voices screamed at him that this was a trap, he was in danger, he should run.

"Who are you, really?"

His heart stopped. The beats were quiet, snuffed out of existence by Rosalie's question. Did she know?

He chose his words carefully. "Who do you think I am, Rosalie?" He bit his tongue to keep himself from clenching his jaw.

The leader of the resistance stared back, her one eye unflinching. "You're Red Guard."

He wouldn't confirm Rosalie's accusation. He couldn't.

She seemed to understand he wouldn't reply, and continued. "Truth be told, Beck, I've known since day one. I saw the tattoo, and I knew."

But he'd masked the tattoo. He'd covered it with flowers and vines and birds. No one should be able to see what lay beneath.

Rosalie tapped beneath her eye. "I may only have one, but my eyes are special. They see things that are touched by magic. Your tattoo glowed like a beacon on your neck."

The prison mark was a hidden spell, old blood magic that was undetectable by modern spells. The tattoo was enough of a giveaway in normal circumstances, but many indentured people like him covered their tattoos with more.

Usually, it was enough. How was she able to see through it?

He said nothing out loud. His silence must have been confirmation enough for Rosalie, as she didn't pry. Instead, she leaned back once more in her chair, weaving her fingers in her lap.

"But we aren't here to talk about me. We need to discuss you."

Selwyn and Az didn't look astonished by Rosalie's surprising power. In fact, they hadn't even moved while she'd spoken. They'd already known—about her *and* about him. They'd backed him into a corner, corralled by these people who'd already known everything about him. They were here for something, he just needed to know what.

Az spoke again after several moments of uncomfortable silence. "I'm sure you've heard what the Shadow and his pact were doing in Spiral City four years ago." They paused, waiting for his confirmation. He only nodded, which seemed enough for them. "He was creating demons. Not waiting for them to die and come to him—no, he was artificially creating demons from mortals before their time. Although Kellan and Cassian fought against him, they were unsuccessful in their attempts."

Kellan's name clanged through him. He'd known Kellan had been involved, but he'd never realized his best friend had *fought* that horrible creature. He knew he wasn't keeping the pain from his face when Selwyn's eyes narrowed. She said nothing as Az continued.

"He wants to do the same to the world, Beck. His goal is to tear down the Veil and join the Infernal Plane with the Material. We've been doing our best at fighting back the encroaching demons, but it's getting harder. And Leo is only getting stronger the longer we take to fix this."

Beck shoved the pain coursing through his veins down deep into the blackness in his heart, vowing not to let it resurface until long after this conversation was over. He didn't like the look in Selwyn's eyes.

Instead, he turned his gaze on Az. "And you're telling me that the Red Council is involved in all of this?"

Az nodded. "And the White Court. Even though the Red Hunter reduced the number of pact-bearers within the government, he wasn't entirely successful. It's been nearly twenty-five years since they executed him, and we are right back at square one."

Somehow, the revelation that their government was rife with demonic pact-bearers was the least surprising thing to come out of this conversation. Rosalie's framing made sense, then. It was something they knew and understood well. They knew the details of Leo and Alvemach's plans. It was simple for them to recreate the same situation.

A niggling question in his mind persisted, begging to be asked.

"Why are you telling me this, Az? Why you? Why me?"

Az smiled. "The reason I am telling you is quite simple—I do not agree with Leo and Alvemach's plans. And I speak for our king when I say he does not agree with them, either."

"You mean Asmodeus?"

They nodded. "The very same."

Which meant demonic civil war. The implications of a battle of that scale were terrifying and overwhelming in a way that made Beck panic. How would any of them ever make it out alive?

They'd been lucky all those years ago when Hym and Sol had fought. The larger part of the mortal populace had survived. But a war of the Hells that would spill to the material plane? There was no way they'd live through it, not when so many had already died just from the sporadic demonic attacks.

He breathed in, then back out, clenching his hands into fists. "You still haven't answered the other part of my question—why me?"

At this, Az smiled. This wasn't the smile he'd seen before, the one that seemed almost human, with just a touch of the ancient mind he knew must rest behind those pale eyes. No, this smile was something not of this world. Feral. Demonic.

"Because you are going to become the new Red Hunter."

55

BECK

Rivenstorm | 12th of Earth Moon

"I t's not that simple, Beck!" Spider cried. Her voice strained to keep her emotions under control.

He knew that look. It meant she was trying to hide something—a feeling, a secret, anything she couldn't stand him knowing.

Beck would know her footsteps in the dark, just the way he knew her hairstyle was an indicator of her mood that morning—twin braids for happiness, a low bun for tiredness, a high bun if she was feeling angry or sad. Just like the way he knew she hated olives but would never say it because everyone else liked them. Like the way he knew that look on her face meant she was hiding something terribly important from him.

And he would do anything to figure out what it was.

He hadn't made a habit of entering her room often, and Spider didn't invite him inside. It was a mutual sort of agreement—the realization that a bedroom was an intimate space. This time, however, Spider had pulled him inside when he'd shown up, somehow knowing they needed a bit of privacy.

Her room was tidy, just as he'd expected from her. The only items that looked as if they belonged to her were a pair of battered combat boots by the door and an old, tattered blanket on the bed.

Everything else was standard-issue from the inn and no different from the furniture in his own room.

Beck struggled to keep himself calm. "Spider, you and I both know you're making it more complicated than it is. Please, I told you because it's important."

Her cheeks reddened, and he knew it wasn't for shame or embarrassment. She was furious with him. "You can't do this. You'll *die.* Are they seriously so stupid that they want you to fill Vaeril's shoes?"

"Do you think I can't?"

"That's not—" she spluttered, then she fisted her loose locks, pulling on them with a vicious tug that Beck assumed must have hurt. He gripped his fingers tightly, willing himself to stay still, to not reach for her.

Spider released her hair, then rubbed her forehead. "I don't think you're unable to perform the task." She breathed in through her nose sharply, exhaling through her mouth. "It's more like…I know what happened to Vaeril. And I don't want that to happen to you."

He'd heard enough about Vaeril, the old Red Hunter, over his years with the resistance. He knew his story had ended tragically with the death of both his beloved master and himself. It was a tale the older resistance members recounted often. But he'd died over twenty-five years ago, so many of the younger members had never met him.

Spider joined after his death, but the story still affected her deeply. Something about his past had apparently echoed in the caverns of her soul; she idolized Vaeril.

Which was why he'd come to her after the discussion in the basement. He understood why Rosalie had asked the twins to leave when they discussed the situation; Rosalie wanted him to reveal his identity to Spider on his own terms. Now was not the time, but Beck couldn't hide this new mission from her for long.

She sighed, closing her eyes while the frown between her brows stayed. "Listen, I know why they picked you."

He flinched. Did she know who he was too? He willed himself to stay calm as he asked, "And why is that?"

"Because," she said, huffing a laugh, "you're the best of us. It was only a matter of time before they came to you with such an important task."

Beck released an internal sigh. His secret was still safe from her. What would she think if she knew the truth? There was no doubt. She would despise him, hate him for keeping such an important and terrible thing from her.

It had taken years to get her to trust him, and he wasn't sure she fully did, even now.

He mirrored her wry smile. "I…I need you to know I didn't ask them for this."

She laughed again, bitter and exhausted. "I know you didn't. While everyone looks up to Vaeril and everything he did, no one wants to fill his shoes." She finally met his gaze. "I just can't help but feel like your journey with us is ending far sooner than it should."

Beck clenched his jaw. He didn't dare hope she harbored any feelings beyond companionship for him. He couldn't. It would spell nothing but heartbreak and disaster for them both.

He *had* to be happy with what they had—because she couldn't follow where he was going. He couldn't bring her along, he couldn't keep her by his side. It would be selfish to take her away from everything and everyone she loved.

You're going to take some of that away, no matter what you want, a small voice in his heart said. And it was right. He was going to take Rosalie, the resistance, and her security away.

The betrayal was inevitable, a charging tsunami that gave no hope of evacuation. It would come crashing upon the resistance, upon Spider, upon Rosalie and Fox and Wasp and everyone else regardless of what he wanted.

Beck could feel his teeth groaning against the pressure. He was helpless. And he hated it so, so much.

Spider watched him with curious eyes, her head tilted ever so slightly to the side. She blinked once, her lashes brushing against the soft skin beneath her eye before she met his gaze again.

"I wish," she began hesitantly, then stopped. She blinked, breaking their eye contact almost as soon as it had started. She couldn't meet his eyes again as she continued. "I wish I could at least go with you."

Were his ears playing tricks on him? Beck stared at her, her hair a dark curtain around her face. He couldn't see her expression, but he watched her hands twist themselves around each other, the nervous energy in them obvious.

How he so badly wanted to reach out and hold those hands.

"That would require you to leave Harpy behind," he finally said.

Spider laughed. "True, it would. But I think she would be okay without me. She isn't…alone like I am."

He couldn't stand the sadness in her voice. Beck knew how she felt, or at least he could sympathize. He'd been the outsider in the Red Guard, one of the few elite indentured who had been selected to join their ranks. They looked down on him, and it was a lonely existence to be so disliked.

But he didn't think it was the same for Spider. The isolation was a choice, or at least on the surface it might have been. She might play it off like she wanted to be aloof, but he felt maybe she feared deep connection with anyone other than her twin.

He stood, crossing the space to stand before her. She finally looked up, confusion crossing her strong features. Beck crouched down, placing a hand on her face. Her hair fell between his fingers, soft as silk and smooth as water.

"You're wrong, you know," he said softly, his gaze unblinking.

Her eyes darted toward his hand, returning just as quickly to meet his gaze. "About what?"

"That you're alone."

Her dark eyebrows lowered, a question in her gaze. She didn't blink.

He continued. "You have Rosalie, Tigereye, and the rest of the people of the resistance. They're your family, too."

She didn't move, regarding him with a look he couldn't name. "And you? What are you, then?"

His mouth opened, then closed again as he dropped his hand. What could he say? Hadn't he been holding himself back, telling himself over and over he couldn't start this, whatever it was?

He couldn't answer the way he wished. *I'm yours.*

"I'm your friend, Spider." It wasn't enough. "I'm here to support you and to make sure you live through this."

She pursed her lips, and he resisted the urge to keep talking, to backpedal. She wore that same expression from before, the one that meant she was hiding something. His heart fluttered, beating against his ribcage like a bird begging to be freed. He hoped she'd fight him, tell him he was wrong. That there was something more.

She opened her mouth before he could dig his own grave.

"Friends," she began, her voice small, "don't call each other by their codenames."

Beck barely breathed. "I don't know your name."

"It's Jelena."

Starbursts. It was like the sun itself had struck the room, the glow illuminating everything in sight. It was as if he had stars covering his eyes.

Jelena. Jelena, Jelena, Jelena.

He wanted to scream it, to never say another word again in his life but her name, wanted it to coat his tongue like chocolate and fill his throat with its velvet.

It was perfect. It was her.

Jelena.

"Jelena." He allowed himself to experience it once.

Her intake of breath was sharp, almost as if she hadn't expected him to actually say it. He studied her face, watching for any sign that he could continue, that he could ask her to give him just one thing. He was teetering on an edge, one foot still shackled to duty and the life he couldn't escape. The other was straining, desperately pulling him toward a life with her in it. A life he could choose for himself.

Beck watched as she released a breath, her shoulders loosening and her face relaxing. It was as if he'd taken a weight from her with the sound of her name on his lips.

"Beck," she finally said, and the world seemed to click into place.

A knock at the door cut through whatever spell had its grip on them. Without waiting for an answer, Harpy stuck her head into the room, eyes darting between the two of them.

"Sorry to interrupt," she said, not looking all that sorry. "But Rosalie wants you both in the back bar."

Beck and Jelena glanced at each other. There was a tenuous agreement between them now, but the deeper issue—Beck becoming the Red Hunter—wasn't resolved. He knew as much.

But he'd do whatever it took to see a smile on her face again. He just hoped he'd have the chance to redeem himself in her eyes.

Harpy left, leaving the door open behind her. Jelena followed her twin out the door. Before she left, however, she turned to face Beck and held out a hand.

"Let's go, shall we?"

The offered hand felt like an olive branch, and Beck's heart soared as he took it.

56

CASSIAN

Unknown

Cassian was swaying. The rhythm was constant, steady, and comforting, like he was lying in a boat on a calm ocean.

He was also warm, cocooned in a swaddle of soft blankets and rendered immobile. His eyes wouldn't open.

Muffled voices spoke. He couldn't hear what they said—except for one.

"Anything?" They spoke in a concerned tone, their worry and love and exhaustion apparent.

Someone else responded, their voice nearly indistinguishable from the roar of static in his ears. It was as if he was hearing everything through a pair of cotton earmuffs.

A different voice spoke, one that sent chills down his spine in recognition. "How are the veins?"

He felt his legs being jostled around. One was lifted—a brief lick of air, then back to the cocoon of warmth.

"It's progressing," the first voice said again.

He couldn't keep himself awake any longer. The swaying pulled him back under.

🔥 🔥 🔥

You're stronger than this, Cassian.

Light burned the inside of his eyelids. They were still shut, but the light beyond was hot and pink and burned like acid.

Wake up.

He tried and failed to move his fingers.

Just a bit more, come on.

He tried again, mustering up as much energy as he could stand into his pointer finger.

That's it.

The effort was too much. He sucked in a deep breath as the light faded and blackness greeted him again.

🜄 🜄 🜄

The light burned less this time.

It was still hot and pink, still brilliant beyond the thin skin covering his eyes, but this time it was filtered.

"Cassian."

Who was that?

"Cassian, it's me."

Memories, hazy and sluggish, tugged on the corners of his mind. White eyes, dark skin. Ice. Magic. Death.

"You're not dead yet. Wake up. You've slept long enough."

He forced his eyes open. They cooperated a bit, just enough for him to see a swaying ceiling above him. He tested his fingers, too. They barely cooperated, twitching slightly and curling the tips in as he focused on them.

"There you are," Zal said. He realized Zal had been talking to him this whole time. While he'd been asleep, ze'd never stopped. "I'm glad my efforts have finally paid off."

Thank you, he replied, but something felt wrong about their connection. While it was usually like a taut line in his head, it was now slack.

"That's because I'm here," Zal said, and he finally realized what was wrong.

He forced his eyes the rest of the way open and found Zal above him. Zir white eyes stared down at him, directly into his soul. He tried to speak, but his voice stuck in his throat. No sound came out.

Those pale eyes crinkled. "You've been asleep for three days, according to your friends here. Go slow."

Someone else cried out close by. "He's awake?" The voice was Kellan's.

"Awake, but not entirely coherent just yet," Zal replied.

Cassian had so many questions. Why was Zal *here,* in the material plane? Why was ze with the group? Why did the group seem to accept zem completely?

Zal seemed to sense his confusion, and zir lips spread into a coy smile. "Don't worry. I've introduced myself."

He tried to speak again, and this time he got out one word. "How?"

Zal made a flourish with zir hands, holding them up as if ze was casting a complicated spell or maybe performing a dance. Cassian could never tell the difference with the demon, but every move ze made was elegant.

"The rift—and several portals, of course," ze said, snapping zir long fingers. Zir face turned serious. "You scared me with that stunt, Cassian. Depleting your magic entirely like that is both stupid and dangerous."

Cassian frowned, unable to voice his question. But Zal didn't need him to.

Ze sighed. "I'm sorry. I didn't have enough time to warn you properly." Ze rubbed zir temples, then released zir hands into zir lap once more. The coy smile returned. "Don't do that again, okay? I'd like for you to stay alive."

Cassian sighed, relaxing into the makeshift bed. They'd covered him in a pile of blankets and laid him out in the van's backseat. They must have put him here after he collapsed, but he remembered nothing. He wondered where Vaida was, if she was okay.

Sitting up was a challenge, but he managed, his body screaming at him as he moved. It felt like he'd been put through a meat grinder and hastily shoved back together, like any moment he might fall right back apart.

Zal chuckled but didn't move to force him back down. Ze just watched with a careful eye as he looked around the van.

Kellan was in the front seat, twisted around so he could watch with worried eyes. Liv was driving, as expected, but he saw her eyes flash often into the rearview mirror and meet his own.

Vaida was on the bench behind him, asleep. Her skin was ashen, but she looked peaceful. He sighed in relief, glad draining his magic hadn't been for nothing.

Everyone was safe, everyone was alive. That alone was worth the risk.

Zal huffed a small laugh as Cassian's head swiveled back and forth from Kellan to Vaida. "Satisfied?"

He nodded once, then faced Kellan. He tried to speak, but his throat was still dry as sandpaper. Zal handed him a bottle of water, a smirk tugging the corners of zir full lips. He gratefully took it and drank deeply. The coolness sliding down his raw throat was almost painful.

He finally felt like he could speak as he set the bottle down on his lap. A lump in his throat formed as he shuffled through the racing in his mind. He had so many questions, and he didn't know where to begin.

"Vaida's okay?" he said. His voice was barely louder than a whisper, rough around the edges.

Kellan's smile was tight. "She'll make it, but she needs better care than what we could give her in the van."

He nodded. "Good."

Zal cleared zir throat. "I think it's about time we discuss something important, Cassian."

He could feel what Zal was feeling in that moment—the unabashed excitement over the artifacts, the tremble of their veins now that zir goal was in sight.

He'd almost forgotten. In the chaos of Ebenfell, he'd almost forgotten that their mission was done. That *his* mission was about to truly begin. Panic rose in his throat as he thought about it.

The betrayal was closing in upon him. The betrayal he didn't want, the one he couldn't possibly stand to commit.

Kellan's eyes met his, a spark of confusion and hesitancy in them. It was like he knew there was something brewing beneath the surface of this conversation. Cassian supposed he had to have figured out at least a little of the plan; he hadn't been subtle when they'd fought in Rivenstorm or when they'd talked on the shores of that glass lake. Cassian would leave. He wouldn't return. And Kellan would be alone.

But did Kellan know just how deep that rift would be?

"I would like," Zal began, interrupting Cassian's thoughts, "to discuss this matter with Rosalie as well."

Liv frowned. "How do you know about Rosalie?"

"I told you before, what he knows, I know." Zal tapped zir temple.

"Right," Liv said, turning back to face the road.

Cassian swallowed. "Where are we?"

Kellan briefly turned to look out the windshield before looking back at Cassian. "Somewhere in Centrilir. We passed Laka yesterday."

Cassian admonished himself for being so careless. How had they managed with two of their party members down?

Zal nudged his leg. "I've been here since you passed out. They haven't been without protection."

"Not that we needed it," Kellan added quickly.

Cassian's confused frown deepened. "You mean the Red Guard isn't pursuing us?"

Kellan and Liv glanced at each other, their faces grim. "I don't think that's necessarily true, but they haven't caught up to us yet." Kellan's voice was tight. "We…haven't stopped for long since leaving Ebenfell."

He asked nothing more. He knew he was stalling whatever

conversation Zal wanted to have. Even if he had to return, betray his friends, and leave them on their own, he could ensure they were safe. He couldn't live with himself if they were in the line of fire because of him.

Zal's hand came to rest on his knee and squeezed once. It was… reassuring. But why? He shot Zal a confused look. The demon simply gave him another wicked grin.

"May I?" Zal said, inclining his head to Kellan and Liv.

Kellan shrugged. Liv said nothing.

"I'll take your silence as permission," Zal continued, locking eyes with Cassian. "I know you've heard the first part of the tale from Rosalie."

Cassian cocked a brow. "About Hym and Sol?"

Zal nodded. "About Hym and Sol's artifacts, about the angels, and the role humans played in hiding them from the very god who stole them."

Liv reacted this time, flinching hard enough that the van jerked. She murmured an apology but didn't take her eyes from the road as she growled her question. "What do you mean 'the god who stole them?'"

"Sol, of course. Did you really think he was powerful enough to create these things on his own?" Zal said mockingly.

The van was silent as they mulled over the implications of Zal's statement. If Sol had stolen the artifacts, then who did they actually belong to?

Kellan beat them to the question. "So whose are they, then?"

Zal shrugged. "Who knows? Sol brought them over during the Conjunction. He stole them from some other god in his original realm."

"So we have to worry about *another* god crossing over and causing havoc? Don't we have enough gods to deal with already?" Liv said, exasperated.

"I doubt they will cross," Zal replied matter-of-factly. "The rifts between the dimensions have since closed, although this leads nicely into what else I have to say." Ze cleared zir throat, pausing dramatically for effect.

"Get on with it," Kellan said, voice low.

Zal threw him an award-winning smile, but continued. "Sol is not powerful enough to continue to hold the planes apart as he has for six hundred years. He is the reason the Veil is falling. His power is waning, finally breaking apart after losing his relics."

Each person in the van yelled something at Zal's statement, but the demon ignored them.

"We must destroy these artifacts, not use them. They corrupt with their power, and we can't allow them to fall back into Sol's hands either." Zal sighed. "We have been secretive about this plan for so long so Sol doesn't find out where his artifacts are, but now it's of the utmost importance."

"Destroy them?" Liv said, hands tightening on the wheel. "We can't destroy them. Rosalie wants to use them to change the world."

"And I'm telling you," Zal said, shaking zir head, white braids snaking over zir shoulders, "that will not work. The only way to achieve peace is by destroying the artifacts."

Kellan sighed. "Say we agree to this plan. How would someone even go about destroying a god's weapons?"

Zal's grin was feral, spreading across zir handsome face like ice on a calm lake. "Only a god can destroy a god's artifacts."

Cassian bit his lip through the exchange, unable to say a word over the intense guilt riddling his body. But at Zal's last statement, he finally burst. "Oh sure, let's just call up Hym and ask him to destroy these artifacts for us. Or maybe we can convince Sol himself to destroy them!"

He could feel the anger rolling off himself in waves. He was furious. Zal had kept this from him—the whole reason he was here, the whole reason they were searching for these things. But now he was trying to convince the others they wanted to destroy them? The only logical explanation for it was that he wanted the humans to give up the artifacts to the demons. Nothing good could come of this.

He knew when Zal wasn't being truthful with him. It was like an itch under his skin when Zal lied. But nothing ze said had given him that feeling. He couldn't bring himself to believe what Zal was saying, even after all this time. The demon had never been *untrustworthy,* per se, but ze'd never given him a reason to trust zem completely either.

Zal's unnerving icy eyes narrowed in on him, then flicked to Cassian's hands. "Hym is…much closer than you think, Cassian. Although he doesn't have the power to destroy the artifacts right now, there is another option. Let us take the artifacts back to the Hells. Let our good king destroy them."

Liv shook her head. "Rosalie asked us to retrieve them, not destroy them. You're a demon—even if you have a pact with Cassian, we still can't trust that you'll do what you say you will."

The look on Zal's face went from quiet contemplation to a look Cassian was familiar with—meddlesome, mischievous. Something tightened in his gut; he didn't like where this conversation was headed.

"Then why don't you come with us?" Zal said.

Cassian's response was immediate. "No."

Zal pouted. "I thought this would be a good opportunity to allow you to bring your love with you to the Hells, Cassian. Why are you protesting?"

His eyes flickered to Kellan's, full of surprise and hesitance and confusion. "Because. No one needs to come with. I can do it myself. I—"

"I'll come," Kellan said, cutting Cassian off.

"No," Cassian said again, firm. "You don't know what it's like there."

Kellan's face fell, frustration coloring his features. "You can't do everything alone, Cassian. You can't expect us to just…let you, either. Zal's proposition is reasonable. And I doubt Rosalie will just let you trot off into the Hells with the artifacts without some kind of guarantee. I can help."

"I don't want your help, Kellan!" Cassian said, blood pounding in his ears. "Didn't you hear me? You don't know what it's like in the Hells! You could *die*. Easily. It's not safe or easy to navigate like it is here."

"So? I'll have you. You and Zal can protect me."

Zal nodded. "I wouldn't let harm come to him."

"That doesn't matter!" Cassian's blood was hot now, throbbing through him so loudly he needed to scream to hear himself over its rhythm. "I don't want you to endure that. I can't—" He stopped, vision going blurry.

Kellan blotted out before him, but Cassian knew he'd gone silent, knew the tears welling in his eyes had stopped him from saying anything more.

He couldn't let Kellan go with him. Because if Zal was bringing the artifacts to the Hells to let Asmodeus use them, Kellan would surely die. There was no way he'd live through something like that. And while Cassian couldn't betray what Zal wanted, he could do everything in his power to protect the man he loved.

57

KELLAN

Rivenstorm | 14th of Earth Moon

Returning to the Autumn Rose after a month away was a strange experience, especially since Kellan hardly knew it before they left. Zal helped Liv with Vaida, leaving Cassian and Kellan to trail behind them awkwardly. They'd left him in charge of the Sphere and the Staff, Cassian carrying the Sword in its leather sheath.

The responsibility of keeping the artifacts had his skin crawling. It was too much power for him to hold; it felt like he wasn't supposed to touch them. Especially after what he'd experienced with the Sphere, he hesitated to even brush the artifacts with his bare skin.

They went in through a back door, and several resistance members immediately carted Vaida away, a soft purple glow trailing in her wake. Zal and Liv were left to stand awkwardly at the threshold as Vaida disappeared.

Kellan dawdled, hanging back even from Cassian. He'd continued to be icy and Kellan wasn't interested in breaking that down right now. Not when he knew what had to come next.

Rosalie appeared moments later, her eye flashing as she saw them. Her arms went around Liv almost immediately, gripping her in a tight hug that Kellan swore would have popped some joints.

When their embrace was over, she turned to the rest of them

and pulled her lips into a thin line. Her usual neat plait was nowhere to be found, her flaxen hair piled high on her head in a messy bun instead.

Kellan's eyes drifted over the back bar, searching for…who? Beck? There was no way he'd still be here, was there? His heart ached anyway as he found no sign of his best friend.

"Come," Rosalie said, her voice interrupting his fruitless search. "We have a lot to discuss."

She led them to the staircase in the back of the bar, guiding them downstairs to where they'd gathered when they first arrived in Rivenstorm.

Kellan didn't know what to do with his hands. The Sphere was bulky and heavy in his pocket, the Staff too large to be hidden at all. He was self-conscious, knowing he was the most conspicuous of all the people in the room, knowing their eyes would inevitably follow him.

His eyes swept over the room one last time and found exactly who he'd been looking for. Beck. Sitting at a table with one of the dark-haired women he'd seen before. Spider, maybe?

Their eyes met, and Beck's gaze went wide. Shock? Surprise? Kellan didn't know what the expression was. It seemed he didn't know a lot of things about his best friend anymore. He couldn't pull his gaze away, though. He kept staring, afraid that if he stopped looking, Beck would somehow disappear.

"Kellan?" Rosalie's voice was quiet but firm. "We can't discuss without you."

Beck broke their eye contact first, turning his face down toward his hands on the table. Kellan's heart deflated. He turned to face Rosalie, nodding her onward.

The basement room looked exactly the same. Rosalie gestured for them to take a seat as she brought over a chair for herself. Zal floated around the space, oblivious to her summoning. Liv obeyed almost immediately, settling herself next to Rosalie. Cassian was slower to sit, hovering behind a chair like he wasn't sure if it would bite. He kept the Sword sheathed at his side.

Kellan finally sat with a thud, resting the Staff between his legs. Liv broke their silence, her voice tight. "What's this about, Rose? Why is it so…" She gestured vaguely at the air with her hands.

He'd felt it too—that strange sort of air, the tension in the patrons. He was chalking it up to his mind playing tricks on him over the strain of seeing Beck again. But apparently, it hadn't just been him feeling it.

Rosalie dipped her head. "I know it's strange, but people have been…a bit on edge for a few days. We have some visitors."

Kellan felt himself tense, the silver of anxiety lining the edges of his vision in its cool glow. He met Cassian's eyes and found the same high-strung look reflected in them.

Cassian asked before he could. "Who are these visitors, Rosalie? Should we be concerned?"

"I hope not. You are well acquainted, after all." Her tone was composed, matter-of-fact.

Kellan frowned. Did they somehow know about Beck? No, there was no way they'd simply let him hang around upstairs if they did. He would have been thrown out or killed the moment they found out about him. Then who? The silver was stronger than ever now, nearly blinding in its brilliance. He wanted to clarify, but Rosalie wasn't looking at them anymore. Her attention had shifted to the stairs.

"In fact, here they are now."

He turned, and the silver burst into the pure pink of joy.

Selwyn Morgenstern stood at the base of the stairs, her eyebrows lifted and her eyes bright as she stared at him. Behind her stood a person whose hair reminded him of the foam that would gather at the shoreline of the Astra River in winter. They were devastatingly beautiful, but something about them was…off.

He nearly dropped the Staff on the floor in his haste to rise. "Selwyn!" he cried, voice catching in his throat as he vaulted over the chair to crash into her. Their embrace was tight. "I missed you."

She squeezed him as hard as she could, her hands locked behind his back. "I've missed you too, Kellan."

"He's really back," he whispered in her ear. From this angle, she could see Cassian still standing by the couch. He knew she'd understand.

She squeezed a little tighter. "I told you he would be."

A throat cleared somewhere behind Selwyn, the sound light and clear. They broke apart from their embrace, and Kellan's eyes met pale blue ones, startling him enough to make him take a step back.

"I've heard much about you," the pale-haired person said to him, voice deep and cold.

Kellan cocked an eyebrow. "All bad things, I hope?"

They smiled. "More of the good than the bad. Come, young one, we must do introductions."

The pale person swept past him breezily, not sparing him a second glance. Selwyn made a face at him apologetically and followed them toward the chairs. Kellan sighed, then trailed behind them back to his place with the Staff.

The newcomer didn't join them right away; instead, they approached Zal, giving zem two swift kisses on each cheek. Their interaction was almost like siblings. Familiar, loving, warm—words he definitely would not use to describe either of them.

Selwyn caught his gaze again as they returned to the gathering area, her smile still slightly off kilter.

"I suppose I should introduce myself, although I believe you are in the minority of those who don't know me," the pale person said, pointing an elegant finger at Kellan. "I am Az'Gomack, also known as a demon prince."

The pieces clicked into place. They weren't mortal—that was what had seemed off about their smile, their friendliness with Zal. He looked toward Cassian, who seemed unsurprised by the revelation of Az'Gomack's identity. Instead, he looked tense.

Az'Gomack chuckled as Kellan's head swiveled around, taking in the reactions of everyone else in the room. Rosalie already knew, it seemed. Liv was surprised too, at least, which made him feel less like the dumbest person in the room.

Obviously Selwyn knew, judging by how Az'Gomack seemed to never stray too far from her and how they exchanged glances Kellan had come to recognize as internal dialogue. They looked just like Cassian did when he spoke to Zal.

"Are you," he began, observing their silent interaction, "are you in a pact, Selwyn?"

"No," she replied quickly. "I don't have any magical power. It's a partnership, of sorts. Trust me when I say it's nothing like Zal and Cassian."

He frowned, unsure of what to make of this relationship. Unfortunately for him, there was nothing he could do about it.

Rosalie cleared her throat. "You've found the artifacts." Her voice was even, almost monotone. "So now, we need to discuss what happens next."

What *was* next? Their argument in the van had resolved nothing, even though Zal made it seem like they'd agreed to destroy the artifacts. Liv hadn't seemed convinced that Rosalie would give the artifacts up. Although Zal had done a lot for them, Kellan didn't trust zem completely. Ze *was* a demon, after all.

Zal seemed amused, zir lips curling into a smirk. Az looked uninterested, but they kept their gaze on Selwyn.

Liv spoke first. "They want to take the artifacts to the Hells to be destroyed," she said to Rosalie.

Rosalie nodded. "Az told me about that plan."

"You don't want to use them, Rosalie?" Kellan asked.

Az'Gomack's icy eyes narrowed, their brow furrowing at his words. "It's madness to wield the power of a god. You would be dead if you tried."

He knew they were right; that moment he'd held the Sphere in the treasury had been overwhelming and awful, like his entire being had melted into the stone. And trying to use any of the weapons to start a revolution wouldn't do much, especially if they couldn't control them.

"Then what's the advantage to destroying them?" Liv asked.

Az and Zal looked at one another, then lowered their eyes after a moment of prolonged eye contact that made Kellan wonder how much went on between them that the rest of the group couldn't hear.

"If we destroy them," Zal began slowly, "then Sol can't use them to aid the Court and the Council. It will only help your cause."

They stayed silent, some nodding with Zal's proclamation. If they couldn't use them to further their goal, it made sense for them to get rid of them so the others couldn't benefit. It evened the playing field.

But it didn't feel like the complete story. Something was still missing from that logic, but Kellan couldn't put his finger on it. Were Az and Zal holding something back? No one else seemed concerned, although Cassian's brows had drawn together in a pinched look.

"So you will take them to Asmodeus," Rosalie said, "and he will destroy them?"

Az nodded. "I assure you, our king is powerful enough to perform the job."

Rosalie looked contemplative, but she didn't show any signs of physical discomfort. Liv was pensive, one finger over her lips and her gaze fixed on Az. Kellan shifted, a question burning in his throat.

"Az'Gomack," he began. When they turned to him, he felt a chill roll over his skin. "You said if we wielded the artifacts we'd die, but I used the Sphere back in Ebenfell."

Az'Gomack's mouth dropped open. "You…you did?"

Kellan nodded, explaining the balls of light and how the orb had injected itself into the Sphere and the fire had burst forth. Az'Gomack's brows only furrowed further as he explained, but Zal's face remained impassive.

"Tell me more about this ball of light," Az'Gomack demanded.

Kellan held up a hand, forming a circle with his fingers to show the orb's size. "It was only about this big, and it seemed like it understood me, I guess?"

Az swore under their breath. "That was…well, I don't exactly know how to describe what that was, Kellan, but you didn't use that orb. Hym did."

Kellan balked. "What do you mean? Isn't he dead?"

"Not dead, just sleeping, separated from themself. In pieces. The orb was…well, part of Hym." Their eyes drifted to Cassian.

"Is that why Cassian passed out? He used the orb too," Liv asked.

Kellan watched Az's expression darken, their lip twitch. Zal seemed unaffected, but Kellan saw zir hand flex. They were keeping something from the group. He couldn't fathom what it was, but something about their silence made the skin on his neck crawl.

Cassian frowned, turning his attention to Zal. "I thought it was because I drained my magic?"

Zal shrugged, but it was Az who replied. "It was mostly that, yes, but—"

Rosalie waved her hands. "We're getting off track, Az. I'm sorry to interrupt you, but time is of the essence. We should discuss who will take the artifacts."

Kellan wanted to ask about Cassian's use of the orb more, but by the set of Rosalie's jaw, he knew he wouldn't get away with bringing the conversation back to that topic.

Cassian didn't wait; he stood from his seat when Rosalie finished speaking. "I'll take them. Alone."

Kellan shook his head. "Over my dead body, you'll go by yourself."

"It's too dangerous, Kellan; we already discussed this." He crossed his arms over his chest, the picture of defiance.

"I don't care," Kellan replied. "It's a terrible idea to do this on your own."

Rosalie nodded. "He's right—you shouldn't go by yourself."

"I'll have Zal with me," Cassian said.

"Three is better than two," Kellan rebuffed.

"Two is plenty, three's a crowd." Cassian turned his face away.

"Stop it, you two," Rosalie said. "Kellan is right. You shouldn't do this on your own. Take him with you."

"The more the merrier," Zal said smoothly, and Cassian shot zem a look that Kellan swore could melt paint from metal.

Kellan bit his lip. He couldn't stay here, not when he didn't know if he'd ever get Cassian back. He'd let him go once, he wouldn't—*couldn't*—make that mistake again. Not when he had a choice.

He had too many questions for Zal and Az. He couldn't let them slip away either, not when he had the chance to go with them.

It wasn't like he was unaware of the risks. Although he'd never seen the Hells, he knew what kind of place they must be after fighting demons for so long. Their actions and presence alone had given him a pretty good picture of what their homeland must be like. It wouldn't be pleasant. He knew it wasn't a vacation.

But he had nothing to lose. He knew Vaida was in good hands, judging by Liv's concern for her. He knew the resistance would function fine without him, as it had for many years.

Cassian, however much the others protested, still looked unconvinced. "No," he said firmly, black eye flashing. "No one else needs to risk their lives for this."

It was the same argument Kellan had heard in the van. Cassian couldn't let anyone else experience the Hells, couldn't allow the others to be put in danger. According to him, the Hells were a dangerous place for even Cassian himself to be.

It made Kellan want to go all the more. He didn't trust Zal, even though ze had helped to save Vaida. It was simply too convenient. Every statement ze made gave no room for protest, no way for anyone to disagree.

"I let you go once, Cassian. I won't do it again."

The room was silent. Cassian stilled, his fists softening at Kellan's words. He knew how much this meant—*what* it meant.

"Kellan…"

"You are my heart, Cassian," he said, breathing deeply before continuing. "I'd go anywhere for you. I thought you knew that."

Cassian nodded slowly, his gaze never leaving Kellan's.

The room was quiet, as if no one wanted to interrupt whatever was happening between them. It was Cassian who broke the silence.

"Okay." His voice was tender, the edges of tension from before softened by the weight of Kellan's words.

Az cleared their throat, breaking the spell over the room. "Then it's settled. Zal, Cassian, Kellan, and I will take the artifacts to our king in the Infernal Plane."

Selwyn cleared her throat. Unlike most of the other people in the room, she was the picture of calm. "Now that we've decided who's taking the artifacts, I think it's time we discuss the other piece no one has brought up yet." Her arms were still crossed, one leg thrown casually over the other.

Cassian nodded. "The time difference."

Kellan sucked in a breath. How could he have forgotten? Four years had passed since Cassian had gone to the Hells, but he hadn't been there for that long.

Rosalie nodded. "That's an important factor, yes. How quickly can you travel through the Hells, Az'Gomack? Zalmelloth?"

Zal shrugged. "We'd be starting from the top, since we can't go back through the tear in Denten. We'd be traveling through eight planes before we'd arrive. In Hells' time, it could be up to a month, maybe longer."

Rosalie made a contemplative noise, scratching her chin as she thought. "We'd have at least a year here, then, if my math is correct?"

Az'Gomack nodded. "That is correct. Will that be enough time?"

Selwyn frowned. "It may be too long."

"It won't be," Rosalie said. "I'll make sure of it. So will Reaper."

Kellan looked between them, confused. "What are you guys planning on doing while we're in the Hells? Who is Reaper?"

"Reaper has a very important mission as one of our best operatives," Rosalie began, then trailed off. She thought for a moment, then cleared her throat and started again. "We'll be supporting his efforts from behind the scenes."

It wasn't the truth, and Kellan knew it. She'd avoided giving him any information, leaving him more confused than he'd been before he'd asked. Before he could press, a sound erupted from above them. An explosion, then a chorus of loud, angry voices. The thunderous cacophony of many booted feet on hardwood.

Rosalie looked up, unconcerned. "It's time," she said, nodding to Selwyn. "Az, Zal, get out of here. Now."

Az turned to Selwyn and snapped their fingers. Behind her, a portal appeared. Before she stepped through, she turned to Kellan.

"Find my brother. Please. Remember what you promised me."

Kellan watched, dumbfounded, as she stepped through the blue swirl and out of sight.

"I sent her back to Spiral City," Az said. "They cannot catch her here. Not now."

"Why didn't the rest of you go?" Kellan said, looking at Rosalie. "It doesn't exactly sound like anything good is happening up there."

Rosalie shook her head. "I will not abandon my people. You four, leave. Now. Tigereye, come with me."

They scrambled to prepare themselves. Kellan watched as Rosalie steeled herself. But there was a glimmer in her eyes, one he'd never seen from her—pure, unaltered fear.

And as Az snapped their fingers again, something upstairs exploded.

58

BECK

Rivenstorm | 15th of Earth Moon

He watched Kellan disappear down the stairs after Rosalie and thought his heart might stop. He couldn't be here, not today. Not *right now*. Brisea was coming, and he couldn't let her get away with Kellan.

Jelena sat across from him. He could feel her eyes boring into the side of his head, watching him as he stared after the group that had just walked past.

"Do you know him?" she asked.

How could he answer? He had little time left—did he really want to destroy the trust she'd placed in him now? Or did he want to savor it for as long as he could? It had an expiration date, one that he was ignoring as long as the universe would allow.

He scratched his chin with the side of his thumb. "No. I just thought I did." It was a weak excuse.

Jelena nodded, a lock of silky black hair falling over her shoulder. He wanted to reach for it, to tuck it behind her ear. His hand twitched as he suppressed the desire.

The curtain to the back bar lifted, and through it strode two figures, Az'Gomack and Selwyn Morgenstern. They didn't give a single passing glance as they strode through the back bar and headed down the staircase after Kellan and Rosalie. He watched them go, too, wondering what they were all gathering to discuss. Rosalie hadn't asked him to join, but she had warned him of the meeting.

Jelena watched them, too. He knew she was confused, wondering why there were so many secret meetings she wasn't involved in. He could see the frustration in her eyes, the slight wrinkle in her forehead.

But she moved on, turning back to face him and sighing.

"Regardless," she said, picking at a knot in the wooden table, "we haven't resolved our argument from before. You can't do this mission alone, it's suicide."

Beck shrugged, a halfhearted lift of his shoulder. He'd been avoiding this conversation, too. Guilt ate away at him for it. What right did he have to know Jelena's name when he'd been keeping so much from her?

The expiration was creeping up on them, on him. It whispered in his ear in Brisea's voice. It tickled the back of his neck, tightening a ghostly noose. He didn't deserve Jelena. He didn't deserve her trust, not when he was avoiding telling her everything important.

"I won't be alone," he finally replied. He wanted to cover the finger she was using to pick at the wood. "I'll have your support from here. That's enough."

"It's not enough, though," she argued. "What can I do from here?"

Beck put a hand over hers, covering her fingers and stalling her fidgeting. "You can keep the revolution going. Without you, they'll have no one to turn to."

Jelena made a face but kept her hand under his. "The Phantom Flame has Rosalie. They wouldn't miss me if I went with you."

Beck tightened his grip, feeling the delicate bones of her hand under his fingertips. Her calluses were thick, but the skin on the back of her hand was soft. She turned her hand palm up, brushing her fingertips against his. Goosebumps raced up his arm.

A ruckus outside gave them pause, stopping Jelena's fingers and pulling their attention to the front bar. All the patrons in the back bar had frozen in their tracks, turned toward the door like prey in the forest, stiff, at attention, and ready to fight or flee when they spotted whatever was lurking.

Jelena stood slowly from the table. Beck followed suit.

An explosion rocked the building, throwing them off balance. He went for Jelena before anything else, wrapping his arms around her and spinning her away from the curtained entrance. She didn't resist, but he heard her squeak as he held her close.

"Jelena, I know you're angry," he began, speaking into her ear, "but I need you to listen."

The back bar erupted into chaos as the patrons flew from their seats, grasping at swords and holstered guns. The ones closest to the entrance raced through the doorway, weapons drawn.

Finally, Jelena seemed to register what was happening. She squirmed in his grip, but he held her even tighter.

"Please, listen to me," he begged again. She stilled in his arms, so he continued, his words a breathy rush from his chest. If he didn't say it now, he'd never get the chance. "Everything *will* be all right, regardless of what happens here today. Do you hear me? I won't let anything happen to you."

"What about you?" she said, gripping him back as the shouts grew louder. "Will you be all right?"

Beck said nothing. He squeezed her tighter, then turned toward the staircase, where Rosalie was reappearing, Tigereye at her heels. No one else resurfaced from the basement. A tiny droplet of relief slid down his stomach—Kellan had gotten out, somehow.

The floorboards creaked with the weight of many descending footfalls. The Red Guard, in their blood-red uniforms, poured into the room as if they were sand fed through an hourglass. Beck tried counting them, but he couldn't keep up with the steady stream of people filtering through and fanning out before the front exit.

Many people had stayed in the back bar, weapons drawn. But the Red Guard wasn't attacking. He knew they wouldn't—not if they got what they'd come for.

Two more people appeared between the uniformity of the Red Guard, one dressed in black from head to toe, face partially obscured by a hood. The other was Brisea, standing out from the sea of red in a brilliant neon green bodysuit.

The person in the hood reached a blackened hand up to pull it off. When their face came into the light, Beck regretted every plan he and Rosalie had made.

Leonardo Whitburn, the man they called the Shadow, stood before them, surrounded by a pack of the scaled demons they'd fought at the port.

"Rosalie Delacour, you are under arrest for suspected collusion with a demonic prince of the Hells to carry out the murder of innocents in Rivenstorm." Brisea's voice dripped with venom, satisfaction winding through every word.

Jelena cried out in protest. Her hands went to the weapons at her hips. Tigereye jumped in front of Rosalie, holding out a protective arm as if that would somehow stop what they had set in motion.

Beck held on to Jelena tightly; she wouldn't advance unless someone else did. He knew his time was running out as he squeezed her shoulders.

"What evidence do you have against me?" Rosalie said, chin held high as she stepped around Liv's arm.

Leo laughed, the sound grating, like metal on metal. "Evidence? Aren't you the picture of justice? You'll see at your trial, queenie."

"I hope it will be fair," Rosalie said, almost contemplative. "I have done nothing wrong, so I will go peacefully. But I would like your word that the rest of the people here will be left alone."

Jelena flinched, nails scratching at Beck's skin. He squeezed her once, hoping to convey the same message he'd given her earlier. *Everything will be all right, I promise.*

Brisea shrugged. "Sure. We'll leave your membership alone. All we want is you."

Leo growled, the veins on his face pulsing, but he didn't contradict Brisea.

"No!" Jelena screamed, releasing Beck. "Rosalie, you can't!"

"If she doesn't," Leo interrupted her, almost hysterical, "then everyone in this bar will die. Don't you see?" He gestured to the group of armed guards behind him, each with a gunblade in their hands, then down to the demons drooling onto the floor. "My pets would obliterate you before you could so much as scream."

Jelena gritted her teeth and moved to speak again. Beck held out a hand before she could, and she looked at him curiously.

"Then I suppose we should get going, shouldn't we?" Rosalie said.

A snake-like smile spread across Leo's face. He stepped back, melting into the crowd of Red Guards. His demonic monsters slunk back with him.

Brisea held a hand out to the guard beside her, gesturing for them to present her with something. Beck's blood turned to ice when he saw what it was.

Shackles.

Brisea turned toward him, a sultry and deadly smile spreading across her lips. "I see now why you so spurned my advances, dearest Beck." She tossed the shackles toward him. "Now be a good dog and chain her."

Jelena froze as Beck caught the shackles. Her head turned slowly toward him, confusion written on her face. Brisea didn't miss her reaction.

"Oh yes, Beck is one of our finest indentured servants, isn't he?" She laughed, waving a hand at the guards dismissively. "Secure the path to the truck. This won't take much longer."

Rosalie was simply waiting, her eye trained on him. Jelena didn't say a word, but Beck could sense her fury. It threatened to bubble over, a pot left too long on the stove. He knew what she'd say if Brisea wasn't here, watching her every move like a predator waiting to strike.

She'd curse him, throw something, maybe even punch him. And he wished she would. He deserved all her fury and more. After all, he'd deceived her. Lied to her. Led her astray and made her believe he was someone she could trust. He was no more worthy of her affection than a parasite to a host. He'd taken safety and security from her.

He gripped the shackles, the cold metal biting into his flesh. And now he was about to take her best friend—her leader—from her.

"Beck?" Rosalie called. "It's time."

He nodded, not daring to look at Jelena as he closed the distance between him and Rosalie. Not daring to look at Liv or the other resistance members, who'd been watching the exchange in furious silence. Not daring to look anywhere but at Rosalie's eye, fierce as she watched him approach.

Her expression never changed as he clamped the shackles to her wrists and pressed the button to activate the plasma chain between them. She seemed contemplative.

"She will never forgive you, and for that, I am sorry." Rosalie's voice was barely a whisper as he finished his work. "I'd hoped…"

Brisea appeared beside them, cutting off whatever Rosalie was about to say next. She gripped Rosalie's arm tightly, her sharp chrome-colored nails drawing small spots of blood. "Seems like our star pupil wants to say his last goodbyes." Her smile was nasty, full of malicious joy and glee. It sent chills down his spine.

He finally turned, allowing himself to look at Jelena's furious expression. Her eyes glowed, their deep brown boring a hole into his soul. Looking at those eyes, he knew Rosalie was right—she would never forgive him.

"Jel—"

He never got to finish. She slapped him, hard, across the face.

Her voice shook as she failed to contain her anger. "You don't deserve to call me that. If you ever show your face around here again, *Reaper*, I *will* kill you."

He knew a lost cause when it stood before him, trembling in anger. This situation was always on the horizon; he'd known it was coming. But he hadn't realized it would hurt this much.

THE PHANTOM FLAME

The reality of it was so much worse than he ever could have imagined. It stung, it needled at his heart and left him gasping for breath. The breath only she could breathe into him.

Beck said nothing. He didn't reach for her; he didn't beg for her forgiveness. The only way he could protect her would be through his silence.

So he simply nodded, turning to face Brisea and Rosalie.

He did not look back.

EPILOGUE

UNKNOWN

Unknown

She was drowning. Water filled her lungs, her nose, her eyes. Everything turned black and cold.

But she was warm.

Blood ran quickly through her veins, smoothing out her sharp edges and polishing her into sea glass. It ran over years of dust and grime and fire and cleaned out the cobwebs behind her eyes. It pooled in her ears and in her hands. It covered her wings.

Her…wings?

Voices. Hundreds of them. A single voice above the rest. Sweet, melodic. Like a song in her bloodied ears. Blonde hair tickled her cheek, and a finger smoothed down her arm, leaving a trail of blood in its wake. Lips caressed her forehead; a hand tangled in her braids.

The voice was back, but it was different, somehow. It called her name, low and syrupy. It begged her not to go. Hold on, it said. Hold on.

Then she was in a cavern. Water dripped from the ceiling onto her cracked lips. It slid down her throat and extinguished the fire in her belly. Hands were on her forehead. Were they hands? They were as cold as ice.

They were utilitarian, not like the hands that left trails of blood down her arms. They touched her softly, as if they were afraid she

495

might break. She wasn't that weak—they wouldn't hurt her.

She wanted to open her mouth and tell them so, but her lips were frozen shut. Her tongue was heavy and dry in her mouth.

A flash of brilliant light and she was deeper in her dream.

Golden clouds surrounded her eyes, their brilliance blinding. The blood and water and ice were gone, replaced by soft cotton and the brush of clouds along her arm.

Someone walked ahead, clothed in a cloak of pure gold and a crown of light on their curls. She knew them, but she couldn't call out. Her lips were still frozen.

They did not stop for her; their strides were long and smooth, as if they glided upon the clouds. She strained her ears to hear if they were speaking, but silence was her only reply. She could feel wind brushing past her, ruffling the soft chiton she wore, but it made no sound. No rustle of cloth, no whisper from the golden clouds.

The gold-cloaked person eventually stopped, their movements as fluid as liquid in a glass. And when they turned to her, she saw molten golden tears falling from their eyes.

Before she could reach out, something tugged her away, falling down, down, down to the earth below. Ground rushed up to meet her; she could not stop her fall. She knew this. She did not avoid it.

Then she was cold and bloodied again, her wings broken and her chiton soaked. The ground was muddied, full of decay and death. The smell choked her. Although she still could not open her mouth, the taste of it flooded her. It was inescapable; no matter where she turned, death was the only thing she saw.

A flash, then flames cloaked her body. Like her blood, it smoothed her out and burned away the death and mud and decay. She felt her lips thaw; the blood on her skin melted and pooled and turned to glass.

Then, the angel opened her eyes.

ACKNOWLEDGEMENTS

Writing acknowledgements for the second book in a series is a strange place to be, but here we are. And I'm incredibly thankful to have the support system I had through this book. They say it takes a village, and I'm so thankful for my village.

Of course, I can't start my acknowledgements without writing about my #1 supporter and rock—my husband and life partner, Ryan. You've been there through all the difficult times, the self doubt, the writer's block I've experienced throughout the drafting of this book. You have been a constant in my life, and I am so thankful to have you by my side.

To my incredible business partners, RaeAnne, Lindsay, Hannah, Rachael, and Stef—you once again have made this endeavor as easy and smooth as I could imagine. Your support, incredible work, and professionalism has made my publishing journey so much easier than it would have been on my own.

To Judith—I said it before and I will say it again. I would not be an author without you. How I managed to get so lucky to find someone like you is a gift from the universe. I don't know what I did to deserve such a fantastic friend, critique partner, and fellow writer, but I am eternally thankful for your presence in my life. Thank you for being there for me.

To Paulina—not only have you supported me from the very beginning, but you've made my life so much richer just by being in it. You are the inspiration for so many of the friendships I write about in my books. Thank you, forever and ever, for being you.

To Mori—I can't express enough how thankful I am for you and your friendship. Your complete obsession with my little gremlin children is the number one reason I've had any modicum of success in this endeavor. You have, single-handedly, kept me afloat when I felt like I couldn't continue. Thank you, thank you, thank you, for so much more than I could ever express in words.

To my author circle—Alex, MJ, Brit, Caity, Jess, Lindsay, Rachel, Gina—you ARE my village. Without any one of you, I would be much, much worse off. You are my lifeline, the buoy that kept me afloat, the sprinkle of sugar that made life so much sweeter. Thank you, always, for being there for me.

To my parents—because without either of you, I never would have followed my dreams. My love of books was born because of your passion for stories, because I followed your lead and found something that was worth keeping. Thank you, for being there every single damn time it mattered, and for never letting me forget that you love me more than anything.

To every person who purchased OBBT and TPF—you are what made my dream come true. I am an author because of your support, excitement, love, and commitment to getting my book in your hands and reading my words.

PRONUNCIATION GUIDE

CHARACTERS

KELLAN MANCHESTER: *Kel-ann Man-ches-tur*

CASSIAN EVERMORE: *Kah-see-ehn Ever-mor*

VAIDA LARSEN: *Veye-duh Lar-sen*

ROSALIE DELACOUR: *Rose-ah-lee Del-la-cor*

LIVA AUCLAIR: *Lih-vay-uh Oh-clair*

BRISEA: *Brihs-say-uh*

GAVNITH ICEHEART: *Gahv-neeth Ice-hart*

AMARIS: *Uh-mar-iss*

VAERIL GILDOVE: *Vair-ill Gil-duhv*

DEMONS & PRINCES

ASMODEUS: *Az-moh-dee-us*

ZALMELLOTH: *Zahl-mehl-oth*

AZ'GOMACK: *Ahz-goh-mack*

ALVEMACH: *Al-vuh-mock*

GODS & GODDESSES

Hym: *Heim*

Sol: *Saul*

Enya: *Ehn-yuh*

Lyra: *Lir-uh*

Avani: *Uh-vahn-ee*

Boreas: *Bor-ee-us*

WORLD & SETTING

Albiga: *Al-bee-zjuh*

Balindao: *Bah-lean-dow*

Alderburn: *All-dur-burn*

Rivenstorm: *Rihv-ehn-storm*

Centrilir: *Sahn-trill-ear*

Raliah: *Rah-lee-uh*

Lachia: *Lah-chee-uh*

Uswye: *Oos-way*

Midlset: *Middle-set*

Ebenfell: *Eb-en-fell*

GOVERNMENT, POLITICS, AND LEADERSHIP

LUNAR CALENDAR

The calendar in Ileron is based upon their lunar calendar and follows the cycles of the moon. A new moon marks the beginning/end of a month, the full moon marking the middle. There are thirty days each month, and twelve months in a year.

The first Moon: Frost

The second Moon: Dawn

The third Moon: Earth

The fourth Moon: Blossom

The fifth Moon: Cresting

The sixth Moon: Day

The seventh Moon: Flame

The eighth Moon: Cerulean

The ninth Moon: Wind

The tenth Moon: Jupiter's

The eleventh Moon: Dusk

The twelfth Moon: Evergreen

Dates in Ileron are written as such: the X day of XXX Moon.

POLITICAL SYSTEM

Although named the Empire, the country runs on a democratic system. Spiral City is unique in its structure as a city-state, thus, its governmental bodies are different.

THE EMPIRE:

The Red Council is the Empire's ruling authority. It is a group of six individuals, nominated by their respective cities, to serve on the council for fifteen to thirty years. The nomination process happens every fifteen years. Three members are elected to stay on the board, two become seniors, and one becomes the Prime. The other three members retire from the council, and three new members are elected by the citizens of the realm to serve on the board. It is possible for a brand new member to become a senior immediately, although you cannot become Prime without serving as a member first.

In addition to the leadership of the Red Council, the White Court was established to serve as the secondary leadership council for the Empire. This court is a lifetime appointment, very similar to how the Supreme Court works in the U.S. The members, however, are not selected by members of the Red Council, but rather are also elected by the citizens of the Empire.

SPIRAL CITY:

The Governor is an elven man elected ninety-two years ago, named Caern Fenwyne. He is a strict and passionate man who is not necessarily adored, but most definitely revered by his citizens. Caern is a cautious man as well, rarely choosing to appear in public for fear of an assassination like that of his predecessor, Zephyr Dornwen. Although nearing the end of his term, he is still passionate about the protection of his citizens.

CURRENT DISTRICT COUNCILORS:

LUNADERE: Led by a shifter by the name of **Hazel**. She's a conniving and secretive woman, but is fiercely protective of her clan. The Councilor of Lunadere is also known as the Commissioner of Public Buildings and City Planning, and is in charge of development projects within the city as well as maintenance of public and government buildings.

UPPER CLOUD: Led by a seraph named **Bethor**. He's a kind and gentle man, if not a little proud. The Councilor of Upper Cloud is also known as the Commissioner of Public Finance and the Treasury, and is in charge of the city's finances.

Northwind: Led by a seraph named **Roland**. Aloof and far removed, he is more interested in grooming the next leader of his district rather than actually governing it. The Councilor of Northwind is also known as the Commissioner of Public Health and Family Services, and oversees the city's public health services.

Tethgir: Led by a Dragonborn named **Arice**. She is just as kind and gentle as her great-great-grandfather, Riveras, who was the original Councilor of Tethgir when Spiral City was established. She leads her district with a just and steady hand. Also known as the Commissioner of Public Information and Technology, this commissioner oversees the flow of information in and out of the city, and ensures technological advancements used by the government are safe and reliable.

Rookford Down: Still led by the extremely old dwarven woman, **Gen**. She was a young woman when Spiral City was established, but is now old and gray. She is senile as hell, although her daughter, Erwen, has been helping her mother for the last one hundred years or so. Also known as the Commissioner of Public Trade and Consumer Safety, this commissioner oversees trade in and out of Spiral City and ensures standards are met to deliver high-quality and safe products to its citizens.

Bloomside: Led by a water elemental named **Exto**. He is incredibly proud of his district, focusing most of his efforts on conservation and water purification to keep the beautiful gardens flourishing. Also known as the Commissioner of Public Lands and Natural Resources, this commissioner oversees the Grand Gardens and other public parks within Spiral City and oversees any agriculture within the city's limits.

Spira Mirabilis: Although technically not a residential district, Spira is represented on the council by none other than the Legion's **Commissioner**. Uniquely referred to as "The Commissioner," his official title is the Commissioner of Public Safety and the Legion. This is also the only member of the council not elected by their district's citizens, simply because there are none to elect.

THE LEGION

The Legion is made up of twenty-five total divisions, varying from accounting and magical facilities to the divisions like law enforcement, security, and investigatory units. In the law enforcement divisions, there are individual units, made up of Privates, Corporals, Sergeants, and Lieutenants.

RANKING STRUCTURE

PRIVATE: Indentured ranking

Same jacket style as the corporals. Each private is designated with the prison mark on the back of their necks. This is not unique to the Fallen. Every Fallen has a prison mark, every private has a mark, but not every private is a Fallen.

CORPORAL: regular/general members of the military divisions of the Legion ten and up, most common rank

Open-jacket style, worn with a white or black undershirt and matching necktie in their division's color.

SERGEANT: the leader of a unit within a division, corporals report to sergeants

Closed jacket style that buttons on one side of the chest and high neck, no undershirt or necktie. Matching solid color epaulets in the color of their division.

LIEUTENANT: the highest rank within a division, sergeants report to lieutenants

Closed-jacket style that buttons on one side of the chest with a folded down panel in the color of their division. Matching striped epaulets.

VICE COMMISSIONER: second-in-command of the Legion, functions as the Commissioner's right hand

Same jacket style as the lieutenant, but has three stars on the epaulets.

COMMISSIONER: the leader of the Legion, all positions report to him/her

Same jacket style as the lieutenant, but has six stars on the epaulets.

Medica: the secondary rank of all members of the tenth, eleventh, and twelfth divisions, nicknamed the Meds

> *Their first rank (Corporal, Sergeant, or Lieutenant) will determine their jacket style*

> *All Medica have an infinity-shaped ouroboros pin incorporated into their division pin*

THE DIVISIONS

The First Division: white piping; reports to the Legion Commissioner

> *Legal work & administrative law, mostly lawyers & judges, some paralegals, and admin assistants.*

The Second, Third, and Fourth Divisions: gray piping; report to Bethor, Roland, and Gen

> *Administrative work such as accounts payable/receivable, mailroom, purchasing, HR, employment relations, etc.*

The Fifth, Sixth, and Seventh Divisions: yellow piping; report to Hazel, Exto, or Arice

> *Facilities work such as maintenance, public works, civil engineering, magical security, etc.*

The Eighth and Ninth Divisions: green piping; report to Exto

> *Scientific research divisions, mostly in charge of exotic flora and fauna. Frequently works in cooperation with the University.*

The Tenth, Eleventh, and Twelfth Divisions: bright red piping

> *All first responder divisions, paramedics, firefighters, etc.*

The Thirteenth Division: black piping

> *Currently vacant. Has not been used as an active division for nearly a hundred years*

THE FOURTEENTH AND FIFTEENTH DIVISIONS: navy piping

Private investigation units, can be hired by private citizens but primarily works for the government. These divisions do not have units, and each member has the rank of Lieutenant.

THE SIXTEENTH, SEVENTEENTH, AND EIGHTEENTH DIVISIONS: cobalt blue piping

Regular law enforcement divisions. Traffic maintenance, domestic disturbances, security, etc.

THE NINETEENTH DIVISION: blood-red piping

Labeled as another private investigatory unit, but most everyone knows this is a lie. They are essentially a "clean-up crew." Made up exclusively of draftees. The 19th also does not have a unit structure; each member reports individually to the Vice Commissioner and Commissioner.

THE TWENTIETH DIVISION: purple piping

A division that functions like a national guard. They are mobilized in extreme emergencies; otherwise, their members are split up into the other divisions when not mobilized.

THE TWENTY-FIRST, TWENTY-SECOND, TWENTY-THIRD, AND TWENTY-FOURTH DIVISIONS: sky-blue piping

Special units, mostly investigatory, homicide, sex crimes, drug busts, etc.

THE TWENTY-FIFTH DIVISION: orange piping

The leadership division. Technically the Commissioner and the Vice Commissioner are the only full-time members of this division, but all Lieutenants have the Twenty-Fifth as their secondary division.

Milton Keynes UK
Ingram Content Group UK Ltd.
UKHW050705270324
440147UK00020B/316/J